Temptation to Sin

Adriana Parrinello

First published by Dog Ear Publishing
4011 Vincennes Rd
Indianapolis, IN 46268
www.dogearpublishing.net

ISBN: 978-1-45754-883-3

This book is printed on acid-free paper.

This book is a work of fiction. Places, events, and situations in this book are purely fictional and any resemblance to actual persons, living or dead, is coincidental.

Printed in the United States of America

Editor: Marcy Mangino

Dedications:

- *To my parents, Antonino and Benedetta Monaco—thank you. Thank you for protecting, guiding, teaching, caring, and for loving me. I pray I will be to my children, what you are to me.* ***Ti voglio tanto bene!***

- *To my siblings, Caterina, Angela, Peter, and Nella—thank you. You've helped to mold me into who I am today. There is no thing, no person, no evil that will ever come between us.* ***I love you all.***

- *To those who suffer or have suffered* ***any*** *kind of abuse—never lose hope. There is a God who loves you and can bring you to complete healing.* ***His name is Jesus Christ.*** *Give yourself to Him, and observe as miracles begin to transpire in you and in your life.*

Prologue

It was high-time he set his scheme in motion. His diabolical and perfect plan for revenge could not fail. Entering Don Mario Galante's office, his heart thumped loudly.

"Why do you come to me?" asked Mario. He sat in a large leather chair at the desk of his extravagant home office. The room was large, dark, and stiflingly hot.

"I've come to warn you of Nino Valente's imminent revenge," he began, trying to ignore the heat.

"And *you* expect *me* to believe . . . that Nino is planning revenge? Why . . . after years of loyalty to him . . . do you betray him?" Mario stared him down. The intimidating gaze was intended to find weakness.

"I have no qualms about betraying him. *He* betrayed *me*. I was next in line to receive the title of 'Don'. He promised *me*. Now he's got Giacalone under his wing, Giacalone as his apprentice. I'm telling you the truth. They do plan revenge." He shifted his weight from one heavy leg to the other. The dark room was so warm it almost nauseated him. He felt a bead of sweat form on his forehead and wiped it quickly. He was to show *no* sign of weakness. Mario was a dangerous man and if Mario knew what he was really up to, *he* was as good as dead.

"You better be telling the truth. I can see where the union of Valente and Giacalone is a possibility—Valente seeking to avenge the deaths of his granddaughters and Giacalone the deaths of his family. Though I considered their demises a business transaction, it is likely that they have not. If this is so, this means war." He sat forward and strummed his manicured fingers on the red oak desk.

Mario sought out his eyes—they were piercing, seeking, questioning. "Though I must tell you, I have my doubts," he continued. "The last time Valente came to me, he came in good faith on behalf of his granddaughter, Giacalone's fiancée. Valente paid off their debts and left peacefully. He supposedly retired. Now you want me to believe that he has gone back on his word? Can you prove this?"

He shifted his weight again. A heat rushed to his face and he knew he needed to get out of the room or fail his mission. Trying to compose himself, he answered, "Yes, I can. They hide under the guise that Giacalone is mentally unstable. But it's just a ploy. He is as sane as he'll ever be. Nino's training him, showing him the ways of the business. When everyone least expects it, they *will* retaliate."

Mario rose from the leather chair. He walked to the window and opened the blind to allow in more sunlight. He finally turned to face him after a considerable amount of time. He could tell that he had gotten Mario Galante's wheels spinning.

"This may be the only opportunity I have to stick it to Valente after all these years. You bring me physical evidence of what you say and not only will I double the annual salary that Valente was giving you, but I will open up a position for you within my organization, if you are interested. Is this fair?"

For a moment, he could not speak. His mouth felt parched and he could not believe that he had succeeded. Finally, he shook his head and extended his hand. Mario Galante firmly clasped his hand and pumped it. He should have been overjoyed with the final outcome. Instead, he felt as though he had just made a deal . . . with the devil.

CHAPTER 1

I John 4:18

"There is no fear in love; but perfect love casts out fear."

November 25, 1978

Tony sat on the couch in the bright blue office of his psychiatrist, Dr. Marcus Parnell. It was a Saturday morning and he was in for his last session of the week. He had grown accustomed to coming to see him weekly. But as of late, Doc was pressing him to come to session three days a week. Tony could not understand it. He felt as though he was making great progress. In fact, his life could not have been better.

He was going to marry Laura, the woman he loved, in a few short months. They were expecting their first child in May. Her family had accepted him and was a wonderful support to him as well. His relationship with his future father-in-law, John, was going so well that the man even hired him to take over the management of his rental dwellings. Tony felt that he was finally at peace within himself and all around.

Except . . . except, for the infamous Nino Valente, Laura's newly reconciled maternal grandfather. Something just did not ring true about him.

Tony believed him not to be as sincere as Laura thought. After how Nino had meddled in her life, causing the death of her adoptive sister, Tammy, and Laura's previous fiancé, Paul Roberts, Tony just could not trust him. Accident or not, Nino Valente had the blood of the innocent on his hands. Now, he had somehow managed to get Laura to overlook and forgive all this. But Tony could not forget.

Nino Valente was a former mob boss supposedly turned 'good'. He claimed to have given his heart to Jesus. *But was he sincere?* Tony did not believe so. *After years of being in the Mafia, could he have cut all ties and become this sweet grandfather Laura wanted him to be?* Tony thought *not* and Nino sensed Tony's suspicions. There was some serious tension in the room when Nino came to visit.

Tony's attention diverted to the turning doorknob in the office. His doctor waltzed in. "Tony!" He smiled and extended his hand.

Tony took it. "Hey Doc, how's it goin'?" he questioned, while shaking his hand.

"Doing good. How 'bout you?"

"Great."

"Glad to hear it. Your holiday went well?"

"Thanksgiving was awesome, thanks. With a fiancée like Laura, how can it not be?"

"She *is* wonderful."

"I couldn't agree more."

Dr. Parnell sat down in his chair. After adjusting his suit jacket, he grabbed Tony's chart, along with a pen. He was a stocky little man, with stringy hairs that sparingly covered his balding head. Setting a pair of light blue eyes on Tony, he began. "Okay, tell me, any progress? Have you been able to recover any childhood memories since we spoke last Wednesday?"

Tony let out a frustrated sigh. "Look Doc, I'm serious when I tell you that there's nothing to my childhood. My father was a harsh man. He had high expectations for us, especially me, being the oldest male. But other than that, we lived normal lives. Everyone has slight dysfunction in their childhood, right?"

Doc ran a hand over his head from one ear to the other mechanically adjusting a few stray strands. "Unfortunately, yes. But we are not talking about your average dysfunction here, Tony, and you are avoiding my question. I asked you if you could remember anything. We left off this past week with a great deal of memory loss. You have large gaps in your memory bank. Tony, I know you don't agree, but we really need to fill in these gaps. The only way to really get you to complete healing is to find the core reason you created this alternate personality."

"Doc, I thought we already did this." Tony's aggravation was now evident.

"Uncovering the gaps from the torture you suffered during your imprisonment with the Galante *famiglia* was only half the battle," Doc explained.

"So, you're saying that the last six weeks of therapy hasn't even put a dent in the healing process?" Tony's chest began to heave. He had worked so hard at getting better.

Doc placed Tony's chart back on the desk and leaned forward in his chair, placing his elbows on his knees, his fingers to a point. "Tony, you've come a long way. But I have been doing more research on your disorder and the majority of patients with Multiple Personality Disorder are victims of some kind of child abuse. I truly believe the reason most of your childhood memories are a blur is because you have suppressed them. Most likely you developed this disorder when you were a child."

Tony's head was spinning. *Could this be?* "Are you saying that I was abused as a child and don't even remember?" His breathing had accelerated and he struggled to keep his head from swooning.

"It's very likely, Tony. The most important thing that you need to keep remembering is that you are okay. The worst is over. You are at a place in your life where all is well. If we uncover something that is painful, you will have the help and support you need to get well, not only from my staff and I, but from your entire family. Remember, recovering those memories and dealing with that hurt and pain will only help you to live a more complete and happy life."

Tony thought about Doc's words. He was so afraid to let those feelings loose. He did not want his 'alter' to come out. "Doc, look . . ." Tony's stomach trembled, while trying to continue with his sentence.

"What is it, Tony? What are you most afraid of?" Doc asked with concern. He stretched a caring hand forward and touched Tony's knee.

Finally, Tony blurted forth his true fear. "I don't want Max to come out and take over again! I don't want to put Laura in harm's way! Every time he has emerged, he's endangered her life and I can't allow that to *ever* happen, again. I don't trust him! Shoot . . . I don't even know why he hates her so much. She's never done anything to harm me. All I know is that he's a time bomb waiting to go off!"

Dr. Parnell looked upon Tony with understanding. "I totally understand your fears. Here is the difference—Max will only emerge under hypnosis, not in an attempt to defend you. Max is your defender; we've already established that, right? He 'comes out' when you feel you are in a situation you can't handle emotionally or physically. When he emerged from your subconscious for the first time in front of Laura, he was protecting you from an attack he felt you were under. Though you never felt your physical being at risk, Max wanted to defend your emotional state. Now that you are at a more secure place in your life, Max has no reason to stay. But under hypnosis, I can draw him out and see if perhaps he'll be able to recall those childhood memories you've obviously suppressed."

Tony felt fearful and anxious. He could not keep his fidgety hands and feet still. "You still don't understand, Doc. Once he's out . . ." Tony found that he could not even finish his sentence. He lifted his eyes to the ceiling to keep the tears from falling.

Dr. Parnell did seem to understand. "No Tony, he will not be able to take over. When I call your name . . . you'll dominate again."

Tony sighed with little relief and ran his fingers through his wavy hair. "Looks like I don't have a choice in the matter, do I?"

"Not unless you don't want to get better."

He pondered on this a moment. There was too much at stake—too much to lose—Laura, the baby, their family. "Of course I want to get better. I'm gonna be a dad. I gotta get my crap together."

"Well then, when do you wanna start?"

****

Laura tipped the espresso cup toward her lips and took in a sip of the rich dark coffee. It slipped down her throat, warming her insides. Its flavor was thick and its aroma strong. Putting her cup down, she picked up the coffee pot and offered more to her grandfather, who sat adjacent to her.

"No, *bella mia*, two cups is my limit," he stated in a heavy Sicilian accent.

"Are you sure Nonno? I made a pot full."

"*Grazie amore*, but I'm good."

"Have another cookie then," she insisted, lifting the tray of sweets toward him.

He chuckled, lifting his hand in protest. "I'm good, I'm good. Thank you for this wonderful visit. I'm happy to see my *bambina* is getting bigger and bigger." He gently rubbed her slightly protruding belly. "You look beautiful. Just like my Vita."

"Thanks, Nonno. I love it when you visit. I feel like a piece of my momma is with me when you're here. I wish I could have gotten to know Nonna Vita. I'm sure she was wonderful."

Sadness fell across his face. Laura regretted her words. She did not want to make him feel sad. He was already more than remorseful for having excommunicated his only daughter Cara, at 18, when she ran off to marry her *'Americano'* boyfriend, Laura's father, Matthew Duke Marcs. Refusing to forgive her, put a wedge between him and Nonna Vita. The strife and hardship caused Nonna Vita to fall into a deep depression. She struggled with the illness for years. Finally, their daughter's untimely death gave her little hope to live, and soon after, she died as well. Nonno had so many regrets. Laura hoped he was on his way to making amends for all the heartache he had caused.

"I'm sorry, Nonno. Don't look so sad. The past is the past. You can't change what happened. You can only make better decisions for the future and it looks like you've done that." She gave a sympathetic smile.

"*Amore*, you're right. But my heart . . . sometimes it hurts. I don't know what I was thinking when I brought her remains back to the old country. Sometimes, I just want to sit and talk to her. I need to feel her near me. I miss her. She was my life and I hurt her so much."

Laura looked with compassion upon her grandfather. At 64, he was as handsome as he was in his youth. Though slightly rounder around the edges, thanks to his love for pasta, he was still quick on his feet. The slightly thinning hair on his head was still dark brown, speckled with silver at the temple and sides. His graying mustache tickled Laura's cheek each time they exchanged a kiss. His big brown eyes reminded her of the richest chocolate. They filled with love every time he was with her, which really was not often enough. That is why she treasured every visit with him. She loved his Sicilian accent and loved the way he called her '*amore*', meaning 'his love'. He made her feel like she was the world and Laura believed that she was to him.

"Nonno, you said that all Nonna ever wanted was for you to come to Jesus and leave the Mob. You've done that! You've made a promise to God to change and in doing so, Nonna's lifelong prayer has been answered. Right now, she's smiling down at you from Heaven and is celebrating with my momma and all the angels, your return to God. Let go of the guilt and live the rest of your life at peace." Laura reached across the table and placed her hand over his wrinkling fingers.

Nino grabbed it and held it. His eyes shimmered with unshed tears. "You always know the right thing to say!"

Laura placed a napkin in his hand and smiled, while he dabbed his tears. "Don't cry Nonno. We've only good things to look forward to now—the baby, the wedding."

Now a look of concern washed over his lined face.

"Oh no . . . please don't start, Nonno."

"No, Laura *mia*. I'm happy for you that you fiancé is getting the help. But I can no help but to worry. Marriage is for life. What if you make a mistake? You see what happened to you momma."

"Nonno, when my mother ran off, she was young and quite immature. From what you told me about her and from what little I remember she told me, she was treated like a princess at home. You and Nonna Vita did everything for Momma. No disrespect to you or to her, because she was the best momma in the world, but frankly, you spoiled her and she was very naive. She didn't know my father long enough to realize that you may have been right about him." Laura waited for a response from her grandfather. She searched his eyes and found that she spoke the truth. Still, he did not reply. He gazed at her intently as she continued.

"I realize I'm not much older than she was when she ran off, but I have known Tony since I was 14, when my family was killed. Fourteen, Nonno! I have known him for five years. He took me in and cared for me in the darkest days of my life. We've been through Hell and back together! I know his faults, but I also know that he is a good, honest man. He's a hard worker and will do whatever he must to provide for this family. He'll take good care of the baby and me." Laura took in a deep breath. She hated having to defend Tony to her grandfather, but she understood his concerns. Tony had a great deal of emotional baggage he was bringing into the marriage. But Laura loved him and was willing to marry him regardless.

"What happens if he can no get better? What if he goes crazy and hurts you or the baby? You have too much to lose, Laura *mia*. All I will say to you is what my papa, God rest his soul, used to say to me. Keep you eyes '*aperti*' . . . open. Don't rush into this kind of life because you have the little baby. Take you time, *amore*. Don't make a mistake. You new momma will help you with the baby and I will give you any money you need."

A door slammed shut, startling them. "Thanks, but no thanks!" Tony stated.

Laura turned to find Tony strutting into the kitchen from the back door of the house. His face was flushed. His eyebrows knit together in the center with anger. Laura stood to greet him. His face softened as he embraced her and planted a gentle kiss on her lips.

Then he turned to Nino. The look of irritation returned. Still holding Laura he said, "I appreciate your concern for my future wife and child, but let me assure you, I would rather die than bring any harm to either of them. If you can't see that by now, that's your problem. I would appreciate if you could take your opinions *and your advice* elsewhere."

Nino recovered quickly and stood. "I mean no disrespect to you, Tony. I believe you love my granddaughter, but I just want the best for her." He stretched out his hand to Tony, who only looked down at it. Nino sighed heavily. He dropped his hand and picked up his hat on the chair next to him, gently placing it on his head. "Laura *mia*, I thank you again for the time you spend with me. *Grazie per il café*."

"You're welcome, Nonno. Anytime." Laura leaned forward and kissed her grandfather's cheek. He squeezed her shoulders softly and whispered that he loved her. Laura felt sad. She loved him, too, and told him so, while she walked him to the front door. *Would Nonno and Tony ever see eye to eye?*

She watched until Nino entered his vehicle in the driveway. His driver drove off. After closing the front door of their new house, Laura entered the little kitchen decorated in bright yellow and pale green. Tony sat at the round oak table in the corner by the bay window. He looked tired, while pouring himself a cup of espresso. He downed it.

"Slow down, boy. That stuff will grow hair on your chest," Laura teased.

Tony scooted his chair back and patted at his lap. Laura happily sat. "I thought you liked a man with a hairy chest?" he teased back.

"Is that what you call those three little hairs?"

Tony almost broke into laughter. Instead, he gave her a wide grin. "Maybe that's why I'm drinking this stuff."

Laura ran her hands through his sandy-brown hair. *He was such a babe—the dark eyes, his chiseled jaw, the little dimple on his left cheek.* But as beautiful as he was on the outside, he had a heart like no other that she loved so completely. "Don't worry. I love you just the way you are."

"Crazy nutcase and all?" he questioned.

"Stop that. You're not crazy." She smacked his muscular arm.

"That's what your *nonno* thinks," he said it in a joking manner. But Laura knew it really bothered him that Nino did not approve.

"*Nonno* is a close-minded old man, who thinks he's doing me good by meddling in my life. I'm really all he has left here in America. Just let him talk. He thinks he's looking after me. Believe it or not, his heart's in the right place."

Tony scoffed, then growled and quickly kissed her neck. "Man, you have a hard head! You insist on loving the unlovely. I don't know how you do it. You're a better person than me to forgive him and find the good in him. But then again, I guess you did the same with me, so who am I to judge?"

"I learned my stubbornness from you. I won't give up on the people I love. Not *Nonno*, nor you. I promise you, Tony, sooner or later *Nonno's* gonna realize just how wonderful you are. Besides, he *also* knows I have a hard head. If you're what I want, no one can convince me otherwise." Laura cupped his face in her hands. She loved the feel of his freshly shaved skin and the masculine scent of his aftershave. She leaned forward to kiss him.

Tony responded, holding her even closer. When their lips parted, he took in a breath. She could see the tears forming in his eyes.

Her heart sank. Tony rarely cried.

"Tony, what's wrong?"

He struggled to maintain his composure. His face turned slightly red. "Maybe your grandfather's right."

"That's ridiculous."

"I'm serious."

"Why would you say that? Your disorder doesn't make you crazy. It's a real illness—one that you didn't ask for. Don't talk like that," she pleaded.

"I went to see Doc today," his eyes finally met hers. She could see his pain.

"I know . . . and?"

"And . . ." Tony struggled to continue.

"Go ahead . . ." She urged.

"He tried a new procedure on me."

"Okay? Like what?"

At last, he explained. "He wants me to recover some childhood memories I've suppressed. He thinks that I developed Max back when I was a kid. So, he wanted to try hypnosis." Tony wiped his eyes and took in another deep breath. His face was still flushed and his eyes looked worn.

"Did it work?"

"No."

"Why not?"

"I wouldn't let myself go under."

"Tony, why?"

He tenderly picked her up and helped her to her feet. Laura found her footing and stepped aside. He stood and began pacing the kitchen floor. His tall frame moved with grace. The muscles flexed in his jaw. Laura was sincerely concerned now.

"Tony, why didn't you let yourself go under? It might really help you." She stepped in his path and grabbed his hands. She looked into his brown eyes. His long lashes blinked and Laura observed a single tear slip down his cheek. She wiped it with her fingers and waited for him to respond. "Tell me," she whispered.

"I'm scared," he finally managed.

So was she, but she could only encourage him to do what he must to heal. "I don't blame you. What did Doc tell you?"

"That the worst is over and that no matter what we uncover, I've already been through it and I'm okay." Tony seemed to breathe a bit easier. He took her hands and kissed them. "But I'm still scared."

"He's right, as usual. I still say it's okay to be scared. But you do have to trust Doc. He knows what he's doing. If he says this is what will help, do it. If you're scared, do what you always told me to do . . . pray."

"You're right." Tony hugged Laura to him. She embraced him and kissed him again. Pulling his face back, she looked deeper into his eyes. She could feel the love, the fear, the pain, *and* the confusion he was feeling.

In a voice, just above a whisper, she said, "When you found me, the night my family was killed, I thought I could never get over the grief and the pain. But you helped me through it. I just want you to know that I am here for you. I will not let you down. I want to help you the way you helped me. Please let me."

Still holding her in the cozy little kitchen, Tony succumbed to her. He promised to be as open as he could. Laura understood that this would not be easy and that struggles were sure to lie ahead. But she would be prepared. She would be for him everything that he had been for her during her darkest hours.

Laura believed in Tony. She believed in him certainly more than he believed in himself, and that puzzled her. He did not recognize within, the true man that he was. She was determined to show him otherwise. She would help him to realize just how happy she was to have him back . . . and that, God alone was responsible for.

CHAPTER 2

Deuteronomy 7:9

"Know therefore that the LORD your God is God;
He is the faithful God, keeping his covenant of love to a thousand generations of those who love him and keep his commands."

In December of 1973, when she was 14 years old, Laura lived with her family in a lowly cabin in the woods of the small town of Brewerton, New York. Having lost her mother, Cara, during the harrowing birth of her little sister, Sabrina, four years prior, Laura and her older sister, Patty, were forced to take on adult-like responsibilities. Their father, Matthew Duke Marcs, the good-for-nothing '*Americano*' who Nonno Nino so despised, had at long last, sobered up and was finally taking care of the family. But his employment with the infamous mobster, Mario Galante, set him on a path to the family's destruction.

Within that same time frame, Antonio Giacalone's *(aka: Tony Warren)* father, Vito, made the lethal mistake of borrowing a quarter-of-a-million dollars from the same Mario Galante. His inability to repay the debt cost him and his family their lives. Only Tony was spared, because he was the sole heir to a half-a-million-dollar life insurance policy on Vito. The policy, purchased years prior, could pay off the debt to the Galantes and then some, thus their reason for sparing him.

After having lost his family at their hands, Tony was placed in foster care. When he turned 18, he was released from the last foster home that cared for him. His plan was to head to California to meet his uncle, Frank Blandino, Tony's only living relative and trustee to his father's estate. Uncle Frank, who had been recently widowed, resided in California. That fateful day, before Tony was able to board the plane, the Galante *famiglia* abducted him and demanded the name of the trustee.

When the flight arrived in California without Tony, Uncle Frank flew to New York in search of his nephew. Tony, fearing for Uncle Frank's life, remained silent, unwilling to give him up. It was then that he was tortured at the hands of one of the Galante's most ruthless thugs . . . Laura's father, Matthew.

The beatings and the torture Tony sustained were believed to be what led him to suffer a psychotic breakdown. His mind created a second personality who could better sustain the pain he was suffering. In the end, Tony's alternate personality, Max, helped him escape from the *mafioso's* prison.

Laura's father's job was then in jeopardy. Though he could not accomplish the assignment he was given, he felt that Galante should have compensated him. Greedy for money, Matthew embezzled $250,000 from him. On December 14, 1973, he came home from work shouting instructions at Laura and her sisters to pack their things for a hurried move. Unknown to Matthew, the Galante *famiglia* was aware of his treachery.

As Laura helped to gather their few belongings, one of the Galante's henchmen thrust through the door and killed her family. It was by the grace of God that Laura survived. When she came to the realization that her family members were dead, she stumbled out of the cabin for help.

It was then that Tony found her. From the time that he had escaped Galante's prison, until that very moment, Max, his alternate personality, had been running his life. Upon seeing Laura's distress from the loss of her family, Tony overcame his dangerous alter. His compassion for the grieving girl and the fear that he had somehow caused the deaths of her family, compelled him to do what was necessary to care for her.

He befriended her and offered her his help. After much convincing, Laura decided to trust Tony and he led her to his grandparents' home where he and Uncle Frank fostered her for three years. Tony and Laura ultimately fell in love and were promised to one another. Unfortunately, that was not the end of Tony's alternate personality, Max.

One evening, an innocent questioning of his past from Laura brought out Max. He assaulted her and locked her in the basement of the home. However, Laura was able to escape. Heartbroken and battered, she went to the police and the Chief of Police, Massimo Desanti *(aka: Sam)*, took her under his wing. Tony was incarcerated for harming her. Laura, still underage at 17, was put in foster care where she roomed with three other girls her age. Tammy Springer, one of her roommates, became her best friend.

Consequently, Laura and Tammy were fortunate enough to be adopted into the same home. Marlene and John Knight made a place for them in their lives. Laura's life seemed to finally come to order, until she got notice of Tony's upcoming parole. Once he was freed, having lost control to Max again, he inevitably found his way to Laura's new home.

Max plotted and waited for a moment when he could get Laura alone. He threatened to physically harm her, until Tony fought for control in time to realize that, once again, Max had hurt his beloved. Laura was able to escape Max, but emotionally was in disarray. She had finally come to the realization that Tony was suffering some kind of mental disorder.

Nevertheless, this cemented Tony's decision to rid Laura of Max indefinitely. Though it broke his heart to do so, Tony staged his own death, aware that this would free Laura of him forever. This would also free himself from the ongoing pursuit of the police and the Mafia. He went into hiding, while Laura grieved for the love of her life.

His 'death' led Laura into a downward spiral of depression that even young medical intern, Paul Roberts, (whom she met at the hospital on the night Max had attacked) could not pull her out of. For months, he pursued her to no avail. Even Tammy, her adoptive sister, had shown Paul more interest.

Eventually, a bout with lung cancer sent Laura's adoptive mother, Marlene, to the hospital. There, Paul was present to help pick up the pieces. Laura witnessed his kindness and compassion and allowed him to continue his pursuit of her. As Paul and Laura grew closer, Tammy found herself struggling with feelings for him as well.

Though Laura vowed to move on without Tony, she refrained from giving her heart completely to Paul. Paul could sense Laura's distance and grew frustrated with her keeping him at bay. This distance led him into Tammy's awaiting arms.

Suddenly, little incidents began to occur to Paul. Mysterious men warned him to take the next step with Laura or pay the consequences. At a doctors' ball, Paul reluctantly proposed to Laura, breaking Tammy's heart and his own. After discussing a long engagement, Laura accepted.

The attraction between Paul and Tammy grew stronger, still, despite their will to stay away from each other. And as Paul heard the threats to the lives of his family and himself, he realized that his attraction to Tammy had also endangered ***her life***. It was then that Paul felt the true terror.

The mysterious Alfonso Rengali became a short distraction for Tammy as she fought her feelings for Paul. Alfonso was a diversion sent by *the one* who threatened Paul. Paul then understood that he must leave town with Tammy, before danger struck. But before they had a chance to skip town together, a staged accident—meant for Paul—took Tammy's life instead.

Paul was concealed within the Witness Protection Program and Laura and her parents were left in devastating grief.

Yet, danger lurked around every corner, as someone was seriously considering Laura's happiness and was willing to do anything to see that she got it. A week after Tammy's death, Laura drove in to work, parked her vehicle, and suddenly her world went dark. She woke up in the bedroom of the house she lived in with Tony. Tony had no choice but to come out of hiding, for Laura's life was in peril again. With some convincing from Uncle Frank, she allowed Tony to tell his story.

Tony finally had the opportunity to explain that he was suffering from Multiple Personality Disorder. At last, Laura was able to understand Tony's altering behavior. Laura also learned of her father's employment with the Galante *famiglia*. She discovered that he had helped to hold Tony against his will. She listened to all of Tony's confession and admitted her undying love for him.

Unable to deny themselves one last chance to be together, Laura and Tony fell into temptation that evening, later resulting in her pregnancy. The following morning, Tony's last warning to Laura, before turning himself in to the authorities, was that of Paul's relationship to Tammy. He encouraged her to find out the truth behind Tammy's death. Then, Tony willingly turned himself in to the authorities. But brutal forces by the Cicero Police Department hurled forth Max, who vowed to never let Tony 'out' again. Tony was institutionalized with no hope for a cure.

Laura reluctantly returned home to her adoptive parents, hoping to pick up the pieces of her shattered life. She convinced her friend Sam, the Cicero Police Chief, to bring her to where Paul was in hiding so she could try to understand the mysteries surrounding her. Sam agreed and brought her to Paul, who eventually admitted to his love for Tammy. He gave Sam the name of the *mafioso* who had threatened him. An Antonino Valente was to blame for Tammy's unfortunate death.

Determined to draw out the mobster, Sam involved the FBI and a falsified wedding between Laura and Paul was arranged. At the altar, Paul was to call off the wedding, leading those who raised the threats to follow through.

On the day of the wedding, Tony finally fought off Max, overcoming his alter, while still in the institution. He convinced Dr. Parnell that he had taken back control, and Dr. Parnell allowed him a reprieve to put a stop to Laura and Paul's nuptials, not realizing that the wedding was a facade. Interrupting the sting, Tony became the target of Valente's thugs. Standing at the altar, Laura sighted the gunman's target and ran to save her lover.

Tony and Laura were spared of the rapid flying bullet, thanks to Paul's heroism. He took the bullet for Laura and died in her arms.

Though the gunmen were arrested, Mr. Valente was still under their protection. Laura indomitably set out to find a way to rid Tony and herself of the Mafia. She had to find a way to pay off the debt of the now pursuing Galante *famiglia* and get protection against this Antonino Valente, who caused the deaths of both Tammy and Paul. She prayed her biological mother's estranged and wealthy father could help. After further investigation, Laura found that her mother's maiden name was also Valente. The man who sought all means to see to her happiness *was* her grandfather, Antonino Valente *(aka: Nonno Nino).*

Laura set up a meeting with her grandfather. He tried to make Laura understand that his motives were genuine and his intent was to never let anyone get hurt. In good faith, he paid off the debt to the Galante *famiglia* for Laura and Tony and offered his protection against them. Laura sought God's help to find forgiveness for her grandfather, as Nino made a promise to leave the Mafia for good and to give his heart to God.

Just as Laura came to forgive Tony for the harm Max had done to her, she forgave the only living biological member of her family. In two short months, Nino had become an intricate part of her life. Though he did not approve of Laura's decision to marry Tony, she continued to rely on him for love and support. Somehow, Nino *had* to come to realization that Tony was a respectable, loving man and that he was not crazy, nor a threat. Laura would take this second chance God had given her with Tony, regardless of his disorder.

Now was Laura's chance to show the Lord that she was going to stand firm in faith. She was going to be strong for Tony and give him back all the faith and hope he had given her. She *could not* fail Him.

****

The following Monday, after Laura met with Nonno Nino for coffee, a freshly showered and shaven Tony drove to the Knight home in his Ford F-150 pickup. He felt confident in the crisp white shirt and tie he threw on to match his dark blue Dockers. To make the outfit more complete, he wore a matching sport coat. It being his first day on the job, he even had his hair cut to a shorter length, the day before, to try to tame the thick waves. He felt ready to tackle the day.

Upon pulling into the driveway, he gave a quick honk and exited his vehicle. He took the porch steps two at a time and rang the doorbell. He could not contain the excitement he felt about his first day on the job with

John. He heard the pitter-patter of dainty feet and smiled. In a moment, he would have his arms wrapped around the love of his life. Just the thought of her made his heart double in rhythm.

The door opened and as usual, she greeted him with her cheerful smile. "Morning, handsome."

"Good morning, beautiful." Tony stepped in and embraced her. She smelled as sweet as any flower might and looked just as beautiful. Her hair was swept up in a ponytail, her face painted perfectly, and she was dressed in a lavender pantsuit, for work. "You look delicious enough to eat," he added in a hush.

"Oh, you're only trying to be nice, because I look like a moose," Laura answered, while blushing. He could not believe she still blushed for him. *God, how he loved her.*

"Are you kidding? If I didn't know you, I wouldn't even know you were pregnant. Just a little rounder in the middle," he joked. Tony held her closer and kissed the hollow of her neck.

"Just a little? Thank you, but I feel like a cow." She reached for his hand and guided him into the kitchen nook.

"Hard headed," he mumbled loud enough for her to hear. "You're four-and-a-half months pregnant. I've seen twigs fatter than you."

She giggled. They entered the kitchen where John and Marlene sat, finishing breakfast. Tony greeted his future in-laws, sat down, and accepted the warm cup of coffee Marlene offered. After adding a little cream and sugar, he got comfortable next to his bride-to-be.

"Are you ready for your first day as manager?" John excitedly asked. He had a fresh, clean look about him today and Tony noticed that he had shaved off his beard. John was always dressed in a suit and tie. He never looked a day over 40, even if he was going to celebrate his 50th birthday in January. He was tall and lean, and kept a strong stance about him.

"Can't wait to get my hands working again." Tony sipped the warm coffee.

"We'll head back to the office, just after I drive you around some of the rental dwellings and apartments we own," John remarked.

"Sounds like a plan." Tony reached over and caressed Laura's back. "What'll you two lovely ladies be doing today?" He smiled at Marlene as well.

"Off to work for me," Laura stated. She still continued to run the law office of defense attorney, Jasper Stone.

"Well, since you're all so busy working, someone has to plan this wedding," Marlene offered. "That's what I'll be working on."

"Now that the date is official, we have to make the arrangements. Short and simple; small but sweet," Laura added.

"February 24th, right?" John asked.

"That's right," Tony said. "Not a day later. I've waited too long for this."

Laura's eyes filled and Tony pulled her into a hug.

John and Marlene stole a glance at one another and smiled. Marlene lifted a graceful hand and patted Tony's shoulder. "She never gave up on you. I'm so happy that you both ended up together. You deserve all the love and happiness this world has to offer."

"Thank you." Tony reached up and grabbed Marlene's hand in thanks. She was so dainty, almost fragile looking. Her struggle with lung cancer left her slightly thin, but almost a year into remission gave them hope that she would stay strong and beat the odds.

Marlene rose to clear the breakfast dishes and Laura helped. They chatted in excitement about the upcoming nuptials. Tony observed at how easily Laura blended with her adoptive mother. They appeared total opposites, but the love was visible to any eye.

Marlene had short, straight, black hair in contrast to Laura's golden-brown wavy locks. Her eyes were round and big—a dark-brown color, versus Laura's almond-shaped hazel eyes; surrounded in long dark lashes. Marlene was petite and thin, while Laura was not short, nor was she tall. She was an average 5' 4" tall, with what Tony thought was an incredible body—curves in all the right places, even pregnant. It did not hurt that Laura's heart-shaped face was the most beautiful he had ever seen. He could not wait to make her his bride.

The men listened a little more to their chatter, before getting up to leave. John reached for his briefcase and kissed Marlene goodbye. Tony did the same to Laura, and they drove into the city in John's 1978 Lincoln Towncar.

There was a comfortable silence in the car, while they pulled into the parking lot of the financial firm, after having visited a few of the more prominent dwellings. John walked Tony through the building's doors and to the elevator that took them to the second floor. Entering the office, they stopped at the front desk for the first introductions.

"Good morning, Beth." John greeted.

"Mr. Knight, good morning." The young woman behind the desk was attractive in her own way. Her long blonde hair was styled in a modern fashion, framing her round face. She had pretty blue eyes and a nice smile.

"Beth, this is my future son-in-law, Tony. Tony, this is Beth, our newest employee. She started with us just a couple weeks ago, replacing our previous assistant, an older woman, who passed suddenly. Beth has done an unbelievable job, considering having to fill such big shoes. She can help you with whatever you need." He turned to Beth and explained, "Tony's going to be using the empty office space to help run my other ventures. Though he's not working for the firm, I'd appreciate if you can aid Mr. Giacalone in whatever . . ."

Beth's face lit up and she looked at Tony intently. Interrupting John, she stammered aloud, "Tony? Did you say Tony Giacalone? From Syracuse?"

Tony looked at her more closely. "Yes," he answered almost questioningly.

"Oh my gosh! Tony, don't you remember me? It's me, Beth, from North Syracuse Junior High! We were in science class together. Mr. Hagle's class."

"Yes, I remember Mr. Hagle, but I'm sorry, I don't remember you." Tony tried to recollect the face and the name.

By this time, Beth stood and walked out from behind the desk. She leaned up against it. Her waist was tiny, yet she had a full figure. She threw her hands in the air in excitement. "Okay, picture this—Mr. Hagle's class—you sat in the first row, second seat. I sat in the second row, third seat. I had dirty-brown hair, Coke-bottle glasses, and was quite heavy. Now do you remember me?"

"I'm sorry. I have a terrible memory."

"Oh!" She moaned. "That's okay. I wasn't much to look at. It's no wonder you don't remember me."

"That's not it. I really do have a terrible memory," Tony insisted. "And you don't look anything like you're describing."

"Thank you," her eyes shone with pride. "After you left in ninth grade, I lost over 100 pounds and I've kept it off since."

"That's awesome. What a small world. So, what brings you here to Albany?" Tony quizzed, glancing at John who seemed amazed at their association.

"After graduation, my parents moved further east so my father could be closer to my grandmother, who was ill. Later, she passed, but we stayed and established ourselves here about four years ago. I can't believe this. After all these years. You know . . . I had a crush on you in junior high!" Beth gave him a huge smile and poked his arm with her finger. Tony blushed and she continued. Beth then glanced nervously at John. It was as if she had forgotten he was there. She then added, "Boss, I hope you don't mind my chatting. I can't believe this is your future son-in-law! It's truly a small world."

"Yes, it sure is." John laughed.

"Well, I love it here!" Beth cried. "And so will you." She pointed a painted fingernail at Tony and gently laid a hand on his forearm. "Tell me, what brings *you* to Albany?"

Tony, uncomfortable under her touch, smoothly moved his arms while he answered her last question. "Laura brings me to Albany, obviously. I moved from town to town in foster homes, after my family passed, until I finally landed in Cicero. That's where I met her. Later, she was adopted by John, as you know, and here I am now. I bought a little house for us, right here in town. We'll be getting married in February."

"Yes," John added. "Just a couple months away and Tony will be both a husband and a father. Luckily for me, he has awesome handyman and managerial skills, so I'll be using them to run my rentals. You two will be seeing a lot more of each other and will have plenty of time to catch up. Let's get busy, in the meantime."

"Great!" Beth stated. Though she had long since dropped her hand, she seemed to seek any cause to touch Tony. She patted his shoulder and gave him a wide smile. "I'll look forward to that. Come find me if you need anything. I'd be happy to help." She gave him a wink. John turned to lead the way for Tony.

Tony smiled politely and said, "Thanks." He followed John around the front desk and down the hallway. "Thank *you*!" he whispered to John, under his breath.

"You're welcome. I didn't think she was gonna let you leave." John gave a low chuckle. "You must have turned 10 shades of red, under her touch."

"I wasn't expecting her to openly flirt with me, while my father-in-law stood watching. Is she 'a-sandwich-short-of-a-picnic-basket', or what?"

John laughed aloud, placing a strong hand on Tony's back. "I'd have to say so. But she can make a mean cup of coffee!"

The rest of the afternoon went by quickly. John explained the different rules and regulations that came with each dwelling, so that Tony knew what to expect from the tenants. His job would consist of collecting rent, keeping the books, affirming their renter's insurance policies, taking care of maintenance needs, and assisting them with any other issues or problems. His office was just down the hall from John's, next to his associate and best friend, Marco Apolone's. It was a smaller office, but had a beautiful view of the outdoors.

Tony sat at his desk and arranged a few pictures Laura had given him of the two of them. He did his best to settle into his office and make it his own. He heard a rap at the door, which was opened.

Beth sauntered in.

"Making yourself at home?"

"I'm trying," Tony hinted.

"I won't keep you, then. Just thought I'd come and check up on you—see if you'd like me to fetch you a cup of coffee."

"Thanks, but I just want to get finished here, so I can get home."

"Rushing home to your girl, are you?" Beth questioned.

"Absolutely."

"Well, that's sweet. I'm still looking for my 'Mr. Right'," she said with a pout.

Tony gave her a quick glance and smiled. "I'm sure you'll find him sooner or later."

"I hope it's sooner than later." She gave him a smile with a hard stare, before gracefully turning on her heel and leaving the room.

Tony was happy to have her leave his office. If there was one thing she would soon learn, it was that Tony only had eyes for Laura.

****

That afternoon, after returning home from work, Laura and Marlene sat at the nook table and excitedly planned John's surprise birthday party. They put together a guest list with all of John's family, friends, co-workers, and employees. They would trick him into believing that it would be the office Christmas party. Meanwhile, the party would be the celebration of half a century of birthdays.

"So, we have two weeks to pull this together. Between the wedding and this party, I'm going to need a vacation," Marlene cried.

"You can join Tony and me on our honeymoon to sunny Mexico!" Laura offered.

"Oh, I wouldn't dream of tagging along. Though if you two don't mind, I might head up to Cicero and spend a week at the house, while you're gone."

"By all means, Mom. That house is magical, the way it can put us all at such ease. I love going there," Laura claimed.

"Me too." Marlene gathered the papers from the table and hid them in a drawer. "I'm going to get dinner started. Our men will be home soon."

Laura rose from her chair and began helping Marlene with supper. Before long, Tony and John arrived, laughing and making ample noise, as they entered. "I swear you looked red as a pepper," John ridiculed.

"Do you blame me?" Tony exclaimed.

"Blame you, for what?" Laura inquired. Tony came to her and planted a kiss on her cheek. "What's so funny?"

"Tony bumped into an old friend at the office," John began. "It turns out that Beth is an old classmate of his, way back from junior high. Let's just say she wasn't shy in telling him that she had a crush on him, back then."

"Oh, really," Laura sassily jested.

"Relax. I don't even remember her. John's just razzing me because Beth *is not* shy. I turned a few shades of red and he thought that was funny." Tony tried to give John the 'cut throat' signal, while Laura was turned the other way. She caught him and smacked his arm.

"Great! Now I'm going to be worried about her coming in to bring you coffee, with an extra short skirt and high heels," Laura pouted.

"She could come in naked and I wouldn't notice her," Tony reassured.

John laughed even harder. Laura pouted and John hugged her. "Sweet Laura. Don't worry." He pulled her closely and in a more serious tone, though still jesting, he whispered, "If you want, I'll watch them like a hawk!"

"John!" Marlene chided.

"Dad! That is not funny!"

"Don't worry, Laura," John coaxed. "Beth is harmless. She wouldn't dare mess with the boss's son-in-law. I just love getting a rise outta you!"

Laura playfully smacked his arm and returned his hug. "You're such a clown."

They ate dinner together with more laughter and chitchat. They finally settled down in the front family room where they sat to watch some television. John put on the evening news and they all watched.

Laura snuggled up next to Tony. The thought of any woman throwing herself at him actually really angered her. She could not even try to imagine what she might do if she had witnessed it herself. She gazed up at him and he looked lovingly down at her. He mouthed the words 'I love you' to her. She hugged his arm closer.

The news reporter on TV went on to tell of the ongoing Mafia crime in central New York. It seemed the Mafia even had a say in who ran and who won political races. They had infiltrated their way into every facet of society. They had grown in power: trafficking weapons, drugs, and anything that would increase their supremacy and money. Laura felt disgusted thinking that that was the life her grandfather used to live. She was thankful he had turned from it.

John changed the TV station, also disgusted with what the news had to say. "I can't stand to hear about that anymore. To think, we lost our Tammy to that. It makes me so angry." His face reddened as he spoke.

Laura turned her head downward in shame for her grandfather's past behavior. John and Marlene had long since forgiven him, as the true Christians they were. But the pain was still raw and any human could understand their anger and need for justice. Laura recognized that they only tolerated Nonno Nino for the love of her.

"I hear you, John. Those pigs cost me my sanity," Tony admitted.

"Almost," Laura corrected.

"Almost," Tony agreed. "I still don't feel that I can say the worst is over."

John lowered the volume with the remote control and made himself more comfortable next to Marlene. "Why do you say that, Tony? You appear to be doing so well."

Tony glanced from John, to Marlene, to Laura. He seemed almost hesitant to continue. Suddenly, it was as if he opened up the dam and let the flooding waters through. "Dr. Parnell wants me to undergo further treatments. I already talked about this with Laura and Uncle Frank and would like to talk to the both of you as well. I can use the support. Doc seems to think that my personality didn't split off when I was held prisoner by the Galantes. He believes that my condition developed back when I was a boy."

"How and why does he believe this?" Marlene asked with concern in her eyes.

"Apparently, he has researched my condition. It's more common in abused children."

Laura was amazed he had actually said the words. She knew how difficult it was for him to talk about these things. She imagined this was just one step closer to healing for him.

She added carefully, "Tony is scared to undergo the treatments because they may have to bring out Max."

"Doc reassured me a million times that he cannot take over. Max will be called out under hypnosis or a drug—whatever works. He already tried hypnosis, but I think I was so afraid to let myself go under, that that's why the session failed. After talking with Laura, I feel better about doing this. My next appointment is tomorrow afternoon. I could use a few extra prayers."

John reached across and patted Tony's knee. "You can count on it, son. We'll keep you in our prayers, as we always have. God will see you through. You must not let Satan get a hold of you. Fear comes only from him."

"Absolutely," agreed Marlene. "Remember the Bible verse that tells us, 'Jesus will never leave you nor forsake you.'"

"Thanks so much. You have no idea what it means to me."

It never ceased to amaze Laura, the kindness and love that John and Marlene offered Tony. After everything they had witnessed Laura go through with him, she imagined they would have found it hard to accept him. Any other close-minded folk might have forbidden her to see him, like Nonno Nino. Instead, they supported her every decision.

Before Tony left for home that evening, Laura escorted him to the front door. Marlene and John wished him God's blessings and went upstairs to bed. Tony slowly strode to the door holding Laura's hand. Stopping, he lifted it to his lips and kissed it. He held her gaze for a moment before speaking.

"I know I'll see you again tomorrow, but I still don't want to go," he whispered.

"Before long, we'll never have to say goodbye at night again. We can crawl up into bed together, the way we used to in the old house."

He pulled her closer and whispered again, "Only this time, I don't have to keep my hands to myself."

Laura giggled, "Like that really worked." She pointed to her protruding stomach.

"That shouldn't count!" Tony breathed. "One night! Only one night, we gave into our love for one another. Yes, it was wrong. Yes, we should have been stronger and waited. But we lived pure for three years! When I think about it, I must've been made of stone!" Tony added, his voice rising a tad.

"Shh! Yes, you're right. We did do good for so long. But we did mess up! And now, I'm getting married with a 'bun in the oven'."

"Can I help it if you're 'Fertile Myrtle'," he teased.

"I'm serious," she chided again. "I've disgraced my family."

Tony suddenly grew serious. "You know Marlene and John hate it when you talk like that. What happened when you and I reunited was not deliberate or planned. Besides, you can't keep punishing yourself for the past. We've been forgiven, God has blessed us with a baby, let's make things right as soon as possible. February 24th couldn't get here fast enough, as far as I'm concerned."

Laura reached up and held on to his neck. She ran her hands through his hair and pulled him into a kiss. His lips were warm on hers. She loved the feel of him so close to her. "I love you," she murmured into his ear.

"I love you, more," Tony found her gaze. His face was still serious. "I always will."

"Tony Giacalone, you sound like you're never gonna get a chance to tell me that again. Don't be so solemn."

"I'm sorry. I'm just worried about tomorrow. Keep praying for me."

"I promise. Would you feel better if I accompanied you to your appointment?"

"No!" he snapped. "What I mean is—I don't want you anywhere near where Max may be. I know you want to come for moral support, but please understand, I can't take the risk of something happening to you or our baby on account of me. Your prayers are all I need."

"Of course, Tony. You're always in my prayers."

He gave her a slow last kiss and trailed out the door. Laura let out a long sigh. She would surely get to her knees and talk to God that night.

CHAPTER 3

Ephesians 6:4

"Fathers, do not provoke your children to anger, but bring them up by training and instructing them about the Lord."

Tuesday, November 28

"Don Nino, how are you?" Alfonso Rengali extended his hand to Nino Valente. Nino took the hand of his friend and pulled him into a bear hug.

It was an unseasonably warm day and Alfonso found Nino sitting in his kitchen nook, surrounded by large windows, absorbing the sun. Nino had moved from his miniature mansion in Long Island, to a cozy yet elegant house south of Albany, in Nassau. Alfonso, having been living in the vicinity the past six months, helped to find the home for his boss so that he could reside closer to his granddaughter, Laura.

In a deep voice, Nino greeted him. "Fonzie, I'm good! How you doing?" He pointed to a chair at the table and offered him a cup of espresso.

"I'm doing, *grazie*," Alfonso took the cup and sat down across from Nino.

"Tell me, how did it go with my friends?"

Alfonso lied, hating the fact that this man had just brushed him off to a few so-called friends for a job. "I got in touch with them, but I'm gonna be honest with you . . . I decided to go on my own, for now."

"You mean to tell me that they did no take you in? I specifically told them to take care of you!" Nino exclaimed.

"Well, after working for someone like you, no one else can really compare." Alfonso did his best to cover the spite he felt. "After all, you're an awesome boss."

The corners of Nino's mouth turned up and a smile lit his face. "*Grazie*, Alfonso! That is nice thing to say. I do admit, some of the time, I miss the way things were. But I have more important things now. I have my *famiglia* back and I would no change that for nothing."

Alfonso nearly choked on his espresso. He took a napkin to his lips and blotted the drops of coffee that threatened to explode from his mouth. "That's great. I'm happy for you. So . . . there is *no* chance for your return then, ehh?"

"No, *amico mio*. I'm retired now. The business is done. No more. Whatever was left, I sold to other families. Except for the transporting business. This I will leave to you one day, as I promised, when it is my time."

"That means the world to me, Boss. But I'm going to miss working side by side with you."

Nino stared intently at Alfonso, seeming almost to read into his thoughts. Alfonso fidgeted and pretended to enjoy the cup of espresso, while staring out into the outside world. Finally, Nino broke the short silence. "I'm sorry, Fonzie."

Puzzled, Alfonso looked at Nino. "Sorry? For what?"

Nino turned his chair, so to face him. He looked at him intently. "I know you hoped to one day run this *famiglia*. I'm sorry, because I love you too much to let you fall into the same kind of life I lived. You are like the son I never had. That is why I referred you to those *amici* of mine. They live the clean life. This is what you momma would want for you—to have the life outside the Mafia. And the same goes for me. I don't want this for you. You go make a better life for yourself. Mafia life will get you killed."

Alfonso felt his blood begin to boil. *How dare he pretend to care about his well-being! How dare he claim to know what his mother wanted for him! Did Nino think that the measly $500,000 bonus he gave him, along with the legitimate business, when he passed, was going to be enough to compensate for the position of 'Don'? Especially after what he had done for Nino—after how hard he had worked for him! Not to mention that Nino was walking away with millions of dollars more. And what of the authority and the control?* Alfonso wanted the name and the power behind it all.

He calmed himself and quietly probed, "No offense, Don Nino, but isn't that a choice I should make for myself? I'm almost 24 years old. I appreciate your concern and yes, you're right, my mother never wanted me to be involved in the Mafia. Yet, she sent me to you, just before she died."

"Yes, because you have no one else in you *famiglia*. You father, Gabe, was one of my best men. She know I felt an obligation to you and to her. I promise to take care of you both and Nino Valente never break a promise! I will take care of you, even if you no like it!"

This man was absurd! He wanted management over everything! Alfonso vowed to end it. Nino would *not* have control over his life. No matter what his mother's death-bed request had been. "You're not obligated to take care of me. Though I appreciate the sentiment, I can take care of myself. I know what I'm doing. Boss, I look up to you. You're a man of power, poise, and respect. When you tell someone to jump, they ask, 'How high?' You're a savvy businessman, a leader in the trade's biz. I really wanted to take over for you."

"And sentence you to a life of crime, *per sempre*? Forever? No! No! Fonzie, you mean too much to me. If you want help, I will help you to start a legitimate successful business of you own. One that will keep you outta the Mafia. Don't you want a *famiglia* of you own, someday? Don't you want to live stress-free with no worry to look over you shoulder all the time? No! My mind is a made up." Nino sat back and played with his mustache, waiting for Alfonso's reply.

It took all that Alfonso had in him to not reach over and choke the man he once loved like a father. This only fueled his revenge more. Now he was certain he had made the right decision in turning to Nino's archenemy, Mario Galante. *Nino would pay for his arrogance and for going back on his word!* Alfonso thought carefully for a response. He must not give Nino even the slightest inclination that he was upset with him.

"Yes, I do hope to have a family of my own, someday. Perhaps, even with that gorgeous granddaughter of yours," he joked. "In fact, the more I think about it . . . you're right. A life of crime could get me killed or endanger a future family. I can be just as successful owning a legitimate business, right?"

Nino reached over and patted his shoulder, "You make me a happy man today, Alfonso. I will help you in any way."

Hook, line, and sinker. Alfonso had Nino right where he wanted him. Now it was just a matter of deceiving Mario Galante into believing that Nino was devising a plan of attack against him.

****

Tony rested his head on the pillow of his assigned bed for the procedure about to take place. The walls of the room of the Catholic hospital were plain, aside from the cross that hung above the door. Tony released a slow long breath and said a silent prayer. Laura's last words to him had been, *'If the Lord can bring you to it, the Lord will see you through it'*. He thanked God for her and prayed for Him to watch over and protect her.

He glanced down at his bound arm and watched the IV drip administer a drug by the name of Sodium Amytal. Glancing at his other arm, it gave him relief to see that it was also bound. Max could not escape, *if* he was to 'come out'. Nurses walked in and out of the room monitoring him steadily. The door opened and Dr. Marcus Parnell entered. He instantly gave Tony a reassuring smile and sat down next to the bed.

"Getting sleepy yet?"

"Kind of."

"Relax. Listen to the sound of my voice and just let go. You're safe here. I promise you'll be okay. Trust me. Do you trust me, Tony?"

Tony nodded, already feeling the drug begin to take effect. "Yeah, Doc, I trust you."

"Good. I believe in you. Relax and close your eyes."

* * *

Dr. Parnell watched Tony finally release restraint and fall into near sedation. He kept an eye on the blood pressure monitor and heart rate. Tony was stable and the procedure could begin. Unbuttoning his hospital jacket, he sat on the foot of the bed. He motioned for the nurse to press the record button on the tape recorder near the bed.

After clearing his voice, he announced into the recorder the name of the patient and the procedure. Laying a gentle hand on Tony's leg, he began.

"Tony? Tony can you hear me?" Dr. Parnell could see the rapid eye movement behind the eyelids of his patient. Still, Tony did not respond. "Tony, it's me, Dr. Parnell. I'd like to talk to you. Do you know what today is?"

It seemed as though Tony almost struggled to speak. His lips twitched and his eyes continued to flutter. "What is today, Tony?"

"Tuesday," he answered in a muffled way.

"Very good. And how do you feel? Do you feel like talking to me today?"

"About?" Tony questioned.

"Let's talk about your mother, Tony."

"Don't want to talk about her."

"Why not? Can you tell me why you don't want to talk about her?"

"She . . . she . . ." Tony would not continue.

"She what? What did she do?"

Tony's eyebrows knit together in frustration and he raised his voice to answer the question. "She did nothing! Absolutely nothing!"

"Okay, I can see you're getting upset. Can we talk about something else? How about your siblings? You were very fond of your little brother, Vincey," Dr. Parnell attempted.

Tony became further upset. He whimpered in his sleep at the mentioning of his little brother. "Vincey, poor Vincey," he moaned.

"You miss him, don't you?"

"Yes, so much."

"What of your sisters? Do you miss them as well?"

"I couldn't help them. I couldn't help them," Tony cried.

"Why did you need to help them? What happened to your sisters, Tony?" Tony would not answer. His crying intensified, until his body shook with sobs. Dr. Parnell tried again, "Tony, tell me what happened?"

"I can't."

"Yes, you can. It's okay. You're safe. No one can hurt you here. Tell me," he insisted.

"NO!" Tony's voice immediately changed.

"Why not?" The doctor pushed.

"Because, he doesn't want to remember."

He looked up from his notepad, recognizing the voice immediately. "Hello, Max. It's been a while since you and I talked. How are *you* feeling today?"

"Just peachy. I want you to stop prying into our past. It's none of your business," Max answered.

"Well, Max, I'm afraid it is my business. It's my job to make Tony well again and you're going to help."

"Why? So he can go off happily-ever-after with that chick he wants to marry?"

"Precisely. We're going to make it so that Tony is aware of all that you withstood to protect him. He'll know what happened and this will help to bring about healing for the both of you." Dr. Parnell checked Tony's blood pressure and noticed a small spike in the numbers. Max was affecting Tony's heart rate as well.

"He can't handle the truth. Why do you think I'm here?"

"What is the truth? Tell me about what Tony's life was like."

Max began . . .

****

Syracuse, NY 1950s

Maria Fontana, daughter of Paolo and Lisa Fontana, migrated to Cicero, New York, with her family in the mid-1940s.

Vito Giacalone and his two brothers were also immigrants from Italy. They came to America in search of carpentry work. Carpenters by trade, they began a business of their own in Syracuse, New York, and were successful for a while. Vito became friends with Maria's sister Margherita's husband, Frank Blandino. Through their friendship, Vito became interested in Maria and the marriage was arranged. In 1951, young Maria, at the age of 17, wed Vito Giacalone.

Frank and Margherita eventually moved to sunny California, in hopes of finding a warmer climate and with a dream of opening their own fruit market. Paolo and Lisa Fontana, unable to part with either daughter, kept a house in New York for summer vacations, and moved to California with Margherita and Frank.

This left Maria in New York alone, with only Vito as her family. Hoping the opportunity would bond the couple, Maria tried to reach out to her new husband. But she soon found that Vito was a quiet and reserved kind of man—one who rarely showed emotion or feeling, aside from faultfinding criticism. Her loneliness made excuses for his coldness, and though he came across as aloof, she reasoned that he was a good provider.

Shortly after they wed, Maria became pregnant with their first child. Antonio Giacalone was born on December 4, 1954, bringing the only joy into Maria's life. Her relationship with her husband continued to be just an arrangement for him. Her duties as a wife were to cook, clean, and care for their son. She could have no other interests outside of her duties. Luckily for her, she enjoyed her time with her infant son.

Maria cherished Baby Tony and this caused a deeper wedge between her and Vito. Vito seemed jealous of the attention Tony received from her. He began to treat the child in the same cold manner. As Tony grew, even he came to realize that in order to gain his father's love, he could not demonstrate his love for his mother openly.

When Tony turned 3, Maria had another child with Vito, and Caterina was born. Being a female, Vito immediately lost interest in the child. Two years later, Nellie, another female child, was born. Tony had plenty of playmates now, but only during the hours in which his father was not home. Vito made it clear that Tony was not to be babied and that he needed to be taught to be strong and manly. There was no playing with girls.

Trying for another male heir, Vito impregnated Maria again. When Tony turned 7, Rosemarie, whom Tony nicknamed, Rosie, was born. Tony was at an old enough age that he could recall the disgusted look on his father's face when they announced another female child.

Vito even went as far as accusing Maria of failing as a wife. It was then that the real abuse began.

****

Nino and Alfonso sat on the leather couch of the cozy study in Nino's new house. A soccer match played on a station of the 26-inch TV placed before them. The men enjoyed the game after eating a filling lunch prepared by Nino's housekeeper and cook, Josie.

Alfonso patted his stomach and yawned. "That Josie sure outdid herself today."

"A wonderful cook I have, ehh?" Nino added.

"Awesome. Thanks for asking me to stay. I wasn't planning on spending the afternoon here."

"Fonzie, you come to my house anytime. You like family to me."

"Same here, Boss. I didn't get to know my dad. But if I had to pick one, he'd have been just like you."

Nino felt himself choke up. He smiled and patted Alfonso's knee. "He was a good man, you father."

Alfonso nodded with a distant look in his eyes. "Tell me something," he suddenly quizzed. "Why did my mother move us to California after he passed? I asked her this question a million times when I was a kid. She never gave me a straight answer. Her family was here—my father's family was here. What provoked her to go to Cali? If we would have stayed here, I would probably be a great deal closer to my parents' relatives. Instead, I'm like a stranger to them. How could she up and leave? You guys were close. Do you know why?"

Nino's face turned ashen. He thought back to nearly 25 years ago. *How could he tell this kid what really went on?* He did not want to hurt him. Yet, his conscience told him that he could not lie, either. "There was a lot of pain here for you momma after you father die. She went to California to get away from the memories of Gabe. I think this is why she go. She picked California because a lot of *Italiani* who immigrated to New York did no like the cold weather. And many of them moved there. Paula flew west with a group of *Italiani* I know. I made sure you was settled in nice home."

Alfonso stared into the elegant rug, still seeming to be off in a different world. Unexpectedly, he snapped back and agreed. "That makes sense. I can see how it was hard for her to stay here with the loss of my father. I must admit—she did love the warm weather in sunny Cali."

"Yes, she always loved the beach," Nino smiled

"You're right! How did you know?" Alfonso enquired in surprise.

"Oh . . . well, Paula and Gabe, and me and Vita, used to go to the beach all the time. Vita would hide under the umbrella and Paula would be in the sun. She always had the dark tan."

Alfonso laughed upon remembering his mother. "Yeah, that sounds just like her. The Sun Goddess is what I used to call her." They laughed in unison. "Mom was lots of fun—the life of the party. Even when times were tough, which was often, she tried to make it a game. If the gas was shut off 'cause she couldn't make a bill, she'd say, 'Let's build a fort of blankets and pretend we're trapped outside in the snow'. We'd put on our coats and rough it until she could scrape up the money to pay the bill."

Nino fidgeted in his seat uncomfortably, while listening to Alfonso talk about how hard he and his mother had it in California. "I wish she told me it was so hard for you both. I would have help anyway that I could."

"It's okay. How could you know we were struggling? Besides, as a kid, I was oblivious to how difficult it was for her. She hid her worries from me, too." Alfonso smiled upon reminiscing, "One time, the bank almost took our car. Mom was scrambling to find money to make the payment. She told me to search the house for anything we didn't need. Within a day, she managed to set up a garage sale and sell enough items to pay the bill. You know how she convinced me to get rid of some of my toys? She said we had to pretend we had just opened up a store and she made me the cashier. I was so happy to collect the money that I forgot it was my toys being sold. She was amazing at making what could have been a hard childhood, into one big game of fun and laughter."

Nino abruptly lowered the volume of the TV with the remote control. He turned to Alfonso and rested a hand on his shoulder. "Son, I've been thinking this afternoon. How would you feel if I give to you the transporting business now?"

Alfonso sat for a moment with his mouth agape. "Whoa, where did that come from? I thought you wanted to give it to me when you passed?" he questioned.

"Now that I think it through, it make no sense. I will no be able to see you do well for yourself if I'm dead. I change my mind. You take the business now. I don't need it. I have money for the rest of my life. You are still young. You make a life for yourself now. Okay?"

"Boss, I don't know what to say. That's very kind of you. I would be honored to take over that business. I promise . . . I won't let you down." Alfonso gave Nino a hug, patting his back heartily.

Nino's eyes filled up and a smile fell across his face again. "I love you, Alfonso. You make me remember my youth. I was a hard worker like you, too. If you need anything, you come to me, okay?"

Alfonso laughed and his cheeks blushed. "Well . . . there is one thing I'd like to ask you, since you're being so generous and all." His eyes cast downward in embarrassment.

"Go ahead, tell me," Nino urged.

"Hook me up with your granddaughter, man. She's beautiful. When I met her a few months ago, I'd wished you wanted me to lure *her* away from that doctor, not Tammy."

"Oh no, *amico mio*. This is something I can no do. My *nipote* is with a baby. She is going to marry that Giacalone. He is the *papa`*."

"What? Oh, man! You never told me that! I knew she wanted Giacalone, but I was hoping you could take care of that."

"Oh, my friend, I try to tell her. It almost backfired to me. I cannot lose my *nipote*. I can no take the risk. Trust me, I no like that Giacalone. He is *pazzo*! Just crazy! But if I push too hard, I will lose her," Nino explained.

"No disrespect, Don Nino, but man, she has you right here," Alfonso pointed to his pinky finger.

Nino burst out laughing. "You right. I'm crazy for her. Since I make mistakes with my daughter, Cara, I learn my lesson for Laura. I love her too much to take the risks. If she make a mistake and marries Giacalone, I pray that God will help her."

"Whoa! Whoa! Whoa! Now I really can't believe my ears. What's this God stuff you're talking about? Since when?" Alfonso questioned.

"Why do you think I leave the Mafia? Alfonso, I'm getting to be old. I want to be with my Vita when I die. Vita is with God, I don't doubt. If I want to see her again, I must change my ways. You should, too. That is why I tell you to leave the Mafia. Join me. God will forgive you, too."

"Wow, Boss. This is heavy stuff. I'll have to think about it more. All this came about because of your granddaughter?"

"*Si*. She is a good Catholic girl. Too good for that punk Giacalone."

"She sounds amazing. Maybe I can help you get rid of Giacalone without spilling any blood?"

Nino looked at Alfonso and considered what he had suggested. The thought tempted him to take matters into his own hands. After a moment, he shook his head in no. "I have to leave it in the hands of God, Fonzie. But if something should change, I will let you know."

****

"Max, you're doing great," Dr. Parnell encouraged.

"Yeah, pat me on the back, why don't ya? It's not Tony here, just me. No need for all the cheering," he added sarcastically.

"Well, the fact is . . . you went through whatever Tony endured as well. Everyone needs to hear a reassuring word, now and then."

"Yeah, well, you weren't going to get that at the Giacalone house," Max divulged.

"Why not?"

"Even if Maria wanted to be a more positive parent, she didn't have the backbone to stand up to that animal she called a husband."

Dr. Parnell was stunned he was getting this far with Max. He had not expected such success with just the first session under medication. He was going to take this ride for as long as it could go. "So, Maria seemed to be the submissive and subordinate wife, huh?"

"That's putting it mildly. She feared Vito, as did the rest of the family. Especially, Tony. He wanted that jerk to love him so bad." Max laughed mockingly. "The ironic part? Nothing . . . and I mean nothing, could win over that pig. Tony could've jumped through hoops. Vito hated his son."

The doctor rose and paced just near the bed for a moment. He snatched the notepad and swiftly jotted down a few notes. "That's a strong word. Hate. Maybe Vito was just a detached man—afraid to show emotion?"

Max scoffed, "It was beyond that. The man had ice running through his veins. Nobody was ever good enough. Nobody could ever do anything right. Everyone was a loser. The truth? *He* was the real loser. He couldn't even run the business successfully. When everything started to go under, he had to resort to those thugs for financial help."

"Mario Galante," Dr. Parnell guessed.

"Exactly. He even made Maria go get a job."

"Maria worked?"

"Yup. She waitressed at a nearby restaurant for a couple years, actually."

"What about the kids? Who watched them?" Dr. Parnell probed curiously.

Max became uneasy. "Well, who do you think? They stayed home with that animal."

"This seems to upset you. Why?"

"I told you. He was a sick, sadistic pig!"

"You really despise him, Max. What else happened that causes you to feel this way?"

"I don't like where this line of questioning is heading," Max suddenly exclaimed.

"Why not? You can't go on protecting Tony forever. He needs to learn the truth sooner or later. What's so bad, that you can't just tell me?"

"Okay, you wanna know the truth? You wanna destroy Tony? Fine, you're the doctor. If this is gonna get you to shut up and stop asking me so many questions, then I'll tell you."

Dr. Parnell sat back on the bed next to Max. Tony's blood pressure was raised and his heart was racing. The doctor could feel the blood pumping through his own heart. This was it. "Go ahead. I'm waiting."

"During those years that Maria worked the afternoon shift at 'Louie's', while the kids were home with *him* . . ." he said the word with such spite, it made Dr. Parnell flinch. "He would put them all to bed at 7 p.m. First, it started when Caterina was about 5. Tony was 9 years old. One night, he heard 'the pig' call out to Caterina to come to his bedroom. This continued for a time. Tony was ignorant to what was happening behind *his* bedroom door. Another night, after he heard his father call out to her again, he heard his sister scream out. Tony ran into the bedroom to see what the matter was. That's when he discovered the truth."

Dr. Parnell scribbled on the note pad. His hands shook, as he took in the reality of the nightmare that Tony bore. "What happened, Max?"

"Do I need to spell it out for you, man? The dude was sick! Sick! He was hurting Caterina. When Tony busted into the room, the pig told him to never enter his room again, or he would kill him. Tony believed him. He closed the door, went to the bathroom, threw up, and crawled back into bed. Tony was so petrified and so shocked, he didn't know what to do. He wanted to help his sister, but he was scared to death of that animal. As he should have been. As he should have been!"

"Tony was just a boy, himself. He couldn't have helped his sister if he tried," Dr. Parnell spoke his thought aloud.

"You're right," Max agreed. "For a week or two, he could've been in shock. But not for two years! For two years that animal molested Caterina and then, once he tired of her, he started on Nellie. He deserved to die a worse death than the Galantes gave him. We hated him! But most of all, Tony hated himself for being a spineless jellyfish. He let it go on so long, before . . ."

"Hold up," Dr. Parnell interrupted, "First of all, I can't believe you expected Tony to be able to do something about it. Secondly, Tony was just a child himself."

"Tony was a coward, I tell you!" Max shouted.

Dr. Parnell eyed the monitors and took notice of the significant increase in Tony's heart rate. His blood pressure increased as well. He suddenly feared for Tony's health. The medication had stopped being administered for almost a half-hour.

"Stop right here, Max. Enough for today. Thanks for being such a big help. You did a good job protecting Tony. Now, Tony will return back to us." The doctor placed a hand on Tony's shoulder and gently nudged him. "Tony? Tony? I'm going to count to three and you must come out. Do you hear me? One, two, three . . ."

Tony's heart rate immediately began to decline. His demeanor seemed to be calmer. He sounded jumbled up, but replied, "Yeah, Doc, I hear ya."

"Tony, go ahead and sleep off the meds. Rest, and when you wake up, we'll talk."

Tony followed his doctor's orders and rested. Dr. Parnell watched his chest move up and down, rhythmically in sleep. Tony would have plenty to deal with when he awoke.

CHAPTER 4

John 8:32

"Then you will know the truth, and the truth will set you free."

Frank Blandino maneuvered his vehicle out of the hospital parking lot. Tony quietly sat in the passenger's seat. His eyes were red-rimmed from crying and he felt emotionally drained. After the lengthy session, Dr. Parnell had Tony sleep off the drug. When Tony finally woke, the reality of what they had learned during the session was revealed and Tony was not sure he could handle it. Doc reassured him that they were making serious progress. Now that the truth of the abuse was out, they could help Tony to come to terms with it. Tony practically trembled at the thought of his little sisters' abuse. He felt sickened that he did not help. In fact, the more he doted on it, the more guilt he felt.

Frank reached over and patted his nephew's shoulder. "Whatever it is . . . whatever you discovered in there, you're going to be okay."

Tony shook his head and the tears fell. "No, Uncle, it's not okay. I don't know if I'll ever be okay. I don't know if I can live through this. If I didn't have Laura and the baby to think about . . ." he gritted his teeth. His anger seething as he spoke, ". . . I swear I'd just put an end to it!"

"Don't say that! Nothing's worth losing your life over. You know you don't have to tell me anything. But one thing is for sure—what happened in the past, happened. All you need to do now is focus on dealing with it," he encouraged.

"Uncle, you were friends with him—my father. My parents met through you and Aunt Margherita, right?"

"Yeah, I met your father at one of the Italian clubs we belonged to. We started talking business and became friends. He met Margherita and Maria at one of the functions. He liked Maria and they hooked up. A bit quickly for my taste, but that's how it happened. Why?"

"What was he like? Did you ever notice anything strange about him?" Tony continued to dig. He was desperate to understand it all.

"Your father didn't have many friends. He was a quiet and reserved kind of guy. Not many of my friends wanted to hang around him. Even his brothers eventually stopped talking to him. Once he met your ma, our friendship kind of diminished. When Margherita, the in-laws, and I, left for Cali, he still made an effort to keep in touch. I think I was one of the only people he could trust, and despite the distance between us, he eventually made me trustee.

"Strangely enough, your mother distanced herself from us, once we left. If it weren't for your grandparents making trips out during the summer, we would have never seen you all. Shoot, she rarely even called."

"Sure, she was too busy catering to *him*—too busy working her tail off so she could pay off *his* debts. You're right about one thing, Uncle, my father was a cold-blooded man. My mother deserved a better man than *him*."

"Tony, I'm sorry. I don't know what to say. Your grandparents never liked him either and they warned your mother quite a few times to think it over before marrying him so quickly. There was something about him that never sat right with any of us. Why do you think your Nonno and Nonna left her their secluded house off Crabtree Lane in Cicero? They were hoping that if she decided to up and leave him, she'd have a place to stay, away from him. Still, your mom never told us that there may have been trouble with him."

Trouble? That was putting it delicately. Tony's head swam with all the information that had battered him that day. He could not understand how he had let two years go by while his sisters suffered. He started to cry again, angry with himself for giving in to so many tears.

"Tony, you should have stayed the night, like the doctor told you. You're too upset. Should I take you back?" Frank offered.

"No! I don't want Laura to know any of this. If I would have stayed, she would've come to the hospital and I don't want her to see me like this."

Frank stole a glance at Tony, while he drove. "What do you mean, 'You don't want Laura to know'? Please tell me you'll open up to her. She's going to be your wife, Tony."

"You want me to tell her that my father was a mad, twisted pervert, who molested my sisters for years, while my mother went off to work. Meanwhile, I sat back and allowed it to happen because I was too afraid he'd kill me. Will Laura even want me when she finds out what a coward I was?"

Frank paled. He pulled into the driveway of Tony's new house. He turned the ignition off and leaned his head on the steering wheel.

"Shocked, aren't ya? Didn't know that the sick-o you set your sister-in-law up with was a child molester, huh?" Tony's eyes burned with rage as he spewed out the information to his uncle.

"My God," Frank whispered. "I'm so sorry."

"How could you have known? No one could have known. He was a recluse. His brothers got out of the business because they wanted nothing to do with him, so we saw no family. What bothers me most is why didn't my mother ever notice this was going on? What was wrong with her?" Tony opened up the door to the truck and stumbled onto the driveway. The drug left him feeling slightly fuzzy and disoriented. He stalked gracelessly into the garage, searching his pocket for the keys, and then entered his house. Frank followed immediately behind him, in case Tony was to lose his footing.

Upon entering the kitchen, Tony opened the fridge and grabbed a bottle of soda. He flipped off the top, letting it fall to the floor, and guzzled half the bottle. "How rude of me. Would you like some, Uncle? Maybe it will help you to swallow the big pill I just gave you."

Frank looked up at Tony. His eyes were filled with unshed tears. He sat at the kitchen table and took a napkin to his eyes. "This must be a nightmare for you," he finally managed.

Tony took an unopened bottle of soda and placed it before Frank, before falling into a chair. "Uncle, I can't believe that I had suppressed that. Do you understand the enormity of it? He abused my poor little sisters almost every night for two years. I discovered the truth and did nothing."

"Tony, you were just a kid. What could you have done to help them?"

"Why didn't I tell my mother? Why didn't I go in there and demand that he stop?" Tony pounded an angry fist to the table, shaking the bottles of soda. "I remember him calling me a 'wimp' and a 'loser'. He was right. I was a wimp."

"Stop. You're wrong. If he was calling you those names, that's because that's what he thought of himself. He was obviously not a mentally stable man to do what he did," Frank explained.

"All I know is that I can't tell Laura right now. I have to process this first. I need time. If she calls, can you tell her I'm sleeping?"

****

Laura glanced at the clock. It was three that afternoon and Tony was sure to be home from the hospital. She finished filing the last of a batch of paperwork and sauntered over to Mr. Stone's door. She knocked and opened it.

"Hey, did you need me for anything else today?" she asked.

Jasper Stone looked up from his desk and peeked at her above the lenses perched on his nose. "Go on ahead, honey. I've got it covered from here. Are you running off to go see Tony?"

She fully entered his office, but stood by the door. "Yup, he had a special session set up for today and I want to make sure he's okay."

"Well then, what are you still doing here? Go on!"

Laura thanked him and left. She thought of calling the house first, but decided to go directly there. Even if they were still at the hospital, she had her own key. She would start some dinner for him and wait there.

Traffic was still light, as she drove anxiously to her future home. The baby stirred inside her, surely feeling her anxiety. She rubbed her belly gently to soothe her little baby. She wondered how the session turned out. *Did they uncover any of his childhood memories? If so, how bad were they that he needed to develop a 'helper personality'?* She said a silent prayer for God to be with Tony.

As she approached the house, she spotted Uncle Frank's truck in the driveway. *Why hadn't they called when they got home, as she requested?* Laura parked the car, snatched her purse, and ran up the walkway to the porch. She grabbed the doorknob and tried to turn it. It was locked. Puzzled, she knocked and waited, growing impatient. As she fumbled for her keys, the door slowly opened.

Uncle Frank answered, "Laura, come in." He put a finger to his lips to suggest that she be quiet. "Tony's resting," he whispered.

"Can I see him?"

"I don't think he really wants visitors today, babe. Maybe you should just head home and let him rest."

Was he serious? Laura peered at Uncle Frank for a moment. The stocky man seemed agitated and even nervous. "Uncle Frank, how bad was it?"

He shook his head and Laura could see his eyes fill. "It's not for me to tell. When Tony's ready, he'll open up."

"Uncle Frank, you're scaring me. I won't bother him, but I must see for myself that he's okay." She placed her purse on the living room couch and walked past Uncle Frank, making a left to get to the bedrooms. She passed the bath on the right. At the next door, she gave a soft tap before entering. Tony did not reply. She tried the doorknob, found it open, and entered. The room was dark—the curtains drawn. In the dimness, she could still see that he kept his room tidy. Laura found Tony lying on the bed, face down. His head was thrust between two pillows, hiding his face from her.

She entered the room and sat on the bed. Laura rubbed his back gently and whispered his name. Tony did not budge. "Are you okay?" He was still, aside from the recurring motion of his breathing. "I'm here for you," she continued. "I won't let you down. I love you," she finally added. Since Tony did not reply, Laura gave a soft kiss on his head and exited his room. She quietly closed his door and walked through the living room to get to the kitchen where Frank prepared a small meal.

She felt as though she had been kicked in the stomach. Her heart literally ached, as she came to the realization that she could not fix this. Laura wanted to be understanding and give Tony his space, yet she did not want him to feel as though she had abandoned him. Something was wrong. They had uncovered something during the session and Laura knew it could not be good. Even Uncle Frank looked terribly distraught. Yet, she wanted to honor his need for rest. *Certainly, he would call her first thing in the morning.*

Laura kissed Uncle Frank goodbye and drove home perplexed. It would be a long evening without Tony for company. She made a mental note to say some serious prayers . . . again.

* * *

Tony listened carefully. He heard Laura's car speed away. Fresh tears fell from his eyes. He sat up in his bed and looked up. "God, why?" he whispered. "Why is this happening to me?" He fell back and pounded his fist into the mattress. *How was he going to get over this?* He just could not tell Laura. He would have to do this alone.

****

The next morning, Laura rose to get ready for work. Her heart felt heavy upon recalling the lonely evening she had spent without Tony. She felt relief, knowing she would see him shortly, when he would arrive to go to work with John. Laura took extra-special care getting ready. She always wanted to look her best for him.

In the kitchen, John and Marlene prepared a small breakfast. Laura strolled in and kissed them both. "You look extra beautiful, this morning," John stated.

"Thanks, Dad," she answered dismally.

"Hey, for someone who looks so good, you sure are gloomy. What's wrong?" he inquired.

It was moments like this when Laura truly missed Tammy. She was always there to listen to Laura. But since her passing, Laura mostly relied on her parents for support. She could not keep anything from them, even if she tried—for it seemed they could read into her soul. Marlene put the orange juice carton down and looked more carefully at her daughter. "Laura?"

"I'm okay. I'm just worried about Tony."

"Why, because he didn't come over last night? I love Tony and all, but a little distance never hurt anyone. You two are constantly glued at the hip," John commented.

"I know that he just needs some time. I need to understand that, but it's hard. I want to help him and I can't." Laura slumped into a chair and pouted.

"Laura, the only thing you can do is 'let go and let God'," Marlene finally added. "Tony's really going through so much. This is going to be challenging for both of you. Hang tight, give him time. He'll come around."

"I just can't wait to see him this morning, so I can see for myself that he's okay."

"Oh, he won't be coming here before work, Laura. He called while you were in the shower. He said he'd drive in and meet me at the office," informed John.

Laura's heart sank. "What? He's not coming here?"

John shook his head and bit into an apple danish. He chewed and swallowed quickly, chasing it down with a sip of coffee. "Laura, don't look so sad. It's not like you're never going to see him again."

"No. Something's wrong. Tony would never avoid me like this. I know it. I can feel it."

Marlene sat down next to her and took hold of her hand. "Laura, you're panicking. Give him time."

"Mom . . ." Laura whined.

"Listen to us. It'll be okay," she soothed.

Laura grabbed a danish, not even sure if she was hungry enough to eat it. Her stomach was tying up in knots. She thought of the baby and took a bite. Staring out the window of the nook, she watched light flurries begin to fall. Something was just not right. She could sense it down to her very bones.

****

Laura would give him his space, if that is what he wanted. But as she sat at her desk in Mr. Stone's office, her insides were doing somersaults. She knew the only way she could calm her nerves was if she could speak to

Tony. It was near noon and she was due to leave for lunch. As her heart raced in her chest, she picked up the phone and dialed the number to John's firm.

"Thank you for calling Northeast Financial Planning. This is Beth. Can I help you?"

Laura cringed at the sound of Beth's voice. She had not forgotten how Beth openly flirted with Tony. "Hi Beth, it's Laura Knight. Can I speak with Tony, please?"

"I'll check to see if he's available, please hold," she answered coolly.

Laura waited impatiently, while soft music played on the phone. Moments later, Beth returned. "Laura, he's just getting ready to leave for lunch. He said he'll call you when he returns."

Her heart sank even further. He *was* avoiding her. "It'll just take a moment. Do you think you can catch him before he leaves?" Laura knew she was getting desperate. But she did not like the feeling that was washing over her.

"I'll try. One moment, please." The line clicked back over to the music and Laura was now sitting on the edge of the seat. Her legs shook and she felt sick. "I'm sorry, Laura. He told me to tell you that he does promise to call you back when he returns."

"Any idea where he'll be heading for lunch?"

"He asked me if I needed anything from Snapps, so I assume that's where he'll be."

So now he was asking Beth if he could pick her up something for lunch. Or was Beth just rubbing it in?

"Thanks, Beth. Have a good day," Laura quickly added, waiting for a response. Instead she found that Beth had already hung up. *How rude!* Laura closed down the office, put on her coat, and dashed out the door to Snapps.

The restaurant was just in town off the main road. Laura entered the fiftyish-style eatery and glanced around. Records and posters of the recently passed Elvis, Marilyn Monroe, and other famous celebrities, covered the walls in a decorative fashion. A bar counter made a U in the center of the room, with fixed bar stools for those who preferred to eat at the counter. Booths lined the U, covered in red plastic and chrome.

In the far corner, near the window, she spotted Tony sitting alone in a booth. His head was down and he looked deep in thought. Just seeing him made Laura's heart thump. She walked quickly, yielding her will to run down the aisle to him. As she approached him, she realized how truly awful he looked.

His head rose to the clicking of her heels and his dark-rimmed eyes clashed with hers. Her heart leapt. For a moment, a familiar sparkle returned to his eye, but vanished very quickly. She reached the table, realizing she did not know what to do next.

"Hi," she finally managed.

"Hi," he said in return.

"I'm sorry . . . I just couldn't stay away. Do you want company? Can I sit with you for a minute?"

He nodded slowly and pointed to the seat across from him. Laura leaned forward, unsure if a hello kiss would be welcomed. He kissed her quickly on her lips. "Are you hungry? Do you want me to order you a burger?"

"Looks great, but I don't think so," she decided.

"Why not," Tony seemed irritated.

"I just can't eat, right now," she stated.

"Why not, Laura? You shouldn't get yourself all worked up. You need to think about the baby. I would've called you when I was ready."

Laura sat in the booth and fought the impulse to succumb to tears. "I'm sorry. I've been so worried. I felt so lost without you last night. I couldn't get my mind off of you."

"I'm okay. I have a great deal to work through. I'm just not ready yet to accept what I've learned." Tony looked down. Laura watched him mindlessly play with a fry.

"I can respect that. I just don't want you to avoid me like this. It hurts. All you had to say was that you needed time. I understand."

Tony seemed to get angry now. "I wasn't avoiding you!" he claimed, in a slightly raised voice. He looked around at the turning faces. He lowered his voice and continued, "The last thing I need, right now, is you getting yourself all worked up for nothing. Don't be hurt. I've enough to deal with. I don't need you having panic attacks on me."

"I'm sorry, Tony. I just want to help you. I want to be here for you," Laura whispered.

"I'll be fine. I just need time. Can you give me that?" he uncharacteristically snapped. Laura could feel her insides turning and grinding against her chest.

"Of course."

"Thank you." He shoved the plate with an untouched burger and fries toward her and rose. After throwing a $10 bill on the table, he bent forward, quickly kissed her cheek, and stormed out of the restaurant.

What had just happened? Laura sat in the booth in shock. Looking at the burger, she covered her mouth and made a dash for the bathroom.

****

It was evident that Tony was upset and needed time. For two weeks, the detached behavior continued. Laura was beside herself with anguish. She hung on for every phone call, hoping he would return to his old self. She found out more about him through John and Uncle Frank, than through his short-and to-the-point telephone conversations.

John stated that he was doing well at his new job. He did everything that was asked of him and more. But John did sense his dissociated behavior. He came into work, barely talked to anyone, and kept the door to his office closed at all times.

One morning, after this continued for almost two weeks, John could see Laura suffering. His need to want to protect her overcame the desire to give Tony time, and he decided to step in. He lightly rapped on the door of Tony's office.

"Come in," he called out.

John entered, "Hey, you got a minute?"

"Sure, have a seat." Tony put his pen down and moved the paperwork he was working on aside. "What's up? Is everything okay?"

John gave him a reassuring smile and said, "Yes, Tony, you're doing a great job here. I couldn't have found a better manager. But work matters aside, I'm very concerned."

Tony knowingly looked at John and then cast his gaze downward. "I'm sorry. I'm not handling this very well."

"Look, I don't know what you're going through. We're praying for God to strengthen you, every day. You know I'm in your corner rooting you on. We all are. You aren't alone. But we can't help you if you're going to push us all away. Laura is beside herself with fear. She's so afraid of losing you again. You avoiding her like this is only confirming her worst nightmare. I hear her crying in her dreams at night. Is there any way you can pull it together enough to not put her under so much stress? This can't be good for her or the baby."

Tony sat back in his chair and covered his face with his hands. He blew out a long breath and slowly sat upright again. "I'm screwing up, aren't I?" John looked at him with empathy. "I'm sorry. I will try not to be so distant. Please understand. I've discovered something that I cannot deal with properly. Doc says therapy will help. I've been going there daily. I thought that if I kept my distance, then I wouldn't have to explain what we've learned."

"That's not true. You can still come by and visit with us, visit with Laura, and not have to tell us what's going on. Perhaps her presence can help lift your spirits and get your mind off things. Not to mention how much it would thrill Laura. She would love it if you came over tonight for dinner. What do you say?"

Tony looked away. He fiddled with the cord of his telephone, winding it through his fingers subconsciously. "I don't know. Maybe not for dinner, but I'll come by for a little while after."

"Tomorrow night is the firm's Christmas party. You're bringing Laura, right?"

"Yeah . . . yeah, of course."

"Good. We can have a few good laughs when Laura sees Beth openly throwing herself at you. I'll have to hold her back."

They both chuckled.

John rose from the chair and extended his hand. Tony stood and firmly shook it. "I hope I haven't offended you in any way. You know I've gotta look out for my girl," John grinned.

Tony walked around the desk and finally cracked a smile. "She's very blessed to have you and Marlene."

"Not as blessed as she is to have you. You're the light of her life. Without you, Laura's spirit goes dark. Hang in there." John pulled Tony into a hug. When they stepped back, John thought he caught a tear fall from Tony's eye.

****

That evening Tony did come, but he stayed for only a short time and it was not the reunion she planned. She put down a Christmas ornament from in her hand, to run to the door. She was helping John and Marlene decorate for the coming Holiday. Opening the door, a smile instantly fell across her face. Tony smiled at her and walked in to give her a quick hug. It was not the hug she longed for, but he came to see her and that was a first step. He greeted John and Marlene, who continued to decorate the real Frasier Fir that stood eight-feet tall in the living room corner. Christmas music played in the background, setting the mood for the preparation of Christ's birth.

Laura took his coat and offered him a hot cocoa. He vacantly smiled at her and said yes. As she entered the kitchen, her insides began to twist again. John's talk with him made no difference. He still was acting distant. She would do anything to get him to return to his old self.

When the tree was finally decorated, John and Marlene said goodnight, giving them some time alone. Laura watched them climb the staircase and disappear upstairs. Suddenly awkward and unsure, she sat next to him on the couch, though their bodies did not touch. Tony stared at the blinking lights of the tree, but Laura could see that his mind was elsewhere.

"Can I get you a warm up for your cocoa?" she asked.

He glanced down at the full cup of cocoa, probably realizing that he had not touched it. "No thanks." He leaned forward and placed the cup on the coffee table before him. "I should probably get going. It's getting late."

Almost too quickly, Laura responded, "Oh, please don't go. You just got here an hour ago."

"Laura, I'm tired and I need to get up in the morning for work."

"That's never stopped you before, from staying a little later with me."

"Before. Exactly. That was before. Things are different now," he blurted.

"Nothing's changed between us. I still love you."

"I love you, too, but you need to understand that you're pushing me too hard, Laura."

"Pushing you? I haven't questioned you once what happened at that session. How do you feel that I'm pushing you?"

"It's there, in your eyes, every time I look at you."

"So sue me if I want to make sure you're okay. I wouldn't love you if I didn't. But I do love you and I feel like I'm losing you again."

Tony looked at her for the first time that night. She struggled to keep the tears from falling. The look on his face confirmed that she was right. She *was* losing him. "I'm sorry. I just feel like you'd be better off without me."

Laura's heart pumped the blood through her body so fast, she began to feel lightheaded. "What? What are you saying?"

"Maybe we need to postpone the wedding?"

The couch seemed to pull out from under her. His words struck her like a slap across her face. "Are you serious? Tony, no!" She burst out and gave way to tears. "You don't really mean that, do you?" she cried.

"I don't know what I want anymore." For the first time his demeanor softened and he pulled her into his arms. "Don't cry. I'm sorry to upset you like this. I'm so confused. I don't know what to do."

Laura fell limply into his embrace and openly wept. "Tony, please don't give up on us. We've worked so hard to be together. We're so close . . . so close to happiness."

He held her tightly to his chest and she finally felt like she had reached him. He gently pulled her hair away from her face and tilted her head so he could see her eyes. His fingers lightly stroked her wet cheeks.

"Don't cry. I hate it when you cry."

"Please don't ever say that you don't want to marry me. It would kill me."

"I'm sorry. Just be patient with me, please. I'm really confused."

Laura sniffed and wiped away the wetness from her face. "I'll never give up on you, Tony."

He gave her a genuine smile for the first time in a while. "You have such a hard head."

"Don't forget it!" she cracked through tears.

Tony stood and Laura walked him to the door. He whispered to her, "I'll pick you up tomorrow for John's party, okay?

Tears filled her eyes with joy and she hugged his waist. "I'd love that!"

He held her for a moment, kissed the top of her head, and walked out into the cold winter night. She observed him enter his vehicle and pull away. Closing the door, Laura leaned her back to it and slid down into a heap. Her shoulders quivered and the sobs racked her body.

He suggested postponing the wedding! This was not good. She needed to find a way to convince him that they belonged together. For starters, she needed Jesus. She put her hands together and prayed as she had not in months.

* * *

Tony steadily drove the vehicle toward his new house. *What was he thinking upsetting her like that? Why did he even suggest postponing the wedding? Is this what he really wanted?* The thought of living his life without her made him want to pull the truck off the road and hurl. Yet, he could not bring himself to tell her about the abuse. *What was he so afraid of?*

He could hear a voice inside of him telling him what he was to fear. Laura deserved a real man—someone who would not 'chicken out' when 'push came to shove'. Someone who did not have to create an alter ego to deal with every painful situation. *How cowardly! Why didn't he just suck it up and do what any other man would have done?* He should have stomped into that bedroom and demanded that the abuse stop. He should have taken matters into his own hands and proven himself to be a man, once and for all.

But he did not, he shrank away. He hid in his room, while his sisters suffered unimaginable abuse.

No, Laura could not know the truth. If she knew, she would look at him and see a weakling. He could not live like that, either. Somehow, he had to convince Laura that this wedding was not meant to be. He needed to do it in a manner in which Laura would decide that he was not fit to be a husband, let alone a father. He would have to be pretty nasty to turn her away. He did not think he could hurt her like that. *But he had to!* For her own good.

She would then find someone better. He felt a sharp pain to his chest. He could not imagine her with someone else again. Yet, if he loved her, he could not be selfish. She would have to find someone who could be a real father to their baby. He would have to give up all rights to the child. The baby deserved to have a father who was confident and strong. Not some spineless jellyfish that ran away from every tough predicament.

Yes, he needed to do whatever was necessary to break off the engagement.

CHAPTER 5

Proverbs 31:30

"Charm is deceptive, and beauty is fleeting;
but a woman who fears the LORD is to be praised."

Saturday, December 16

Tony woke Saturday morning with a heaviness he could not sustain. That night would surely be a disaster if he could actually follow through with his own plan. *Laura would not want anything to do with him . . . if she knew what was good for her.* It would be near impossible pulling it off. He did not think he could intentionally hurt her. Ironically, this is the reason he worked so hard to get better—to protect her. *Wasn't he getting help for his illness, so Max would never return, thus keeping Laura out of harm's way?* Now he was making plans to turn her away. It sounded absurd, but things could not continue on the way they were.

He gazed out the window of the bedroom he had planned to share with her for the rest of their lives. Light snow trickled downward, leaving a white haze over everything it hit. This would have been a perfect day to pick Laura up and spend the afternoon together, just frolicking around outside. Or even to stay home and sit near a fire, relaxing. Instead, he was home alone, concocting a plot on how to let her go.

He thought back to the old house. Their first three years there were like a dream to him. They were the best times of his life, so far. His chest ached. He could not help but wonder what he would do, when she finally dumped him. *Did he even want to live?*

* * *

Laura stared out the bay window of the warm family room. For the first time in weeks, she felt hope. The lingering snowflakes reminded her of the days she spent with Tony at the old house. Throughout all of her life, she had never experienced such happiness, as she did then with Tony. Tonight, she would remind him of all the reasons they belonged together. She planned to do something special for him.

In her haste to prepare for the evening, Laura scooted out the door shortly after breakfast. At the mall, she found her favorite jewelry store, the place where she had already purchased John's 50th birthday present. This time, she shopped for something special for Tony; a gift she would give him at the end of their evening together. After sorting through the many selections, she found what she was looking for. It was the perfect ring. Grooves were carved into the gold, leading to a single little diamond on the top left of the ring. She asked the jeweler to engrave an inscription on the inside. He was to inscribe the words, '*Forever! Love, Laura*'. After doing so, he polished the ring and placed it in a blue velvet box for her. Laura paid him with cash and eagerly left the mall.

At home, Laura and Marlene excitedly prepared for the party. John seemed oblivious to their deviousness. The plan was set. All his family, friends, and co-workers were already at the banquet hall they rented, awaiting John's arrival. Marlene, Laura, and Tony would lure John to the hall for the 'Office Christmas Party'.

Laura dressed in a black evening gown that hid her pregnancy well. She was not trying to disguise it; it simply fell right into place. She pulled her hair up into a twist and made-up her face to precision. To finalize her look, she put on a pair of drop earrings and a necklace to match. Her black satin heels completed her ensemble. Soon, Tony would arrive and she wanted the night to be special for everyone.

Laura glanced at the clock with worry. Tony should have arrived by that time and still there was no sign of him. She picked up the phone and dialed his number. The line rang a few times, and moments later, he actually answered.

"Hello?" His tone was dry and cold.

"Hi Ton, you're still home? I was just wondering if you'd left yet. We're waiting for you."

"Oh, sorry, I should have called. You go on without me. I'll meet you there when I can," he suggested in a frosty voice.

The same sinking feeling from the days prior set in. Laura sat down in a nearby chair, before her legs could give way. "But I thought you said we'd go to the party together?" she asked in a weak tone.

"Yeah . . . well, something's come up. I'll be there. Don't worry. Just go."

Before Laura could say another word, the line clicked and a dial tone rang. Her anger suddenly flared. She decided that it was John's night and she was not about to let anyone ruin it. Not even Tony.

* * *

Tony cradled the phone to the receiver. He hated this. He felt sick, but he finished dressing for the party, deciding that a suit and tie were appropriate for the occasion. He combed back his hair, adding gel to keep it tamed. Still, the dressy clothes and freshly shaven face could not hide the dark rings that circled his eyes. He looked away from the mirror in disgust.

After taking his coat and John's gift, he left his house, and drove to the hall. Laura, Marlene, and John had yet to arrive, so he had not missed the surprise. He found Uncle Frank, who greeted him with a hug. Soon, other co-workers said hello and Tony made his rounds with Frank. John's brother, Joe, was there with his wife, Bernadette, and their boys, Peter and Michael. They greeted Tony and Frank, as well. Paula and Marco Apolone, John's partner and best friend, waited anxiously with the rest of the crowd.

Before he could hide, Beth sauntered her way toward him. Uncle Frank stood watching in disbelief, as she boldly hugged Tony and kissed his cheek. She wore a flashy red dress that was cut far lower than it should have been at the chest, and far shorter than it should have been at the hem. Her stiletto red heels looked almost painful, yet she walked in them with grace.

"I was wondering if you were going to come," she whispered into his ear. She held onto his arm with both hands. Frank looked at Tony, then to her hands, and then back again to Tony. He seemed speechless that the woman was staking her claim on him so openly.

"Well, what made you think that I wasn't coming?" Tony asked.

"You've been so quiet lately. I was starting to get worried that you didn't want to be my friend anymore," she pouted with a tease.

"Now, why would I want to do that?" he encouraged.

Beth excitedly welcomed his banter. "Oh, I don't know. Maybe your girlfriend might get jealous."

"That's nonsense. What's a little teasing amongst friends, huh?"

Beth squeezed his arm harder, whispering in a breathy tone, "Just teasing, right?"

"Yep," he tore his eyes from her gaze, to find Frank looking disgusted.

Frank then quickly interrupted, "Excuse me. Can I borrow my nephew for a moment?"

"Sure, but only for a moment. I'm living on borrowed time here," she teased.

Frank gave her a wry smile and pulled Tony into a corner. His eyes were blazing by the time they were far enough away from Beth to talk. "What are you doing?" Frank grilled angrily.

"Nothing," Tony stated. He could not keep his uncle's piercing gaze.

"I don't know what's going on inside you. I believe you're going through a tough time, but you better not screw up what you have with Laura over *her.*" Frank tried gazing deeper into Tony's eyes. Tony looked away. "Look at me, Tony!" he stressed with anger. "What's going on?"

Tony finally looked at Frank. He had never talked back to the man who was more a father to him than an uncle. "Uncle Frank, I'm asking you nicely to mind your own business. I know what I'm doing," he answered matter-of-factly.

"Oh, really? Fine! You wanna mess up your life again? Well, I won't stand around here and watch you do it. Give John my best. Tell him that I went home because I felt sick to my stomach." Frank strode past him and left. Tony's insides ached. *What was he doing encouraging Beth?* Then he remembered—Laura could not find out the truth.

* * *

Despite the despair Laura felt in her heart over the manner in which Tony was treating her, she put a smile on her face and entered the banquet hall doors alongside John and Marlene. Marlene led the way through the foyer. She held John's hand. A sign near the entryway doors read, 'Northeast Financial Christmas Party'.

"Here it is," John cheered. "Ladies first!" He held open the door for the girls. There was a dead silence in the room. Laura entered after Marlene. John finally stepped foot into the dark room, a puzzled look on his face. The lights flickered on and the whole room shouted their surprise.

The crowd broke out into the 'Happy Birthday' song, while John stood at the door in shock. Marlene held him and pulled him into the room. Laura reached for his other hand and the women brought him to the crowd.

"You mean to tell me this is all for me?" he shouted over all the voices.

"Happy birthday, darling!"

"Happy birthday, Dad!"

John swept the women up into his embrace and held them tight. Marlene lavished his face with kisses. Laura could not stop the tears from falling. She held on to him, tightly. Finally, Uncle Joe stepped in.

"Hey, share him with the rest of us!" He hugged his brother, wishing him a happy birthday. The crowd seemed to swallow up both Marlene and John, during which everyone gave congratulations with hugs and kisses.

Laura finally stopped a moment to catch her breath from all the excitement. She blotted her face with a tissue, hoping she had not smudged her makeup. She glanced around the room at the crowd in search of Tony. She came to focus on Beth first. Her red dress was unmistakably noticeable. Her arm was looped through someone else's. She could not see who it was, at first. He gave his back to the crowd, leaning on the bar in an enticing pose. Suddenly, Laura recognized the hair. Her heart doubled in rhythm. *It could not be.*

As if he could sense her stare, Tony slowly turned toward the boisterous crowd. The smile quickly fell from his face, when his eyes clashed with Laura's. Laura stumbled back for a moment, securing her balance with a nearby chair. An expression of hurt had surely fallen over her face. He gave her a weak smile and excused himself. Beth's eyes grazed the room and she recognized the object of Tony's distraction. She followed Tony toward the crowd and they waited their turn to congratulate John.

Laura's emotions went into overload. She was angry and hurt. *Tony could not find time to come to the party with her, but he had found the time to make it to the party early enough to hang out with Beth?* She watched both Tony and Beth greet John with hugs. Laura found the table reserved for them and placed her purse on it. She suddenly was not sure if she could last the rest of the night. Her head felt light and her legs weak. Just as she was about to pull out a chair to sit, two strong hands grabbed her shoulders from behind.

"Are you okay? You look kind of pale." There was sincerity and concern in Tony's voice.

Laura turned and gave him a frown. "I'm fine."

"Hi," he whispered, nuzzling her neck with his nose. She looked at him in surprise. His eyes were remorseful, deep, hurting.

"Hi," she whispered in return. He pulled out her chair and Laura sat down.

"Looks like he was completely clueless, huh?"

"Yeah, we really got him good." She looked down at her hands and fiddled with her engagement ring. Tony's ring sat in her purse. *Would she be able to tear him away from Beth long enough to give it to him?*

"Is there room enough for me at this table?" he asked.

"Of course," Laura answered.

Tony pulled out a chair next to her and sat down. He sat facing her, his legs trapping hers between his. He lifted her chin with his finger. Their eyes met. "You look so beautiful, tonight."

"Thank you."

"One would never know you were carrying my baby in that dress."

"Well, I am," Laura could not help but snap.

Tony sat back a moment at her words. "I haven't forgotten. I think about it every moment of every day."

"Well, Beth certainly seemed to be doing a fine job of distracting you."

Tony looked down, now avoiding her eyes. "She's just a friend. Nothing more. You know that."

"I don't know anything, anymore," Laura whispered, tears filling her eyes. "I don't know where we stand. I don't know if you want me. I don't know if we're going to make it to our wedding."

"Well, this isn't the place to be discussing it. This is John's night. Let's forget our problems for one night and enjoy the party," Tony pleaded.

"Fine," Laura stated.

John and Marlene approached the table. John was smiling from ear to ear. Marlene was glowing with love and happiness. Everyone sat down. The waiters prepared to serve the meal. Joe, Bernadette, and the boys sat at their table. Marlene noticed that Frank was missing.

"Tony, where's Frank?" she asked with concern.

"He came down with something last minute. He sends his best and congratulations, but he couldn't make it." Tony rehearsed.

"Oh, I'll have to call him tomorrow and see how he's feeling," John added.

"I'm sure he'll be okay," Tony quickly threw in.

From the corner of Laura's eye, she could see a bright red dress coming toward them. She looked up to find Beth standing over the two empty seats at their table. "Are these seats taken?" she quizzed.

"Actually," Marlene jumped in, "One is for Father Bill, who is ready to say 'Grace' and the other belonged to Tony's Uncle Frank."

"What happened, Beth? Couldn't you find a seat?" John asked.

"I must be too slow. The only table that has an available seat with people I know is yours."

"Well, since Uncle Frank's not coming, just sit here," Tony invited.

"Of course, Beth. Sit down," John insisted. She slyly smiled at Laura and took a seat next to Tony.

Laura's pulse was racing. *Was there something there that she should be picking up on?* The last time she had this feeling, Paul and Tammy were falling in love with each other, and Laura pretended not to notice. Fear and love had blinded her. She would not make the same mistake twice. If Tony was starting to fall for Beth, she would not be the last to know.

Father Bill disrupted her negative thoughts and began to speak. The young priest stood on the DJ's platform with the microphone in his hand.

"Before we say 'Grace', I'd like to speak on behalf of Marlene and Laura, who came to personally invite me to John's 50th birthday party. As you all know, being close family members and friends of John, the Knights took a horrible blow this past summer, with the loss of their beloved daughter, Tammy . . ."

Laura looked up and caught Marlene's gaze. They knowingly exchanged glances that revealed the pain that was still so fresh from their loss. John, sitting between the two women, reached out and held their hands. Father Bill continued.

"Any other family might have fallen apart after such a horrendous tragedy. Not the Knights. I've never seen a family so rooted and strengthened by God's love. Marlene and Laura didn't know if having this caliber of a party was appropriate after suffering such a great loss. I told them that if they are going to learn anything from Tammy's death, it's to celebrate life. John, my friend, I know I can speak on behalf of all of us when I say, may the Lord bless you with another healthy and happy 50 years. Now, if you would all bow your heads for the blessing . . ."

Before long, dinner was being served. Laura glanced across the table. Everyone seemed engaged in conversation, laughing and carrying on. She smiled and pretended to be following along, but her mind was racing. A few times, she thought she caught Beth gazing at Tony. Tony would spot her eye and wink or smile in return. Laura barely touched her meal. Her stomach felt uneasy.

Was he doing this on purpose to upset her? What were his intentions? Laura asked herself.

When dinner ended, the crowd left their tables to linger to the bar or dance floor. The DJ played disco and rock-and-roll music, inviting the crowd to 'boogie'. Laura nearly ran from the room to get away from the nausea that threatened to take her. She rushed into the Ladies' Powder Room and closed the door. Fresh tears filled her eyes.

The door opened, and of all people, Beth slinked in. She noticed Laura's tearful expression.

"Are you okay?" she quizzed.

"I'm fine. Just happy tears," Laura lied, planting a smile on her face.

"Yes, this certainly is a happy occasion."

Laura opened her purse in search of some cover-up to hide the fact that she had been crying. She also powdered her nose and applied fresh lipstick. Beth did the same, occasionally stealing a glance toward Laura. Finally, she probed, "So, how far along are you in your pregnancy?"

Laura felt uncomfortable divulging any personal information to Beth, but she did not want to appear unkind. "Five months now."

"Wow, you can hardly tell you're even pregnant. Are you sure?"

Laura almost did not catch her innuendo. When the words sunk in, she could not believe her ears. *This woman had nerve.* "I think the doctors would know whether this is a baby or just an extra 15 pounds that may have accumulated," she added, sarcastically.

"Well, you never know what women will do these days, to hang on to a guy like Tony."

Laura's anger blazed and she could no longer hold back. She put the lipstick in her purse and gracefully walked up to Beth. Beth easily towered over Laura, but Laura was not intimidated.

"Sad, isn't it? But you're right. Some women stoop below God's standards to sink their nails into another woman's man. It's women like that, that'll have to answer to Him, in the end." She walked past Beth, whose mouth hung agape, and exited the bathroom. She felt like a load had been lifted from her shoulders. Perhaps now, Beth would know that Laura was on to her and she would back off Tony.

At first, the evening seemed to pass uneventfully. Tony sat quietly next to Laura at their table, while they watched the crowd dancing on the dance floor. The DJ slowed down the pace and played a ballad. Tony reached for Laura's hand and pulled her up into his embrace. They danced together slowly. He could not tear his eyes from hers. Laura knew he loved her. It was evident in his gaze. *Why ruin something so beautiful?*

Tony pulled her even closer. Laura melted in his arms. "I love you, Tony." He squeezed her tighter. They danced to two additional songs and then the DJ picked up the pace with music from the Bee Gees. Tony was ready to escape the dance floor, but Laura insisted they dance.

"Are you sure it's okay for the baby?" he asked with concern in his eyes.

"Of course, come on!"

Tony clumsily tried to keep up with Laura, who knew the moves to the new song. She laughed at how he struggled to keep up. Suddenly, Beth was behind him. She lifted his arms with hers and guided him through the dance moves. Laura stepped back a moment to give them space, since Beth seemed to hijack the entire dance floor. Tony helplessly laughed. The crowd cheered them on. Laura was becoming more and more uncomfortable with the way Beth moved against Tony. Tony was not resisting. Across the dance floor, a circle of guests formed to watch Beth professionally dance with an uncoordinated Tony.

John's eyes suddenly collided with Laura's. He could see that she was upset. He grabbed Marlene's hand and pushed his way into the center of the circle, swinging Marlene around like a true professional. The crowd cheered for the birthday boy. Tony and Beth were pushed out of the center.

Finally, Tony told Beth that he was done. "No more! You're killing me out there."

"Oh, you big baby! It was fun! Admit it!"

"No way!" Tony laughed.

"Well, it had to be more fun than sitting around with 'skinny' over there."

Beth said it loud enough for Laura to hear. Tony looked from Beth to Laura, finally understanding that words had to have been exchanged. "Hey now . . . 'skinny', as you put it, has a baby to think about. She can't be bouncing all over the place in her condition." Tony pulled Laura into a hug.

Beth gave Laura a smug smile. "She don't look like it."

Tony grew more serious, obviously not liking Beth's implication. "What are you insinuating, Beth?"

"Forget it!" Beth turned on her heel and walked away.

Tony looked down at Laura, whose fiery eyes followed Beth as she sauntered away. "What's going on?" he quizzed.

"Why don't you go ask your old friend?" Laura pulled away, grabbed her purse, and walked out of the banquet hall, through the foyer, and into the dark brisk night. The cool air hit her like a freight train. Laura did not care.

Tony followed closely behind, calling her name. "Laura, it's freezing out here. Come back in!" He ran to catch up to her. "What happened in there?"

Laura stopped and twirled to confront him. "Your friend accused me of lying about my pregnancy just to hang on to you. Maybe that's something she would do, but that's certainly not something I would ever think of doing."

"Why would Beth do that?" Tony asked. He took off his suit jacket and draped it over her shoulders.

Laura's body shook with rage and from the cold. "Are you serious? Are you that blind? She wants you for herself! She can care less that you've made a commitment to me and that you have a child on the way. Frankly, I'm starting to wonder if you even care!"

"Laura, don't be ridiculous!" Tony blasted.

"Ridiculous? I've been faithful and supportive of you in every way. I've never led you to believe for even a moment that I might find interest in someone else. On the contrary, you flirt with that woman, encouraging her behavior!"

"I do not! I can't help it if she's throwing herself at me!" Tony shouted.

"You can so! You can tell her that you are committed to me. But you won't! You like the attention she gives you!" Laura accused.

"Again, that's ridiculous!"

"No, what's ridiculous is that I was going to give this to you tonight." Laura opened her purse with trembling hands. She took out the blue velvet box and placed it in his hands. "Read the inscription, and then tell me if I'm ridiculous!"

Laura pulled off his jacket and shoved it in his arms. She stomped back into the building.

* * *

Tony wished the night would open up and swallow him whole. He had made such a mess of things. He put his jacket on and walked back into the banquet hall. In the light of the foyer, he opened the little blue box. The ring inside made him feel all the more guilty. He pulled it out of the box and read the inscription. *Forever! Love, Laura.*

He put the ring on the fourth finger of his left hand. It fit perfectly. He would go inside and make things right with her. Determined to repair the damage he had done, he brazenly walked into the party. His eyes grazed the room in search of her. Suddenly, John was at his side, forcibly pulling him back out of the room.

"We need to talk," John insisted.

Tony almost resisted, but he did not want to upset John on such a special occasion. John stomped out of the hall into the foyer. Tony followed behind him. John turned and pulled Tony into an empty cloakroom.

"Tony, what's the meaning of all of this? After everything that has happened, Marlene and I have forgiven all the pain you previously caused Laura and accepted you into our home with open arms. I even took you under my wing and gave you a job as manager of my rentals. Please don't make me regret these decisions." His chest rose and fell with quick breaths.

Tony looked at the man he admired and had grown to love. He was disappointing everyone with his unstable behavior. "I'm sorry."

"That's it? You're sorry? What about Laura? Are you sorry you embarrassed her out there with *Beth*?"

Tony knew he was wrong. He could not explain to John the turmoil that was tearing him up inside. Yet, he could not let him believe the worst of him. "John, you have to believe me when I say, I have Laura's best intentions."

"You're kidding, right? Because you could have fooled me. I think you need to leave, Mr. Giacalone, before you make this night even more of a disaster for her." John walked toward the door with disappointment on his face. He turned once more to face him. "Don't come back until you're ready to apologize to this family and especially to Laura. I'll tell her I sent you home. Get outta here and clear that head of yours or you're going to lose the best thing in your life."

Tony watched John leave the cloakroom. The door closed, leaving him alone for the first time that night. John was right. He was not acting as if he had Laura's best intentions. If he continued on this way, he would lose her. *Yet, isn't that what he set out to do?* Tony was so confused. He needed a friend to talk to.

****

Tony pulled up to Uncle Frank's bungalow. The cute little house sat just outside of the city limits of Albany, not more than five miles from Tony's house. The front room light was on. Tony jumped up the porch steps. He knocked on the door and waited. He could hear Frank's feet scuttling to the door. When the door opened, Uncle Frank was still in his dress shirt and slacks. The tie he was wearing was loosened and he held a beer in his hand.

"I knew you were gonna come. Get in," he demanded.

"I came to apologize," Tony whispered.

Frank pulled him through the doorway and closed the door. Tony shivered from the wintry chill. He saw Frank stumble back onto the couch. "It's not me you need to be apologizing to," he accused.

Tony entered the living room, after removing his shoes. He plopped down on the couch next to his uncle. "I made a mess of things tonight. I ruined your night and I ruined John's night. But worst of all, I destroyed Laura's night."

Uncle Frank looked at him in anger for the first time. "I don't understand you sometimes. What you have with that girl is rare. It's a gift from God. You have a love—an unconditional, true love with her. Why are you working so hard to get rid of her?"

"Because I don't deserve her, Uncle. I already told you this. Laura and the baby are better off without me," Tony frankly stated.

"So, you'd rather give her up because of something that already happened, you can't change, and you couldn't help? Do you know how crazy that sounds?" Frank shouted.

"Well, that's me, isn't it? Crazy Tony!"

Frank sat up, softening a bit. "Ton, you're not crazy. You did not ask to witness what you did and to suffer all that pain. But you *are* crazy if you're going to let her go because of your fears."

Tony leaned back and smacked his hands to his head. "Ahh!" he shouted in frustration. "Uncle, I don't know what to do! What's the right thing? Is it right to sentence her to a life with a man who has all this emotional baggage? Or do I set her free to find someone normal?"

Frank put his beer down and rose from the couch. He paced in front of the TV. His stocky little figure moved quickly. He set a pair of warm brown eyes on Tony. "Tony, I don't have any children. Therefore, you are a son to me. So, if I come across harsh, take it in a fatherly fashion. You need to get your life together, son. You need to understand that you have a baby on the way and a woman who loves you unconditionally. You make this work! That's your God-given duty! You talk about God all the time. Have you bothered once to stop and think what He wants of you?"

Tony stood as well. He walked to the window and stared out into the night. "I've thought about Him more than ever. Does He really want me to hinder Laura with all these problems?"

Frank touched Tony's shoulder, forcing him to look into his face. "Do you really think God would want you to abandon your future wife and child? You made a baby with her. You're both already bound to one another. You cannot walk out on her!"

Tony looked into his uncle's sincere face. "You're right," he finally agreed. "Tomorrow night, I'm going to go over there and make this all right." Tony paused a moment, catching a glance of the ring on his finger. "Look . . . Look at what she gave me tonight." Tony wiggled the ring off his finger and gave it to Frank. "Read the inscription on the inside."

Frank pulled a pair of reading glasses off the end table and placed it on the tip of his nose. He lifted the ring into the light of the lamp and read. Removing the glasses, he handed the ring back to Tony. Tony put it on and sat back down on the couch. Frank playfully lifted his hand and hit his nephew in the back of the head. "And you wanted to break up with her? *Stupido*!"

Tony and Frank broke into laughter. Frank sat down and Tony hugged him.

CHAPTER 6

Mark 14:38

"Watch and pray so that you will not fall into temptation. The spirit is willing, but the body is weak."

Laura helped carry John's gifts into the house that night after the party. She did not want to put more of a damper on the evening, so she pretended that nothing had happened to trouble her.

"Well, did you suspect anything, at all?" she playfully questioned John. They both juggled gift boxes in their arms.

"Not a thing, you little sneaks!" he teased.

"That's why they call it a 'surprise'," she jested.

"You and your mom really got me this time. This is something *I* would normally pull."

"That's why we planned it. It was so perfect. You looked completely shocked," Laura giggled. John placed his packages on the nook table and helped Laura with hers. They paused a moment, looking at one another, and John then placed two gentle hands on her shoulders, pulling her into an embrace.

"You don't have to pretend anymore. I know you're hurting."

She looked up into his handsome face and smiled. "I'm fine, Dad. Stop worrying. This is your night. I don't want anything to ruin it for you."

"Believe me. Nothing could spoil what you two did for me. But I know you're upset."

Marlene entered at that moment with more gifts and both John and Laura helped to empty her hands. "What's going on? Are you upset?" Marlene inquired.

"I'm not upset. I'm fine," Laura insisted.

John and Marlene exchanged glances and both reached for her hands, pulling Laura into a chair. "I told him to leave, Laura. I pulled him aside and told him to get his life together. I also told him that he couldn't come back here unless it was to apologize."

Laura took in an unsteady breath and threw her hands in the air. "I don't know what to do for him, anymore."

"There is nothing for you to do. This is all Tony. He needs to decide what *he's* going to do," John answered.

"The boy is just so lost and confused. I feel sorry for him," Marlene added.

"But not at Laura's expense!" John chimed in.

"Absolutely not! He cannot use his illness as an excuse to hurt you, honey. At the same time, we need to find compassion and understanding in our hearts for him." Marlene gave John a hard glance.

John smiled and shook his head. "You old softy!"

Marlene and Laura both smiled. "Just keep praying for him. He'll come around. If there is one thing we know for sure . . . it's that he does love you."

Laura made her way up the stairway to her room. She mulled over Marlene's last words. She wished she felt that confident of Tony's love for her. Deep down, she knew their love was strong, but his behavior was beginning to confuse her. She pulled back the bedspread and sat on her comforter. Looking into the vanity across from her, the reflection in the mirror displayed her true emotions. Laura's face fell into her hands and she cried. She cried for Tony and all his suffering. She cried for all the agony that he was trying to endure alone. Laura cried for the baby and for their uncertain future.

Still, despite all that had been happening, Laura held on to hope. She believed that Jesus would not have brought them together, after all this time, to have them break up. Just to be sure, Laura decided to put her trust in Him, once again. If there was one person who could make this right, it was Jesus.

****

Sunday morning, Nino walked through his lonely house and decided he was not going to let anyone stand in his way of seeing his granddaughter. Two weeks had gone by and he was missing her desperately. Sure, he had filled up his time helping Alfonso with the transporting business, but his heart longed to see Laura. He decided to call her and set up a time to meet her.

Remembering suddenly that his driver had taken the day off, Nino sulked. He had long since stopped driving, years prior. His vision for distance was not what it used to be and he had become reliant on his driver for transportation. *How could he manage this?* He did not want Laura to have to drive down by herself.

The phone rang and Nino heard Josie answer it. Moments later, she entered the study and announced a call from Alfonso. Nino struggled to rise from the couch. He was suddenly feeling his age. Slowly, he walked to the desk. He clenched the phone and breathlessly spoke to Alfonso. As it turned out, Alfonso had the day off and was seeking Nino's company.

"Actually, Fonzie, I was gonna see if I could see my *nipote* today. But my driver has the day off. I don't know how I can go see her. But this was my plan."

"Why don't I go pick her up for you?" Alfonso offered.

"Oh no, that's okay. I don't know if she will be okay with this idea."

"Why not? I've never done anything to hurt her."

"Yes, but you was involved in the whole Tammy situation. It might bother her."

"Boss, she won't even know it's me. I'm just a driver, remember?"

"Are you sure?" Nino asked.

"Positive," he reassured.

"Okay, I will call her first and let you know. Okay?"

Nino hung up with Alfonso and called the Knight home. It was still slightly early. He hoped he was not waking them. To Nino's dismay, Laura did not answer the phone. Still feeling uncomfortable around John and Marlene, he liked to avoid any confrontation with them whatsoever. John answered and informed Nino that Laura was still resting. He promised to have her call when she rose. Nino thanked John and hung up.

He understood the Knights' reluctance to warm up to him. He created a great deal of damage to see to Laura's happiness. Two lives were unintentionally taken. This was something that Nino sincerely regretted. He prayed for God's forgiveness and hoped that one day Marlene and John would see his sincerity.

Meanwhile, he was so thankful that Laura had forgiven him and that she had become such a significant part of his life. He lived for the days that he could spend some time with her. He hoped today would be one of those days.

* * *

When Laura woke that morning, she felt as though she had not slept a wink. Her body ached and she wondered how she was going to get through the day. After making her bed, dressing, and refreshing her face in the bathroom, Laura entered the kitchen nook. John was sitting at the table reading the Sunday paper. Marlene had yet to rise.

"Morning," John's voice sang with a chipper.

"Morning," Laura kissed the top of his head and passed him to get to the fridge. She poured herself a glass of orange juice and sat down next to him.

"You've already received a phone call this morning," John disclosed.

"Tony?" Laura guessed with a slight raise to her tone.

"Sorry, no. Not Tony, your grandfather."

"Nonno called this early?"

"Oh, I'm sure he wants a visit with his favorite granddaughter," John added.

Laura rose from her chair and quickly dialed his number. After discussing the arrangements, she decided to visit with him after attending church with John and Marlene. He promised to have his driver pick her up at 11 a.m. Laura needed a change of pace. Anything sounded better than sitting around at home, waiting for Tony to call.

As Nonno promised, Laura spotted the Cadillac pulling up the driveway. She kissed her parents goodbye, thankful that she spent the morning with them. She walked out the front door into the sunny, yet cold winter morning. The driver exited the vehicle and quickly came to open her door. Laura sat on the soft leather seat, as he closed her door. She still was not used to such treatment from her grandfather's staff. She watched the large man walk around the front of the vehicle. He was dressed in a dark suit and wore a driver's cap that hid his eyes. He reentered the car and began to back it out of the driveway.

Laura looked out the tinted window of the beautiful Cadillac, as it drove away. She welcomed its warmth and coziness. Outside, a light snow had fallen covering everything in white again. The vehicle easily maneuvered its way down the slick roads. Its interior was a light-crème colored leather that was in mint condition. Distracting her thoughts, Laura realized the driver had asked her a question.

"I'm sorry, did you ask me something?" she questioned.

"Yes, Miss. I just asked if the vehicle was warm enough for you."

Laura took a good look at the driver. He was not Nonno's usual driver, yet his voice was familiar—the accent familiar. She looked at the back of his head, trying to place a face with the voice and the curly dark hair that poked out from under the hat. Finally, she realized she had not answered his question.

"Oh, yes. It's fine."

"Good, I'd hate for you to be uncomfortable," he added.

"Thank you."

She looked at the driver even more closely. He was young—much younger than the other driver. Before she could finish her thought, she watched him remove his hat and run his fingers through his dark hair.

Laura's heart crashed into her chest. She had not seen Alfonso Rengali since just before Tammy's death. Seeing him again brought all the emotions right back to the surface. Unable to get the words out right, Laura stuttered. "W-w-what are *you* doing driving my grandfather's car?"

"It's good to see you, too," he teased. "It's been a while," he added.

"Not long enough!" Laura exclaimed.

"Ouch! Well, I guess I deserve that. Though, you haven't heard my side of the story."

"I asked you a question. Where is my nonno's regular driver?"

"He has the day off. Nino needed a favor and I was happy to oblige. I hope you're okay with it," he added, seemingly sincere.

"I don't know. I thought you were arrested after what happened to Tammy."

"I *was* arrested . . . under false pretenses. They had no evidence against me. I had no part in Tammy's or Paul's deaths. Your grandfather asked me to be a distraction for Tammy and that's all I did. I feel terrible for what happened to her."

Laura did not know how to respond. She would have to verify it all with her grandfather. She was not comfortable around Alfonso, knowing that he was never sincere in his interest in Tammy. "If you'd have known her like I did, you wouldn't have had to pretend that you liked her."

"On the contrary, I truly enjoyed my time with her. Tammy seemed like a wonderful person. That's why I'm so sad for how it all turned out. Nino's intentions were for no one to ever get hurt," he defended.

"There's no need for you to defend my grandfather to me. I know he's sorry for what he did. I just don't know if I believe that you are so innocent, Mr. Rengali."

Alfonso nodded in understanding. "That's fine. You can ask Nino. He'll vouch for me. I enjoyed meeting you and your sister. I was hoping we could look past all that happened and be friends. I'll be working closely with Nino until I can run his transporting business on my own. He's been kind enough to turn it over to me. So, we'll probably be seeing a lot of each other."

Laura was caught off guard with all that Alfonso was telling her. She certainly was going to confirm it with Nonno Nino. Paul never liked

Alfonso, but of course, that could have been because he did not approve of Alfonso's pursuit of Tammy. Still, Laura's gut told her that he was not to be trusted. She hoped he was sincere in his relationship with Nino and that he would not be a bad influence.

When they arrived at Nino's house, Alfonso parked the vehicle in the driveway. He exited the car and walked to Laura's door. She had already opened her door. He extended his left hand. "Allow me," he said with a charming smile.

Laura was unsure, but took his hand to rise from the seat. She glanced at his face. He held a smile on his lips. His eyes seemed sharp, intense. She quickly pulled her hand from his and walked up the driveway to the front porch. In the front room, the curtains drew back and she spotted her grandfather. Before she had a chance to knock, the door was pulled open.

"*Bella mia*!" Nino exclaimed.

"Hi, Nonno," Laura entered the house, falling into her grandpa's warm hold.

Alfonso lingered in behind her, handing the keys to Nino. "She drives like a beauty, boss."

"Ah, you like, ehh? *Si*, she is my favorite car." Nino took the keys from Alfonso and invited them in. He took Laura's coat and hung it in the foyer closet. Alfonso had not removed his coat and Laura wondered what he was still doing hanging around.

They came into the kitchen, where Laura found the table set and Josie cooking at the stove. She was a cute little Italian woman, with brown graying hair, rounded cheeks, and a genuine smile. She waived hello to Laura and continued preparing the meal. Nino pulled out a chair for Laura and urged her to sit.

"Smells great, as usual Josie," Alfonso complimented.

"Thanks, Fonzie. I don't know if you're staying, but I can pack some up for you to take home," she offered.

"Oh, I wouldn't think of intruding. Thanks, anyway."

"Alfonso," Nino stated. "How rude of me. You like to stay to *mangiare*?"

"Thanks, boss, but I already ate. I'll give you some quiet time with your granddaughter. When do you want me to return to take her home?"

Laura quickly jumped in. "You're driving me home?"

"Yup. Remember? Mr. Valente's driver took the day off today?" He flashed a set of white teeth Laura's way.

"If you can come about three this afternoon, that should give us enough time to catch up," Laura estimated.

"Certainly, I'll see you then." Josie handed a container of food to Alfonso. "Thanks, Josie." He kissed her cheek.

"Thank you, again, my friend," Nino gratefully stated. "See you soon."

Laura warily scrutinized Alfonso's every move, while he made his way around the home as if he owned it. It was obvious that he was very welcome there and that frightened her. *Who was this man to Nino and why did it seem they were so at ease around each other?*

Alfonso left. Before Laura could speak her mind, Nino leapt in, "I know what you thinking. What's this guy doing here?"

Laura did not want to come across as being judgmental. "Nonno, it's none of my business. But I'm not going to lie, I was a little shocked to see him. I had almost forgotten about Alfonso. I guess I just thought that he was held after Tammy's death."

"Alfonso had nothing to do with what happened to you sister. I just ask him to help take her eye off the doctor for you. That is it. They no put him in jail because he is innocent," Nino defended.

"Innocent?" she scoffed. "I guess, Nonno. I just don't feel comfortable around him, knowing that he wasn't really sincere in his interest in Tammy. Who is he, anyway? What I mean is, he seems to be so relaxed here . . . has he been working for you for a long time—because he seems so young?"

Nino sat back and Josie served minestrone soup to the both of them. He nodded to her and she gave him a wide smile in return. "Come on, let's *mangia* first. Say thank you to God." Laura gave thanks and they began to eat. "Alfonso's papa, Gabe, was one of my men, 25 years ago. He had just gotten married to Paula, Alfonso's momma, when he came to work for me. We all became *amici*, with Nonna, too. Gabe died when Paula was with child. We try to help her. She wanted to move to California. Me and Nonna give her some money to help. Alfonso was born just before she go."

Nino blew onto the hot soup and took a spoonful. Laura also took a nibble, curiously observed him, as he continued his story. "Three years ago, Alfonso show up to my door. He say, 'I'm Paula and Gabe's son. My momma die. She told me to come to you and you help me to get on my feet.' And because I feel the obligation to take care of Gabe and Paula's son, I take him in."

Laura took another spoonful of the delicious soup and then gently wiped the corners of her mouth. "That's sad. How did she die?"

"Cancer," he answered.

"Well, that was very kind of you to take him in. What worries me is the fact that Paul remembered him being involved in some serious crimes in the past. Was he working for you at the time? 'Cause, I'd really hate for him to be a bad influence on you."

Nonno Nino laughed aloud. "You think he's the bad influence for me?" he chuckled. "No, *figlia mia*, I was the bad influence on him. Now I convince him to stay away from the Mafia. This is why I give him the transporting business. I want him to stay clean. I even told him about Jesus."

Now, Laura burst into laughter. "Nonno, that's wonderful! You're witnessing to Alfonso?"

Nino's eyes were sparkling at Laura's laughter. "*Si*! I make him change his ways!"

Laura felt a sense of relief. Perhaps God was already working through Nonno to bring others to the Kingdom. She felt elated.

The rest of lunch passed quickly. They spoke more of the type of business Alfonso would soon take over. Laura found that her grandfather's heart *was* generous, like her mother had once told her. This made her heart soar. He may have made his mistakes in the past, but he was not the monster that he could have turned into.

After lunch, Nino and Laura drank tea in the nook that overlooked his beautiful backyard. The bushes and trees were still masked with white little crystals of snow, making it look like a painting out of an art gallery.

"So, tell me, how was John's party? Was he surprised?"

Laura cringed at the mere thought of the party and though she quickly recovered, she was afraid Nino had noticed her recoiling. "The party was a success. Dad was completely surprised."

Nino's brows came together at the center. "Tell me more," he insisted.

Laura blew out a slow breath. "Well, he got wonderful gifts . . ." she paused, trying to think of anything else to say, so to not give herself away. ". . . He . . . the . . . the food, yes—the food was great." She gave him a weak smile.

"You know, when you momma used to no tell me the truth, she used to stumble on the words, like you. What is it? What you no tell me?"

Laura did not want to burden him with her troubles. But more than anything, she did not want to tell him what was going on with Tony. If he knew the trouble she was having with him, it would only fortify Nino's opinion of him and she did not want him to dislike Tony even more.

"Really, Nonno, that's it. There's nothing more," she hated lying.

"Laura, you no have to tell me. But I think I know you. Something is wrong with you. If you need me, I'm here for you."

Needing his loving support, Laura instantly caved. "It's just, Tony," she released. "He's going through a really hard time, right now. They must have uncovered something horrible in therapy and he can't deal with it."

"What do you mean, 'they *must have* uncovered something'? Did he no tell you?"

"Well, no. He's not ready to talk about it yet," Laura hesitantly replied.

"Why, no? Are you no his fiancée? He should tell you everything," Nino insisted.

"It's not that easy for him, Nonno. He's holding back for some reason."

It was obvious that Nino was distressed. Laura could tell that he was treading thin waters trying to keep his opinions to himself. "Laura, I must tell you, I no like what you tell me. There should be no secrets between you."

"I don't like it either, Nonno. But I must be patient and understanding. That's not even bothering me as much as that woman who works for my father," she admitted with disgust.

"Who?" Nino probed.

"The secretary at my dad's office turns out to be an old schoolmate of Tony's. She's made it no secret that she's interested in him. Even at the party, she was practically throwing herself at him, making rude comments to upset me."

Nonno suddenly stood and began pacing in front of the window. "Laura, this no good!"

"Relax, Nonno, it will all turn out. I have to trust that God will help us," she added.

"No, you no understand me. I no like this because I know how things work. She no give him attention unless he receive it. You *capisce* me?"

"Are you trying to tell me that Tony is encouraging her?" Laura's heart doubled in rhythm.

Nino sat back down and clasped Laura's hand. "I don't know that for sure and I no want to make you more nervous, but you keep you eyes *aperti* . . . remember? Open!"

Laura gazed into his loving face. He was truly concerned for her. She could not help but feel grateful that she had him in her corner, looking out for her. She considered his words. As she had recalled before, she would not be naïve to the fact that something could be going on between Tony and Beth. It killed her to even consider it. In fact, it set her insides grinding, once again.

"Nonno, believe me. I've got my eyes wide open," she reassured.

"If you want, I can keep an eye on him, too," he suggested.

"No, Nonno! I don't want you getting into any trouble over me."

"I will just have somebody watch him. To make sure he no be unfaithful to you."

"No, Nonno. At least not yet. If I suspect something further, I'll let you know. But I believe that he's telling me the truth when he says that he loves only me."

Nino looked at her skeptically. "Okay, you tell me if you need me. I will help you and no make trouble," he promised.

"Thank you."

Before long, Alfonso arrived to take Laura home. Nino gingerly gave him the keys to the Cadillac before kissing his granddaughter goodbye. He walked Laura to the front door. In the closet, he withdrew her coat and helped her to put it on. As Alfonso held the door open, Nino gave Laura a big squeeze. He kissed both of her cheeks and lifted a pointed finger to her.

"Don't forget what I say! If you need me to help you, you call me right away!"

"Thanks, Nonno. I love you." She gave him a big kiss and left the house.

The sun had finally broken through the clouds, making the snow sparkle on the ground. Alfonso held his arm out for Laura to hold onto, while making their way to the car. He helped her in and then entered the vehicle himself. Laura looked up at the house and smiled upon seeing her grandpa waving at her in the doorway. She had grown to love him so much.

Distracting her thoughts, Alfonso's voice rang out. "Did you two have a nice visit?"

She could tell that Alfonso was looking to make small talk. Truthfully, she wanted to be alone with her thoughts, but again, she did not want to come across as rude. "As always," she answered.

"Yeah, that man is incredible. Like a father to me, ya know."

It suddenly hit Laura, "A Californian. Yes, that's it!" she stated aloud.

"What's it? What are you talking about?" Alfonso asked.

"You have a Californian accent. I couldn't pinpoint it, before. But I just remembered Nonno telling me you were from California."

Alfonso flashed her another wide smile. "So, you guys were talkin' about me, *ehh*?"

Laura could not help but blush. "It wasn't like that. I just asked how you two came to know each other, is all."

"Aww! Don't crush me like that. For a minute there, I had hopes that maybe I was the hot topic of conversation between the two of you," he flirted.

"Sorry. I was just curious," Laura tried to conceal a smile. She did not want to encourage him in any way, even if he did make her laugh.

"Curious is good," Alfonso encouraged.

"Impossible," Laura whispered aloud. Alfonso caught her grin in the rearview mirror and laughed.

"That's what my ma used to say 'bout me," he revealed. "She used to say I was relentless when I wanted something, even as a kid."

"I hate to disappoint you, Mr. Rengali . . ."

"Please, you make me sound so old. Call me Al or Fonz or something," he insisted.

"As I was saying, I hate to disappoint you, but you can't always get what you want out of life," Laura lectured.

"You can if you try hard enough!"

"Some things are just not in God's will. You can't twist God's arm," she preached.

Alfonso stared at her in the rearview mirror for a moment. "Your grandpa was right. You *do* talk about God a lot."

Laura smiled, "He said that?"

"Yeah, he even tried converting me," Alfonso said with a deep laugh.

"Well, what's so funny about that?" Laura enquired.

"Me becoming converted is hilarious!"

Laura became serious. "Why is that?"

"God don't want a bum like me. The thought of even asking God, would surely send a bolt of lightning down on us. I promised to get you home safely. How would I explain that one to Nino?"

"I was right, you are impossible."

The chitchat continued this way until they reached the Knight home. When Alfonso pulled the vehicle into the driveway, he parked the car, and immediately ran to Laura's aide. She gripped his strong arm and pulled herself from the vehicle onto the slick driveway.

"At your service, madam," he chided.

"What a gracious chauffeur you are, Mr. Rengali," Laura teased in return.

"Only the best for the Boss's lovely granddaughter," Alfonso bantered. He helped her up the porch steps. "Easy, milady," he teased.

"I'll take it from here, thanks."

Laura glanced up to see Tony standing at the top of the porch steps. Her heart skipped a beat at the jealousy fix on his face. He reached down and gently took hold of Laura's arm. Alfonso continued to walk her up the steps.

"I said, I got it," Tony's voice elevated.

Alfonso's face grew serious. He looked to Laura and whispered, "You okay?"

Before Laura could respond, Tony answered for her. "She'll be okay, once you let her arm go. I said I got her!"

"That's okay, Alfonso. I'm okay. He's my fiancé. Thank you for the ride. I appreciate it."

He glared irritably at Tony and then turned to Laura and smiled. "You're welcome. Anytime. Have a good one." He tipped his hat and casually walked back down the steps.

Laura watched him reenter the vehicle, turn the engine, and drive away.

"Who was that goon?" Tony spat.

Laura turned her gaze back to Tony. He was being rude and it annoyed her. "That was my grandfather's friend, who was kind enough to pick me up to take me to see him." She pulled her arm from his grasp and entered the house. No one appeared to be home.

Tony followed Laura in. "Where are my parents?" she asked.

"They had some errands to run. Since they knew I was anxious to see you, they let me in to wait."

Laura really looked at Tony for the first time since she had arrived. *Why did he have to look so beautiful, even when he was infuriating?* He had prickly whiskers on his face from a day without a razor and his hair was slightly tousled. He wore a pair of fitted jeans and a button-down shirt that revealed a few strands of the hair on his chest. He was gorgeous even though his eyes were dark and troubled.

She removed her coat and hung it in the closet. They stood a moment looking at one another in the hallway. "Well, are you just going to stand there, or are you going to come in?" she finally asked.

"After you," he offered.

CHAPTER 7

Zechariah 8:16-17

"'These are the things you are to do: Speak the truth to each other, and render true and sound judgment in your courts; do not plot evil against your neighbor, and do not love to swear falsely. I hate all this,' declares the LORD."

Laura entered the living room and sat on the couch. Tony followed and took a seat next to her. She pretended to adjust her shirtsleeve, determined to make him speak first. She felt that she had nothing left to say to him, unless he opened up.

Tony gently clasped her chin and forced her to look upon him. The expression on his face made her instantly regret her coldness. What she really wanted was nothing more than to jump into his arms. But she resisted. Tony needed to make the first move.

"I miss you," he simply stated. "I'm so sorry about last night. I was a big fat jerk."

Laura took his hand and held it. She recognized her ring on his ring finger. "I see you put on my ring."

"I love it. Thank you. The inscription is beautiful. I just wish it could be true," he glowered.

"Why wouldn't it be? Through Christ, all things are possible. Did you forget that, already?"

"I don't know anything anymore. I don't like strange guys driving you to far places. I do not like the way that punk was looking at you and touching you. Yet, I don't deserve you, either."

"That's crazy talk. We belong together," Laura insisted. Despite his erratic behavior, she wanted to continue to support him. Although, somehow, she had to help him recognize that his behavior was unacceptable. "This is just so not you," she finally managed. "There was no need to be rude to Alfonso."

Tony's eyes protruded. "Alfonso? Alfonso Rengali? You mean to tell me that that's the same goon who was dating Tammy?"

"Don't be like that. Why do you have to be so judgmental? Not everyone is a bad guy," Laura defended.

Tony pulled his hand away and sat back. "I'm not trying to be judgmental. But forgive me for not immediately trusting everyone who has connections to your grandfather."

Laura sat back as well. The conversation was not headed in a good direction. "I can see where this is going and maybe it's best we just change the subject. I don't know what more to do to make you and my grandfather get along."

"I'm not saying that he doesn't love you. I believe that he does. But I'm not the one with the problem. He hates me and I've never done a thing to him. I wouldn't put it past him to do something that will break us further apart," he waived his hand in frustration.

Laura was growing more and more frustrated with Tony. "First of all," she began, "For you to say 'further apart', that would indicate that we are already on the verge. If that's the case, it's not my grandfather's doing, and frankly, neither is it mine. If we are falling apart, it's because you're shutting me out. It has nothing to do with my grandfather. He has been loving and supportive."

"Oh, sure, and I'm guessing he's just loving the fact that I'm acting like a fat jerk, doesn't he? You went there today and told him what's been going on, didn't you?" Tony accused.

Laura's chest began to hurt. The twisting and turning of her insides began to make her nauseous. "I went to see my grandfather because I love him. If the topic of conversation came up, that's between him and me. I'm sure you ran to Uncle Frank and opened up to him. What? I can't have someone to confide in?"

"Not him!" Tony now shouted. "All you're doing is dangling the carrot in front of him to take matters into his own hands and don't think that he won't."

"Nonno has changed. He's not the man he used to be. If he promises me that he'll stay out of it, I believe him!"

"Then you are playing a very dangerous game, because—like it or not—he was a dangerous man. I think it's great that you've forgiven him and I pray that he *is* changed. But don't think that a leopard changes its spots quite that easily. You give him reason to, and he'll break us apart, indefinitely," Tony warned.

"If you love me the way you claim you loved me, then nothing and no one will break us apart. But if you continue to push me away, then I can't do anything to help us. I'd hate for this to end, when we've fought so hard to be together." Laura struggled to get to her feet. Her mouth felt dry and she needed something to drink. Suddenly, remembering a valid point, she turned and pointed a finger to him. "If there's someone who's bound and determined to see us break up, it's not Nonno. It's your old pal, Beth."

Tony rolled his eyes and shook his head. "Beth's harmless."

Now it was Laura who waved her hands in frustration. Her breathing came in short quick spurts, as she belted out her expressions. "She—is—far—from—harmless. She flat out accused me of pretending to be pregnant. That's the worst kind of insult. If you cared, you'd be angry with her that she could say something so vile about me," Laura heaved.

"Beth is an insecure, spoiled brat. She doesn't like you because you're everything she wishes she could be. But Beth won't send you 'sleeping with the fishes' to get rid of you. She doesn't have *that* kind of power."

"That's not the only kind of power that can pilot this relationship into the toilet!" exclaimed Laura. She stalked into the kitchen and retrieved a gallon of orange juice from the refrigerator. With quaking hands, she poured some into a glass and quickly lifted it to her parched lips. After taking in half the liquid, the glass slipped from her hands and crashed to the counter. Tony was instantly behind her grasping her shoulders.

"Hey! Are you okay?" he asked.

"Fine!" Laura tried to order her now wobbly legs to take her to the table. Suddenly, it seemed to stretch a mile away. She was shaky and could feel herself rapidly falling forward. Tony took hold of her before she plummeted to the hard ceramic floor.

"Laura, honey, what is it? What do you feel?" Tony questioned with alarm.

"Dizzy," she managed.

In a swift instant, he gathered her into his arms and carried her back to the couch. He laid her down gently and brushed her hair from her damp forehead. "You're all clammy and pale. Are you okay?"

"I don't know," she whispered.

"Should I call a doctor?" he asked.

"No, just give me a minute." She closed her eyes, loving the feel of his hands on her. He caressed her arm. His hand traveled downward and he rubbed her round belly.

"Please, be okay," he whispered. "I can't lose you."

Laura kept her eyes closed, willing the dizziness to go away. She tried concentrating on Tony's nearness. He claimed to not want to lose her, but probably not nearly as much as she was horrified of losing him.

His touch sent her reeling. "Don't stop touching me," she begged.

She felt him stretch out next to her on the sofa. He weaved his arm under her and pulled her onto his chest. She could feel his heart beating unpredictably beneath his ribs. He pulled her hair back with ease and touched her neck lovingly. "Better?" he asked.

"Much."

For nearly a half-hour, they laid down together on the couch. Though their conversation curtailed, the way he held her that moment, transcended every unspoken word. When she finally felt herself again, she lifted her head from his chest and looked up at him. He was staring at her intently. The expression on his face was unreadable—a mixture of regret and guilt or pain and hurt.

"What?" she finally pressed.

He shook his head and gently pushed her head back down to his chest. "Don't move," he whispered.

"Why?"

"Stop asking so many questions. I'm just enjoying holding you, right now."

"But you looked so . . . so . . ."

"So, what?"

"So sad, or hurt . . . I don't know," Laura probed.

"Guilty."

"What do you mean?" she questioned.

"I feel guilty. I've been a big jerk. Guilty, because I got you so upset you nearly passed out. Guilty, because I don't deserve you and instead of treasuring you, I keep screwing up. Guilty as sin," Tony finally emitted.

Laura propped herself up on her elbow. Her body pressed against his. She leaned forward and placed her finger to his lips. "Just shut up and kiss me."

Tony seized her head and pulled her to him. Their lips crashed in a passion-filled kiss that sent Laura swooning. Her body reacted to him in an intense way. Feelings that only Tony could stir up, made Laura instantly forget her anger. She felt him react to her in the same manner. There was no denying that the love between them was something that could not be ignored. Tony struggled to sit up, his lips never leaving hers. Laura held him for dear life, as they hugged and kissed, expressing their love with no more restraints.

"Laura, I'm so sorry. I hate myself for hurting you." He pressed his lips to hers.

She pulled her head back, mumbling, "Say no more. I forgive you."

He pulled her onto his lap and hugged her to him. "I just can't deny myself. I'm too selfish. I can't be without you!" He kissed her again.

"Why would you want to be?" she muttered between kisses.

"Not for my own selfishness, but to spare you. I'm no good, Laura. You're better off without me," he cried, kissing her neck. "I'm so selfish, so selfish!"

"I won't give up on you. Never!" She pulled his messy hair back and kissed him with passion.

When their lips parted, he panted breathlessly, "You have such a hard head!"

"And you're such a big fat jerk!" she mocked in return. Laura erupted in laughter. Tony followed suit.

Though he had not opened up, they took one step closer to one another. This was more than Laura had expected from the way the visit had initiated.

****

"What you trying to tell me, Fonzie?" Nino demanded.

Alfonso had driven back to the Valente home and picked up Nino. They drove to Nino's warehouse, where the majority of the transporting of goods took place. Both Nino and Alfonso walked down the open aisle ways of the building, between coffee bean crates and olive oil containers.

"I'm sorry, boss. It really irked me the way that nut held ownership over your granddaughter. It was as if she couldn't have a mind of her own. I was simply walking her up the slippery porch steps. If looks could've killed, he would have popped me right there."

Nino shook his head in dismay. The thought of Giacalone grabbing her as if he owned her made his blood boil. *Nobody would treat his granddaughter like that. Not while he was alive to stop them.*

"What did *she* say?" Nino inquired.

"Nothing. She simply told me that it was okay and went in the house with him. I swear, if you had given me the okay, I wouldn't have left her with that *pazzo*!" Alfonso stopped walking and folded his arms across his wide chest. "It's still not too late, Don Nino. You give me the word and I'm on that punk like sap to a tree."

Nino considered Alfonso's offer. *What was he to do?* He promised Laura he would stay out of it. He did not want to do anything that would require being devious or cunning. But if she was not thinking of herself, if she was allowing him to mistreat her, he could not stand by and let it happen. Perhaps she was used to abuse because of the conditions in which she was raised. Perhaps she did not recognize that it was unnatural to be treated indecently.

He stomped his foot furiously, angry with himself for having permitted his only daughter and granddaughters to live in the hostile environment that they had. His pride and mercilessness led him to make unwise decisions that now haunted him for as long as he lived. He could never forgive himself. He must make up for the mistakes he made.

He put his hands together and waved them back and forth in frustration. "I am so torn! Tell me, Alfonso, what do I do?" He was beside himself with grief.

Alfonso shook his head. He placed a hefty hand on Nino's shoulder in an affectionate manner. "Boss, it's your call. I don't want to tell you what to do. But I will say this. She's special. She's very special. She deserves a real man. Not that basket case with two screws loose. I really hate to see her get hurt. I'm not just talking about having her heart broken. That cracker has a mean streak a mile wide. I don't like him. If he flips, he'll kill her."

Everything that Alfonso was saying was exactly what Nino feared. He knew that Alfonso was right. He did not trust Tony and he could not—*NO*, he *would not* lose his beloved Laura. His mind was made up.

"Okay, Alfonso. I know you will listen to me. I don't want you to do nothing without my orders. You keep the tabs on him. Follow him and find out if he is what he say he is. If he even look to another woman, we will catch him. If he steps outta the line with Laura, I want to know. You will no hurt him. Do you understand? You are to stay clean. No funny business," Nino ordered. His heart raced in his old chest, while he spouted orders for Alfonso to, once again, do his dirty work. He hated this. He hated going against his better judgment, but he could not lose Laura. *He just could not.*

* * *

Alfonso watched Nino walk ahead. He was so happy—he could have shouted it from the rooftops. Things were going better than he had expected. *Nino was playing right into his hands!* If it continued to go this smoothly, his plan would go off without a hitch. He would get rid of that banana Giacalone and Nino would get his just pay.

That would leave Laura free. Free of Tony. Free from that hovering old coot!

He followed Nino, observing his surroundings. Soon, he would have it all. 'Valente Imports' would be signed over to him and he would be the sole owner. He would turn down the Galantes' offer for a job, after using them to finish off the old man and Tony. Then, the business *and* the girl would be his.

Oh, he could not wait! But he warned himself that he must be patient. Things needed to be handled delicately. He could not rush it. If he pushed too hard, he might turn her away and that was the last thing he wanted. For as much as he desired the money and the power, he desired the girl. He needed to be sure that he came out of it all smelling like a rose. If she suspected any foul play, he would mess up his chance, forever.

Nino began rattling off some business information and Alfonso tried to concentrate. He caught up to the man and pretended to find interest. Although his body was present, his mind was elsewhere. He could not stop thinking about her. Her long brown hair and how it shimmered golden in the sun that afternoon. It had taken everything in him not to reach out and touch it.

He was mesmerized by her laugh, her smile. When she blushed, it made his heart jerk. *Oh, he had it bad.* Sure, he liked her before. When he met her the first time at the apartment that Tammy and Laura were temporarily living in, he was immediately attracted to her. But he was on a mission and because he was so loyal to that scoundrel, everything else came second to following orders.

Now, seeing her again that day, it was like taking in his first breath ever. It was as though he had been dead until now. The feel of her dainty little hand on his big arm awoke a sleeping giant and now Alfonso did not want to go back to feeling dead again. He wanted to feel what she made him feel. Alive.

****

Monday, December 17

John strolled into the office Monday morning feeling as though a weight had been lifted off his shoulders. Knowing that Laura and Tony's discussion had been somewhat civil eased his worries a shred. But he was not done meddling in his daughter's business. He had words for both Tony and Beth. First, he needed to express to Beth that her behavior was tactless and that she needed to back off.

When the elevator doors finally opened to the second floor, he made his way into the office. Punctual as usual, Beth sat behind the front desk. The telephone seemed glued to her ear, as she directed a phone call to its destination. She waived to him and flashed him a bright smile. Upon seeing that he stopped at her desk, she gave him a signal to hold a moment.

When she finally hung up the phone, her voice chimed bright, "Good Morning, Mr. Knight."

"Morning, Beth," he reluctantly answered.

"Can I get you a coffee just how you like it?" Her excessive helpfulness was sometimes nauseating.

"That actually sounds great. I'll join you in the break room." John followed Beth down the hall toward the break room. She wore a tighter black skirt that fell just above her knees. Her sweater accentuated her figure as well. There was no doubt she was out to please someone.

As they continued down the hall, she gushed about how wonderful the surprise party went. She complimented both Marlene and Laura for an incredible job. "The food was wonderful," she insisted.

They entered the room and John watched her prepare his coffee, continuing her senseless chattering. Finally, he cut a sentence short, to get his point across. "Since you brought it up, Beth, I really feel I must talk to you."

Her face grew serious and ashen in color. "Oh no. What did I do wrong?"

"Why do you automatically assume you've done something wrong, Beth? I just said I wanted to talk to you."

She seemed at a loss for words for a moment, stirring his coffee mechanically. She handed the cup to him and tried to recoup quickly. Instead, she stammered, "W-w-well . . . I-I-I just assume from the look on your face, that you're upset with me."

John took the cup and thanked her. "Look, relax. Your job is not in jeopardy, if that's your concern. You do a fine job here at the firm. Although, I do want to make one thing clear; Laura and Tony may be going through their struggles, but they are in love, and do intend to make this relationship work. The last thing they need is someone else in the mix, looking to make matters more complicated."

Beth opened her mouth to protest, but John held up his hand. "Please, let me finish. I may be getting older, but I am not dim. I have been around the block a time or two. I can see that you find Tony attractive." Beth blushed and cast her eyes downward. "Frankly, I can't blame you. Despite his struggles, I've grown to love him myself, because he's one heck of a guy. I guess I'm just asking that you back off. Laura doesn't need this extra stress. She's already been through enough. Agreed?"

Beth chewed on her lower lip and pouted. "I'm so sorry, Mr. Knight. I didn't realize that my crush on Tony was so obvious. My job here means everything to me. I don't want to jeopardize it for anyone. You have my word. I'll stay completely out of Tony's way."

"Beth, you must understand how awkward this is for me. I normally mind my own business and stay out of people's lives. But this is a fragile situation. Tony has a great deal on his mind and doesn't need the distraction. And Laura, well, like I said, she's had a hard life," John explained.

"Enough said, sir," she crossed her heart with a red-painted fingernail. "I get the picture."

"Thanks for understanding, Beth. You're a loyal employee and we do appreciate you." John watched her give him a humble smile and walk away. *One down and one more to go.*

* * *

Beth marched to her desk to sulk. *This was preposterous!* She did nothing wrong. She innocently flirted with Tony, and finally, he was responding. Sure, she loved her job, but to have a chance with Tony . . . she could get a job anywhere as a secretary. She would have to be more careful. If she was going to give Tony the inclination that she was interested, it'd have to be in private. Once she got him alone and offered what she had to give, he would be stupid to turn her down.

Besides, what did that sack of skin and bones have to give to him that she did not? She had worked so hard, lost weight, took care of herself, and—she was not a rigid, stuck-up snob like Laura was. If she could prove it, she was almost certain that *that twig* was not even pregnant. With no baby tying him to her, Tony would not take a second glance at Laura. *But how? How could she prove it?* She had some thinking to do.

* * *

A sticky note on John's desk instructed him that Tony needed his assistance. *Perfect!* With that opportunity, John could talk to him, too. He came to Tony's door, surprised to find it ajar. "Knock knock," he rang.

"Hey, John. Come on in," Tony sang.

"You're looking much better this morning," John praised.

"Thanks, I'm feeling much better than I have in a while."

"Good to hear, my friend. So, you said you needed me? What's up?" John questioned.

"Just thought I'd let you know that the vacant rental on Beamer Drive has had some water damage. I assessed it this morning, on my way in, and found some damage to the interior walls and unfortunately even to some of the furnishings," Tony explained.

"Oh, shoot!" John exclaimed. "That's right; the rentals on Beamer are furnished. How bad is it?"

"Not too bad," Tony described. "I've written an estimate for repairs." He handed the estimation to John, who quickly scanned it over. Tony continued, “Luckily for us, the neighbors who live next door called to tell us they had water leaking into their apartment. I went there first thing this morning and shut the valve off. The damage to the neighbors’ is minimal. But we need to repair the burst pipe and all the damage it caused. I want to get working on it right away. It will help to keep me busy and get my mind off things.”

John put the paperwork down. He studied Tony a moment, feeling completely impressed. Tony had handled the situation exactly as he would have. “Ton, you’ve impressed me this morning. Excellent work, and yes, you can begin the process of repair. As for keeping your hands busy, do what you must to continue on this path. I’m happy to hear that you’ve straightened things out with Laura. I could tell that with just one visit, my daughter is walking on clouds again.”

Tony smiled from ear to ear. “Yes, I must admit, I really missed her. I’m sorry if I caused any of you added stress. That certainly was never my intent. I need to learn how to handle myself better.”

“Keep up the good work. I just want to say one last thing, Ton. It’s a long way down for her to fall once she’s back on those clouds again. I know life isn’t perfect, but if you stand strong together, you can overcome any obstacle.”

Tony shook his head in agreement. “Thanks for cracking the whip. I needed that.”

John let out a loud chuckle and smacked his hand to the desk. “Whenever you need a little cracking, you just come to me.” They both interrupted in laughter.

* * *

From down the hallway, Tony could see Beth staring on. She had a sour look on her face. John rose from the chair and pumped Tony’s hand enthusiastically. John turned to leave Tony’s office to go to his own. Suddenly, Tony watched Beth spring from her desk and run into his office. She glanced into the hallway once more, before closing Tony’s door.

“Some nerve,” she whispered upon clicking the lock.

“Um, what are you doing, Beth?” Tony questioned.

“We’ll never get a moment alone, if I don’t sneak in here from time to time,” she smiled coyly.

“What are you talking about?”

“They’re on to us. John came and had a talk with me, this morning. He told me to back off,” she explained.

“Oh no, Beth, I’m sorry. If I’ve given you reason to believe I was interested, I was wrong.”

Beth's face fell. "What do you mean?" she asked.

"Beth, I'm going through a tough time and I've been very confused. I never intended to lead you on. If I did, I'm sorry, but I'm devoted to Laura. She's the love of my life." Tony stood from his chair and fiddled with a pen. "I hope you understand."

Beth slinked around the desk and sat on the top of it, right next to where he stood. "You were right about one thing. You *are* confused. I know what I saw and I know what I felt. You and I have a connection. You cannot deny that." She playfully pulled on his tie.

Tony gently pried her fingers from his tie. "No, Beth. I love only Laura. You must accept that."

"How can I change your mind?" she insisted. Her hands found their way around his neck.

Tony pulled her hands down and stepped away from her. He walked to the door and opened it. "Beth, you can't. You'd better leave. I'd like to remain just friends. But if that's not possible, then I understand that, too. We can still work together and be cordial."

She sauntered toward him and stopped just before departing. With a playful finger, she traced his jaw line. "You'll change your mind. I'll see to it."

"Don't hold your breath," Tony replied. She blew him a kiss and left.

What had he done? As if matters were not already bad, now he had this woman who would not take no for an answer. He needed to be careful. He was not about to let her ruin things for him.

****

Her fingers flew across the typewriter with lightning speed. Laura finished the rest of the letter she was working on and creased it in three. She slid it into an envelope and sealed the fold. She was done for the day and could not wait to head home in the hopes of seeing Tony. After placing a stamp on the envelope, she slipped it into her purse, reminding herself to drop it in the mail on her way out.

Buttoning her coat, she looped her arm through her purse straps and began pulling a pair of gloves over her hands. The telephone rang, startling her. Flustered, she put her purse back down and clutched the receiver.

"Law office of Jasper Stone. Laura speaking," she answered. Laura waited for a reply. *Nothing.* "Hello," she repeated. *Still, no answer.* She placed the receiver back down and attempted to leave the office once more. Just as she opened the door, the telephone rang again. Laura was tempted to leave the building. *Could it be Tony?* She just could not take the risk of missing him.

Laura ran to her desk and clasped the phone. Again, she repeated the office name. When no one responded, she wondered if she was being pranked. "Hello," she shouted into the receiver. Laura listened carefully. She could hear a presence on the other line, but they were not replying. Spooked, she hung up and decided to depart whether the telephone continued to ring or not.

Mr. Stone had already left for the day and so Laura headed out the door of the office alone. She slid the envelope into the 'outgoing mail' slot and continued to walk out. She could not help but feel a little anxious in the deserted parking lot, for dusk had already fallen. Laura hurried across the walkway, toward her car. As she approached the vehicle, she noticed a large bouquet of roses sitting on her windshield. A smile fell across her face. Still spooked, she quickly plucked the bouquet off the top of the car and entered her vehicle. Laura immediately locked her doors.

Reaching into the bouquet, she found a tiny envelope. Opening it quickly, with jittery fingers, she read:

Love is like a dagger—it will pierce your heart
and make you bleed.

Laura reread the card twice, not really understanding its meaning. *What did Tony mean by it?* She quickly placed the flowers on the passenger's side seat, while nervously glancing around the vacant lot. Something did not feel quite right and Laura peeled out of the parking lot as fast as legally possible.

Once Laura was settled in safely at home, she took the telephone and dialed Tony's home number. He sounded tired upon answering. "Hello?"

"Hi, it's me," Laura answered.

"Hi. How are you?"

"I'm great thanks. Just calling to say, 'thank you'."

"For?"

"Come on, don't play hard to get," she teased.

Tony chuckled, "I'm not. What are you talking about?"

"I love the roses, but I don't get the note. Are you trying to tell me that loving me hurts like a knife?"

For a moment, Tony did not respond. Finally, he asked, "Laura, I don't know what you're talking about. What roses?"

Laura felt the uneasiness fall over her again. "Are you serious?" she quizzed.

"Yes," Tony exclaimed. "You received flowers?"

"Yes, I thought they were from you."

"No, honey, I'm sorry. I wish I could say I'd been that thoughtful, but they're not from me. What does the card say?"

Laura read the card for him, word for word.

"Well, it looks like you have a secret admirer. I don't know if I like this," Tony stated.

"I know I don't. This has me freaked out. Who would send me roses anonymously?" Laura thought aloud.

"Well, you're beautiful and some poor sap probably saw you at the office, hoping to have a chance with you. They'll have to pry you from my cold dead hands!"

Laura felt a warm glow. She loved it when he became possessive of her. "Well, you better come on over tonight and claim your prize before someone snatches me away."

"Oh, Laura. I can't, honey. I have an early appointment with Dr. Parnell in the morning and I've had an exhausting day. I'm just gonna retire for the night. Okay?"

Laura felt her heart sink. "Are you sure?"

"I'm sorry, maybe I can make it up to you tomorrow night."

"Promise?"

Tony hesitated for a moment. "I'll call you tomorrow, okay? Have a good night."

"Okay, Tony. I love you."

"I love you, too."

Laura hung up and stared at the bouquet now sitting in a vase. *Who could have possibly sent it to her with such a strange note?* Laura prayed the ill feeling within would just go away.

CHAPTER 8

James 1:12

"Blessed is the man who perseveres under trial, because when he has stood the test, he will receive the crown of life that God has promised to those who love Him."

Tuesday, December 19

"I just can't do it, Doc," Tony cried. For the second time that week, he found himself sitting in Dr. Parnell's office discussing his problems. He was far past frustrated and confusion clouded his judgment. "I just can't bring myself to open up to her. What's wrong with me?" Tony's eyes pleaded with his doctor's.

In a casual manner, Dr. Parnell lifted his right foot and placed it over his left leg. His hands adjusted his red paisley tie and he sat back in his chair. "Ton, I've told you before and I'm going to tell you again. You need to listen to me if you are going to find some peace in your life. The longer you keep this bottled up inside, the harder it's going to be. You need to talk about this, and not just with me but with your loved ones, too. Laura is a caring, loving woman. She wants to be there for you. What are you so worried about?"

"I'm ashamed! I don't feel worthy of her!" Tony shouted.

Doc tried repeatedly to help Tony understand that he was just a child when he had witnessed the abuse and could not have helped his sisters. "Would you think differently of Laura if this had happened to her?"

Tony thought about it for a moment. Of course he would not feel differently toward her, if it had happened to her. He would understand. Finally, it hit him. "Wow," Tony whispered.

"Yeah . . . wow. You see Tony, this is just one more way for you to let your fears control you," Doc explained.

Confused, Tony questioned him, "What do you mean?"

"There are several reasons you won't break down and tell Laura and it's not because of the reasons you think."

"Like . . ."

"Like the fact that if you tell her what happened, then that might mean that it actually happened. Denial. The second reason . . . the wedding draws closer. You're *this* close to realizing your dream. You're pushing her away because, for one, you don't feel you deserve her, and two, you're afraid that it's too good to be true and that you'll somehow lose her. It's almost like you're preparing yourself for something bad to happen, even though it may not." Doc took in a deep breath.

The truth of what he said sunk into Tony's head. He was amazed. *Doc was right—right about everything. He was afraid. Very afraid.* A life with Laura was all he had ever truly wanted. A life without her would shatter him. "How do you do that?" Tony whispered.

Doc let out a chuckle and slapped Tony's knee. "I read a lot of books! Listen to me, Tony. Go to Laura and spend a nice evening with her. When you're ready, just tell her what we've discovered. You'll feel 10 times better to have her loving support."

Tony shook his head in understanding. He would do just that. He would call her up and ask her over for dinner. He finally felt excited and could not wait to leave to plan the evening. Just as he rose, Doc interrupted his train of thought.

"Whoa, where are you going? We're not done just yet," he claimed.

"Sorry, Doc. I got so wrapped up in thought, I didn't realize our session wasn't over."

Doc pointed to the couch and Tony sat back down. "I wanted to ask you again if you've had any dreams or flashes of memory."

Tony thought carefully and shook his head. "Nope, nothing. Why do you keep asking me that?"

Tony noticed Doc's nervous habit of brushing at his balding head, when ready to drop a bomb. "Well, like I said, after your first session of drug therapy, I suspect that there's more to your story."

"Come on, Doc. Haven't we discovered enough bad news?"

Dr. Parnell firmly held Tony's gaze. "Tony, I interrupted and ended the conversation with Max in the middle of a serious account. You didn't just develop this additional personality because of your sisters' abuse. I expect memories to start coming back to you either in the form of dreams or in quick flashes."

Tony swallowed. He certainly did not like what Doc was implying. In fact, it was crazy to even consider. His father would have never . . . not to a boy. Tony felt like vomiting. "Doc are you saying that you think I was abused in the same manner my sisters were?"

"There's only one way to find out," Doc stated.

"No! No more! I don't want to know any more!"

"Tony, I don't blame you. This is terrifying. But it's beneficial to your mental health that you find out the whole truth and nothing but. We need to put you under the drug therapy one more time."

Tony stood from the couch, unsure if he was going to storm out, hit something, or jump from the nearest window. Doc stood, as well, and placed his calming hands on Tony's shoulders. He was a shorter man, but his strength held authority.

"It's going to be okay. The worst is over. You're okay. The danger is gone and you never have to worry about being hurt again. Do you understand this?"

Tony's heart raced in his chest. He understood it, but he could not help but feel like he was choking. He slowly shook his head and sat back down.

"Are you okay?" Dr. Parnell asked.

It took a moment for Tony to speak. His tongue felt glued to the roof of his mouth. "I don't think I'm ready to find out just yet."

"That's okay, Tony. We'll take this nice and slow. One thing at a time. Talk to Laura and let her help you over this first obstacle. When you're ready, I'm here. Now go home and rest and call me if you need me."

Tony left the office with a dull ache in his chest. Once again, Doc was right. He did not develop a second personality just because of what he'd witnessed. Something worse had happened to him. *But what?* The whole way home, he strained his memory *trying* to pick up even the slightest recollection of anything. He kept coming up with nil.

Turning the vehicle down a different street, Tony headed for Uncle Frank's. He still was not sure what to do.

****

"Antonio! Come in. What brings you by?" Frank patted his nephew's back and Tony entered the front door. The kitchen smelled incredible. A mixture of aromas filled the air—lasagna, fresh bread, and oregano that seasoned a green leafy salad—tantalizing Tony's taste buds. "How did you know I was cooking today?"

Tony took in another deep breath and a smile actually fell across his face. "Nonna's lasagna recipe—how can I resist?"

"It's still baking in the oven. Sit down and join me," Frank invited.

"Oh man, I'd love to. But I might have plans with Laura."

"What do you mean, *might*?"

"That depends," Tony stated.

"Oh no, what's going on?"

Tony tried to explain the session he had with Dr. Parnell. Though Doc gave him every reason why he should open up to Laura, Tony still had his doubts. "Do you think she would be better off without me?"

Frank grew frustrated. Tony could tell from the way he stood up from the kitchen table to begin fussing with the already prepared salad. "Son, I don't know what to do with you anymore," Frank admitted. "I'm trying really hard to understand you, but I must confess—I can't figure you out!"

"It's not hard, Uncle. I'm afraid I'm going to mess up her life, so I'm panicking before the wedding. I don't want to be responsible for breaking her heart," Tony explained.

"But that is exactly what you will be doing!" Frank shouted. "Whether you break up with her before or after the wedding, you'll still be accomplishing the same thing. You'll be breaking her heart, Tony! How can you do that to that girl, after everything she's been through to be with you? I know you're not this selfish!"

Tony stared at Frank's reddened face. Frank made sense, but Tony felt that he made a good point as well. He would be sentencing Laura to a life with a man with a sordid past. "Uncle, I am doing this for *her*! She'd eventually forget about me and find someone normal to love."

Frank shook his head in disagreement. He smacked his hands together in frustration and stomped toward the table. Placing both hands on it, while leaning over Tony, he spouted, "Get this through that thick head of yours! You are normal! You have nothing wrong with you! You were a victim! You deserve love and happiness! I will not have this conversation with you anymore, son. Don't you dare hurt that girl! If you hurt her, you can forget you have an uncle!"

"Okay! Okay!" Tony could not help but burst into laughter at Frank's need to protect Laura. "Geez, bite my head off, why don't you?"

The seriousness fell from Frank's face. A smile tried perking up the corners of his mouth. "That's right! Now, git outta here and go call her. Git your head screwed on straight or I'm going to knock it off!"

Tony stood from the table and put his fists up in playful fight. "Come on, old man. I'll take you."

Frank threw a quick jab at Tony and hit him in the arm. Tony flinched. "Look out now!" Frank teased.

"You think you still got it?" Tony danced around the kitchen like a boxer. Frank grasped his nephew's torso and tried to take him down. Tony and Frank laughed, as they wrestled in the small kitchen. Tony pinned Frank to the floor. "Do you give? Do you give?" He breathlessly panted.

"You *would* hit an old man, you scoundrel!" Frank shouted. He pounded his hand to the floor three times. "I give!"

Tony released his uncle and stood, extending a hand to help Frank up. "Come on, gramps."

* * *

Later that evening, Tony's hands trembled with anticipation, while he prepared dinner for Laura. After his wrestling match with Uncle Frank, he went home and called to invite her. Laura immediately accepted and promised to come straight from work. He decided to make a batch of the same lasagna that Frank had prepared, using his Grandmother Lisa's recipe. For the second course, he made a salad and cooked a few slices of breaded meat as well. The kitchen table was set with a glowing candle in the middle. He was ready to make right what he had done wrong.

When the doorbell finally rang, Tony was surprised. In light of all that had happened, she no longer felt comfortable enough to just walk on in. Tony felt sad. He had done this. After tonight, he was sure things would be back to normal. He ran to the door and greeted his fiancée.

* * *

Laura trembled out in the cold, on the porch of Tony's house. *Could she even consider this their house again?* She hoped so. So far, things seemed to be getting back on track. Tonight would be the true test.

Tony finally opened the door. His face seemed to light up upon seeing her. He reached out and pulled her into the home, sweeping her into his warm arms. Laura felt a lump rise in her throat at the joy she felt.

"Hi," he whispered into her ear.

"Hi," her voice muffled from his strong hold.

He loosened his grip just enough to kiss her fully on the lips. Laura was stunned. So far, she was happy with the start of their evening.

Tony helped her with her coat and then led her into the kitchen. "Smells wonderful," she complimented.

"My Nonna's recipe," Tony interjected.

"Oh, yes! Just what the baby wanted!"

"The baby or you?" Tony teased.

"Both!"

"Well, I hope you're both hungry. Come on . . . let's eat."

Sitting at the table, Tony cut a piece of the lasagna and placed it on her plate, then did the same for himself. He extended his hand to hold hers. His eyes lit up with a smile and he began the blessing. "Lord, I want to thank you for this evening, for this beautiful woman before me, for our love, our baby, and for all the help you continually give to us. Please bless this food and bless this little family in Jesus' name. Amen."

Laura's eyes filled at his prayer. It was simple, yet sincere. She had much to be thankful for. "Amen," she nearly shouted. They ate in a comfortable silence. Occasionally, Tony would ask about John, Marlene, or her work. Though the evening was going smoother than Laura expected, something still tugged at her heartstrings. Tony had yet to come forward and talk about himself. So Laura kept her patience in check and told herself to not fall into the temptation to ask him how he was doing or anything even related to the issue.

When they had cleaned up after dinner, Tony invited Laura over to the couch to watch TV together. Laura snuggled up a little closer to him than she had dared to in a while. Tony seemed to invite her closer. Still, his silence was deafening.

At last, at nearly 8 p.m., he tore his eyes from the tube. His demeanor became slightly rigid, as he struggled to open up. He looked down at her and gave her a weak smile.

"I . . ." he began, "I . . . I'm sorry. This is so hard," he stated.

"What? What is it, Tony?"

"I want to talk to you. I want to tell you about what I now know. I'm so afraid you will see me differently," he finally admitted.

Laura sat up and gathered his hand in hers. She forced his gaze, while she spoke. "No matter what you've found out, no matter what you say, I'll always love you. I will not think differently of you. I have a good idea of what you might have endured. I've done my own research on your disorder. Don't you believe in my love for you?"

Tony took a moment to answer her question. "It's not that I don't believe in your love; it's me that I doubt."

"You doubt your love for me?"

"No, that came out wrong. I know I love you. But after you find out what I know, you may not think so highly of me."

"Can you just trust me?" Laura finally pressed.

"Laura . . . I . . ." Tony's face reddened and she could see his emotions move. Unexpectedly, tears began trickling down his face.

Laura's heart instantly went out to him. She placed her arm around his shoulder and held him. Uncontrollable sobs suddenly seized his body. "It's okay. Stop. You don't have to tell me, yet. You're not ready. Don't force it. I'm here for you whenever you need me. Just take your time."

Laura held the love of her life, while he wept like a child in her arms. After a moment, he rested his head on her lap and lay down on the couch, grasping a hold of her legs. Laura's fingers ran through his tousled hair, calming and soothing, until his cries subsided. When she glanced down, Laura noticed that he had fallen asleep. As her hands rested on his precious head, she began to fervently pray over him.

* * *

Her fingers felt magical, as they gently stroked his head. Tony could feel his body releasing every last bit of tension. He closed his eyes and held on to her legs. Drowsiness suddenly took him. As he fought off the desire to fall asleep, he could hear her whispering. She was praying for him and he felt safe again.

He let go and fell into a comfortable repose. He even began to dream. The memories from the time they shared in his grandparents' house, played as on a movie screen in his mind. Her nearness had brought him to the best days of his life.

Suddenly, the pleasant dreams faded and he found that he was in the house in Syracuse. He slept next to Vincey in their bed. He heard a scream that jolted him right out of his sleep. He could hear crying and muffled screams. Tony covered his head with the pillow. He could not stand it anymore. *Something had to be done!*

Suddenly, he was running through the hallway, determined to stop that monster from terrorizing his sister. He entered the door. There was yelling. This time it was not his father, but it was coming from Tony. He demanded that the abuse stop. He threatened to tell the authorities, his mother, whoever would listen. Rosie ran from the room. Vito rose from the bed with a belt in his hands. Tony's heart raced in his chest. He ordered his legs to run, but they did not move. *He would show him that he was not afraid anymore!*

Vito grabbed his son and threw him on the bedroom floor, slamming the door closed. Tony scrambled to his feet. The next images his dream played out caused Tony to scream. He ordered his eyes to open, to wake up from the horrible visions he was seeing. Vito was beating him—whipping his little body… and then . . . he did the unthinkable, the unimaginable.

Tony screamed and jumped from the couch off Laura's lap. He looked at her with crazed eyes. She instantly stood, laying her hands on him, trying to calm him. He screamed out, "Don't touch me!"

"Tony, what happened? What did you see?"

"No, just go! Just leave. This is never going to work! You need to leave."

Laura pleaded with him. "Tony, please, don't shut me out. I want to help."

"Just go!"

Laura's face crumbled. "If that's what you want." She gathered her coat and purse. The tears slowly slid down her face.

Tony felt terrible. It was not her fault. "I'm sorry," he explained, in a whisper. "I can't deal with you right now. I need to get back to bed. I have an early appointment tomorrow at one of the rentals."

She nodded and walked past him toward the door. Before leaving, she turned around and whispered, "If you need me, I'm here for you. Just call me. I'll be waiting."

Tony watched her walk through the door, brokenhearted. The door closed after her. He walked to the door wondering whether to stop her or let her go. He did the latter and then ran to the telephone, instead. Dialing Dr. Parnell's emergency number, he held the phone, praying not to find a busy signal. When Doc's voice rang through the line, Tony immediately blurted out what he had seen in the dream.

"Do you think it was a dream or was it a flashback?" Tony frantically queried.

"From the sound of your emotional state, I believe it may be the breakthrough we've been waiting for."

"Breakthrough? Do you understand what I just told you? He . . . he did it to me!"

"Tony, listen to me. Calm down. Let's set up an appointment to do the drug session early tomorrow morning. That's the only way you're going to get any rest. We have to let Max finish telling us what happened. Until you discover the whole truth, you'll have no peace. Get someone to bring you here in the morning. Is 8 a.m. good?"

"I'll have to double check with my uncle, but I'll say yes, for now. I'll be there."

* * *

Laura decided to pull her car over before she caused a car wreck. After parking in the parking lot of a local grocery store, she broke down and let the tears fall. Witnessing Tony's behavior that evening had helped her to truly realize how serious the situation was. Tony was far from getting better. Whatever he had sustained as a child, might take him years to overcome. Laura did not have years. The baby was to be born in four short months. *Could she wait to marry Tony until after the baby was born? Of course she would wait for him—until the end of the Earth. But what about the baby? Would she have to raise the child without him until he was ready to be a father and a husband?*

Laura was so confused. Every time she envisioned the pain in his eyes, when he woke from the nightmare, she broke into fresh hot tears. It pained her so much to see him hurting. What pained her more was the fact that she could not comfort him—that once again, he had shut her out and chosen to endure his suffering alone.

Laura reached into her purse and withdrew a tissue. Wiping her eyes and nose, she came to focus on the clock. It was nearing 10 p.m. and she did not want to worry John and Marlene. As she put the vehicle back in gear, she noticed another car across the parking lot. It was parked separate from the other vehicles and was facing her. She strained her eyes to see the person sitting in the driver's seat. Almost automatically, the vehicle's lights gleamed on and the car peeled out of the parking lot. The dark sedan sped away.

Laura drove her vehicle in the opposite direction and headed for home.

****

Tony did not sleep a wink that night, horrified to fall back into the terrible nightmare. By the time Frank arrived at his home at 7 a.m., Tony felt exhausted. Frank drove him to the hospital again and then took his place in the waiting room, while Tony went in for his procedure. His heart raced faster this time, knowing what to expect as the outcome. Once the drug began being administered into him, Tony panicked. *Did he really want to know the whole truth?* He could not live with the fact that his sisters were abused. *How could he deal with this?*

Just before the nurses strapped him down, Dr. Parnell entered his room. "Feeling okay, Tony?"

Tony's chest rose and fell in quick short breaths. "No! I changed my mind—I don't want to do this!"

"Relax, son. It's going to be okay."

Tony noticed Doc give the male nurse a heads up to bind him down. Before he reached the bed, Tony jumped from it, determined to walk out. Dr. Parnell and the male nurse quickly seized him and pulled him down to the bed, before he could tear the IV from his arm.

"Stop! I don't want to do this!" Tony shouted.

"Tony," Doc reasoned, "You must. This is part of your healing process. Trust me. Just let the medication do its job."

Both hands were bound now and Tony pulled and yanked, wiggling and squirming in his bed. "No! Untie me! Untie me! I don't want to! Let me go!"

* * *

Dr. Parnell could tell that Tony was having another flashback and though it pained him to see his patient under such distress, the truth had to come out. "Tony," he tried to soothe. "Let the medication help you. Please, relax. You're okay. No one will hurt you! You're safe!"

"No! I'm not. He's going to hurt me! He's going to kill me!"

Suddenly, Tony's demeanor changed. He calmed down almost instantly. "What do you think you're doing?" grilled Max.

"I'm helping Tony out," Dr. Parnell explained. He ran to the nightstand and hit 'record' on the tape recorder he used to document the case. "Would you mind telling me why you came out? Tony was in no real danger."

"You know very well that he felt the danger was real. As usual, I'm stepping in to clean up the mess."

"But we didn't even get a chance to let the medication kick in. You know you are only the subservient and not the dominant personality. You'll return to talk to me when I call you out. For now, it's adamant that I talk to Tony. We have some important issues to discuss."

Max laughed aloud in a cocky and arrogant manner. "Do you really think you'll get anywhere with Tony? He's so horrified of what he's discovered that I might have to take over indefinitely."

Now, Dr. Parnell laughed, "Fat chance of that happening, my friend. Tony has too much to lose and his happiness will reflect your happiness. He has to come through this for the sake of his future wife and child. Now you rest and I'll talk to Tony." Dr. Parnell watched Max close his eyes and fall into a restful sleep. He took in a deep breath and wiped his large forehead with a handkerchief. He monitored Tony's heartbeat and blood pressure and documented them on Tony's chart.

Finally, he took a seat next to Tony's bed and gently shook his arm. "Tony, it's me, Doc, as you call me. I'd like to talk to you. Don't be afraid. You're safe now."

Tony's eyes fluttered open and stared blankly at Dr. Parnell.

"Tony, you're a strong man. You've been through tougher times than this. You're a survivor. I want you to remain strong and talk to me. Can you do that?"

Tony licked his lips to moisten them and whispered, "I'll try."

"Good man. Now tell me . . . tell me your story."

CHAPTER 9

Colossians 3:21

"Fathers, do not embitter your children, or they will become discouraged."

As Tony's horrifying story gushed forward, it more than explained the reason for the splitting of his mental state and the jarring of his emotions. Dr. Parnell sat closely, absorbing the very dark tale that moved his heart and stirred his own sentiments. A tale . . . he would *never* forget.

****

Tony's Tale

Nobody knew of the abuse we all received at the hands of our father. Nobody knew and it seemed as though nobody cared. Mother was rarely home when we were and so if she gathered that something was not right, she never let on. Father had all the control. He could do with us as he pleased and none of us could do a thing about it.

I grew more sick with every passing day, knowing that Caterina was being abused. When nightfall came, I would cringe when I heard him call out for her. A few times, I hid her in my closet. When he came looking for her and found her crying in the shadows, he not only beat her, but he beat me, as well.

We all trembled at the sound of his thunderous voice. Even his footsteps sounded menacing. Because he was tall and somewhat lean, he towered over each of us. His grip was like a vise and rough as the wood with which he worked. For someone with such evil intent, he had the face of someone you could easily love. His thick hair was a sandy brown color, his eyes dark—appealing to any stranger, but sinister to those of us who knew him well. He had high cheekbones that gave his presence authority and a square jaw that was always set firmly.

I hated him. I hated everything about him, even his good looks. I hated them because, as I grew older, my features began to change and I looked more and more like him. I did not want to be *anything* like him. He had no compassion. He had no love inside of him. He was nothing like my mother, who always had a sympathetic ear and a loving caress. But mother was blind. Blinded by his beauty and blinded by her need to please him.

When my father's brothers broke off and sold their part of the business to him, he arrogantly assumed he would be able to run it more efficiently without them. When the economy began to plummet, we were *all* drowning. Mother, wanting to help, found the waitressing job at Louie's, and then *our* nightmare began.

Mother would never leave for Louie's without preparing dinner for us. We would come home from school to a home-cooked meal, which our father would begrudgingly serve every day. Our dinners had to be eaten in silence. No one would talk and no one dared to make a mess. We found that out the hard way.

At 7 p.m., it was bedtime for everyone. After I had discovered what was happening to Caterina, my nights of restful sleep were over. I would lie awake in bed every night praying for the muffled cries to stop. I felt sick. I hated myself. I stopped caring about my grades at school. Letters from my schoolteachers would come home almost on a daily basis, asking my parents if they had noticed my unusual behavior. Father never read them. He threw them away before Mother could see them.

I did not think I was acting out of character, aside from not caring about my schoolwork. It made no sense to work so hard for good school grades when no one noticed. As far as my character was concerned, I was finally standing up to some of the bullies at school. *Wasn't it bad enough to be bullied at home?* When I began defending myself and the school received no response from the letters they sent, they called the house. When I got home from school that day, I thanked God that I had been suspended, because I would not have been able to walk to school if I tried. Father took the belt to my butt and legs, leaving Mother home for a week to tend to me. This only made him angrier.

He hated me. You could see it in the way he looked at me. The feeling was mutual. When he finally had me alone again, he called me every name in the book. I was so afraid of him that I jumped at every sound, flinched at his every breath. The rage grew and festered inside of me with every day that passed.

After nearly two years of horrible fear and constant anxiety, I could not tolerate the stress anymore. I was coming near my breaking point. I was 11 years old in the fall of 1965. He had already begun to call Nellie into his room at night. Caterina was now 7; Nellie, 5; Rosie, 3; and Vincey was only 1. Because I feared him so incredibly and because I had received such a brutal beating for fighting at school, my plan to try to save my sisters faltered. I chickened out and allowed the abuse to continue.

Shortly after Mother took that week off to tend to me, Nellie became sick. Mother requested some time off, so she could stay home and care for her. Father was not happy about this. He argued with her that she needed to work to help pay the bills and keep us above water. He said he would tend to Nellie. But Nellie cried all the time and Mother just could not leave her.

The first evening that she was home with us, Nellie's fever spiked. Mother begged Father to take her to Emergency. He claimed that they could not, because he had failed to pay the medical insurance and that we no longer had coverage. Mother did not care. She knew Nellie needed a doctor, but he still insisted they care for her at home. To help keep the fever down, Mother stripped Nellie and put her in the tub with lukewarm water. That is when she finally caught wind that something was terribly wrong.

"Vito!" she screamed. "Come here!"

Father sat on his recliner watching TV with a beer in his hands. He huffed, "What do you want?"

Mother stormed out of the bathroom, her face was pallid—her eyes protruding. "What happened to my baby?" she screamed.

He looked at her.

I sat at the kitchen table coloring with Caterina and Rose. Vincey sat in his highchair, happy to be scribbling on a piece of paper with us. I looked up and bore my eyes, full of hate, into the back of his head. I could not wait for him to get busted. I hoped Mother would realize the truth and send him packing.

Mother's words came out in short puffs "What—happened—to—my—baby?" she seethed, asking him again.

He looked away from her and back to the TV. Sipping his beer, he muttered, "She fell."

Mother trembled, standing but a few feet from him. Her arms were at her sides, her hands curled into fists. "She fell? Where? How? How did she get bruises all over her thighs? All over her back? What did you do to her?" she demanded.

He looked up at her again. His eyes sent daggers into her. Mother certainly was not expecting what was coming. Her concern for her baby clouded her judgment. She stood there accusing him of having hurt Nellie.

That is all I remember her saying. He rose from the chair so quickly that all four of us jumped. He began punching Mother anywhere his fist could strike. She started screaming and tried to run from him. I grabbed Vincey and the girls and we ran in the bathroom, where Nellie sat shivering in the tub. I locked the door and quickly took Nellie out of the water. I wrapped her in a towel, trying hard not to look at the black and blue marks all over her little legs and back. My stomach felt queasy. I hastily helped her to dress into her pink ruffled nightgown. By this time all four of them where crying, clinging to me for protection. I sat them down on the floor near the toilet and huddled with my little sisters and brother, determined to shield them.

Vincey and the girls wailed at the horrid screams we could hear coming from our mother. I kept trying to shush them, fearful that he would come in and start on us. When the noise finally stopped and we heard his bedroom door slam, we sat straining our ears for the slightest noise.

"It's okay. It's over," I whispered. "Mom's going to need my help. Can you sit here quietly for a minute?" Caterina and Nellie shook their heads. Rosie had her head leaning against the wall—her eyes closing with sleep and her thumb securely in her mouth. Vincey found his pacifier and greedily sucked on it. I stood to check on Mother. I told Caterina to lock the door behind me and keep the little ones quiet.

Trembling with fear, I noiselessly tiptoed across the hall into the kitchen. Mother was on the kitchen floor, on her knees, picking up a shattered plate that must have been knocked over in the struggle. I could not see her face yet, because her dark hair had come loose from her ponytail and was hanging all tangled in front of her face. I quietly snuck to her, gently placing my hands on her shoulders. She let out a small startled scream.

Upon seeing me, she covered her face and whispered for me to leave. Upon seeing her beat-up and bruised face, tears filled my eyes and fury—my heart.

"Mom," I cried in a whisper. I ran to the sink and wet the dishtowel with cold water. Running back to her, I lifted her chin and gently applied the towel to her already swollen black eye. Tears coursed down our faces. Words were not needed. The way she had cared for me, when Father had hurt me, I would care for her. The more I tried to soothe her, the more Mother cried. I made her go into my bedroom to lie down and I promised to get the kids to bed and clean up.

When the girls were all in bed and Vincey drinking a bottle in his crib in my room, I brought a fresh cold cloth to apply to Mother's face. I found her in my bed, staring up at the ceiling.

"Why do you stay with him?" I whispered. "You see what he does to us. Look at what he has done to you, to Nellie. Let's get outta here. Let's go to live with Nonna," I begged.

Mother put her finger to her lips. "Shh. Son, you're so sweet. You're a good boy and I love you so much. But you have to understand, your father's under a lot of stress. The business, working all day, then coming home to care for all of you at night. It's hard for him," she explained.

"Mom, that's no excuse for his hateful behavior. He's so mean. He hurts us. He . . ." I didn't know how to tell her. I did not know how I could explain such an unspeakable thing. Before I had a chance to finish my sentence, the door swung open. Mother and I both gasped. Even Vincey dropped the bottle from his hands.

"Get out there," he commanded her, pointing out toward their room. Then his sinister stare fell upon me. "Stop fillin' her head with lies, boy! You're nothin' but a lying bully. Did you know he's getting into trouble at school? Beating up on kids and getting bad grades?" he told her.

Mother looked at me. Her gaze said so many things. One thing was for sure, it said, 'Don't say a word'. I looked down and said nothing. Slowly, Mother rose from my bed and limped toward the door. As she neared him, she quickly scampered past him, cringing in fear. He slammed my door shut, leaving Vincey and I alone. I breathed out the air that was nearly bursting from my lungs. I prayed Mother would be okay. I prayed we all would be okay, but while he was in the picture, evil was ever present.

After Mother healed and Nellie's cold got better, Mother needed to go back to work. All five of us were petrified to see her go. We knew what was in store for us when she was gone. On the Sunday night before her first day back, we all gathered in the girls' bedroom. Caterina and Nellie slept on the end with Rosie in the middle. I crawled in with them and sat Rosie on my lap. Vincey held onto Mother, as if he could understand that it was her last evening with us for a whole week.

Mother prayed with us and then read us a bedtime story. I held onto Vincey, while she tucked the girls in. Nellie began to wail and held onto our mother's neck for nearly 10 minutes. Mother tried to explain to her that she would still see them off to school in the morning.

"Will you be here when we come home?" Nellie asked in the littlest voice.

"No, *bella*, but I will come into your room and kiss you when I get home, okay?"

"No, Mommy! I will miss you! I don't want to stay home with him!" she cried.

Mother tried to quiet her down. Finally, I took Vincey to our room and placed him in his crib. Later on, Mother came in and kissed us both good night. I hugged her and told her I loved her.

For the first week of our mother's return back to work, the evenings were quiet. Father put us all to bed at the usual time and kept to himself the rest of the night. On the weekend, we felt grateful to have Mother home with us. I prayed that Mother's discovery of Nellie's bruises would keep him away from the girls, forever. But that was asking too much.

On the following Monday night, something ominous materialized in my father's eyes at dinner. I could feel the tension in the air. I helped Caterina clear the table and wash the dishes. He yelled at me for doing women's work, but I did not listen. It was not fair that Caterina was stuck with the dishes every night. He called me names and said that Mother was turning me into a pathetic weakling.

The words pierced my ego like a sword. If helping out my sister made me a pathetic weakling or a wimp, as he put it, then I guessed that is what I was. I had made up my mind, not to let his words stop me from doing what I thought was right.

What I did not know, was that my strength was soon to be tested.

I climbed into bed at the usual time, after making sure the girls were all tucked in. Vincey lay in his crib drinking a bottle. The thought that falling asleep was getting easier, knowing that the girls were safe, quickly vanished when I heard his bedroom door creak open.

"Rosie, come here. Come in Daddy's room. I have candy!" he called out merrily.

NO! NO! NO! Not little Rose! Not a little 3-year-old. I could hear crying coming from both Caterina and Nellie, as they tried to convince Rosie not to go. That evil devil knew just how to lure the little girl in. Rosie was a sucker for candy. She loved chocolate and sweets. My insides felt on fire and the rage inside me was nearly bursting from my very core. I knew what awaited me if I dared interrupt him. I knew that my very life could be at stake if I entered that room and stopped him from hurting Rose, too.

Could I live with myself knowing that I had allowed that monster to abuse my little sisters? *No! Then I would be exactly what he always called me . . . a wimp!* I did not want to be a wimp anymore. I did not want to be the weakling he thought I was—the weakling that I believed myself to be.

As the minutes ticked away, I debated what to do. I prayed to God for the courage to get up and stop him. But I shuddered with terror . . . until I heard Rosie start to cry. I threw the covers from my bed and flew to my feet. I ran out of my room and into the hallway. Before I could think twice about it, I threw his bedroom door open.

"Stop it!" I shouted. "Don't touch her. Leave her alone!"

He sat up in the bed, the covers falling from his body exposing his bare chest. His eyes pierced mine with hatred. "Walk out, now!" he commanded.

"NO! Enough! Run, Rosie! Go in your room and shut the door!" I screamed.

Rosie hesitantly glanced from him to me. I told her to run again and she slid from the bed, running out of the room crying. Father stood as well, slipping on his pants at the foot of the bed. He tore the belt from the pant loops and swung it with a whooshing sound.

"So, you want to be a hero, huh?" he whispered in a looming voice.

"I just want you to leave my sisters alone!" I said with a quiver in my voice that betrayed me.

"What are you goin' to do about it?" he challenged.

"I'll tell Mom. I'll tell the police!" I threatened. By this time, he was inching toward me, slapping the belt against the palm of his hand. He let out a loud howl and laughed at my answer.

"Oh, you are so tough! Goin' to tell Mommy!" he mimicked.

"She'll believe me. She saw the bruises all over Nellie's body."

"Maria doesn't have the courage to stand up to me. She's a weakling. Just—like—you!" He poked a finger in my chest to emphasize the last three painful words. My heart raced in my chest. He was less than a foot from me, but I refused to step back and run. I would not be the wimp he accused me of being. I did not care what was coming my way. But I should have . . . I should have.

Despite my newfound courage, I shook uncontrollably with alarm. I knew he could kill me with one blow. Suddenly, he seized my arm and threw me into the bedroom, slamming the door shut. I stumbled to the floor, but quickly rose to my feet. Before I had a chance to protect myself, he attacked me with full force. The belt tore into my flesh, even through my clothes.

He hit my head, my back, my legs—any part of my body that he could. I felt a warm wetness dripping down my leg and wondered if it was blood. Somehow, between the blows, I was able to see that it was not blood. I had accidentally relieved my bladder from the terror. He taunted me and laughed, saying that I was an 11-year-old baby who still peed his pants. I did not care about the name calling anymore, I was calloused to it. But the blows to my head and back were burning and it was evident that I needed to get out from under him or I would not survive.

That is when the unimaginable happened. He stopped hitting me. Suddenly, he was picking me up screaming something about how I was going to live to regret that night for the rest of my life. I was so shocked at what was about to happen. I froze.

I do not remember what happened after that. The next thing that I could recall, it was morning and Mother was waking me up for school. After she saw the swollen welts to my face and body, she kept me home with her and took care of me. We did not talk about it. In fact, we never discussed it again. Mother never knew that instead of calling on the girls for the next year, he abused me. This was the only way I could save my sisters.

The best part? I could never recall what went on in that bedroom. Somehow, God made it so I did not have to know all the gory details.

When Father went to the Galante *famiglia* for the loan a year later, Mother quit. His going to the Mob for money, spared me from the repeated abuse. But the damage was already done. Large gaps of time began missing from my memory. The school frequently tried contacting my mother to tell her of my strange behavior. She would ask me if everything was okay and I would not answer. I became isolated and spoke only when necessary. Because Mother refused to get us out of that house, knowing full well that something horrible was happening to all of us, I began to resent her, too. At the same time, I pitied her. Just as we were hurting—she was hurting. The signs of depression were evident. They were evident in nearly all of us.

Every time I looked at my sisters, I could see how he had hurt them. Caterina was perpetually sad. She rarely smiled, and though she was as beautiful as a flower, she never cared for her self-image. He had destroyed it. She would walk around the house hiding her body under layer after layer of clothing. Her hair was always a tangled mess and the darkened circles under her eyes gave her a haunting expression.

Nellie was the same. Mother was always after the girls to wash their faces and do their hair. But Mother had to be careful how she addressed them, especially Nellie. She was ever sensitive and constantly crying. Mother never raised her voice to her, ever cautious of her feelings. Any one thing would set Nellie off and the tears would not stop until she felt safe again. Her fears and insecurities caused her to cling tightly to Mother whenever Father was present.

Thankfully, Rosie forgot about that fateful night when I stepped in to protect her. She was the only one of the girls who bounced around the house singing and laughing. I could see how Father looked at her. I could see how he hated her happiness, her pleasant personality. I could tell he wanted to annihilate it. Despite what it cost me, I was happy to have spared her.

Little Vincey was my only ray of hope. Because Mother was a stay-at-home mom again, Father was rarely home, spending most of his time at the shop that continued to spiral downward. Vincey and I spent our time together doing the things that I wished Father would have done with me. We played catch out on the lawn and tag in the yard. I was constantly inviting the girls to join us. Rosie would run out into the yard with her pretty little dress floating behind her. Nellie would watch from the family room window with a smile tickling her lips. Caterina would not even glance our way, as she followed Mother around the house constantly looking to be of assistance.

We all sought acceptance from her so much, because we knew we would never get it from him. Not with his spiteful demeanor and hateful attitude. Not with his evil mind and blackened heart. Not when he sought every opportunity to knock us down and make us feel less than human. No, he knew only anger and hate and he wanted everyone to feel what he felt. There was no room for love in his heart.

I can only speak for myself when I say that I wanted to be the exact opposite of him. I prayed that God would give me the strength to take all that we had suffered and make us better people for it.

One thing was for sure, Father taught me to hate—because I hated him with every fiber of my being and with every ounce of my soul. I hated him so completely, that after the abuse started, anytime I was within five feet of him, I blocked him from my mind. Something inside me would take over to deal with him, so I did not have to.

As I got older and began to hit puberty, I shot up and grew, it seemed overnight. I was not quite as tall as Father, but he would not dare touch me anymore, because he knew I could fight back. I worked out every day during gym, happy to see that my body was taking the shape of a man. When I was strong enough, I would take revenge on him for all the hurt he had caused us. I would make him pay for damaging my sisters' souls—and mine.

CHAPTER 10

Romans 12:19

"Do not take revenge, my friends, but leave room for God's wrath, for it is written: 'It is mine to avenge; I will repay,' says the Lord."

Dr. Marcus Parnell sat back in his chair amazed at what the man before him had suffered. While Tony explained his story, he felt a compassion for him that he had never felt for any of his patients before. Dr. Parnell always viewed his patients as an opportunity to grow in experience—as a way to gain knowledge. Though he had a decent bedside manner, he always remained detached—until now. Tony had truly touched his heart, and though the man had endured inconceivable pain, Dr. Parnell envied him. For Tony had an inner strength, a reckoning force from within, that pulled him through and made him more potent than any man he knew. The doctor finally pinpointed that strength. It was Tony's faith.

Any other man may have turned an angry fist to God, but not Tony. Any other man would have certainly laughed at the face of God and doubted His existence, but not Tony. His faith never faltered—never wavered.

"Okay," Dr. Parnell interjected. "Tony, I'm going to give you a break for now. Max needs to come out so we can fill in just a few more blanks. Max, are you ready to talk to us again?"

Again, there was a slight change in Tony's heart rate and blood pressure. Max turned to Dr. Parnell and gave him a wry grin. "You called?"

"As you well know, Tony was able to recall much more than I thought he could. But still, I'd like to hear your version of what happened the night Tony stepped in to protect Rosie," The doctor explained.

"Do you really need all the gruesome details?" Max asked.

"How about if we start off on a question/answer basis? I ask, you answer."

"Okay," Max sang. "Shoot."

"Well, it's evident that when Vito attacked Tony that night you were created, at that very moment, to shelter Tony from the 'gruesome details', as you put it," Dr. Parnell concluded. "What were your thoughts—your feelings?"

Max finally grew serious. "Does it matter? I did what I had to do. I kept Tony from realizing the true danger that Vito emitted. I took the disgusting torture for him. I endured being tied up, night after night, to be his slave. Me, Maximillian."

"Why? Why do you call yourself that?"

"Maximillian was a holy warrior. One of the greatest of warriors. That's what I felt when I stepped in. I was—a great warrior."

"That makes sense," Dr. Parnell agreed. "So, when the abuse continued, he took to tying you up?"

Max fidgeted in the bed uncomfortably. "Do we really need these?" he asked, directing his eyes to the straps that held his hands down.

"I'm sorry, but it is necessary. Just precautionary, in case Tony tries to hurt himself."

Max continued to fidget, avoiding the question. Finally, Dr. Parnell quizzed again.

"So, did Vito tie you up every time?"

"YES!" Max screamed out. "Yes, that repulsive pig tied us up because I would fight him with all that I had. I would kick and hit back. He would say, 'You wanted to be the hero. Well, it's them or you.' So, I put up with it," Max explained.

"You did it not only for Tony, but for the girls, as well?" Dr. Parnell questioned.

"I didn't have a choice. There are some choices that even I can't convince Tony of changing or making, for that matter."

Dr. Parnell jotted a note down, finding it remarkable how Tony actually had the final call. "Does this upset you?" he asked Max.

"What do you think? Yes, *it upsets me*!" he mimicked. "Tony always has to do the right thing. He puts everybody else first. He doesn't care about what *he* wants or what *he* needs. If it wasn't his mother he catered to, it was his sisters. And when they were gone, we had to worry about someone else . . . Laura!" he spat.

"Tony is a loving man. He has noble characteristics. That's rare in a man, nowadays. Especially a man who has survived this type of abuse. Tony's special because of the difficult circumstances he sustained," Dr. Parnell complimented.

"A lot of good it's done him to be noble. It's caused him nothing but pain."

"Tell me, Max, is that why you hate Laura and wanted to hurt her?" Dr. Parnell dug.

"Yes! She was one more person that we had to worry about protecting. I was getting sick of being the doormat. Tony only used me when he couldn't take the heat."

"What did you need to protect Laura from?" The doctor probed.

Suddenly he could see a struggle taking place between the two personas within Tony. "No! I'm going to tell him!" Max shouted.

"Shut up!" screamed Tony. "Don't tell him! That secret would kill Laura. Let the past stay in the past!"

"He needs to know and I'm going to tell him!" Max insisted.

"You will not! *I* will tell him why you hate her!" Tony stated.

This was a first for Tony and Max, and Dr. Parnell was fortunate enough to witness it. Tony finally broke through and was conversing with his alter. He was taking possession of authority and this was a positive sign of healing. "Go ahead, Tony," he encouraged. "You tell me why Max despises Laura."

Tony's chest heaved as he tried to regain control. "I need a glass of water," he stated.

The male nurse quickly leaned over the bed and placed a Styrofoam cup with ice water and a straw to Tony's lips. He drank eagerly, most likely feeling drained from the entire process.

"Thank you," Tony moistened his lips and explained. "When I was being held in the Galantes' prison, Laura's father consistently assaulted and battered me. He wanted to get the trustee's name from me. But I knew better than to give it to him."

"Why not?" asked Dr. Parnell. "Perhaps they would have taken the money and finally left you alone."

"No, we knew better," Tony claimed.

"We?" Dr. Parnell asked again.

"Yeah, we," Max jumped in.

"Stop butting in!" Tony screamed.

"No! If the truth is going to come out, then let it *all* come out!" said Max.

"What are you talking about?" Tony questioned.

"You know why we could never tell Matt, Frank's name. You know why!"

"No, I don't. I don't know!"

"Fine, then I'll tell you why. I overheard the Galantes say they were going to kill the trustee and then kill you, and in turn, me, as soon as they got their money." Max divulged.

"When?" Tony doubted.

"When I went there and told them that Father had a life insurance policy steep enough to pay off the debt and more."

"You did what?" Tony shouted.

"You heard me! I'm the one who went to the Galantes. That's how they knew about the policy. I told them to kill off the old man, and when we cashed in, we would pay them. Mother would be free and all of us would be rid of him. Only, as I left the cozy little restaurant in which the meeting took place, I overheard the one with the dark mole say that they'd collect the money and kill you and the trustee! We showed them, didn't we? We got away and Frank's name was never disclosed."

"You idiot!" Tony shouted. "That animal with the dark mole killed the entire family! Mother and the little ones didn't have to die!"

"I didn't know they would kill everyone. We wanted to get revenge. Don't lie and say you didn't want Father to pay for all the pain he'd caused. Besides, I did you a favor! All you had to worry about was yourself after they were all gone." Max stated.

"You selfish animal! You didn't care that they had planned to kill the whole family. That's what you wanted, so you didn't have to be responsible for anyone any more. Mother, Caterina, Nellie, Rose, and Vincey! They didn't have to die!" Tony cried.

"That's why I agreed to help you take care of Laura and her sisters!" Max slipped.

Dr. Parnell finally interrupted the ongoing dispute. "Why would you need to take care of Laura and her sisters?"

"I can't believe this! I'm responsible for the death of my own family. Oh, God!" Tony cried aloud.

"Tony," Dr. Parnell comforted. "You couldn't control what Max was doing. You're not responsible for Max's actions."

"He's a part of me and he acted on my need for revenge. It's my fault!" he sobbed.

"You weren't in the right mind frame. You were ill. You need to forgive yourself. You've been through a horrible ordeal. Now if you continue on this way, we're going to end this session, right now. But we'll have to have one more of these sessions to get the rest of the truth out. Or you can hang tough and finish the session today. How do you feel?" Dr. Parnell asked.

Tony continued to cry silently. The male nurse wiped his tears for him with a tissue. The doctor gave him the okay to loosen the straps holding down Tony's hands. Tony pulled his hands out and wiped his eyes.

"Are you okay?" Dr. Parnell examined.

Tony nodded.

"Well then, can you continue? Would you like to tell me a little bit more about Laura and her father, Matthew?"

Tony took in a deep breath and nodded again. He slowly began explaining, "During my imprisonment, Matt was trying to pry the trustee's name from me. Because I refused to break, he grew frustrated with me. He would actually spew his thoughts aloud, telling me how when he got the name out of me, he would come into more money than he'd ever seen. He told me that he planned to leave town with his girls. He said he had three of them. Well, that pulled at my heartstrings. I once had three sisters." Tony's eyes filled again and the salty liquid spilled down his cheeks. He wiped them and continued.

"Then, one day, he told me he came up with an incredible plan for his girls, once they left town. Only, it wasn't an incredible plan. It was a diabolical plan and the thought of these three girls suffering at the hands of their father, made my insides churn. He even showed me an old church family photo, taken when their mother was alive, before the youngest was born. The two little girls called out to me. I wanted to help them. Especially, when I found out what he planned to do with them. I thought to myself, that because I couldn't save my own sisters—perhaps I could save these girls."

Dr. Parnell checked the tape in the recorder, making sure there was enough ribbon to continue the session. Meanwhile, he completely stopped the intravenous drip, so the medication would begin to wear. The session would soon be coming to a close.

"Tell me, Tony. What did Matt plan to do to his daughters?" Dr. Parnell probed.

"Laura must never know this. It would pain her too much."

"Tony, you cannot keep withholding information from her. It's detrimental to your relationship if you're not completely truthful. Somehow, secrets have a way of finding their way to the surface, as you are painfully finding," Dr. Parnell explained.

Tony shook his head. "It's only because of my need to protect her that I don't want her to hear this. If you feel that it will somehow help to have this truth exposed, than I guess I'm going to have to trust you."

Dr. Parnell nodded. "You can trust me, Tony. I'm here to help you and all of those around you to heal."

Tony nodded and continued. "Thanks to Max, we escaped the prison. It took a long time before we found our way to Uncle Frank. When we did, Max pretended to be me. Uncle Frank helped us to get a fake identity and Tony Warren was fabricated. He moved us in. We kept my grandparents' house boarded up and seemingly abandoned, as a last-minute hideout, in case somehow the Galantes had caught on to Max's trail.

"Meanwhile, because Matt had yet to be paid the money he expected, Max took his time preparing. He set up the house, filling it with clothing for girls ranging from the ages of Matt's youngest daughter to his eldest, just in case Matt planned on following through with his idea. Max kept carting things in for the girls, discarding the empty boxes in the basement."

Dr. Parnell interrupted again, "I'm sorry, Tony, but you have yet to tell me what the plan was."

"I'm getting there," Tony stated. His red-rimmed eyes closed off to a time and place only he could see. He resumed with his story. "Max followed Matt often. When Matt realized he wasn't going to get paid the money they had promised, he decided to take it. On one of the days when he was given a job to run some money, he took off with it. Max was fortunate to have been on his tracks, that day. He went back to the house and grabbed the camping backpack already filled with goods and warm clothes. Max knew I wanted to stop Matt from taking those girls out of the country."

"Out of the country?"

"Let me explain."

"And why did you need the backpack of things?" Dr. Parnell curiously asked.

"We wanted to make sure that we could provide for the walk back to the boarded up house. If the three girls were going to come with me, I couldn't expect them to have the proper clothing for that kind of a hike. I needed to be sure we had food to get by, until I could buy enough to stock the house. If the Galantes found the house supposedly abandoned, yet stocked with food, they would have figured it out. We had to think of everything," Tony explained.

"That makes sense," Dr. Parnell agreed. "Please continue—why was Matt taking the girls out of the country?"

"He planned to take the girls to Mexico. In Mexico, two families were waiting." Tony swallowed, trying to continue. "One family wanted Sabrina and were willing to pay him $100,000 to keep her as their own. The other family needed a good servant and sought a teenage girl capable of handling a household. They were ready to pay him $25,000 for Patty. As for Laura, he didn't want to let *her* go. He planned to put her good looks to use. He intended on selling her out for prostitution."

Tears fell from Tony's face, as he continued to reveal Matt's malevolent arrangement. "Why," he cried, "Why do fathers do these things to their children? How could I have *not* stepped in to help Laura and her sisters? Unfortunately, Max was too late. The Galantes had already gotten to Matt and the two girls. But God spared Laura. He spared her for me. Because when *I* saw her . . . when *I* saw Laura running in the woods that night, I immediately fell in love with her. I was bound and determined to help her. Max went away and didn't return until three years later.

"I didn't know that she would actually help to heal me. I didn't know that taking her in was going to be the best thing that ever happened to *me*. God gave me three of the most wonderful years of my life. I forgot about my past, forgot about my pain. I was so focused on helping her through hers, that I kept putting my own hurts aside. I guess they were bound to come out eventually, and they did. The night Laura began to question me about my father, Max stepped back up to the plate."

"If it hadn't been for you, I would have finished the job! I would have gotten rid of her, too!" Max barged in.

"Max," Dr. Parnell added, "You have got to let it go. Tony's dominant. He doesn't need protection anymore. Laura's not someone he needs to save, anymore. Laura's someone he wants to love."

"What do you think love leads to? More and more pain!" Max shouted.

"Well, the course of love never has run smoothly, but that's not a reason to run from it. Nor is it a reason to remove the source from which it comes. Max, you need to say goodbye to Tony. Tony, you can tell Max thank you for getting you through those difficult years, but you won't need him anymore. We've discovered the entire truth and now it's time to heal. To get past these hurts and look forward to a future—one with Laura," Dr. Parnell counseled.

"How? How do I get through this?" Tony cried.

"You'll have plenty of help. You have the rest of your life to heal," The doctor explained.

"It's going to take me the rest of my life?" Tony exclaimed.

"No, but now that the truth is out, you can start to put the past behind you. Look at what we have accomplished today. You were finally able to get into Max's head, so to speak. You were able to read his thoughts and converse with him. You really were able to do that all along. Those voices in your head were most likely Max. Especially the voices hell-bent on revenge or seeking a way out of a situation where you were likely to get hurt—emotionally or physically." Dr. Parnell paused to allow Tony a moment to absorb his words. "I think it's time you thanked Max for his help and that you let him go."

"But I hate him. How can I thank him? He helped get my family killed!"

"Maybe so, but he was created by you, so you didn't have to endure the physical and emotional pain of being sexually, physically, and emotionally abused by your father. If he has done anything right, that was it," Dr. Parnell added.

"After everything I did, that's the thanks I get—that he hates me," Max whispered in a surprisingly sad voice.

"Will you just go away?" Tony begged.

"That's up to you," said Max.

"Go away. Thank you for your help, but go away," Tony stated, while the tears spilled downward.

There was a silence in the room for the first time since the session began. Tony quietly sobbed, his hands covering his face. Dr. Parnell sat next to Tony. He placed a gentle hand on Tony's arm. Tony leaned forward and cried on the doctor's shoulder. It took a moment before either of them could speak. Dr. Parnell could not believe his own reaction toward Tony. He had fought the urge to cry throughout the session, but once Tony broke down, he could no longer contain himself.

This was a special man, as he had told Max, and he would do everything in his power to help him. When he felt that Tony had the proper grieving time, he questioned him a little further.

"Would you like to rest? Do you want to sleep off the rest of the drug?"

Tony shook his head in no. "Thanks, but I'll go home to rest."

"Tony, you did great today, considering what we've discovered. I'm proud of you."

"Thank you."

"What are you feeling, right now?"

* * *

Tony felt emotionally and physically drained. He was so confused. So lost. Sure, they had discovered the entire truth and they had said goodbye to Max. But the truth remained. Tony had been raped . . . repeatedly. He had played a part in the death of his family. Not only that, but the truth behind Matthew Marc's plan was revealed and it would tear Laura apart. *How was this supposed to be good?*

Dr. Parnell interrupted Tony's train of thought. "Tony?"

"Doc, what can I tell you about how I feel? I feel so many things. I feel violated, neglected, hurt, fury, hate. I hate myself for wanting revenge. I hate myself because my need for revenge backfired on me and took my entire family. I'm scared for Laura. I'm horrified. I don't know where I'm going—what I'm going to do—or how I'm going to do it! This is impossible!"

Doc nodded, seeming to truly understand. "You're right. It's not going to be easy. So, let's tackle one thing at a time. First, your feelings toward your father. Think of it this way—the man was seriously ill to do what he was doing. He was most likely abused in some manner as a child and/or had a chemical imbalance that went untreated. It will take time, but you must come to terms with what happened and forgive him. Seeing him as a mentally unbalanced man will help you to find even a fragment of compassion in your heart for him and forgiveness will follow. Seek God to help you with that one."

"I don't know. How does someone become like him? Why was he the way he was?"

"If it helps, find out. Contact your uncles. See if they can shed a little light on his story. It will surely help you to forgive," Doc suggested. "Now, as for what happened with Max and his going to the Galantes, we're going to work on this the most in the cognitive therapy that we will continue. Tony, you have to forgive yourself. You carry around *way* too much guilt. Do you understand that you couldn't control what Max did? I know he was a part of you and that you created him to help you through the abuse, but Max had his own thoughts and he acted on them. You know," Doc pondered a moment on a thought, "You're a religious man. I've seen that you have an unshakable faith. Your God demands that you forgive. This applies to you, too. This is another area in which God can help you."

Tony looked down. It all seemed so easy when Doc put things into perspective. But it was not so cut and dry. It was not that simple. He did not feel that he was worthy to have a wonderful wife, a child given by God. He had two personalities, was mentally unstable, had killed his family, and had hurt Laura before in the past. He was going to ruin her. *And what of the baby? If his father had been abused, didn't he turn into an abuser? Could that happen to Tony, too? What if he hurt his own child?* Then he could NEVER forgive himself.

"Finally," Doc continued, "I believe it'll be best to bring Laura into a session. We can play back the tapes and she can hear everything, or you can tell her yourself. Either way, I want you to be comfortable with it. A few sessions together to work out these issues will help you both."

Tony nodded, not really listening anymore. His own thoughts were jumbled. His mind was racing a mile a minute.

"I will see you tomorrow for a regular session and we'll continue with your therapy. Rest up for the night and take it easy. Remember, no operating any type of machinery." Doc patted Tony's leg and slipped out of the room.

Tony watched Dr. Parnell leave. He lay back on the pillow and closed his eyes. *Lies, deceit, rape, abuse, pain, murder, unforgiveness!* The weight of all that they had discovered, crushed his soul. He thought of his mother and a sob escaped his throat. She had turned a blind eye toward her children. She *had* to notice that something was off. *Why couldn't she have found the courage to remove them from the situation?* Yet, he cried for her. She did the best she could, considering her circumstances.

She had come to this country, not knowing a word of English, but learned to speak the language. She was married at a young age and separated from her parents and only sister, when they moved to California. She bore and raised her five children with little help and worked hard to help her family financially. Still, she was able to instill in Tony the nurturing nature that was within him. She had shown him how to love and Tony knew that he had already forgiven her, in his deepest heart.

His thoughts moved on to his siblings. His heart ached at the fresh memories that he had long since forgotten. The session helped to bring out the bad, but it also helped him to recall the good that he had blocked out as well. Like the scent of Rosie's hair, fresh out of the tub. He remembered the way she would crawl up on the couch, always next to him. Tony would hold her and love the feel of her soft hair on his arm. Tears coursed down his cheeks at these memories.

Caterina was always his partner in crime. She would follow him around the house and together they would find trouble. Tony let out a chuckle, through his tears. He recalled a time when they decided to surprise their mother by making homemade bread. By the time Maria rose that morning, both the kitchen and the children were covered in flour.

He pondered on Nellie for a moment, picturing her rosy rounded cheeks and the longest pair of eyelashes he had ever seen. Nellie was different from the other girls. She was quiet and would be content playing by herself. Yet, when Tony walked into a room, she followed him around like a lost puppy. He remembered nicknaming her, 'his shadow'.

Finally, his thoughts fell upon Vincey. His face fell into his hands and fresh tears seared his cheeks. He had failed Vincey, too. He failed to protect him in the end. The night of the fire came rushing back to him and Tony could recall every wretched emotion. Now he could understand why he had blocked it all out. It *was* just too painful. *How could any man overcome such pain?*

Dr. Parnell had mentioned God. He laughed at Doc's comment of having an unshakable faith. Tony looked toward Heaven and cried out, "How? How do You expect me to do this? I am only a man! What do You want from me? I've never doubted You! I've always believed in You! You said You'd never give us more than we can handle. Is this possible? Can I carry this burden—this pain, alone?"

Tony could feel himself drowning. He had many struggles ahead of him. He had way too much baggage to burden any one person with. Especially a person with so much to live for. There was only one obvious solution—he would call off the wedding and free Laura for good.

CHAPTER 11

Psalm 119:153

"Lord, look upon my suffering and deliver me,
for I have not forgotten your law."

Wednesday, December 20

John strolled in through the door of the garage that evening, feeling weary after a long day at work. It was oddly hectic, it seemed, since Beth had called and was unable to make it in. She complained something about car trouble and having her father help tow the vehicle in to her mechanic's shop. Despite the uncomfortable tension she had recently brought upon the office, John realized that day, how much he truly relied on her.

As he hung his jacket and removed his shoes, he could hear Laura and Marlene preparing dinner in the kitchen. Sliding on his slippers, he quickened his pace when he heard Laura whispering in a tear-filled voice.

She stood at the counter chopping onions. Her eyes and nose were red from crying. Marlene had a stalk of celery in one hand and the other hand on Laura's back, gently rubbing. They both looked up when he entered the room.

"Hey, what's going on here?" he questioned, while planting a kiss on both of their cheeks.

Laura looked down and Marlene went to the sink to rinse the celery. "Not much," she stated.

"Not much? I can tell something's wrong. Laura, you've been crying," he insisted.

"It's just the onions," she covered, flashing a phony smile.

"Come on now. That's as old as me. Aren't you going to share with old Dad whatever's on your mind?"

Laura sighed and glanced his way. "Aren't you tired of hearing my problems?" she answered his question with a question.

"No," he simply answered.

"I'm just worried about Tony," she finally summed it up.

"I thought things were better?" John asked in confusion.

"Last night, while I was there for dinner, he must have had some kind of flashback. After spending a wonderful evening together, he practically threw me out."

"That doesn't sound like something he'd do. But lately, Tony hasn't been himself." John wrapped his arm around her shoulders and squeezed. "He's going through a very difficult time. We all know that now. Before dinner, let's say a prayer for him and continue to pray for him, whenever he comes to our minds."

"Then I should be on my knees, 24 hours a day," Laura stated.

"Whatever it takes. He needs our help."

"That's what I told her," Marlene added. "Tony needs God and our love and support. More than anything, he needs our prayers."

****

They gathered around the table and held hands. Marlene began the prayer.

"Heavenly Father, we gather together this evening to give You thanks for this food and for all the blessings You give to us. But mostly, Lord, we lift up our Tony. He needs You more than ever. He's hurting and needs Your comforting touch, Your healing hand. Please, restore him to a sound mind and body. Bring him peace and help him to know he is loved—not only by You, Lord, but by us as well. Thank you, Jesus. In Your name, we pray. Amen."

Everyone crossed themselves. John held onto Laura's hand a minute longer. He gave her a sincere smile and promised, "We're going to get you through this, too. You just hang in there and have faith."

"Thanks, Dad," she whispered.

"Now, dig in. I'm starving," John exclaimed.

"Didn't you eat your lunch?" Marlene asked with motherly concern, while dishes of food were being passed.

"We were swamped today. Beth was gone and the office phones were going mad. I worked right through lunch!" John scooped a spoonful of mashed potatoes onto his plate.

"Where was the rest of the group?" Laura questioned between bites.

"Marco had appointments. Tony was out. Paula and I were the only ones handling the office," he stated.

"Tony was out?" Laura inquired.

John thought about it for a moment while chewing, then answered, "Yes, I didn't see him all day."

"Well, he did mention something about having to wake up early to get to the apartment that needed a repair," Laura thought aloud. She worked on cutting her meat.

"Oh, good, he probably went to the apartment on Beamer, where we had water damage," John guessed.

"What happened?" Marlene quizzed.

John went on to explain how impressed he was with the way Tony was handling the repairs to the damaged apartment. Marlene commented on how damaging water can be to a dwelling if not taken care of immediately. John listened and occasionally threw in a comment or two, but something troubled him. He did not like the idea of Beth and Tony missing work at the same time. First thing in the morning, he would go to the apartment on Beamer and see if the damages had been fixed.

* * *

Laura could see that John was not truly participating in the conversation. He had a far-off look in his eyes and it worried her. He thought it had not concerned her that both Tony and Beth were not at work. But it had, and Laura felt an ill chill wash over her, immediately losing her appetite. Tony had not called her all day. Because of the way they parted the night before, she vowed to give him his space.

When dinner ended, Laura cleaned up the kitchen. John and Marlene left to do some Christmas shopping. She cleared the table, washed and dried the dishes, and was sweeping the floor when the telephone rang. *Tony, she hoped.*

"Hello," she answered. Laura waited for a response. "Hello?" Again, she heard no answer. Laura hung up and returned to sweeping the floor. A moment later, the telephone rang again. Frustrated, Laura stomped to the phone, raising her voice a notch, she shouted, "Hello?" Straining her ear, she could hear that whoever was calling was still on the line. "Who is this?" she shouted. "Why do you keep calling?"

Still, there was no response. Laura grew nervous. This was happening too often for it to be a coincidence. She waited anxiously for the slightest sound. Finally, she heard a click. Laura looked into the telephone receiver, perplexed. Whoever it was, knew both numbers in which to contact her. She hung up and looked nervously around the room. She walked toward the nook windows and shut the shades. Laura was feeling spooked again. She finished up, checked the locks on all the doors, and went up to her room. She sat at her vanity table, unsure what to do next. She pondered whether to call her friend, Sam Desanti, the Chief of Police of Cicero, her hometown. *Was it simply coincidence and Laura was just paranoid?* She decided to give it more time. If the anonymous calls continued, she would tell someone.

She sat still for a moment, her thoughts immediately going to Tony. She wondered where he had been all day and wondered if it had anything to do with Beth's absence at the office. She shook her head and thought how suspicious she was becoming. She needed to do what John and Marlene were telling her to do. She needed to have faith and pray. Laura knelt at the side of her bed and put her hands together. She asked God to comfort Tony and to help bring peace to his heart and mind.

Amidst her prayers, Laura cried. Her heart ached for Tony and all that he was suffering. She also asked the Lord to restore their relationship and to help them through this time of testing. Laura crossed herself and undressed for bed. She was tired and weary.

The telephone suddenly rang again. She slipped on her pajama shirt and ran to John and Marlene's room to answer it. "Hello?" she chimed. Laura could hear someone breathing on the other end. She waited a moment longer and hung up. Alarmed, she ran into her room and closed the door.

****

John rose early the next morning, eager to find the underlying cause of the Beth/Tony situation. He drove to the apartment on Beamer, disappointed to find that none of the repairs had been completed. John's mind was working overtime. He sped to get to the office, before either Beth or Tony arrived. As luck would have it, John made it in before anyone. He plugged in the coffeemaker and planned his day. After pouring a cup of the fresh brew, John curiously entered Tony's office. He glanced around. The office seemed in order and as untouched as the day before. His eyes fell upon a picture of Tony and Laura embracing at Thanksgiving dinner. He remembered Marlene taking the photo.

John's heart ached for Laura. They looked so happy in the picture. *How had it gone from that—to the way things were now?* He wanted to help make it right for her. John stepped from Tony's office into his own, putting the coffee mug down, to go to the restroom. As he placed a hand on the bathroom door, the elevator doors dinged and Beth and Tony exited together. He could hear Beth's boisterous voice telling Tony what had happened to her car. Tony kept his gaze down, while she continued to ramble, assuming her usual role as flirt. John quickly slipped into the bathroom. His insides boiled.

It seemed almost feign the way she carried on. He quickly finished in the restroom and reentered the office.

"Morning, Mr. Knight. I see you made it in early. I could smell the coffee as soon as I walked in," she announced.

"Good morning. Yes, I have plenty to do to keep me busy today. Did you get your car fixed?" John questioned.

"Yup, she's up and running," Beth said.

"That was quick. What was wrong with it?" he grilled.

"Oh, what do I know? My daddy took care of it for me."

John nodded, not really satisfied with her answer. "Glad you're back. It was tough yesterday without you," he smiled.

"It's good to know I'm still needed," she returned his smile.

"Absolutely," John tapped a finger on her desk and walked away. Walking toward his office, he glanced at Tony's door. It was closed. John was tempted to knock. He marched forward and rapped on the door.

"Come in," Tony yelled.

"Hey, good morning," John called.

Tony looked up from his desk. His eyes seemed vacant. His smile was empty. "Good morning," he whispered, his voice barely audible.

"You gonna be around all day?" John asked.

"Actually, no, I'm heading over to Beamer in a few minutes. I went out to purchase a few things for the repair and am meeting the plumber in an hour."

John nodded, "Well, if I don't see you, have a good one."

"Thanks, you too," Tony murmured.

John closed the door slowly, but not before stealing another glance at Tony. His eyes looked haunted, or was it guilt? John was sure of one thing; the feeling in the pit of his stomach was waving red flags before his eyes.

He entered his office and closed his door. Dialing the number for 'Information', he asked the operator for the number to the Cicero Police Department. John jotted down the digits and sat in his chair. Dialing the number as rapidly as his finger could, he waited for an answer.

"Chief Desanti, please," he requested.

Moments later, Sam's voice rang through, "Desanti, here."

"Hey Sam, it's John Knight."

"John! How are you?"

"Doing good. And you?"

"All is good. The family is well? Laura and Marlene?"

"We're okay," John affirmed.

"What can I do for you, buddy?"

"Sam, we seem to be having some problems and I was hoping you might be able to refer me to someone who can help."

"Uh oh, what's going on?"

"It's Tony," John announced. He could hear Sam cussing under his breath.

"Please, tell me he hasn't done anything to hurt Laura."

"Not physically, but he's going through a very difficult time with his therapy recently, and his behavior has been a bit peculiar," John went on to explain to Sam all that Laura and Tony were going through.

"So, you suspect him of being unfaithful?"

"I don't know, Sam. I just want to protect Laura. I'm considering hiring a private detective to keep an eye on him, but I don't know if it's necessary and if I'm just being overprotective."

"One thing I've learned after all these years, John, is follow your instincts. Tell you what; don't worry about spending your money. I'll take care of this for you. I can call in on a few favors and have someone monitor him for you. I'll keep you posted with what I find," Sam offered.

John sat back in his chair and rubbed the back of his neck. "That sounds great, Sam. You've just lifted a huge load off my shoulders."

"Anything for Laura. That girl has had enough heartache to last her a lifetime."

"Amen," John said. "Thanks so much. It's good to know I can count on you. You're a great friend to her."

"Thanks, John, I'll talk to you soon."

John placed the receiver down and sighed. His shoulders felt tense and his neck muscles tight, but he was happy he made the call.

****

Saturday rolled around and Laura had yet to hear from Tony. John and Marlene did what they could to occupy her time and she went along with it, so not to worry them. They shopped together, baked cookies and cakes, all in preparation for the coming celebration of Christ's birth.

Although, deep inside, Laura felt a piece of her heart was dying. John had reluctantly told Laura what he had discovered or rather what he *failed* to discover at the Beamer rental. Laura did not know what to think. He could have been at Dr. Parnell's office or he could have been with Beth. Either way, the distance Tony was putting between them, intensified her insecurities. She missed him and longed for his company.

As she lay awake on her bed, too early for a Saturday morning, she wondered how she would fill her day. After making her bed and showering, Laura descended into the kitchen for a bite. The baby was awake and moving within her, probably waiting to be fed.

"Morning, sunshine," John called out.

"Hi, Dad," she kissed his freshly shaved face. "You smell so good!"

"Thank you. Your mother up yet?"

"I heard her moving around in the bedroom. I'd say, yes," she said, while pouring a glass of orange juice for herself. She placed it on the table and prepared her breakfast. "How about some hotcakes," she offered.

"Sounds great."

Laura mixed the batter, unexpectedly feeling light-headed. She quickly ran to the table and clenched the glass of orange juice. Spilling some of it down her chin, she guzzled half the glass. Alarmed, John quickly handed her a napkin.

"Are you okay?" he asked.

Laura nodded, immediately sitting down. She wiped her face.

"Laura, what happened?"

"I felt a little dizzy. The little one must be really hungry," she said with a not-so-reassuring smile.

"Has this happened before?" he questioned.

"One other time, but as soon as I drank something it passed," she explained.

"You better tell your doctor. When's your next monthly visit?"

"Between Christmas and New Year's."

"What's the matter?" Marlene entered the kitchen. "Are you alright?"

"Really, it's nothing. I just get dizzy here and there," Laura covered.

Marlene began to lecture her about the importance of eating and resting while pregnant. "This stress isn't helping, either. Take your mind off things and think of that baby, first."

Laura understood Marlene's concern, since Marlene had previously lost babies of her own. Laura could sense her fear. "I'll be fine. I promise to take better care of myself."

During breakfast, the telephone rang. Laura was reluctant to get it, afraid to receive another prank call, but answered the ring. She was happy to hear her grandfather's voice. He asked her of her plans for the day, wondering if he could take her to dinner. She answered, yes, and looked forward to spending the day with him. He promised to be at her home at four o'clock.

Precisely on time, the doorbell rang and Nino arrived. Marlene and John made plans of their own and had already left for the evening. Nino came in with kisses and hugs for Laura. She happily returned them.

"It is so good to see you," Nino exclaimed.

"Nonno, it's good to see you, too."

"Are you ready? I have the reservation for the restaurant at 4:30," he explained.

"Sure, let's go," Laura agreed. She pulled on her coat, with Nino's help, and locked the door before exiting. It was a sunny day, cloudless, yet cold. Laura shivered, while descending the porch steps.

Alfonso stood at the back door of the vehicle, waiting to assist her. "Good evening, milady," he said with a tip of his hat.

"Alfonso, have you taken up chauffeuring as your permanent profession?" Laura quizzed with a tease.

"My chauffeur is sick. He has no been able to drive me and so Alfonso offer to help me," Nino interjected.

"What a nice guy," Laura stated while stepping into the car. Alfonso's smile widened.

Nino slid in next to her. Alfonso sat behind the steering wheel. He maneuvered the Cadillac onto the main road with ease.

"How has you week been?" Nino questioned.

"Busy, busy," Laura fabricated. "How about you?"

Nino told Laura about how well Alfonso was doing with taking over his company. He explained all the different phases to shipping and receiving imported goods. "There is no food like the food from *Sicilia*. Restaurants and stores pay top dollar for what we sell. The olive oil is one hundred percent extra virgin. Tell her, Fonzie, how does that *olio* taste?"

Alfonso turned a second and glanced at Laura, as he drove. "You've never had anything like this, Laura. It smells so good; your mouth begins to water before you even taste it." He said with a laugh, "I don't know if it's such a good idea, my taking over. I may eat the entire inventory."

Laura genuinely laughed. She was happy to be enjoying herself despite the trials she was facing. The thought of Tony sent a chill down her spine. Laura shivered.

"Are you cold?" he asked her. "Alfonso, put the heat high. My *nipote* is still cold."

"I'm okay. It was just a chill," Laura protested.

Alfonso stole a glance at her and raised the heat. "Don't like the cold much, do ya?" he probed with a smirk.

"Never have, never will," she revealed.

"You picked the wrong place to live," he chuckled.

"Isn't that the truth? But I wouldn't leave my family, even if winter came to stay forever." She placed a gloved hand over Nino's.

A tear glistened in his eye and he whispered, "*Amore*."

Laura smiled with him. In her peripheral vision, she caught Alfonso staring. The smile on his face had faded at the sight of Laura's hand over Nino's. Laura looked at him more intently. A troubled feeling swept over her. Laura wondered what Alfonso's real agenda was.

Twenty minutes into the drive, Nino announced their arrival at the upscale restaurant. Laura opened the door before Alfonso could come around to her. She stepped back to allow room for Nino to exit as well. Unexpectedly, she felt another rush of heat to her face. She broke into an instant sweat. Her head began to spin and Laura felt the ground moving beneath her.

"Laura!" Nino shouted.

She heard feet scurrying and a set of muscular arms caught her before she dropped to the ground. "Laura?"

* * *

"Laura? *Ma che successe*?" Nino cried aloud, asking what happened.

Alfonso lifted Laura easily and carried her limp body into the restaurant. She felt warm in his arms and he felt a thrill just holding her. Her skirt blew in the wind and he caught a glimpse of her legs. He looked away, afraid to give his obsession away. Alfonso was falling hard.

The woman at the door quickly opened it and helped guide him to a chair. He gently sat Laura down and called out her name.

Someone shouted for a glass of water. Another asked if there was a doctor present in the restaurant. "Should we call an ambulance?"

Alfonso felt horrified for the first time in a long time. He brushed her soft hair back and applied the wet cold cloth someone had handed him to her forehead and neck. Her hair felt soft on his hard-callused hand. He could get used to touching her this way.

"Perhaps, her blood sugar dropped. Some apple juice . . . get a glass of juice," a man shouted.

Laura seemed to be coming out of it. She rolled her head back and drew her eyebrows together. "What happened?" she whispered.

Alfonso's heartbeat doubled. He was so happy to see her come to. "You passed out. You alright?" he questioned with sincere concern.

"Laura, Laura *mia*, what happened to you, *amore*. You scare me," Nino cried.

"I'm okay now," Laura said after sipping the juice Alfonso offered her.

* * *

Laura looked at the crowd around her. She felt embarrassed for having drawn so much attention. A nurse, who had been dining in the restaurant, came, and was taking Laura's pulse. She asked her questions about her pregnancy and if the dizzy spells were happening frequently.

"Honestly, I think I'm just hungry. I had a few pancakes this morning at about 9:30 and haven't had anything since."

"Young lady, you need to take better care of yourself. Eating properly is essential to your child's development," the woman chastised. She pointed to Alfonso and continued, "You make sure you take your wife to the doctor, first thing. Monitor her this weekend and make sure she's eating well and more frequently. Oh, and pancakes are the worst thing you can have for breakfast. It breaks down into sugar and has no real sustenance. Give her eggs with her hotcakes, or sausage. Something with protein."

Alfonso had a smirk clear across his face. "Yes ma'am. I'll make her a hearty breakfast every morning. No more pancakes for you, young lady," he pretended to reprimand.

Laura narrowed her eyes at him. Returning his smirk with her own, she added, "Don't listen to him, ma'am. He's not my husband. Just my chauffeur."

"I'm sorry, I saw your ring and just assumed that since he carried you in, he was your husband," the woman remarked, now looking at Alfonso skeptically.

"That's okay," Laura said, "Thank you for your help. I appreciate it and thank you for the advice. That explains why I felt so light-headed." Laura shook the woman's hand and the crowd around them diminished.

She stood from the chair. Alfonso grasped an elbow and Nino the other. "Guys, really, I'm okay now. The juice helped. Thank you for not letting me fall to the ground," she directed her comment to Alfonso. "Are you going to join us?"

"Who, me? No, I'm *'just the chauffeur'*," he stated with a pout.

Laura burst into laughter. "Oh, come on, now. Nonno, you don't mind if Alfonso joins us, do you?"

"Of course, no. *Mangia* with us," Nino invited.

"Only if I can pretend to be Laura's husband again. That was lots of fun," he teased.

"No chance! Chauffeur or nothing!" Laura returned.

"Aww, man. Okay, you twisted my arm."

* * *

Nino had to stop this. He did not like what he was seeing. The innocent banter going on between Laura and Alfonso was scaring him. Since Laura invited him to eat with them, he could not make a fuss about it. But he would watch and see where this was headed. He needed to warn Alfonso to stay away from her. *The question was . . . how? How could he make Alfonso keep his distance?* Any man with half a brain would not pass up an opportunity with her. *And how would he manage to keep an already interested Alfonso from pursuing her, knowing that her relationship with Tony was not sound—not stable?* He had to somehow fix this.

****

Dinner was pleasant. Afterward they ordered desserts and coffee. The meal was filled with Alfonso's jesting and Laura's laughter. They touched on nearly every subject, from the weather, to politics, to world and local news. Somehow, the conversation ultimately led to religion.

"Oh no, you're not going to try to convert me again, are you?" he questioned.

"It would do you good," Laura insisted.

"I grew up Catholic, isn't that enough? I made all my sacraments—Baptism, Communion, Confirmation. My mother did right by me. So I'm a little rough around the edges. That doesn't mean I'm a bad guy," he defended.

"Never said you were," Laura declared. "I'm just saying that it's not enough to say you're Catholic, you have to live it in your everyday life. Talk to Jesus every day. Go to mass on Sunday. Read the Bible to get to know God better. That's what I'm talking about."

"You mean, become a holy roller?" Alfonso laughed.

"Like I've said before, you're impossible," Laura laughed as well.

"Impossible is no the word. Alfonso is almost as hard-headed as you," Nino teased.

Laura giggled. "That's what Tony always tells me," she slipped. She had sworn to herself to not raise the subject to her grandfather. At the mention of his name, her heart stood still. Her smile faded and she was undoubtedly ready to go home.

Nino seemed to catch on and quickly signaled to the waiter for the check. He paid the bill, though Alfonso protested, insisting he pay his part. Nino refused. Alfonso ran ahead and pulled the vehicle around to the restaurant doors. Laura and Nino walked into the cold night and back into the Cadillac to head toward home.

Nino reached over and touched Laura's hand. "You are so sad. How is Tony?" he whispered.

"I don't know. I haven't heard from him. I'm guessing he's not good. Last I saw him, he had a horrible flashback. I worry about him. But he keeps pushing me away," Laura disclosed in whispers.

"And of the girl at the office?" he quizzed.

"I don't know. Wednesday she called in, unable to make it to work, and he was gone all day, too. She claimed she had car trouble. He never gave his excuse for missing work," Laura uttered.

"What does this mean?" Nino asked.

"I don't know, Nonno. I only know that something's not right," she murmured.

"I don't mean to intrude in on your convo—Boss, Laura. But if it looks like a rat and smells like a rat—it's a rat," Alfonso affirmed.

"What are you saying, Alfonso," Laura grilled defensively, "That you believe Tony's being unfaithful to me?"

"Look, it's none of my business and I don't want to speak my opinion unless you truly want to hear it. I don't want to offend you or your so-called fiancé," Alfonso reasoned.

"Let's hear it," Laura challenged.

"Alfonso . . ." Nino cautioned.

"It's okay, Nonno. I really want to hear what he has to say."

"I'm going to tell you the same thing I told Mr. V. I don't like the way he treated you last week. He handled you like a possession. Like he owned you or somethin'. As far as this other woman goes, if you were my girl and this woman was throwing herself at me, she'd know from the get-go that there was no chance I'd be interested," Alfonso expressed.

Laura was moved by Alfonso's declaration. Her eyes filled and she knew that he spoke the truth. Alfonso stated exactly what she had already thought—that Tony could have stopped whatever was going on with Beth from the start—*if he wanted to.* Perhaps he did not and that moved Laura to more tears. She swiftly swatted a teardrop away. Alfonso turned to steal a quick glimpse of her face and frowned.

"I'm sorry. I hope you aren't offended in any way. That wasn't my intention," he conveyed.

Nino wrapped his arm around her, in comfort. Laura fought the urge to break down. She shook her head and replied, "I'm fine. I guess the truth hurts."

Thankfully, they arrived at the Knight home. "Will you be okay, *amore*? I can stay if you need me," Nino offered.

"I'll be fine, Nonno. Don't worry about me," Laura kissed his cheek. "Thank you for an incredible dinner and for such wonderful company. I'm sorry if I scared you earlier."

Alfonso stood near her door, waiting to assist her to the house. Nino held Laura in a long embrace. “You are so much to me. Take care. No worries, okay?”

Laura nodded and kissed his cheek again. She opened the car door and slipped out. Alfonso stood next to her, holding the door open. Upon her exit, he shut it, and immediately offered to escort her. Laura held her hand up in protest.

“Really, Fonzie, I can manage. Thank you.” Laura walked passed him but not before he reached for her elbow to stop her. Laura gazed at the large hand on her arm. She looked up at him in displeasure.

“Are you upset with me?” he humbly asked.

“No, Fonzie, I’m just disappointed with love.”

“I understand,” he whispered. “Hurts like a dagger, doesn’t it?”

He released his hold and entered the vehicle.

Laura stood in the driveway with her mouth agape. Alfonso had sent the roses. Her heart seemed to sink into the pit of her stomach and her breathing suddenly became labored. The car drove away leaving her in the cold. She walked up the porch steps and hastily entered. Chills were making their way all over her body. Anxiety swept over her and she instantly longed for a sense of security—her safe haven . . . Tony.

CHAPTER 12

1 Peter 4:8

"Above all, love each other deeply, because love covers over a multitude of sins."

Safety . . . the protection that came with Tony's loving arms was *my* refuge and my utter definition of sanctuary. There was *never* a time I felt more secure than when I lived with *him* in the old 'abandoned' house. From the very first evening, when he found me in the forest in Brewerton, until that last, dreaded night after Thanksgiving, nearly three years later, I sought only *him* for security.

The first nights, after my family was murdered, were the harshest. I will never forget the way Tony pulled me through those long dark hours . . .

****

December 1973

It was the second day in the 'abandoned' house—the day Tony left to contact his Uncle Frank. He had no choice but to leave me in the shelter of the house, while he ventured out where I believed rioters waged war against our small town. I trembled at the thought that he might not return to me and cried brokenheartedly that I found myself in the nightmare in which I was living. But Tony did return, with the good news that Uncle Frank would help us.

That night, we climbed the stairs to the second level of the house. As I pulled the covers up onto me, Tony slipped into the sleeping bag on the floor, next to my bed, and we attempted to rest. After the first nightmare, it was inevitable—he lay down next to me *in* my bed. There was no other way to soothe my screams, as the visions of my dead family members haunted me.

The third day, after having met Uncle Frank, I ultimately decided to stay. That evening, Tony again made an effort to sleep in the sleeping bag, next to the bed. I was emotionally and physically drained, from the prior restless nights, and was finally about to close my eyes, when a flash of headlights brightened the bedroom. I could hear the quiet hum of a vehicle approaching. Before I could react, I felt Tony's hand reach up and pull me down to the floor. His chest cushioned my fall and suddenly, his body covered mine as he rolled on top of me and put a finger to my lips.

"Shh!" he warned. My eyes protruded in fear. "Follow me," he whispered. I forced my weakened limbs to move and trailed behind him. We crawled out of the bedroom into the hallway. He began the descent down the staircase until I stopped him.

"No!" I whispered urgently. "Don't go down there."

"We have to! Staying up here, we're sitting ducks. There is no way out!"

I reluctantly nodded and held onto one of his strong arms with all my strength. His hand pressed against my body, holding me as closely behind him as he could, while we stole down the stairs and ran into the kitchen. He brought me to the back door and softly pushed me down next to the end of the cabinets. I heard the slam of a car door and gasped.

"Don't move! I'll be back," he encouraged.

"Please, Tony! Don't leave me!"

"Laura, you have to trust me." He kissed my forehead and crept back into the great room. I crawled across the kitchen, ignoring his orders. I pressed against the kitchen wall near the entrance and peeked to see Tony grasp the wood poker from the fireplace. He ran to the front door and pushed his back against the wall. He raised the poker.

A knock on the door startled me and I covered my mouth to keep from screaming. I hid back behind the wall. There was a stretch of silence and then another loud knock.

"Tony!" Uncle Frank shouted through the front door. "It's me . . . open up!"

I felt relief wash over me like a surge. My head fell into my hands and I burst into tears. I heard Tony swear under his breath. He turned on the light and opened the door for Uncle Frank.

"Uncle! You scared the crap out of us!" he admitted, before placing the poker back on its rack and running into the kitchen to find me. He knelt down before me and placed his hands on my shoulders. "It's okay. It's just Uncle Frank," he soothed.

I wrapped my arms around his neck and cried. Tony pulled me up onto my feet and sat me down at the kitchen table.

Uncle Frank entered the kitchen with a look of regret. “I’m so sorry, sweetie! I didn’t mean to scare you both. But the weather man predicted more snowfall tonight and I figured this was the best time for me to come and bring Tony’s bedroom set,” he explained. “After I leave, the snow will cover my tracks, and there will be no evidence that a vehicle took the path.”

“Well, geez, Uncle! It could have waited!” Tony insisted.

“If we’re going to foster her, we do it by my rules. I’m just as responsible for Laura and I want to make this as right as possible. Besides, I had no way to contact you. I certainly didn’t mean to scare you. If you help me, we can get your bed set up and I’ll be out of your hair, so you can get some rest.” Uncle Frank took a second look at me and detected my anxiety. “Are you okay?”

I tried to gather myself, as I did not want him to feel worse. I nodded at the question. To my reluctance, Tony and Uncle Frank then began the process of carrying Tony’s bedroom set into the spare bedroom. Before long, the bed was assembled in the center of the room. The small nightstand was placed next to the bed and the dresser was placed on the outside wall, near the window, opposite of the closet. Finally, the bed was set with fresh linens and a warm comforter.

Uncle Frank apologized once more and then said his ‘good night.’ Tony and I, at last, ascended the stairs together again.

He grasped my hand and whispered, “You going to be okay all by yourself?”

I swallowed the lump in my throat. “Yeah,” I lied.

“If you need me, just shout.”

“Thanks,” I whispered. Tony squeezed my hand and watched me enter my room.

Once under my covers, I felt stiff and uncomfortable, forcing my eyes closed. Still, sleep decided it would not come. When I finally could not handle it any longer, I quietly peeled the covers back and left my room. Tony’s door was ajar. The full-size bed was smaller, in comparison to the queen we had shared the past few nights. Nevertheless, I slipped in next to him, hoping to go unnoticed. His face was inches from mine and suddenly I could see that his eyes were wide open.

“Can’t sleep?” he whispered.

“I’m sorry. Did I wake you?” I asked regretfully.

“No. I can’t sleep either.”

“Do you care if I lay down here with you for a few minutes? I’m still a little shaken up.”

He reached his arm out and pulled me closer. I shivered at his touch. "Not at all. Having you here now, maybe I can fall asleep, too."

I closed my eyes and finally found sleep.

And so, it continued in this manner. Regardless of Uncle Frank's rules and our better judgment, we found that neither of us could get good rest unless we were at one another's side. The bed in the spare bedroom served as nothing more than a way to appease Uncle Frank's intent for some respectability. I ignored the guilt of lying to him, because there was not any other way for me to be able to sleep unless Tony was beside me. His presence and loving comfort helped me to move past the grief of losing my family, and settle into a new life with *him*.

***

October 1975

Two years later, the bond that had formed between Tony and I, was becoming more than that tie of friendship. I had already turned 16 the month prior to our first kiss and though we never expressed it outwardly, Tony and I were falling deeply in love. It had become obvious in our gaze and in the way we touched. Tony was ever mindful with his manners, stepping over and beyond the characteristics of a gentleman. He was becoming my actual soul.

Though we lived alone, our time together was limited. Uncle Frank became the fatherly figure I yearned for—and sometimes annoyed, since I sought out 'alone time' with Tony more than the very air that I breathed. It was only on Friday evenings that we three did not eat supper together, as Uncle Frank remained at the store after it closed to restock for the week. Otherwise, every day, after work, they would both come home to find my home-cooked meals and some relaxation after a hard day.

Uncle Frank was perpetually in my business when it came to my studies as well. He was always making sure that we used our evening time wisely, reading or studying. Ultimately, I was more than happy that they had 'unofficially' adopted me as a family member.

One Saturday evening, he passed the salad bowl to me, while we sat together for a meal. "So, tell me," he quizzed, poking at the last piece of breaded chicken on his dish. "What does Tony have you reading right now?"

Because Tony and I both had a passion for reading, as part of my English curriculum, Tony regularly checked out educational books, novels, and popular magazines from the local library for me to read.

Tony let out a laugh. "You're going to love this one, Uncle."

He looked questioningly at Tony and then to me.

"We just finished Shakespeare's 'Romeo and Juliet'," I answered, placing a few leaves of the salad on my plate.

Uncle Frank immediately put his palm to his forehead. "Oh no," he shouted with a laugh.

"Why," I asked. "What's wrong with 'Romeo and Juliet'?"

"I hate that book!" he cried out.

Tony quickly swallowed his last bite and nonchalantly added, "Uncle Frank thinks it has a stupid ending."

Uncle Frank waved a hand in the air. "It's so depressing!"

"It is!" I exclaimed. "How horrible that they both die! I was devastated!"

"That's the whole point," Tony explained. "Don't you two get it? The circumstances that led to the death of both Juliet and Romeo were precisely what made the story so awesome!"

"All I know is that their families were horrible," I stated. "It was all their fault!"

Tony laughed and stood to clear his dish. "You can't always have a happy ending," he emphasized. "Life isn't always a bowl of cherries."

Uncle Frank threw in, "Look, if I'm going to read a book, I want to escape the ugly of this world and get carried off to another place and time. A happy one, I might add."

"Agreed, Uncle Frank." I winked at him and he winked back. I then ate the last bite of lettuce from my plate.

We all stood to clear the table and our dishes.

"Just keep reading, Laura. Reading will not only take you places you've never been, but reading makes you smart." He pointed to his temple. He always had such sound fatherly wisdom for me.

After clearing the table and washing the dishes, he finally kissed my cheek and was off to head home to his apartment. I stood on the porch steps and watched his figure vanish into the dark forest. He would walk back to the store and drive home from there.

It seemed that was the only way to keep our 'abandoned house' a secret. No one could know that the narrow trail in the woods, led to a home that housed an orphaned kid, who lived with an orphaned adult. I was happy they were taking extreme measures to keep me hidden, even if it meant my solitude. At that point, I wanted nothing to come between what I was feeling for Tony and what I guessed he was feeling for me.

The wind blew an unusually warm breeze through my hair. The leaves had long since started to fall and I watched them scatter across the yard.

Tony came up next to me and leaned forward on the porch bannister. "Warm out, isn't it?'

I nodded, approving. "Strange. Not the temperature you would expect for fall."

He crossed his arms over the rail and flashed me a smile. The wind played with a loose lock of his hair and it softly fell onto his forehead. Looking back out into the lawn, he suddenly frowned. "I know what I'll be doing tomorrow on my only day off," he sighed with exaggeration.

I leaned forward next to him and copied his pose, brushing his arm with mine. "And what's that?" I flirted.

His eyes caught mine. They were deep and he looked at me with intensity. My heart pounded against my ribs. There was a long silence as we held one another's gaze.

Nervously, I broke the quiet. "Tony?"

He blushed and smiled again. "I'm sorry. Your eyes distracted me."

I blushed now and looked down, breaching the hold he had over me. "What were you saying?"

He laughed and shook his head, seeming to recall what the discussion was about. "I've got a lot of work to do out here before the snow comes," he announced with a pout.

I stood straight and looked out into the large yard. "Well, I'll help you," I offered.

Tony stood to face me. "Really?"

"Of course," I replied. "I had some housework to do, but it's nothing that can't wait."

"Thanks. That'd be great! It's a date. We'll have fun," he decided.

"A date?" I complained. "You're gonna make me work? That's not quite what I had in mind for a date," I teased.

Tony chuckled, "I promise, I'll make it worth your while. Then, on another night, I'll show you what it's like to go on a real date," he promised.

My heart began to pump with speed again. The thought of going on a date with Tony, made my whole body tremor. "You got a deal," I finally whispered. I extended my hand and he shook it. Our eyes met again. I could not help but blush. Not even the rustling wind could lure Tony's attention away. I caught a chill and shivered.

"Come on. It's getting chillier. Let's get in." Tony grasped my hand and led me to the door. He opened it for me. His hand fell to the small of my back, sending more shivers down my spine. I could not deny that his touch was electrifying. "Come by the couch and I'll get you a blanket," he offered.

I sat on the couch. Tony snatched a blanket from the closet. He pulled it over me, tucking it in to warm me. "Thank you," I whispered.

He plopped down next to me. "So, you really think 'Romeo and Juliet' stunk, huh?"

I giggled, "Of course not. It really is so romantic and sweet, but if I were the writer, I would have ended it entirely different."

Tony's eyebrows came together, as he reflected. "Okay, Shakespeare. How would you have ended the story?"

I thought about the events in the tale and contemplated. "I would have had Romeo whisk Juliet off into the woods, never to be seen again!"

A smile played on Tony's face. He relaxed his head against the headrest. "Oh yeah, and where would they have gone?" he probed.

I pondered a moment longer, playing with the holes in the knitted blanket. My gaze moved upward until my eyes adhered to his. "He would have found her a place to live in an 'abandoned house', where no one would ever find them."

Tony lifted his head and kept my stare. His eyes were smiling. "Then what?" he quizzed.

"There, they would spend all their time together, getting to know one another, like no two others in the whole world."

"Would they have jobs?" Tony baited.

"Nope! Their only job was to love one another."

"I see," he said with seriousness. "And then…"

I deliberated a moment, and then concluded, "They would secretly get married and spend the rest of their lives living off the land, with their 10 children!"

"TEN!" Tony laughed at my fantasy. "They certainly would keep very busy, making 10 babies." I laughed out loud with him. "I like your version better," Tony admitted.

"Told ya," I played.

"Ten kids, huh?" he chuckled.

I blushed. "Okay, maybe that was a bit much," I answered.

Tony laughed again. "Laura," he whispered, leaning his head back down on the headrest. His eyes never left mine. "You are so refreshing. Where did you come from and how was I so fortunate to have found you?"

My face flushed again at his openness. I lowered my gaze apprehensively. I could not find the words or the courage to meet his sharp watch. I said the only thing I could to relieve the strong tension that had suddenly filled the air.

"You just lucked out."

Tony roared with laughter. He pulled me into a hug.

Later that evening, while resting in our bed, I turned to my right side expecting to find Tony asleep. Instead, I caught his gaze in the light of the moon.

He smiled at me.

I returned a smile.

"Still awake?" I whispered.

"Can't sleep," he admitted.

"What's on your mind?"

"Your version of 'Romeo and Juliet'," he breathed. His face lit with laughter.

"You liked that, didn't you?" I pressed.

"You have a vivid imagination and you're a sucker for happy endings."

"Hey, I'll admit it. I'm a believer that love can conquer all."

"I love your optimism. It's contagious."

"Don't you believe in happy endings, Tony Warren?" I asked.

"Not until you walked into my life." He closed his eyes, letting a smile lift the corners of his mouth.

I fell asleep with a grin on my face as well.

The next day, after a quick breakfast, I threw a load of laundry into the washing machine, while Tony gathered the rakes and gardening tools we needed to clean up the yard. I exited the house through the back door finding that the warm weather had decided to stay another day. The shorts and buttoned-down short-sleeve shirt I tied at my waste, would keep me plenty cool as I worked. Tony had slipped into an old pair of jeans, but wore a white tank without a shirt. I was concerned it might be too cool out for him, as it was still quite windy. Yet, his forehead beaded with perspiration from the work he had already begun.

Throughout the morning, the jesting and flirting that had transpired between us the night prior, kept us in a jolly mood. Tony whistled while he worked. I sang quietly to the radio we had playing through the open window of the kitchen. Now and again, I would catch him watching me, and likewise, he caught me staring at him. It seemed a silent banter had materialized between us.

Meanwhile, we had managed to cut down what we had sown with love that past spring. I had discovered that I had a green thumb and a knack for gardening. Tony then helped me to landscape and decorate the exterior of our house, keeping me occupied in the summer months, while he was away at work during the day.

Finally, we pruned back the perennial plants and flowers and pulled out the annuals in our pots and flowerbeds. We gave one last trim to the bushes that decorated the little landscaping, near the porch, making sure to clean up the trimmings as we went. By midafternoon, we stopped for a quick break to eat a few sandwiches.

After, I quickly placed the first load of washed laundry into the dryer. Tony continued with the work outside and began with raking the leaves. When I finished with the clothes, I exited the house to find that he already had a large mound of leaves gathered.

I grasped a rake and began at one end of the yard. Tony worked the other half. Gradually we made our way to the center, until we worked side by side, having created a mountain of leaves behind us that we would later dump in a nearby woods.

Unexpectedly, a mass of leaves rattled through the air into my face and hair. I turned instantly to find Tony raking swiftly, not realizing he was tossing the leaves on me. I raked fast, spewing the leaves back at him. They landed in his hair and even stuck to his tank top. He turned to see the laughter on my face.

"Oh, yeah?" He quizzed.

Tony raked furiously, quickly burying me in the crisp, dry leaves. I blew the leaves off my face and tried to pitch the dry foliage toward him. When I could not get them on him fast enough, I reached for the pile behind me. Tony dropped his rake and ran at me. He tackled me into the mound and we rolled around, each fighting to get on top of the other. I laughed with my whole heart, while flinging the crunching leaves.

I could not see what I was doing, at one point, and closed my eyes, grasping for his arms. He pulled me to him and we rolled in the mass of leaves now flattened. Tony pinned me to the brittle ground and we laughed breathlessly. Our eyes met and our laughter quieted.

He looked at my mouth. Slowly, he brushed his lips against mine. The sensation of his lips touching mine, sent feelings through me I never knew I had. His body leaned in closer, touching mine. He was now propped up on his elbows; our legs were intertwined. Tony reached up and caressed my face. He held my chin and pressed his mouth to mine in a passionate kiss.

I felt as though my heart would burst with excitement. He gently lifted his head and our eyes met again.

"Laura . . ."

"Wow," I could not help but whisper.

A smile fell across his face and he chuckled. "Yeah, wow!" he whispered in return.

"That was amazing," I admitted.

"That was phenomenal!"

"Better than 'Romeo and Juliet'?"

"Better!" He lowered his head and kissed me again.

Our kiss strengthened until we were both breathless. Tony lifted his head from mine and sought out my gaze. He picked a leaf from my hair and a grin fell across his face. My arms were holding his tightly, afraid he would pull away. But we remained glued to the ground, unwilling to separate. The wind blew and the rustling of leaves was the only sound above our accelerated heartbeats.

"What do we do?" he finally broke the silence.

At first, I was unsure what he meant with his questioning. "Don't stop," I whispered. He started to quietly chuckle at my statement. "What?" I asked.

Tony played with the leaves in my hair. "I don't want to stop kissing you either, but that's not what I meant."

I searched his face for an answer. "What do we do about . . . our kiss?"

He lowered his forehead to mine and kissed me briefly. ". . . About these feelings?"

I was stumped—unable to answer his inquiry. I did not know where our feelings would take us. I only knew that I did not want them to end.

"Is it wrong?" I whispered in a frightened voice.

Tony shook his head in 'no'. "It's never felt more right!"

"Then, I don't understand."

Tony rolled over onto his back pulling me with him. I leaned up on my elbow and stared down into his face.

"Laura, I'm 20. You're only 16."

"So what?"

He placed his free hand behind his head, propping it up so he could better see me. "You're so young."

My heart sank into my stomach. *Was he already regretting sharing a kiss with me?* Tears filled my eyes. "Does that change how you feel about me?"

Tony immediately softened upon seeing my tears. "Laura . . . I'm falling in love with you," he admitted.

A tear trickled down my cheek. I lowered my head and kissed him again. He wrapped his arms around me and pulled me even closer.

"I'm already in love with you," I whispered.

My gnarled hair fell forward. He lifted his hands and pulled it back, cupping my face. "You are so beautiful. I'm so glad you're in my life. But I have to be responsible and protect and watch over you, first. As much as I don't want to hold back on expressing my feelings for you, I have to."

I finally understood what he was trying to convey. "Are you worried Uncle Frank will be concerned about us?"

"Exactly! He's going to want to make sure we can still live here alone, with no funny business going on. You know what I mean?" Tony winked and I giggled.

"Now we'll never get any 'alone time'!" I cried.

Tony laughed with me and we sat up. "He's going to be here soon with that pizza he promised to make. Let's finish cleaning up this mess, and then we'll go clean up before dinner."

He pulled me up. We stood so close, that I could feel the pounding of his heart. He lowered his head and kissed me. My arms found their way around his neck and our kiss intensified. I stood on the points of my feet, while he squeezed me against his strong chest. Suddenly, my feet were lifted off the ground as he spun me around. We laughed and kissed again.

"Uh, excuse me! What's going on here?"

My stomach immediately knotted at the sound of Uncle Frank's voice. Tony held me still, hindering me from making a single move. He turned to Uncle Frank, who stood in the path of our narrow roadway, holding grocery bags in his hands.

"I'm kissing her, Uncle," Tony divulged.

Uncle Frank walked across the yard toward us. His feet crunched the few leaves we scattered in our wrestling match.

"Well, I can see that, Tony. How long has this been going on?" he pressed with concern.

"You just missed our first kiss!" Tony proudly announced.

Uncle Frank's face was serious. "I knew this was going to happen. Do you realize that this can cause all kinds of complications?"

I lowered my gaze, unable to meet his eyes. I really did not understand what all the fuss was about.

"Uncle, I love her," he proclaimed.

"Laura?" Uncle Frank quizzed.

I lifted my eyes and met his hard stare. "I've loved him from the moment he found me."

Uncle Frank glared at the both of us for a moment. "Laura, why don't you go on in and clean up? Tony, you finish up out here. I'm heading inside to make us some dinner. We'll talk about this later."

Tony finally released his hold over me, and Uncle Frank followed me toward the house. I shook the leaves out of my hair and off my clothes before I entered the back door. Uncle Frank walked in, placing the bags of groceries on the table. I quietly entered the kitchen. He seemed upset, while unloading the grocery bags with the ingredients for our pizza. I approached him and rested a gentle hand on his arm.

"Uncle Frank? Don't be mad. Nothing is going on. Tony and I really did just kiss for the very first time today," I tried to explain.

Uncle Frank immediately relaxed. He turned to me, placing a hand on my shoulder. "Laura, it couldn't thrill me more that you and Tony would eventually end up together. But there is so much at stake. You are too young. I just want you both to be very careful and think of your every move."

"I understand, Uncle Frank."

"Go on up and get showered. You have leaves still stuck in your hair," he said with a chuckle.

I leaned in and kissed his cheek. "Thank you for always caring so much. If I haven't told you this lately . . . I love you, Uncle Frank."

His face flushed and he seemed moved by my display of affection. "Go on, git! You're making me get all worked up!"

I grinned at his frustration and left the kitchen. I could hear him mumble to himself about, 'those darn kids'.

The warm shower was exactly what I needed to relieve some of the tension I felt building up in my shoulders. After, I dressed and made myself presentable to eat dinner with my little family. As I descended the stairs into the living room, I could hear whispers from the kitchen. The tantalizing aroma of a home-cooked pizza filled the air.

"I knew this would happen, Tony. It was inevitable! Living here with her—day in and day out."

"What do you want me to do, Uncle? Pretend I don't feel what I feel."

"It was a bad set up from the start. I should have moved her into the apartment with me."

"But she isn't safe there," Tony added.

My heart doubled in rhythm. *Living with Tony, the past two years, had been my salvation!*

"I know, I'm just worried."

I sighed with relief. Uncle Frank released a heavy sigh as well. I could see him now pacing the kitchen floor. I slowly approached the kitchen. "Still, it's not right, Tony! Don't you realize how serious this is? You are playing a dangerous game. Temptation will be lurking around every corner!" he insisted.

"Uncle, I think you're 'jumping the gun' a bit. I just kissed her for the very first time today. You don't have to worry about anything happening. I promise you, it won't. I would never take advantage of her. I love her too much and I don't want anything to happen to mess up a future with her."

My heart leapt at his answer. He wanted a future with me.

"By God, Tony, you better stick to that mind frame! She is an extraordinary girl. Don't you mess this up or I'll have your head!"

Tony feigned grief. "Man, I'm beginning to think you love her more than me."

"I do," Uncle Frank teased. "Now pass me that oven mitt. Dinner is ready."

I used that as my cue to enter. We ate the majority of dinner together in silence. Uncle Frank kept stopping to look at each of us. When Tony finally had enough, he questioned him.

"What?"

Uncle Frank swallowed his food. "I know you may not believe me when I say this . . . but I'm happy."

I looked at Uncle Frank with a questioning gaze. "You are?"

He nodded and added, "I figured this would eventually happen. I watched it every day—just waiting. Now that I see your happiness, it warms my heart. Still, I can't help but feel concerned. You are both young and sometimes feelings are hard to control. I won't have you two living in this house together in sin!"

I nearly choked on my pizza. "Uncle Frank, you offend me!" I finally expressed.

"I'm sorry, dear. I'm a man. I know the ways of the world. You can have the best of intentions and still make mistakes. I just don't want that to happen to you," he explained.

"Uncle, I don't ever want to disappoint you, or my Momma, but mostly God, by breaking that commandment. That's not what I believe in and that's not how I was raised," I defended.

Uncle Frank looked from me to Tony. "You both need to understand. I know you want to do what is right. But being together like this . . . you are playing with fire. I just want to warn you. Be careful. That's all I'm saying."

Uncle Frank had serious reservations. Looking back, I realize that his counsel was wise. At the same time, the circumstances we were in, demanded that I remain hidden, as well as Tony. Uncle Frank was right to worry, only I did not realize then, what his misgivings were truly about. I only knew that that day was the start of something amazing. Something that neither my mind nor my heart could have ever conceived.

I stood on the porch and waved goodbye to Uncle Frank, that evening. Tony stepped up behind me and pulled me into his arms. The warm air was gone, replacing it—an icy chill. He rubbed my arms to warm me. I turned around and looked up into his beautiful face. He leaned in and pecked my lips.

"Bedtime?" he asked. I nodded and followed him back into the safety of our home.

While Tony showered, I climbed into bed and turned on the lamp on my nightstand. I waited in anticipation for him to join me. On the small table, I grasped the next novel he wanted me to read, 'The Count of Monte Cristo' by Alexandre Dumas. Fighting to concentrate, I struggled to read.

Since the very first night we had arrived at the house, I could not recall an evening when I felt more nervous to lie beside Tony in my bed. Uncle Frank's words were shouting out to me. I did not want him to think that we were so weak that we could fall into temptation so easily. Yet, I feared the emotions that kissing Tony awakened within me that day.

When Tony finished showering, he entered the bedroom with his damp hair neatly combed back, and a freshly shaved face.

"Still up?" he asked.

I lifted the book. "Thought I'd catch the first chapter."

He pulled the covers back and sat on the crisp sheets. "Oh, you're starting it already?"

I flipped to the back of the book and looked at the back cover. "Looks interesting," I replied. My voice gave my nervousness away, as it quivered. I tried to clear my throat. "If you're tired, I'll turn the light off. I can start the book tomorrow."

Tony lay down, turning on his side to face me. He propped his head up onto his hand and grabbed the book. He placed it on his nightstand and turned back to me. I played with the covers, trying to remain cool.

"Look at me," he firmly commanded. He gently grasped my chin and forced his gaze. "Why are you so nervous? It's just me."

My hand traveled up and caressed his solid arm. "Tony . . ."

"Laura, our kisses today . . . I've never felt more alive," he admitted.

I closed my eyes, loving the touch of his hands on my face. "You make me feel things, I've never felt before. These feelings almost scare me."

He reached under the covers and pulled me to him. I trembled within.

"What's the matter?" he quizzed. He knew me too well.

I stuttered, "I . . . Nothing . . . Well . . . What Uncle Frank said, really bothered me." I finally blurted.

Tony sighed, "Me too."

"Does he think that little of me?"

"No, he thinks that little of *me*. I'm older than you and he expects more of me. It's because he loves us so much, that he fears we'll fail. But the thing is . . . he's right. We really should be sleeping in separate beds. I should be in my own bed, right now. But I'm not going to lie, I don't want to sleep anywhere but beside you," Tony confessed. He nuzzled his face into my neck.

I quaked from my very core. His touch was exhilarating. For the first time, I was speechless. Tony reached up and caressed my face again.

"Tell me what's on your mind?" he pleaded.

I held his hand to my cheek. So many emotions moved me. I was anxious that Uncle Frank's suggestion would come to pass and I would be forced to move into the apartment with him. Yet, I worried that if Tony continued to sleep in my bed, the feelings that moved me at that very moment, would lead me to act on my desires.

"Laura?" he begged.

"Tony," I respired with sadness. "Lying next to you every night . . . it's the best part of my day. I don't want you to sleep in your bed and I don't want to move in with Uncle. Your company gives me a sense of . . . protection. I realize that things will never be the same now that we've crossed that threshold and we've openly shared our feelings.

"No," I continued, "Maybe it's not right to share a bed when we're not married. But it's just a place to rest. That's all."

Tony nodded in agreement and loosened his hold on me. "And that's what it will continue to be—a place where we can come to rest, to talk, and to dream. I don't ever want you to feel like I'm expecting anything more than what we already share. I love your company; I love your friendship; I love the way you take care of Uncle Frank and me. One day, if it's God's will, we can make this more. The right way."

I lifted my hand and touched his smooth face. He grasped my hand and pressed it to his lips.

"Although, I must admit," he whispered. "Having you this close, I don't know if I can refrain from holding you. We have to be strong enough to be able to lay this close, hold and kiss one another, without getting carried away. I think we can do that. After two years of me hiding what I feel for you—I know I can. What about you?"

I agreed, moving in just a tiny bit closer. My lips touched his, filling my stomach with fluttering butterflies. "Yes, Tony. We gotta do what's right."

He pulled me closer still and kissed me.

I knew at that very moment that there would never be another's kiss that could give me the sense of love and refuge that Tony's kisses did.

CHAPTER 13

Psalm 25:16

"Turn to me, Oh God, and be gracious to me, for I am lonely and afflicted."

Sunday, December 24
Christmas Eve

"What's so important that you come to disrupt my family time?" asked Mario Galante.

Alfonso respected this man. He said what he felt, no matter how blunt. "I apologize, sir, but this was the only time I could get away unnoticed. Valente's been keeping me busy."

"Doing what?"

"Don Mario, I'm moving in closer than I ever thought. He has grown to rely on me. He may not have an empire to give to me, but he has promised me his legitimate business. He's been training me since I last saw you," Alfonso revealed.

Mario sat back in his large leather chair, rubbing his hands together slowly. "Tell me, Alfonso, because I am growing more and more impatient. How does this benefit me?"

Alfonso started to panic. He must not upset this man if he wanted to live. "Sir, it's imperative to the plan that Valente completely trust me. I'll be able to lure him and Giacalone in at the right time and we can take them out."

Mario bore his eyes into Alfonso's. His bodyguards stepped up behind Alfonso grabbing his arms. "Hey, what's going on?" he asked with a tremor to his voice.

"You've yet to show me proof that these two plan to retaliate. You better be telling me the truth. You know what a mistake it would be to lure *me* into an unnecessary war with Valente." Mario's men dropped Alfonso's arms.

Alfonso stepped forward toward the desk. He laughed nervously. "Don Mario, I promise you, you will not regret your decision to be rid of them. You don't need me to tell you how dangerous Valente can be. Not to mention, what a whack-job Giacalone is. Those two together are a lethal combination. I'll get the proof you require. Then all I ask is for one of your men to help me. I'll even set the job up. You need not lift a finger."

Mario leaned forward placing both his elbows on his desk. In a threatening tone, he whispered, "Get the proof or you will *not* live to regret it. My nephew Gino will help you take them out. He'd love to finish the job that Marcs could not." He laughed menacingly, "How ironic. Gino killed Giacalone's and Valente's families and now he'll help bring it all to an end. Don't mess this up."

"You have my word," Alfonso promised.

He walked out of the house on weak knees. Alfonso knew what was at stake. It was time he sent his plan into action.

****

It was Christmas Eve, and Laura had yet to hear from Tony. She prayed that they would have some time together on Christmas Day. As she showered and dressed herself that morning, she thought of the previous year's Christmas. She was still mourning Tony's death and had fallen into a deep depression. Somehow, she found herself in the same despair. She was still in a funk, only now Tony was alive. *How could it be possible?* Had an angel came down and told her last year that Tony was alive, she would have been overjoyed. Now as close as they had come to living their dream, it still was not close enough. *Was she asking too much*?

Laura threw on a pair of jeans and a loose-fitting, baby-doll top. She styled her hair, letting the loose curls free. Finishing, she applied the last touches of makeup to her face and skipped down the stairs. Laura picked her coat from the closet and put her shoes on.

"Where are you off to, this morning?" John quizzed, startling her.

"Oh, hey Dad. Just running out to the mall for some last-minute shopping," she answered.

"You're going to join the millions of crazies at the mall?"

Laura followed him into the kitchen and snatched a banana off the counter. "Yup. I came up with a great idea for part of Nonno's gift. I shouldn't be long. I'll definitely be back to help prepare dinner for Uncle Joe and the gang."

John leaned against the counter top and watched her carefully strip a banana of its peel. "Have you heard from Tony?" he gently pressed.

"No," Laura returned. "It looks as though I'll be spending the holidays without him." Her eyes filled, but she quickly sniffed the tears away. John opened his arms and Laura hugged him. "I'm so blessed to have you and Mom. I would be lost without you," she cried.

"We'll always be here for you."

"I miss Tammy."

"Me too. It's going to be hard without her this Christmas. Mom and I are going to the cemetery tomorrow morning. You coming?"

"Of course," Laura whispered. "I better go." John released his hold and helped Laura with her coat. She grabbed her purse and keys, and left saying goodbye. Laura stepped into the garage and entered her car. As she was about to turn the ignition, John ran out waving his arms. Laura rolled down her window.

"It's Tony. He's on the phone," John called out.

Laura quickly exited her car and ran into the house. John handed her the telephone and left the kitchen to give her privacy. Laura's whole body quivered, as she placed the receiver to her ear.

"Hello?"

"Hi," Tony whispered.

Laura strained to listen. "Hi."

"I called to tell you that I'm going to be leaving town for the next couple days. I have some business to take care of and Uncle Frank will be coming to keep me company. Maybe a little time away will do me good," he considered aloud.

Laura did not know what to say. She struggled to find the right words.

"Laura, are you there?"

She swallowed the protruding lump in her throat. "I'm going to miss you," she whispered.

Silence.

Finally, Tony murmured, "I miss you, already."

His words cut deep. Laura felt the tears slide down her cheeks. "Then don't go."

"I'm sorry, I have to go. I'll call you when I get back."

"Tony wait . . ." Laura struggled to hear him.

"What?"

"I love you," she cried.

"I-I-I'll call you."

Laura heard the dial tone. He hung up. She placed the receiver down and let a sob escape her. She ran into the bathroom and retrieved a tissue. Wiping her tears, Laura found herself growing angry. She did not deserve to be treated this way. She was not about to let him ruin another important day. Sure, she felt compassion for what he was going through. Yes, she loved him and wanted to spend the rest of her life with him. But this roller-coaster of emotions was taking its toll and she was near done.

Laura blew her nose, retouched her makeup, and stalked out of the house. It was Christmas Eve, her favorite holiday, and no one could take that from her. Tonight, she and her parents would spend the evening at home with Uncle Joe, Aunt Bernadette, and the boys. On Christmas Day, they would go to mass, visit Tammy's grave, and head to Uncle Joe's for dinner. She made plans to spend the day after Christmas with Nonno Nino. She had plenty to do to keep her busy.

Yet, her heart ached so much! Laura shook her head and drove away. She would not go down that path.

****

"How did she take the news?" Uncle Frank asked Tony.

"Obviously, she sounded very disappointed. But I have to do this Uncle."

"You couldn't wait until after Christmas?" Frank grilled.

"No. I gathered the courage to call them. They said they would meet with me. I'm doing this now, while it's all so fresh to me," Tony explained.

"What can they tell you that'll make the slightest difference? You can't change the past, Tony."

Tony drove his truck at a rapid speed. He looked at his uncle sitting next to him. "No, but maybe I can understand how he became that way. If I can just comprehend even a little, maybe I can try to forgive him and move on."

"You really think your uncles are going to open up to you?"

Tony thought about it for a moment. He would tell them what he had discovered. As horribly humiliating as it was, he would tell them. "I don't know if they're anything like him—but I'll take my chances."

"I hope it's worth missing Christmas with Laura. You're not pushing her away again, are you?" Frank grilled.

Tony let out a loud sigh. "Uncle, I love that girl so much, that it physically hurts. But I'm so messed up right now, that I don't know what to do. Maybe these couple days away will help me to figure out what I want."

"Ton, you know I love you and I'll stick by you, no matter what. But I've warned you before and I'm warning you now, if you leave that girl, you're making the biggest mistake of your life."

"Precisely! *I'd* be making a mistake, because *I'll* never find another like her. Is that fair to Laura—that I stay with her selfishly, when she could have a chance at a normal life with someone who has it together?" Tony argued.

"Ton, I don't know anyone who has it better together than you. You're a hard worker, a loving man, you own your own home, and you're responsible and respectful. What more can she ask for?"

"For someone without all this emotional junk," Tony claimed.

"You'll get better. You're already getting better. Look at the progress you've made. God will help you," Frank encouraged, placing a hand on Tony's shoulder.

Tony stole a glance at Frank and smiled. "You'd make a great shrink."

Frank burst out laughing. "Yeah, well, you keep this up and I'm going to shrink your head with my fist."

Tony finally laughed.

****

Laura strolled through the mall, looking for a specific gift for Nonno Nino. She had already purchased him a beautiful evening robe to wear around the house. Now she sought a gold necklace with a cross. She walked into the same jewelry store where she had purchased John's gift and Tony's ring. Looking through the display, she found a resurrected Jesus on a handsome cross, with a manly chain. After pricing it out, Laura decided to buy it for him.

As she made her purchase, Laura began to feel a bit shaky. She decided to grab a quick bite and swiftly walked to the mall directory to look for the nearest pretzel stand. A strange feeling came over her and she glanced around sensing eyes on her. *Overly paranoid again!* She continued to look at the directory. Finding the pretzel shop on the map, Laura moved toward it.

The mall was overflowing with shoppers of every age. Everyone seemed to be squeezing in those last-minute gifts. Laura thought about Nonno's gift. She had not intended on spending so much on him, but he had shown her so much love, so much support. She could not help herself. She worked hard and saved her money. *Since she only had a few people to buy for, why not splurge on them? They deserved it!*

Laura strolled toward the pretzel shop, when a memory of Tammy abruptly came to mind. She remembered how much fun they had shopping together the year prior and how they had bumped into Paul that evening. It was so obvious to Laura now, as she recalled that night, how much Tammy was in love with Paul from the very beginning. *How she missed her company and her silly laughter!* She immediately pictured Paul's handsome face. Feeling the absence of both their presence, made Laura stop mid-trek. Tears began to swell in her eyes. She missed them so much.

Sifting through her purse for a tissue, she made herself move forward until she finally reached the pretzel stand. Laura dried her eyes, once more. She stood behind a long line of hungry shoppers and wondered whether to leave and eat at home or stay and wait it out. In front of her, a large man waited patiently. Laura looked carefully at his familiar backside. Stepping to his right, she was not surprised to find Alfonso.

He did a double take and seemed amusingly pleased to see her. "Laura, what are you doing here?"

"Probably the same thing you are," she articulated.

"You here alone?" he asked.

"Yes. How about you?"

"Yup, me, myself, and I," he jested.

Laura smiled, trying to find a way to put into words how she would ask him why he sent the flowers—and why the conspicuous card.

"You feeling alright?" he examined. "Your eyes are red."

"It being our first Christmas without Tammy and all, I was just remembering what it was like last year having her around," Laura confessed.

Alfonso's face grew serious for the first time. "I'm sorry. I remember what it was like the first year without my Ma. It stinks, doesn't it?"

Laura laughed through her tears. "Yeah, you can put it that way."

"Come on, I'll buy you a pretzel to cheer you up," he offered.

"You don't have to do that. Besides, I've gotta get home soon. We're expecting company and I want to help my mom with dinner."

"What are you gonna do, eat your pretzel while you drive? That's an accident waiting to happen. It'll just be five minutes—ten tops. Join me," he insisted.

Laura agreed, hoping that the opportunity would arise for her to confront him. Alfonso purchased two large pretzels and two sodas. He paid the cashier and guided Laura to a table.

"Eat up," he encouraged, "before you cause another scene and pass out. Then I'll have to pretend I'm your husband again. On second thought . . ."

"Very funny," Laura uttered. "You think I like drawing that much attention. I'm a shy girl." She picked a piece of pretzel and put it in her mouth.

"You, shy? If you're trying to not get attention, you better put a bag over your head," Alfonso insisted.

"What's that supposed to mean?" Laura cried.

"Come on, Laura. Don't you see it? I'm sorry. I better just shut up before I open my mouth and insert my foot."

Laura burst into laughter. She watched Alfonso take a large bite of his pretzel. He quickly chased it down with the soda. "What?" she insisted.

"You're so beautiful. You can have any man in this mall, including me. Yet, you wait around for a guy who treats you like dirt. Enlighten me?"

Laura swallowed the pretzel and wiped her mouth. She sipped the soda and leaned into the table to get closer to him. "Do you see this big round pouch right here?" she whispered, pointing to her belly.

"Yeah. Groovy top, by the way. It makes your eyes even greener."

"'Groovy'? 'Groovy' is out."

"Nice?"

"Better, and thank you, but don't try to distract me. I'm in love with Tony. He's the father of my child. You may not understand why he is the way he is, but I do. I love him enough to see past his issues. Because, when the dust settles, I don't want to regret that I didn't wait for him."

"What if he breaks up with you? Are you just going to wait around for him in case he changes his mind?" Alfonso asked.

"If that should happen, I'll cross that bridge when I get to it. Meanwhile, I have something I need to ask you."

Alfonso caught her eyes and knowingly admitted, "Yes, it was me."

"You don't even know what I was going to ask you."

"Okay, ask away," he jested, a smile clear across his face. His dark eyes penetrated hers.

Laura shifted in her seat. She did not like the way he was watching her, even if he looked rather handsome with his curly hair slicked back. He was getting out of hand and she needed to set him straight. "Yesterday, when you left, you said, 'Love hurts like a dagger, doesn't it?' Did you send me the roses?"

Again, he repeated, "Yes, it was me."

"Well, thank you, I guess. But why didn't you sign the card and why did you write that love is like a dagger? It's a bit morbid, don't you think?" Laura ultimately questioned.

Alfonso took a sip of his soda and leaned into the table, closer to Laura. "You really are naïve. Isn't it obvious to you, yet?"

Laura shook her head, "What?"

He leaned back, stretching his thick arms up behind his head. His broad chest expanded with a deep breath. He let the breath out and leaned into the table again. "Laura, I really like you. You're different from other women. You are genuine, sincere—you're . . . just . . . different."

Laura wiped her mouth again, her gaze cast downward. She was sinking, unsure how she had gotten herself into this. "Fonzie . . ."

"You don't have to say another word. I know your heart belongs to someone else. But when and if you wake up someday and decide that you deserve better, I'll be here waiting. You *are* worth it." He stood from his chair, kissed her cheek, and left.

Laura's heart raced. "Wait!" she called out.

Alfonso stopped and returned to the table, "Yeah?"

"You never told me what you meant by the card."

"Exactly what it says. Love is a dagger, because it makes your heart bleed." He stepped back, his eyes never leaving hers, until he spun around and walked away.

****

Laura drove home in emotional disarray. She snuck into the house and quickly went upstairs to her room. She changed into dress slacks and a festive sweater, then dashed into the bathroom. Washing her blotchy face, she reapplied makeup and adjusted her hair. Before long, she found herself surrounded by family and her troubles were temporarily forgotten. Uncle Joe and Aunt Bernadette arrived with the boys to celebrate together. They ate another amazing dinner, made by Marlene, and had plenty of desserts and snacks to munch. They played a few board games, which ended in a battle between John and Joe. Laughter filled the air with their competitive tactics on how to win Monopoly.

When Uncle Joe and the family left, promising to see them the next day, Laura helped with the cleanup. She looked forward to going to church the next morning and to spending the day with them again.

Finally, at her bedside, Laura prayed.

"Father, praises to You for bringing me to this wonderful family. Thank You for Your grace and for Your love. You've given me the greatest gift in them. I love them and I thank You for them. Lord, forgive me for my sins. I'm sorry I have failed You in so many ways. Please help me to be a better Christian. Help me to be a light in this dark world. Finally, Jesus, I come to You with this heavy heart. Help Tony. Please help him to find comfort and peace. Please heal him and save him. Please bring him back to me, the way You intend it to be. Lord, I know it's Your will for us to be together. Send Your angels to protect us from whatever evil stands in our way. Thank You, Father. And please, help me to better handle this situation with Alfonso. Help me bring him to salvation. In Jesus' name, Amen."

****

Christmas Day went by short of a call from Tony. Laura tried to enjoy the day with her family, but the reality of spending another Christmas without him brought Laura further down. She *was* thankful for her family. Still, in the end, she was glad the day was over.

Tuesday morning, Laura prepared for her day. She slid on a black skirt with a red sequin shirt and black shoes to match. Her hair was up in a soft twist and dainty earrings hung from her lobes. She packed up the car with Nonno Nino's presents and the desserts she made for him. After goodbyes, she drove down to Nino's new home.

At Nino's, Josie prepared an outstanding meal. Laura and Nino decided to eat first and exchange gifts after. When the last course was served, Laura was already bursting.

"Nonno, I can't have another bite. I might go into labor."

Nino chuckled, "Ah, *amore*, that's just like us *Siciliani*. We eat until we just can't eat no more!"

Laura agreed with a laugh. "Nonno, I have to talk to you about something," She finally professed.

"*Si*, what is it?" he asked, his eyebrows pulled together in concern.

"I know you really like Alfonso. He seems to be your best companion lately. I can't pinpoint it yet, but something doesn't feel right about him," Laura explained.

"What do you mean, Laura?" Nino questioned, while sipping his coffee.

"Nonno, strange things have been happening to me, lately."

"Laura *mia*, you scare me. What strange things?"

"I've been getting prank calls. The telephone rings, no one responds, yet I can hear that they are there . . . listening, waiting. The other day at work, I found roses on my car. The card read, 'Love is a dagger, it makes your heart bleed'. I thought perhaps Tony had sent them. But he didn't. Saturday, when you took me out to dinner, as Alfonso opened my door to see me to my house, he asked me if I was upset with him voicing his opinion. I said no, that I was just disappointed in love. He says, 'Love hurts like a dagger, doesn't it'? Well, I figured then that he sent the roses.

"On Christmas Eve, he 'happens' to be at the mall. Of course, I 'happened' to bump into him at the pretzel stand. He insists on buying me one, so I can sit down with him. I agreed only so I could confront him and straighten things out. Nonno, he admitted to sending me the roses. He said he likes me and that he'll wait for me in case things don't work out with Tony. What am I going to do?"

Nino placed both hands over his forehead and whispered, "*Mama` mia! Che disastro*!"

"Nonno?"

"Laura *mia*, how do you feel for him?"

"He's nice and he's funny. I like to hang out with him, but I only care for him as a friend. Nonno, you know I love Tony. There's no other man for me," Laura confessed.

Nino seemed to sigh in relief. "I'm happy you told him, *cara*. You keep on telling him. You must never be with him, okay?"

Laura was shocked by his demand. "Nonno, I thought you said he was a changed man. Why do you say this? I mean, I have no interest in him, other than friendship. But I thought you would be overjoyed that he liked me. I thought you would tell me to break up with Tony to be with Fonzie."

"Well," Nino began, "it is too complicated. Fonzie is my right-hand man. I trust him with my life. But I would never put you at risk of danger. I believe Fonzie is changing. But only Jesus know a man's true heart."

Laura thought about what he said. "Does this mean you think he might be the one pranking me?"

"I don't want to believe this. But I don't know, *amore*. I will try to feel him out. Okay?" Nino reached over and patted her hand.

"Thanks, Nonno," Laura whispered. The doorbell rang and Josie ran to get the door. "Are you expecting anyone?"

"No," Nino answered, rising from his chair. Laura waited in the kitchen. She could hear the voices clear across the house.

"*Buon Natale*!" Alfonso bellowed.

"*Buon Natale*, Merry Christmas, Alfonso. Come in. What brings you by?"

"I didn't get a chance to swing by the last couple days and I couldn't let the holiday go by without seeing my best . . ." Alfonso froze when he entered the kitchen. His eyes fell upon Laura.

Laura stood from her seat, "Merry Christmas, Fonzie."

He walked around the table to greet her. He kissed her cheek and gave her a bear hug. "Merry Christmas, beautiful."

Nino's eyes crashed with Laura's. She gave him the 'told you so' look and smiled. Nino winked and they both continued, as if they had not had the conversation.

Alfonso handed Nino a wrapped box. "What is this?" Nino quizzed.

"Just a little something," Alfonso affirmed.

"Just in time, we were about to exchange Christmas gifts in the living room. Come on," Laura invited.

They gathered together in the living room, where a beautiful Balsam tree sat decorated in the corner. A couple scattered gifts adorned the bottom skirt. Laura gracefully knelt before the tree to obtain them.

"Open Fonzie's first," Laura insisted.

* * *

Alfonso watched Laura excitedly wait to see Nino open his gifts. To see her face smiling, was like seeing the sun. She was blinding, radiant. She observed with interest, while Nino peeled back the decorative paper. Opening the oblong box, he retrieved a hunting knife.

"Fonzie, this is the collector's item. It's from Scandinavia. *It's bellisimo! Grazie!*" Nino cried with delight.

"You're welcome, boss. Next time we go fishing or rabbit hunting, I don't want to see you without it! Look at the handle. Go ahead, read it," Alfonso urged.

Nino looked closer at the carving in the opal handle. He moved the knife away struggling to see it clearly. "I no have my glasses. Laura, you read it." He handed the knife to Laura, who quickly found the inscription.

"*Spada del cuore*? Did I say that right?" she questioned.

"*Si, amore*, it means 'spear of you heart'. Me and Fonzie love our hunting knives. We collect them. Thank you, Alfonso. It is too much." Nino rose and gave Alfonso a hug. Alfonso had a smug smile. Neither the old man nor the girl caught on to the inscription. But one day, they would.

Nino put the gift aside. "Okay, you two open up my gifts to you." Nino pointed out the delicately wrapped boxes and Laura and Alfonso tore them open. Alfonso received a new camouflage hunting jacket with his name embroidered on the chest.

"Nino, this is awesome! Perfect fit!" Alfonso exclaimed after putting it on. He was surprised that Nino went through so much trouble for him.

Laura excitedly opened her gift. Her little hands fiddled with the wrapper until a velvet box appeared. She anxiously opened it up to find a gold chain with a heart locket. She let out a gasp.

"Nonno!"

"It is the replica of the one I give you Momma. Look inside," he encouraged.

Laura's hands trembled. She pried open the locket. Inside was a picture of her mother. Laura burst into tears and embraced Nino. Alfonso looked away, trying not to let the scene move him. He was getting too close to his subjects and was afraid it might affect his assignment.

"Nonno, this is so beautiful. I will treasure this, forever!"

"I'm happy you like, ehh?"

"I love it." She wiped the tears from her face and promptly handed her gifts to Nino. "Your turn," she sang.

He tore off the wrapper like a child on Christmas morning. His eyes lit up at the brown plush robe Laura gave him. "This is *perfetto*, for the cold winter days. *Grazie, grazie.*"

"One more," Laura stated. "Hurry, open it. I can't wait."

Nino ripped open the paper and lifted the box lid. "Oh, Laura *mia*. This is too, too much!" He lifted the chain with the cross from the box.

"Just my way of congratulating you on your conversion. Now Jesus is not only *in* your heart, but *on* your heart." She rose from the floor and helped him put it on.

Alfonso had to look away again. He felt a sense of jealousy he could not explain. The love between Nino and Laura was so genuine, so real. He longed for that kind of love—the love of a father, something he never had the pleasure of experiencing. Just when he thought he would found it, Nino betrayed him—taking away all Alfonso ever wanted.

He was angry with himself for getting so emotionally involved. The truth was—he loved Nino like a father. He was hurt, he was angry, and he wanted revenge. Like it or not, love was a dagger and the knife that he purchased Nino was a symbol of the knife Nino put in Alfonso's back. '*Spada del cuore*'. Alfonso knew what he must do to be sure that dagger would not pierce his heart as well.

* * *

Alfonso did not think that she caught on, but she did. '*Spada del cuore*' did not stand for their love of knives, but for the dagger that Alfonso talked so freely about to her at the mall. A foreboding terrorized her heart. Tony could possibly be right. Alfonso might not be whom he claimed to be.

CHAPTER 14

Romans 15:1-2

"We who are strong ought to bear with the failings of the weak and not to please ourselves. Each of us should please his neighbor for his good, to build him up."

Taking off to find my father's family with Uncle Frank was the reality check I truly needed. The nearly four-hour drive to White Plains, New York, was certainly necessary for me to help put things into perspective. It was irrefutable. If I was genuinely going to walk in the steps of Christ, I needed to let Laura go. And this was going to be the hardest thing I would ever have to do . . . *again.*

****

Summer 1975

That first year and a half in the 'abandoned' house with Laura seemed to pass swiftly. In that time frame, Laura and I never once had an argument, or even so much as exchanged a heated word. I could not believe that I would ever find myself angry with her, as she was perfection in every way. In turn, on that first warm summer night in 1975, I caused her to cry for the first time, while struggling to harness my feelings for her. I hated myself for hurting her. Ultimately, it seems that is all I did.

Laura would turn 16 in September and it was evident in every way that she had developed into a full-blown woman over the course of that past winter. As the weather warmed, this quickly came to my attention, for Laura's prior summer clothes were just not fitting quite right. It was becoming more and more difficult for me to see her as that sweet little teenager I had found in the woods nearly two years prior.

Because she was ever mindful of how much money I spent on her, she was silent about needing new clothing. I recalled coming home that unusually hot

Saturday night in June, with Uncle Frank, to find her in a summer dress that clung much tighter to her new curves than before. It was then that Uncle pulled me aside and made me promise to take her out shopping, even if it meant driving her into town and risking the chance that someone would recognize us.

"Tony," she argued. "These clothes are fine. I don't want you spending needless money on me."

I strained to find the right words to explain the reason both Uncle Frank and I were insisting on new clothes. "Laura, look," I began, "If Uncle is offering to get you some new clothes, don't ask questions. Just accept it."

We stood over the kitchen sink washing and drying our dinner dishes. Uncle Frank had already left to retire for the night. Laura dried a dish mechanically while gazing at my side profile. I tried concentrating on scrubbing a soiled frying pan.

"I don't understand. I mean, I know these clothes are a little tight, but I hate when you guys spend money on me. I feel bad," she insisted.

"It's our job to care for you. The same way you care for us. It's final! I'll take you into town tomorrow."

"But, Tony!"

I turned the water off and spun to face her. "Laura, you can't walk around the house like this!" I finally blurted. "It's not right!"

She looked confused. "What am I doing wrong?"

"You didn't do anything wrong, but you need to understand. You're not a kid anymore. We need to get you into clothes that aren't so," I swallowed, ". . . fitted."

Her hand self-consciously moved to her neck. "But they're still new. I only wore them one season."

I tried to find my patience and placed a gentle hand on her arm. "It's not the clothes, Laura. Your body's changing."

"Am I getting fat?" She asked, near tears.

I let out a laugh. "Fat? My God, no! You're perfect! Too perfect . . . and that's why Uncle wants you to get some clothes that will better fit . . . *and* cover you."

Laura did not argue further. After dishes, we studied about an hour, and then ascended the stairs to the suffocating, hot second floor. I opened the windows in every room, hoping for some relief before crawling into Laura's bed. I kept the nightstand lamp burning, while I waited for her to enter the room. Moments later, she appeared, wearing a sleeveless nightshirt that I had seen her wear a hundred times before. Only this time, my mouth fell open in surprise. Laura looked sensual, and despite my valiant efforts, she was becoming the object of my desire, more and more.

Unaware of my sudden complexity, she climbed into the bed and gave me a goodnight peck on my cheek. She curled up next to me and closed her eyes. I could not seem to tear my eyes from her. There would be no way for me to find sleep with her beside me like that.

"Laura," I whispered. "Don't you have anything else to put on for bed tonight?" Her eyes popped open and she looked at me unpretentiously.

"What? Why?"

I did not reply, only looked at her without expression.

"It's so hot up here!" she continued. "This is the coolest thing I own."

"Can you please find something else to put on?" I finally snapped. I could feel my patience wearing thin and I was getting angry with myself for getting mad at her, when it was hardly her fault. She truly was not even aware of the power that she was beginning to possess over me.

She sat up in the bed and pulled the sheet up to cover herself, turning her backside to me, now. She lowered her head shyly and whispered, "I don't have anything else. This is the only pajama that fits me somewhat decent."

"Well, you need to change. Put on a pair of shorts and a shirt or something," I suggested, with a hint of frustration in my voice.

She turned to me with tears in her eyes. "I'm sorry!" She jumped off the bed and flew to her feet. She ran from the bedroom, into the bathroom, and closed the door. Guiltily, I chased after her. I knocked on the bathroom door.

"Laura, I'm sorry. Please open the door." Silence. I knocked again. "It's not you! It's me. I'm being a jerk. Please, let's talk."

She opened the door. Her eyes were red and she was fighting tears. "I can't help what's happening to me. I don't know what you want me to do," she whispered.

"Nothing. You're fine. Come to bed. Forget about what I said. I'm just tired and cranky." I held out my hand. She sniffled and hesitantly took my hand, following me into the bedroom. We both lay down beside one another. Despite the heat, because I had caused her to feel insecure, she pulled the sheet up over her body. Thankful to God that she was so forgiving, I reached over and turned the light off—praying to Him for sleep, and to see her as I once used to.

Instead, I fell into a restless slumber. I tossed and turned, until finally surrendering to my subconscious, in the early morning hours. Reluctantly, I began to dream of her. The feeling of her warm skin near mine was more than tempting. I pulled her into my arms and she did not resist me. I kissed her passionately and we were suddenly taking matters *way too far*! Before I could stop myself, before I had the chance to take in what was happening, I heard her call out my name. I opened my eyes and found that she was still beside me, only she was openly crying for me in her sleep. She was having another nightmare.

I shook her shoulders to wake her. Her eyes flew open and she finally focused in on my face. "Oh, Tony," she cried. Her arms found their way around my neck.

I tried with all my might to not think of my dream and her warm body pressing against mine. I tried so hard to concentrate on that very moment and that she needed me in a different way than I was needing her.

"What happened?" I whispered into her ear.

"You left and I was all alone!"

I shook my head in 'no'. "That's not going to happen. I'm not going anywhere."

I had triggered the nightmare. *I* had caused her to feel fear—fear of angering the only stability she had—*me*. One little fight had sent her into this anxiety. I grew angrier with myself.

Finally, she quieted down and fell asleep in my arms. I could not close my eyes, literally seeing for the first time that changes needed to be made. It was crucial that I move to my own room at night, to avoid my dream from becoming a reality. I could never allow myself to take advantage of her. *Ever!*

The following morning, we ate breakfast, and then left for town. Laura and I each wore a baseball cap to disguise ourselves, so we could shop more discreetly and securely. Laura found what she needed in summer pajamas, dresses, shirts, and shorts. I even encouraged her to purchase whatever girly needs she wanted. She picked out a few pieces of makeup, hair styling products, and perfume, as well as new undergarments and two pairs of shoes to match the clothing we picked. There was not a thing I wanted her to lack.

Later that evening before bed, Laura neatly folded and put away her new clothing. Afterward, I found her in the bathroom organizing her makeup and things. I stood in the bathroom doorway, ready for bed. Somehow, I needed to explain to her that I would no longer be sleeping in her room.

"Ready for bed, yet?" I asked.

"Almost." Suddenly she turned to me with a gleaming smile. "Thank you, again, for all of this. I'm so excited to practice applying the makeup."

"I'm glad you're happy," I started, struggling to say the right thing. "Laura, I've been thinking . . . I'd like to think that by now, you're feeling pretty secure here. Am I right?"

"Of course, Tony," she immediately answered. "You make me feel so safe here. Why do you ask?"

I looked down at the brown ceramic floor, afraid to meet her gaze. "Laura, I think it's time I started sleeping in my own bed. It's only right. You need your privacy, and frankly . . . so do I." I dared to glance at her.

Her smile vanished and concern seemed to fall over her face. "Well," she paused a long moment. "If you think that's best," she whispered. I could see the disappointment in her expression. I did not want to hurt her, but this was all I could do to keep from letting my true feelings for her surface.

"Please understand. You're not the teenager you used to be. You're growing up. You really should have the bed to yourself at night. Besides, if Uncle Frank ever knew the truth, he'd kill me. Starting tonight, I'm going to sleep in my own room."

She nodded slowly and I could see her swallow hard. "I understand."

"Laura. It's the right thing." I walked into the bathroom and gave her a quick squeeze. Kissing her cheek, I wished her goodnight and entered my room. I pulled the covers back on my bed and opened my bedroom window. It would be strange not having her at my flank all night.

In fact, the more the minutes went by without her, I began to feel an ache in my heart and instant regret that I was working to be so noble. I strained to hear her finish in the bathroom. Eventually, the light outside my closed door turned off and then slowly, I heard her make her way toward her room. She paused at my door, and then made more footsteps, until I heard her door close.

I felt sick. I knew I was doing what was right for us. Still, as the next hour passed, I wanted her nearness until I felt physically ill. Suddenly, I heard a quiet rap at my door and then the door creak open.

"Tony?" she murmured.

I sat up immediately. The thin sheet I used for cover fell to my waist, baring my chest. "Yeah?"

She took a step closer into my room. Despite the shadows, I could see her standing in the new silk pajama shorts and tank we had purchased that day. She looked just as alluring to me as the night before. It seemed there was no getting around the attraction I felt for her. My heart abruptly pounded in my ears.

"Can I just say something?" she continued. She had been crying, so I gathered from her nasally speech.

"Of course," I encouraged.

"You say that we should sleep in our own beds and you're right, because that *is* the right thing to do. But if you're doing this because you think it's what *I* need, then . . . you couldn't be more wrong. I'm alone *all day long*, and when you're home, I just want to be with you. I thought that you wanted to be with me, too, and that sharing the bed was just so we could be in each other's company. If I'm wrong and you've decided this because you're tired of being my babysitter, then . . . I guess I'll just have to adjust," she said, as she choked back a crack in her voice.

I succumbed to my heart. "Come here," I invited.

She ran to my bed and jumped on, throwing herself into my embrace. I fell back onto my pillow while I held her head to my chest. Her shoulders shook and she cried in my arms.

"It's not what you think," I tried to soothe. "I can't share the bed with you. Not because I don't want to; I just can't look at you the same." I explained. She lifted her head and searched my eyes in the dark. I wiped her tears with my hands and pulled back her hair that was falling forward.

"Why, Tony? Am I so ugly?" she sniveled.

"Holy Jesus, Laura! It's the exact opposite! I decided to try to make things right around here because . . ." I paused, hoping for the right words. " . . . Because, I'm having a hard time seeing you as that teenage girl I found in the woods. Over this past winter, you've changed. You have become . . . this desirable, even more beautiful, young woman. I have to keep reminding myself that I'm fostering you and not pursuing you," I finally divulged.

I could feel her heart beating quickly against mine. Still, there was silence as we held one another's gaze. I could see her head lowering toward mine. Suddenly, my heart was racing at the possibility of our first kiss.

A car door suddenly slammed, startling both of us. Laura jumped to her knees and I quickly followed suit. "Go to your room!" I hastily whispered. "It's probably Uncle. He can't find you in here."

She scurried out of my room and I followed her into her bedroom. I peeked out her window to see Uncle Frank approaching the porch steps. His truck sat in the roadway.

"Don't worry. It's just Uncle Frank. Stay here. I'll see what he needs." Laura got into her bed. I skipped down the stairs and opened the door to Uncle, who was about to knock. It turned out that he came to let me know that he would be at the store later than normal the next morning, to meet with a doctor for a routine checkup. He also needed me to go over a few numbers with him concerning the store's inventory. We plugged in a few figures, calculated what we needed, and Uncle Frank left for the night.

I walked up the stairs, debating my next move. Before I could stop myself, I entered her room and crawled into bed next to her. She was sleeping soundly on her side—still I pulled her into my hold. She reached out for me. I realized at that moment that there was no turning back. I could not pretend anymore. I would wait for the right moment for that perfect kiss. I would wait until the right time to go from fostering her, to pursuing her.

Until then, I prayed for God to help me sustain and keep my thoughts and feelings for her pure. And then, when we would finally share that first perfect kiss, she would know that she would be mine, forever.

***

October 1975

After that evening, I vowed to make up for the hurt I had caused her. I never let a day go by without letting her know, in some small way, how much she meant to me. Finally, on the night prior to that memorable fall day, when we finally shared our first kiss, I had promised her a date . . . and on a date is where we were going.

Once 'the cat was out of the bag' about our love for one another, I had no qualms about showing Laura how I felt about her, even in the presence of Uncle Frank and his ever-concerned scrutiny. I knew it was not because he did not want us to be together. It was because he was worried that our 'raging hormones' could not be controlled. What he did not understand was that I was not about to let *anything* ruin what we had.

All *I* wanted for Laura was some normalcy. It was strange enough that we fell upon a house she was told had been 'abandoned' and then purchased by Uncle Frank. It was also particularly outlandish that this man, who was a father to both of us, was permitting us to live in the house together . . . alone. Not to mention, that Laura was kept a secret from the rest of world, and remained hidden there, being schooled by me—a guy just a few years older than her. A guy who was falling crazy in love with her.

Yes, Laura needed some normality, and at that point, I was going to give it to her regardless of the risks.

The Friday following our first kiss, I stacked 20-pound bags of imported flour from Italy onto a wooden crate, on the floor, near the door of Blandino's Market. It was quieter that afternoon. A rush of customers had just paid at the register and left, leaving me alone with Uncle Frank. I could hear him humming behind the deli, to the radio playing quietly in the back of the store.

"Hey, Uncle?" I called out, pressing my foot against a bag to straighten it. "You know of any authentic Italian restaurants in the nearby neighborhoods?"

I purposely watched to see his reaction. His head popped up from behind the deli counter. He placed his hands on the countertop and gazed about the store. "Why do you need to know?" he quizzed, with a nod of his head.

I lifted another bag of flour off the dolly and tossed it onto the crate. Flour covered my hands. I clapped them together to dust off the white powder. "Because," I finally answered, meeting his glare. "I'm taking Laura out on a date."

I know I heard cursing. He scurried out from behind the counter to look down the two aisle ways in the store. When he realized the coast was clear, he stalked toward me and shouted, "Are you crazy? Have you completely lost your mind?"

"Actually, yeah! I'm crazy alright . . . about her. I want to take her out on a date."

Uncle Frank's mustache seemed to twitch with anxiety, as he now stood before me. Raising a finger, he lectured, "Tony Giacalone . . . you don't need me to give you the reasons why you can't take that girl out on the town. You are endangering her life and your own. It's not worth it!" he warned.

I picked up the last bag of flour, tossing it with a thump onto the others. I wrestled with it to make it straight. "Uncle," I began to reason, "You have to understand. Laura's in that house 24 hours a day. I gotta get her out every now and then, or she'll go stir crazy. I wasn't thinking too close by. I was hoping you would let me borrow your truck so I could drive her out to Rome for some dinner. She deserves a break!"

Uncle Frank grabbed the empty dolly and turned to wheel it toward the back of the store. He was angry. It was evident even in the way he stomped his feet to move away from me. I followed behind him. Suddenly, he turned and I nearly collided into him.

"Tony, you know how many Italians live in Rome, New York? Why do you think it's called Rome? Now, I've been very patient with you! I know you want to have a normal life, too. Laura is the only thing normal about us. She grounds us both. But you need to stay focused. I see that you love her. Still, we can't screw up! If they catch wind—if they see you . . . it will all be over! You will lose her and they will kill you, too. That will leave me with nothing but heartache the rest of my life, *if* they don't discover I'm the trustee, and kill me, too. Which they might as well!"

I sighed heavily. I knew he was right. An idea suddenly came to my mind. "We'll disguise ourselves. I'll have her put heavy makeup on, making her look older. I'll wear a hat and glasses. Please, let me do this for her!" I begged.

Uncle Frank pushed at the dolly again and wheeled it into the back storage room. From behind the wall, I heard him shout, "I'll think about it."

I nearly jumped in excitement. I could not wait to go home to her and see her beautiful face. I knew what I needed to do to convince Uncle. I would have Laura ask. One conversation with her and he melted like butter.

I nearly raced home to get to her, an hour later. As usual, Friday evenings was Uncle Frank's night to stay late to stock the store. He had always sent me home earlier, as to not leave Laura alone for too long of a day. Therefore, we would not be expecting him to come home for dinner until later.

I found her standing on the porch, looking into the woods for me. Her long hair was down, fanned over her shoulders, curling at the ends. The blue jeans and button-down blouse she wore were not nearly warm enough for the crisp fall day. She greeted me with a smile, while curiously staring at my hair. I took the porch steps two at a time to gather her into my arms. By now, she was laughing. I picked her up, briefly kissed her lips, and finally sought her face for the reason she was humored.

"What?" I panted, out of breath from my run.

I put her down and she ran her fingers through my hair. I watched a white powder float into the air. "I thought you were getting old and gray on me. You're all full of flour!"

I pulled her closer and kissed her neck. "Flour came in today. Thought I'd help out Uncle before I left," I explained, my voice muffled by her sweet skin.

"I see," she whispered. "Hungry?"

I ignored her question and looked down at her. "Where's your coat? It's too cold for you to be standing out here like this," I scolded.

"I literally just stepped out," she replied.

"Come on," I urged.

We came into the house. I washed my hands and face and we sat down to dinner. After a prayer, I broached the subject about our date.

"What are you doing tomorrow night?"

She finished sipping from her glass of lemonade. "Well, let's see … a whole lot of nothing," she answered sarcastically.

"Would you like to go out on a date with me? I promise, I won't make you work," I persuaded with a grin and a wink.

Laura slowly lowered her glass. Her smile was luminous. "Are you serious?"

"Of course I am. But . . . there is a catch," I admitted.

"Uh oh."

"How 'bout *you* ask Uncle Frank?" I blurted.

"I knew it!" she shouted, with a twinkle in her eye. "Sure, you want me to ask, so *you* don't get the blame!"

I laughed aloud. "No, I swear! I already talked to him about it today. He said he'd think about it. I know that he won't say no to *you*, if *you* ask."

Laura picked up her fork and played with her food. "You really think he'll let us?"

I nodded and mentioned, "We just need to disguise ourselves. I can wear a hat and glasses and we'll get you all dressed up to look older. We'll be safe, I promise."

Laura was beaming with happiness. "That sounds like fun. Should we ask him tonight?"

After we finished our meal, we packed up Uncle Frank's food and decided to pay him a visit at the store. As we walked down our trail to Crabtree Lane, I looked up into the sky. It was already approaching dusk. Still, I could see the dark clouds moving in overhead. I grasped Laura's hand and we walked faster. Once we were on Crabtree, I advised her to lift the hood of her jacket to conceal her face, and we nearly sprinted, until we reached the store.

The front door was locked, for the store closed at 7 p.m. I used my key and we entered the dim building, locking the door behind us.

"Uncle?" I called out.

"In the back," his voice carried.

We both entered through the door that led to the backroom. It was a fairly large industrial size structure, built for stocking foods and to cut fresh meat. To the right, a small room was used as an office to run administrative tasks. To the left, a large garage door opened to haul in the imported goods and fresh produce that kept our customers coming back for more. Uncle Frank had the garage door lifted and was making a trip with a crate of fruit from a delivery truck to the storage area. I grasped the crate from his hands.

"What are you doing here?" he questioned.

Laura stepped out from behind me. "Hi, Uncle," she cheerfully greeted. I placed the crate on a shelf.

His face instantly smiled and he went to her. She kissed his cheek and he embraced her. Suddenly, his eyebrows knit together with concern. "Go! Go into the office. Don't let anyone see you. Let me finish up with the driver and I'll be right back," he whispered.

I looked out the garage door and noticed the driver curiously gaping into the building. I grasped Laura and immediately guided her into the office. I closed the door.

"What's the matter?" she asked.

"Just being safe, is all."

We waited quietly for a few minutes. She looked nervous and I wrapped my arm around her shoulder and kissed her.

The door opened. "Oh, geez!" Uncle Frank cried out. "Will you two give it a rest?"

I dropped my arm from around her shoulders, but grasped her hand. "Get used to it, Uncle."

"That's what I'm afraid of. What's going on? Why are you both here? It's going to storm out there any minute! Then I'll have to drive you home, thus possibly exposing our 'safe house'. It better be important," he added.

Laura lifted the care package she made for him with his dinner. "We thought we'd bring you dinner," she revealed.

He seemed to relax. "Well, that was awfully sweet of you." He looked at me and then back to Laura. "What else?"

I chuckled to myself. He knew me so well.

"Nothing," I lied.

Laura stated, "I was itching to get out of the house, too."

"I believe *you*. I don't believe *him*!" Uncle Frank admitted.

I laughed aloud this time. "Why do you think I have an ulterior motive for everything?" I quizzed.

"Because you do!" Uncle Frank immediately replied. "Is this about that date? Have you brought her here to convince me? Because if you did, that was a low blow!"

I smiled from ear to ear. "There's no pulling the wool over your eyes, is there?"

"I'm a lot older than you, Tony. Wise enough to tell you, that you're both getting sloppy. Look," he whispered, taking her hand in his, after placing the package on his desk. "I understand your need to get out. I'm sure the solitude is enough to make you crazy. But I'm so scared for you. I'm so afraid Social Services will find out you're orphaned and they will take you away from us."

"Can't you just adopt me?" she begged.

"Laura," Uncle Frank seemed to choke up. "You are already my daughter without the legal paperwork to confirm it. I wish I could just 'adopt you'. But there is a chance that the adoption wouldn't go through and we *won't* risk losing you. In a couple of years, you will be free to do as you will. Can't you two hang tough a little while longer?"

"Uncle," I intervened. "Just one night. We're not asking for a lot. We will head out, away from town. What are the chances someone will recognize her, especially in a town as small as Rome?"

"Please," Laura pleaded.

He threw his hands up in the air. "Fine. Just this once . . . and be careful. Tomorrow, after work, Tony will drop me off at my apartment, take the truck back here, and then walk to the house to get Laura. Then, you two will have to walk here, like I always do, to get the truck and drive into Rome. I'm warning you—lay low! Don't draw any attention to yourselves. I don't know what I'll do if I lose either one of you."

Laura hugged Uncle Frank, thanking him profusely. *She was so affectionate!* I could not help but feel overcome. *It was impossible not to love her!*

We left Uncle to his food and departed the store in silence. The wind had intensified since we had arrived. Uncle Frank was right. We were bound to get soaked.

Laura and I ran down Crabtree Lane. When we turned onto our hidden trail and were finally safe, I grasped her from behind and spun her in a circle.

"You did it!" I shouted with laughter. "You convinced the old man to let us go!"

She held my hands until I put her down. "He's so mad at us. We're driving him bonkers." She admitted, "I almost feel bad."

I grasped her hand and we continued down our trail. "He'll get over it," I exclaimed. Predictably, I felt a raindrop on my face. I looked at Laura. She glanced at me knowingly. We were about to get waterlogged.

The wind suddenly gust and an instant spray of rain cascaded over us. We began to run as fast as the immediately spongy dirt would allow. Laura nearly slipped and I caught her before she landed in the mud.

She burst out laughing and suddenly stopped. I tugged at her arm, but her fits of laughter hindered her ability to move.

"What?" I finally questioned.

"This . . . is . . . exactly what we deserve!" she snickered.

I laughed with her. By now, we were both drenched. "Come on. We're gonna catch pneumonia!"

A lightning bolt unexpectedly struck. Thunder instantly followed. Laura screamed and sprinted for the house. I followed her, until we breathlessly ascended the porch steps. Finally, under the protection of our porch roof, I grasped my soggy girlfriend. Her nose was red from the cold and her chin quivered. I placed my thumb and forefinger on it, to keep it from trembling. Her eyes closed and awaited my kiss. I lowered my head to hers and tasted her sweetness.

The following day, I was overly anxious, as the day seemed to crawl at a snail's pace while I worked. Uncle Frank appeared more nervous than normal as well. Laura promised to be ready by the time I got home. I would quickly shower, and we would be off on our first date.

At six o'clock, our normal closing time for a Saturday, we locked up the store and I drove Uncle Frank back to his apartment. He gave me a stern look, before leaving the truck.

"On your toes, Giacalone. Be mindful of your surroundings. Don't drown yourself in those beautiful eyes. Don't linger. Eat your food and leave. Most importantly . . . enjoy it. This is the last risk we take like this!" He slammed the truck door and stalked off, fading into his apartment building.

I tried not to drive back to the store with haste, to prevent from getting a moving violation. After parking the truck in the lot at Blandino's, I ran all the way home, thankful that the prior night's rain had stopped and the trail had dried up. I entered the house to find Laura lying on the couch asleep. She was already dressed for the occasion.

The dark blue cable-knit sweater she wore clung to her curves, and went perfectly with the black wool skirt that ended just above her knees. Her dainty feet modeled a pair of black high-heel shoes, which I had recently purchased for her. Her long hair was loose, carefully spread out over the pillow. It seemed to shine in the glow of the small blaze she had kindled in the fireplace.

Stunning as her outfit was, nothing could define the beauty of her face. I had told her to try and make herself up to appear older. Her eyes were perfectly lined and shadowed in a darker color. Her lashes were thickened and nearly fanned across her cheeks. Her lips looked like satin, shimmering with a pink tint. Gazing at her, at that moment, she was the most beautiful creature I had ever seen—the definition of true beauty.

I scurried up the stairs, without disturbing her, to quickly shower. It had been a few days since I had had a shave, and to further disguise myself, I left the growth on my face, cleaning it up at the neck and cheeks. I decided to match her and wore black dress pants along with a dark button-down shirt to match. I gelled my hair back, as it had a mind of its own and would not stay where I wanted it to. Exhausting all effort to discipline it, I placed my old-fashioned imported Sicilian cap atop of it. To complete my disguise, I slipped on a pair of non-prescription glasses I had picked up from a local drug store that morning. Finally, I splashed some aftershave on my face and descended the steps.

Tiptoeing to the couch, I bent over and kissed her. Her eyes fluttered open.

Laura sat up confused. “Oh my gosh! I must have dozed off,” she exclaimed. She looked at me. “Hello, stranger! You’re already ready?”

“Let’s go, gorgeous,” I whispered.

Rome was a quaint little town, with vintage buildings and an old-fashioned characteristic. The Italian population really did rule over the majority of restaurants, so it was not hard to choose a place that offered an authentic meal. I wanted the best for her and chose a restaurant with a reputation for the top pasta recipes. Any kind of pasta was Laura’s favorite dish.

The hostess led us to our table. I pulled Laura’s chair out for her and she thanked me. Sitting across from her finally, I could see how Uncle Frank’s warning to not get lost in her eyes, was accurate. She took my breath away.

We ordered our meals and waited.

“You did a great job with the makeup. How did you learn to apply it so perfectly?” I inquired.

Laura blushed and turned her gaze downward in shyness. “The magazines you bring home to me. Some of them give great tips,” she replied.

“Amazing. You look amazing. Even your hair seems longer tonight. It’s really grown,” I remarked.

“I haven’t trimmed it in some time. It’s too long for me to cut myself now. Patty used to do it for me, before,” she admitted with a hint of sadness.

“I’ll try and get you to a salon, soon, if you’d like,” I offered.

“You don’t like it?” she asked in a small voice.

“Laura, you’re stunning!” I replied flatly. “There isn’t a guy in here that didn’t turn to look at you when we walked in.”

She blushed again at my compliments. “Well, thanks. I really do need to cut it, though.”

I leaned into the table and whispered, “You could be bald and you’d still be the most beautiful woman in the world to me.”

She laughed aloud. “Don’t exaggerate!” she pleaded.

I noticed two men at the bar turn to look at her. Leaning in even closer, I whispered, "Let's try not to attract curious eyes this way. It's enough that your good looks are enticing onlookers."

"They are *not* looking at *me*," she whispered.

"Those guys," I covertly pointed. "Believe me—they are *not* looking at me."

Laura slowly turned in the direction of my pointing finger. She spied the two scruffy looking men having a drink at the bar and shivered. "They give me the creeps," she confessed.

"Those kinds of men—only looking for trouble," I affirmed.

"I believe it. There are some really sick people in this world. You know, recently, on the radio, I heard they convicted a 22-year-old man for raping and killing an 8-year-old girl. Who does these things?" she whispered.

My heart seemed to instantly double in rhythm. I felt sick at the thought of the pain the child she mentioned, endured. Angrily, I replied, "Only a demented person could do that! It only makes me want to keep you in the 'safe house' forever! Away from every harm!"

She brushed her hand over my arm and my rage quickly vanished. "Well then, I guess you're just going to have to stay by my side, for the rest of my life, just in case!"

"Done," I agreed, letting go of the fury.

She did that for me. She eased my pain, calmed my nerves, and brought peace to my soul—at least until later that hour, after our meal. There was no stopping my reaction when it occurred. I had already paid for our dinner when Laura rose to find the restroom. I could see *their* hungry eyes watching her. They were whispering to one another and I sensed that the evening was about to sour if I did not immediately intervene. The two repulsive men at the bar were devising a plan. Only I was on to it . . . *pronto*.

One rose and came my way.

The diversion.

The other walked toward the restroom where Laura was sure to exit at any moment.

The threat.

I did not even give 'the diversion' a chance to open his mouth. I shot to my feet to tear past him. He swung, I ducked. My fist immediately came up in an upper cut and I hit him square in his jaw, knocking him to the ground. The diners around us reacted to the brief run-in.

By the time my glare turned to 'the threat', his arm was on Laura's. She was pulling away from him, trying to get to me. My blood boiled. I do not know quite how I got to her so fast. I could only recall that my fist collided with his wrist and his hold over her was broken. He tried to hit me, but I caught his hand in mid-air. He did not know that years of hard work had built my hands to have a vast strength. I crushed his fingers until he screamed.

"Don't touch . . . what doesn't belong to you," I scolded.

Letting him go, I gripped Laura's hand, snatched our jackets from our table, and ushered her out of the restaurant, ignoring the stares of the diners, waiters and waitresses, and the two detestable men who attempted to handle my girl. We would have run to the truck, if it had not been for the high-heels on Laura's feet and the slight drizzle that had begun to make the ground slick. She was nearly crying by the time I got the truck started and was backing out of my parking spot.

"Are you okay?" I examined. "Did he hurt your arm?" I reached over and pulled her to my flank. I gathered her left hand and brought it to my lips.

She sniffled back her tears and whispered, "I'm so sorry."

The window wipers started to careen back and forth, as the rain strengthened. Now that we were safely on the road to home, I glanced at her. "Sorry?" I asked. "I'm the one who's sorry. I should have walked you to the restroom or something."

She shook her head. "Those men . . . who were they?"

"I've never seen them before. No one I think we need to be worried about. Just a couple of drunks, looking for a little fun and some trouble."

A smile broke across her face. "They messed with the wrong guy," she giggled through her tears.

My soul felt instantaneously lighter. "I saw it coming," I revealed with a chuckle.

She wrapped her left arm through my right and squeezed my muscle. "They didn't stand a chance, did they?" she flattered.

I quickly kissed her lips, while at a red light. "Seeing someone touch you without you permitting it—infuriated me. Like red to a bull. I'm just thankful for Uncle Frank's advice to be aware of my surroundings. Speaking of which, it's best we don't tell him about this little incident. He'll never let us out again!"

She nodded in agreement. Resting her head on my shoulder, we drove back to Blandino's Market in silence. With all the commotion, it had not dawned on me that, once again, we would be walking home in the rain. Only this time, Laura was not adequately dressed for a stroll in the mud. In the parking lot, we sat in the truck for a moment. I did not want to risk driving the truck up the trail to our house. If the troublemakers from the restaurant were following, the 'safe house' would be compromised. And though I was certain no one trailed us home, I would not take any risks.

"Come on," I urged. "I got an idea."

I zipped her jacket up as high as it could go and lifted the hood up over her head. Doing the same for myself, I opened my door and helped her out of the truck. I locked the door and saved the key in my pocket. In the morning, I would drive the truck to Uncle's apartment and take us both back to work.

We quietly walked together, in the rain, until we reached the trail. The night was quiet and not a vehicle cruised the streets. The rain bounced off our coats until they were saturated. Before Laura could step foot on the muddy path, I scooped her up into my arms.

"Tony, you are not going to carry me the whole way back," she insisted.

"Quiet woman, it's my duty," I joked.

She wrapped her arms around my neck. I could feel her penetrating stare. "You are truly a miracle," she suddenly whispered.

I caught her gaze. "Miracle?" I quizzed.

"Yes," she continued. "There is no one else in the world like you! You're a miracle."

I scoffed at the thought. If anyone was a miracle, it was *her*. The way she put me back together, healed my very soul. Nothing could have prepared me for the powerful way her love conformed me. I would have never believed it possible. Yet, as I carried her all the way down the sodden trail to our little 'safe house', I believed.

We reached the porch and I set her down. A raindrop dripped off her hood, onto her cheek. I slowly pulled it back to uncover her head. Our eyes were linked.

"My God, how I love you," I whispered, caressing her face with my hand.

"Tony," she whispered, and we sealed our first date with a kiss.

****

Recalling those memories as I drove to White Plains with Uncle Frank, only tore at my very heart, while I contemplated my next moves. It was futile to ponder on them. I knew only too well the pain to come. And though I had made up my mind, I prayed that Christ would give me the strength to put my selfishness aside and say goodbye to her for the very last time.

I had done it before with success, when I staged my own death; even though I felt I literally went dead inside. I would do it again. To the world, I *was* dead. I realized even then that all I could ever bring to Laura was harm. That truth still remained.

Yet, to save her from the dangers the Galante family imposed, I was now reunited with her. Having her back was a joy I did not think could ever be possible again. Especially after having to watch from a distance, as she 'moved on' with her life, assuming my death.

No one could fathom the torture I felt knowing Laura believed I was gone. No one could have prepared *me* for the blow of comprehending that Paul was then pursuing her—the notion that someone else was seeking her love. It knocked me into the deepest slump. I was drowning. There was no solution to my brokenness. Sleeping in our empty bed, I ached to hold her. Reaching out into the night, I found only desolation. I had forgotten what it felt to kiss her, to feel the life that she breathed within me, to feel her love unconditionally gifted to me. There was only pain . . . and more pain, until I felt I could not survive.

Then, Paul proposed.

It was Uncle Frank who literally saved my life. He shoved a Bible in my hand and forced me to swear I would not put a true end to it all. He manipulated me into living.

"What if the Galantes come after her," he had said. "Who will protect her?"

And so, I lived. I lived to see her live. I lived to be a silent guardian over her. I pressed through the pain when I secretly witnessed Paul, unworthy of her, steal kisses from Tammy. I watched mysterious strangers seek her happiness, regardless of the cost. I observed, as dangers drew nearer to her. Dangers almost as threatening as the 'alter' within me.

I do not know if that was the excuse I used to convince myself that I needed to make my existence known to her. Perhaps it was God's plan so to finally free her of the Galante's pursuit.

Regardless, I would not be making that mistake again. I could not expect her to continue this farce of a relationship. I could not give her what she deserved.

I would do it again. I would let my heart die off, so that she could live.

CHAPTER 15

Psalm 27:14

"Wait for the LORD; be strong and take heart and wait for the LORD."

Wednesday, December 27

"Tony, that woman is nothing but trouble! You better find a way to get rid of her!" Frank advised, while they made their way home from White Plains, New York.

Tony shook his head. Both his hands tightly gripped the steering wheel. His knuckles were turning white. Irritated, he exclaimed, "What am I going to do? How can I get rid of her? And they say I'm a nutcase! Who would've thought that she'd be crazy enough to show up at our hotel room?"

"The question is—how did she know you were even in White Plains?" Frank inquired.

"I don't know. I did make the reservation for the hotel from the office phone. Could she be listening in on my telephone conversations?"

"It's likely! That girl *is* insane! You better be careful. I don't like this, son. I do not like it one bit. She's out to destroy your relationship with Laura. I think you should tell John," Frank insisted.

"What's John going to do? He already talked to her once. Two seconds later, she snuck into my office and practically threw herself at me. I couldn't have told her to get lost more plainly!" Tony sighed in frustration. "This is crazy. What has my mind really boggled, right now, is the ring situation. I'm certain I put the ring Laura gave me on the bathroom counter that night, before I showered. When I came out, the ring was gone. I looked all over for it. It vanished into thin air."

"Was that the night I left to pick up our pizza?"

"Yes! You closed the door behind you, didn't you?"

"Of course."

"I turned that hotel room upside down looking for it. The only thing I can think of is that one of the hotel staff came in and took it. How am I going to tell Laura?"

"I'm sure she'll understand. Having Beth show up at our hotel door, on the other hand, now that's a different story."

Tony reflected for a moment at the disaster this could cause. Though he had ultimately decided to break it off with Laura, he did not want her to believe him unfaithful. The only way out of the Beth situation was to quit his job with John. John was likely to fire him anyway. Once he officially called it off with Laura, John would surely send *him* packing. *Rightly so!* Tony needed to walk away from the Knight family indefinitely. The escalating situation with Beth was confirmation. It was time to cut all ties.

Tony could sense Frank's eyes on him. He glanced at his uncle. "What?" he finally grilled.

"Something's brewing in that kettle of yours. What is it?"

"Nothing, just thinking about our trip," Tony lied.

"Are you satisfied with the results?" Frank questioned.

"It saddens me to find that my father and uncles were terribly neglected and abused as children. It saddens me that the Giacalone family is under this generational curse of childhood abuse. The fact that my father and uncles came to America to escape the poverty and the horrible life they lived in Sicily, is overwhelming enough." Tony stole another glance at Frank. "If it hadn't been for my cousins, I would've never known this. My uncles are still in denial and refuse to get help. Their wives left them. Their kids don't talk to them. It's so sad."

"All the more reason, you should be proud of yourself. That generational curse will end with you and now hopefully for your cousins. You were able to reach them and help them, because of what you've suffered. You're already making a profound impact on others through your experience, Ton. That's awesome! Those kids can seek counseling now for what they've withstood."

Tony thought about it for a moment. He had not looked at it that way before. He had not seen his sufferings as a means to help others who had endured similar situations. *How could he have thought this?* He still felt he could not help himself. Yet, spending a few days with his cousins and aunts helped Tony in more ways than he realized. Though he would not wish his childhood upon his worst enemy, it was comforting to know that he was not alone. It was comforting to know that others, who suffered at the hands of child abuse, turned out okay.

Still, Tony had made up his mind. He would call Laura upon his return, meet with her, and call off the wedding.

****

John sat in his office infuriated. *How was he going to tell Laura the news? How was he going to explain to her what Sam had just revealed to him?* John prayed. He was so nervous. His hands shook, as he put them together in prayer. He begged God to give him guidance. He pleaded for God to give him strength. Lastly, he beseeched God to help Laura.

Glancing at the clock, he decided to end his day. He grabbed his wool coat and keys and stormed out of the office. Walking past Beth's desk, he stopped. She looked up at him questioningly.

"Leaving so soon, boss?" she asked, in a sickeningly sweet voice.

"Yes, I suddenly feel *sick* to my stomach!" He stomped past her and left the office.

On his way home, he had another thought and detoured. He guided his vehicle toward Jasper Stone's law office. He could not wait for Laura to get home. He needed to see her immediately.

****

Laura glanced at the clock. It was nearly three that afternoon. *Two more hours left*, she thought. She felt exhausted from a busy day at work and looked forward to going home. She was overly tired. Being unable to sleep at night was making her drowsy during the day. Her body was having more and more symptoms of 'the shakes' and she couldn't wait to see her doctor the next day.

Of course, she knew the reason for her insomnia. She could not stop thinking about Alfonso. The more she thought about the blade he purchased Nino, the more she panicked. *Was it a sign of some sort? Was he sending Nino some kind of message?* Laura worried about her grandfather. She worried about Tony. She had not heard from him since he left and she wondered if he had returned. She would have to ask John if he was in to work that day.

Laura sighed and stood to file a folder into the tall filing cabinet behind her. She heard the foyer door open, expecting someone to soon enter. A moment passed and Laura turned to see if anyone had come in. She closed the cabinet door and walked toward the entry. Looking down the hall, no one was in sight. Laura walked back into the office, wishing this was one of those days when Mr. Stone stayed later.

She sat behind her desk and continued to work. Feeling a little shaky, she snatched a caramel candy from the dish on her desk and chewed on it. The telephone rang, startling her. Her heart raced. She put the telephone to her ear.

"Law offices of Jasper Stone. Laura speaking." Laura knew what was coming next, when there was a pause on the other line. "Hello?" she called. "Who is this?" she now demanded. "Stop calling me or better yet, get some courage to talk to me." The line clicked.

Laura was growing more and more frustrated. She would definitely call Sam to tell him about the strange calls as soon as she got home. She thought about it a moment longer. *Why wait?* She searched her rolodex for his card. With the telephone in hand, Laura began to dial.

Before she had a chance to complete the number, John entered her office. "Dad, what are you doing here?" she asked with a happy surprise. She rose from her desk and squeezed him, after hanging up the phone.

"Hi, babes. How are you today?" he examined.

"Okay. I'm so happy you stopped by. What's up? Short day today?" she asked.

"Couldn't wait to see my girl," John kissed the top of her head. "I love you so much."

"Uh oh, what's wrong?" Laura assumed.

"Why does something have to be wrong? Can't I just swing in to see you?"

"Dad, it's three o'clock. You couldn't wait two more hours? What's wrong?"

"Man, you know me well, don't you?" John sighed.

"Dad, you're scaring me," Laura held his hands and led him to the chairs before her desk. She sat in one next to him.

"Babe, I don't know how to tell you this," John explained.

"Dad, you really *are* scaring me. What happened?"

"I heard from Sam today. I don't have good news. I came here, because I don't want to unnecessarily worry your mom. When we know for sure what's going on, then we can tell her, too."

"Dad, please?" Laura begged. Her heart raced in her chest.

"It's Tony. Sam said that the undercover agent he had following him was able to shed some light on a few things. One, he did leave town. He went to White Plains, New York. Two, not only did *he* go to White Plains, so did Beth."

Laura stood from her seat. She walked away grasping her chest. *No, it couldn't be.*

"Wait," called John. "Come here, there's more."

Laura returned to the chair. Tears already streaked her face. "Do I really need to hear anymore?"

"Laura, don't jump to conclusions. Frank went with Tony. You know how much Frank loves you. I don't believe that he'd allow or want to be a part of Tony being unfaithful to you. So there could be a logical explanation for things. Sam did say that Tony met up with other people while there. It turns out they are also Giacalones."

Laura snatched a tissue off the box on her desk. She wiped her eyes. "Dad, what's going on?"

"There's more," John revealed. "Your grandfather's buddy, Alfonso, has been caught snooping around Tony. I don't know why, but maybe your grandfather's sending him to look out for you. Laura, this is not good. You know what happened to the last guy who your grandfather was keeping an eye on."

"Paul," Laura whispered.

"Yes, Paul. I know it wasn't Nino's intent, but Paul died. I don't want anything to happen to Tony, because it would push you right over the edge. Not to mention that — bad decisions or not — I love Tony too. I don't want him to get hurt."

"I have to call Sam, Dad. I have to hear this from him." Laura walked around to her desk chair. She sat and picked up the telephone ready to dial. She paused a moment, "You know the strange thing, Dad, I had the phone in my hand ready to call Sam just before you walked in. Look, he's up on my rolodex."

John peered over the desk, while she dialed. "Why were you calling Sam?"

Laura held up her finger, signaling for a moment. "I'll explain to the both of you. Hang on." She looked at him as he stared intently at her.

"I love you, Laura."

A lump rose in Laura's throat. "I love you, Dad," she whispered. She reached across the desk to grasp his hand. He squeezed her fingers gently and held them, while she requested for the police chief.

"Sam Desanti, here, who's this?"

"Hi, Chief, it's me, Laura," she said with a break in her voice.

"Laura! Hey, I'm glad you called. You okay?" Sam asked with sincere love and concern in his voice.

"I've been better. How are you?"

"Don't worry about me. I'm fine. I take it you talked to John?"

"Yes, he's here with me now, explaining what you told him. Please Chief, tell me Tony did not really meet up with Beth," she begged.

"Laura, I cannot tell you what went on, I can only say what my detective discovered on December 25. Beth did go to the hotel where Tony was staying. The detective couldn't follow her in because he got distracted—by none other than Alfonso Rengali."

"What do you suppose he was doing in White Plains?" Laura questioned.

"I don't know. But I'm giving you a heads-up. Laura that man is dangerous. I'm doing more investigating on him and am going to find out what he's all about. In the meantime, stay away from him. Do you understand me?" Sam questioned.

"Actually, that's why *I* was going to call *you*. I had the phone in my hands when my dad walked in," she explained.

"Why were you going to call *me*?"

"There've been a few strange things happening to me, lately." Laura explained the mysterious telephone calls and told him the strange things that were going on involving Alfonso.

John stood from his chair. "What? Why didn't you tell me these things?"

"Dad, please," she whispered, covering the receiver with her hands.

"Okay, okay, Laura this is serious. This is a real cause for alarm. He fits the profile for a stalker. You need to be careful. You better call your grandfather and tell him to call this guy off or you may be in serious danger," Sam warned.

"Really, Chief? I don't think he's that dangerous. I don't believe that he wants to hurt me. Maybe, he just has a crush?" Laura justified.

"Laura, please, listen to me. Go straight home with John and don't leave the house until I call you. Okay?" Sam begged.

"Are you serious?"

"Dead! Do as I say," Sam warned. "I don't want you left alone for one minute. Do you understand? If you're going in to work tomorrow, tell Mr. Stone that it's only under the condition that he's there with you. You're not to be alone in that office anymore. Do you get me?"

"Yes, sir," Laura whispered. "Thanks, Chief. I'll wait to hear from you. Chief?"

"Yes?"

"Please keep Tony safe. Promise?"

"I promise."

Laura begrudgingly hung up, unwilling to face John's wrath.

"You're coming home with me, right now. You're not to leave the house. We're going to call Nino and tell him everything and he better call off that goon, or I am going to handle this my own way," John stormed.

"Calm down, Dad. Come on, let's go home." Laura called Mr. Stone and explained the situation quickly. He told her to take the rest of the week off and call him after the New Year. She thanked him and promised to keep in touch with him on what was happening. After collecting her things, Laura put on her coat and shut down the office. John followed her home.

****

When Laura arrived home, she and John explained to Marlene what was happening. Marlene grew just as worried and made it perfectly clear that Laura was not to be left alone. While things were fresh, Laura called Nino to ask him a few questions. She did not want to reveal all that Sam had discovered about Tony and Beth, so not to worry him.

"Laura *mia*, you okay?" His raspy voice asked over the line.

"Nonno, I'm not sure. I just have to ask you a few questions about Alfonso," Laura simply stated.

"Si, *amore*. What is it?"

"Nonno, please tell me the truth. Are you having Alfonso follow Tony?"

* * *

Nino cringed. He was caught red-handed. He remembered promising Laura that he would not take matters into his own hands unless she asked. *What was he to tell her now? How could he lie to her and risk destroying her trust in him?*

"Laura *mia*, I no want to lie to you. After what happened the day Alfonso drive you home and Tony was so rude, Alfonso took it upon himself to see that Tony be truthful to you. We already know that he likes you. This no secret," Nino told.

"Are you saying, yes, Nonno," Laura frankly pressed.

"*Si, amore*. Alfonso followed Tony to White Plains," Nino revealed.

"I already know this, Nonno. What did Alfonso find?" Laura pressed.

"That the woman from John's office, she was with Tony."

Laura's heart sank. Just hearing it again, confirmed for her what Sam had discovered.

"Nonno, can you do me a favor?" Laura questioned. "Please tell Alfonso to stay out of it now. John has someone already investigating it and Alfonso will only get himself in trouble if he's seen snooping around Tony. Just tell him to back off for his own good."

"*Si*, I will call him right away. No worry, Laura *mia*. Everything will be okay. You have a good father. John is a smart man."

"Thanks, Nonno," Laura whispered. She said goodbye and hung up. Laura explained her conversation to Marlene and John. They seemed more at ease, knowing Nino was going to talk to Alfonso and see to it that he backed off.

"Darling, you look exhausted. Go upstairs to your room and rest. I'll call you when dinner is ready," Marlene offered.

"Don't you need help?"

"I'll help her. Go on up. You need rest," John offered.

Laura slowly dragged her feet up the stairs. Her heart felt heavy. She pulled back her bedspread and lay down on her comforter. Laura cried. She cried for all the heartache she felt; she cried for the betrayal and the hurt Tony was causing her.

Unexpectedly, a sharp pain shot through her back into her stomach. Laura gasped. She clutched her belly, holding her breath until the sharp pain ceased. Slowly, she let her breath out. Concern for her baby washed over her. She was so wrapped up in her relationship problems she was neglecting to care for herself and her baby.

"I'm so sorry, baby," she cried. "I'll never hurt you. I'll take good care of you."

Laura heard the telephone ring. Curious, she opened her bedroom door and listened.

"Tony, Laura's resting. What did you want?" she heard John ask. "Well, I wonder if I should bother her, just so you could speak to her. Haven't you caused her enough pain?"

Laura shouted down the stairs, "I'll talk to him, Dad. Please, I'll get the phone up here."

"Hold on," John reluctantly told Tony.

Laura picked up the telephone in John and Marlene's room. John spoke into the receiver to Laura. "You should be resting," he chastised.

"I will, Dad, please, just give me a moment," Laura begged. John sighed and hung up on his end.

"Hello?" Laura whispered.

"Hey," Tony murmured.

Just the sound of his voice sent her stomach into summersaults. She could not be without him. "Hi," she managed, in a nasally voice.

"I'd really like to see you. If you're not feeling well tonight, maybe tomorrow?" Tony asked.

"Don't listen to my dad. He's just being overprotective. I can meet you. Where and when?" she questioned.

"How about the park in 15 minutes? Dress warm, it's a bit chilly out there."

"See you then," Laura whispered.

She ran into her room, swiftly changed out of her work clothes, and squeezed into a pair of jeans and a thick sweater. She brushed her hair and touched up her makeup. Sprinkling perfume on her wrists and neck, she glanced at her reflection in the mirror. No makeup in the world could mask the worry lines around her eyes. Laura sighed. *How was she going to slip away unnoticed?* John and Marlene were sure to give her grief. Ultimately, she decided to tell them.

Descending the stairs, she found John sitting on the bottom steps. He did not look up to her, but kept his head down. "You're going to meet him, aren't you?" he asked.

"Yeah, Dad, in 15 minutes," Laura sat next to him on the step.

He gazed lovingly upon her. "Laura, I can't stop you and the only reason I'm letting you walk out that door, is because I know Tony will keep you safe and would never harm you physically. Yet, he can do just as much damage to you emotionally."

Laura cast her eyes downward now. "That's a chance I have to take. We can't go on like this, Dad. This not knowing is killing me. I need to know where he stands, no matter how painful."

"I understand. Be careful. Come straight home. Don't be out in public alone, okay?"

Laura nodded. She kissed his cheek and Marlene's, who stood not five feet away, listening. "Be careful," she whispered, giving Laura a hug.

****

Tony paced the park parking lot. He prayed he would be unselfish enough to see this through. He prayed he could find the strength to let her go. Tony prayed that he would not fall apart on seeing her, because he longed to hold her so much, it physically hurt him.

When her car pulled up, he suddenly felt nauseated. She looked beautiful, as always. Her hair was straighter than she usually kept it, falling over her shoulders. She wore a brown parka jacket that came down past her waist and blue jeans. A brown wool hat covered her head and matching gloves protected her hands. She walked toward him, seemingly unsure.

* * *

Laura could spot him a mile away. He leaned against his car. His brown bomber jacket fit snuggly at his tight waist. His lamb's wool collar was pulled up and he sported a hat over his crazy waves. She walked to him, uncertain how she would react. She felt anger and betrayal. She felt love—an overpowering love for him. Tony watched her approach him. Yet, she refused to fall into his arms.

His arms were not outstretched. Laura's heart nearly stopped. He did not look happy. He looked disconnected and bleak.

"Come on, let's take a walk," he offered. He did not extend his hand.

Laura walked beside him, looking around at the strangers at the park. Children played, sliding down a nearby hill on sleds. Others skated in the tennis court turned into an ice rink. The park lights illuminated the entire area. They strolled down the path that encircled the large park.

Laura recalled all the walks they used to take down their trail off Crabtree Lane in the past. Her heart ached for those simpler days. *Why did life always have to be so complicated?*

"Thanks for meeting me out here," Tony said.

"Well, I figured sooner or later we'd have to talk. No sense in putting it off. Do you have something you want to get off your chest?" she coolly asked.

"Look if you're asking about my past . . ."

Laura cut in, "Tony, it's evident you don't want to share your past with me and that's fine. I'm not going to beg you to want to be open with me. It's obvious you don't trust me or don't want to tell me. Whatever! I'm not talking about your past. I'm talking about right now."

Tony seemed stunned by her outburst. "What do you mean?" he quizzed, confused.

"Is there something you need to tell me tonight or not? Why did you call me out here in the cold?"

Tony stopped to face her. His eyes looked tortured—hurt. "You're right," he confessed. "I do have something I need to tell you. I'm sorry, Laura. I'm sorry I led you to believe that we could have a future together. I was wrong. I have too many issues. We can't get married," he finally blurted.

Laura was not surprised at his words. More than ever, she felt angry. "Don't," she whispered in a voice that quivered. "Don't patronize me and don't you dare insult my intelligence with the 'I have too many issues' bit. Because I knew going in that you had issues. We all do! Just tell the real truth. You're not calling the wedding off because of what you've learned of your past. You're calling the wedding off because you have found someone else," she accused.

Tony looked at her in surprise. "What?"

"That's right, I know where you went. I know Beth followed you to White Plains and that she came to your hotel room. What I don't understand is . . . *how? How could you?* I am carrying your baby. Doesn't that mean anything to you?"

"You had me followed?" he questioned, growing angry. He yanked off his hat and ran his left hand through his hair.

Laura could not help but notice that he had removed her ring. Her heart sank further. Focusing back on the subject at hand, she argued, raising her voice, "That's beside the point. You've been unfaithful to me. After everything we've been to each other. After all that I have given you. Forgiveness and unconditional love." She sniffed and continued in a whisper, "I-I-I gave myself to you. My heart, my mind . . ." Laura let out a whimper, ". . . My body. You've hurt me. You won't even wear my ring, anymore!"

* * *

Tears coursed down Tony's cheeks. He felt deplorable for allowing her to deem that he had betrayed her, that he had taken off her ring, when he had really lost it. Yet, this could be the easy way out for her. If she continued to believe this, she would let him go more easily and that is what he wanted for her—to be let down with ease.

"Don't you have anything to say for yourself," she cried.

"I'm sorry," Tony mustered. "But you had no right to have me followed. I'm not a criminal."

"No, maybe you're not, but my family wants to protect me and that's all they were trying to do," she explained.

"I would've come to you eventually. I needed time," Tony admitted.

"How much more time? The wedding was two months away. The baby's birth is four months away. What do you expect me to do now that you don't want to marry me anymore?" she grilled.

"I don't know."

"What is wrong with you? What happened to my Tony? What happened to the man who promised he'd never let me go? Where is he?" she cried.

"I can't do this anymore."

Tony walked away abruptly. He could not stand to see her hurting so deeply. He could not stomach his own actions. Yet, it had to be done. Tony wanted to end the misery and pain inside his heart. Tempted to put an end to it all, he decided to race to the nearest church.

* * *

Laura watched him walk away. "Tony," she cried. "Wait!" She ran to catch up to him. "Please," she whispered, grasping his arm.

He looked down at her with tear-filled eyes. "Don't," his voice cracked. "Don't make this harder."

"Why are you doing this to us?" she finally asked. "I've never loved anyone the way I love you."

He caressed her face softly with his hand. "It's over, Laura. Goodbye." A tear slipped down his cheek and he walked away.

"Please," she called out. "Don't leave me!" People turned to stare. Laura wiped her face and walked toward the parking lot. Sobs shook her shoulders and tears blurred her vision. She could not even locate him. She searched the park for him. He was suddenly out of sight. She heard a vehicle peel out of the parking lot, guessing that it was his truck. Laura lost control and could not stop sobbing.

She searched her pocket for her keys, unable to find them. She checked her purse to no avail. She panicked, afraid to be alone in the park as dusk set in. She retraced their steps down the path, unable to see past her tears. Looking around, she found that the park was emptying out and people were leaving. It was nearing five o'clock and the park was closing.

Laura needed to find her keys promptly, before the park shut down. She ran down the path, fear seizing her. Wiping the tears from her eyes, she struggled to find clarity. The ground was fuzzy. Her keys were nowhere in sight. Swells of tears coursed down her face. She felt confused and suddenly weak. Someone was yelling at her, but Laura was out of focus. They were saying something about her keys, but she could not respond.

She was holding her breath again, because a monstrous pain ripped through her belly. She felt her knees hit the cold wet ground. She heard screaming, not recognizing that the shrilling cries were her own.

Losing complete focus, Laura could only see darkness. Strong arms suddenly seized her and she felt herself floating. Someone was carrying her to safety. Laura gave God thanks, before passing out.

CHAPTER 16

Galatians 6:7

"Do not be deceived: God cannot be mocked. A man reaps what he sows."

The ringing was not only the buzzing in Laura's ear, but the wailing of the ambulance, while it sped toward the hospital. A warm hand held hers, caressing her softly. She felt comforted by this hand. A voice promised her that she would be okay, but it was swallowed by the blaring siren and she was unable to recognize it.

She wanted to open her eyes, but Laura suffered from exhaustion. She had not the strength to lift an eyelid and was anxious that her child might be in danger. Another pain racked her body and Laura could hear the paramedic shouting orders to have a room prepared in labor and delivery.

No! It was too soon. The baby could not be coming. Something sharp pierced her arm and she guessed they were inserting an IV.

"Is she in labor?" the voice queried.

"Yes. How far along is she in her pregnancy?"

"I don't know! Four maybe five months. It's too soon!"

"We'll do what we can to stop the labor."

Laura tried to move her tongue to speak. It felt glued to the roof of her mouth. She struggled to work up some saliva to talk, but it seemed she had not a drop of moisture left in her. "Help," she muttered.

"Ma'am?" the paramedic spoke. "We've arrived at the hospital. Just stay calm. We'll take care of you and your baby." His voice faded, as he moved out of the vehicle. "Sir, you may remain in the waiting room, until we have more news of your wife . . ."

Wife? Laura was confused. She could feel the paramedics move her through the emergency room doors. Doctors immediately approached them, while the paramedics spouted her status.

Someone touched her forehead and kissed her. Laura forced her eyes open. Her vision was blurred. She blinked trying to see more clearly. "Let's get her down to L and D, prompt!" The doctor barking the orders forced her eyes open and shined a light into each one. "Ma'am, can you see me? Just nod if you can't speak."

"You're blurry," she uttered. "Oh!" Laura screeched. Pain seared through her abdomen.

"Breathe," the doctor shouted. Laura blew air out of her mouth, gasping as the pain seized her. She took in gulps of air, panting. As they wheeled her down endless hallways, her pain slowly diminished.

"Okay, you got through it. Rest up," he ordered. "Keep those fluids running through her stat. She is severely dehydrated. Get a urinalysis before having her down the gluc, and then extract two smalls of hemo. Administer 100 mgs of Demerol afterward, for the pain." He took a breath and asked her if she could drink.

Laura nodded. Her mouth was so dry. She wished they had asked that in the first place. Nurses scurried in and out of the room they moved her to. Someone helped her to sit up and Laura tried to open her eyes again. She was finally able to focus. A nurse asked if she could stand. Laura nodded, praying her legs could hold her up and the nurse assisted her into the bathroom to get a urinalysis. Afterward, Laura clumsily entered the bed, thankful the dizziness had ceased.

Her OB/GYN, Dr. Ben Packard, moved into the room. He approached the bed with her chart under his arm. "You're in big trouble, young lady," he reprimanded.

"Dr. Packard, what's happening to me?" she whispered, still unstable.

"You're not taking care of yourself. You're severely dehydrated. You're in premature labor, and we have to stop it." He took hold of the little orange bottle the same nurse handed him. Removing the top, he handed it to her. "Drink all this," he commanded.

Laura grasped the bottle with trembling fingers. Putting it to her lips, she drank the entire bottle at once. It tasted like an orange soda. "That was good. I'm so thirsty," she complained.

"That orange-soda-tasting drink is actually glucose. We'll draw your blood in a while and check your sugars. Laura, I don't mean to scare you, but you've placed your child in jeopardy by not properly caring for yourself. Your body is screaming out for liquids. Let's hope we can get these labor pains to cease."

Again, Laura was taken by another contraction and tried breathing her way through it. When it diminished, she laid her head on the pillow, the tears slipping into her hair. She had allowed the circumstances surrounding her to put her child at risk. She felt angry with herself for letting it happen.

The IV continued to drip fluids into her, rehydrating, and hopefully reversing the labor. The doctor then checked her and found that she was not dilated. This was good news, he reported. The liquids were finally slowing down the labor. He ordered her to rest.

Thirty minutes after having downed the glucose, a nurse drew her blood, and then placed a Band-Aid over the poke. The Demerol was finally administered into her IV and Laura rested, at last.

A short time later, Laura heard rustling about her room. The sounds of beeping and overhead speakers calling for doctors filled her head. She opened her eyes to find that the room was nearly dark. In the chair next to her bed, Alfonso sat with his head in his hand. His hair was in disarray and his pants from the knees down, wet and dirty.

Laura opened her mouth to try to talk. His head shot up. His eyes crashed with hers. He stood swiftly and approached her bedside. "Laura . . ." he whispered. His eyes were red-rimmed.

Laura swallowed, trying to moisten her mouth, still dry. "Fonzie, what are you doing here?" she quizzed.

He pulled the chair closer, ran a hand through his hair, and sat. He grabbed her hand. A grin fell across his face. His dark eyes smiling. "I'm glad you're okay," he whispered again.

"Did they stop the labor?" she enquired, still groggy.

"Yes, the baby's okay and so are you, thankfully. You scared the tar outta me," he confessed.

"Where's my family? Why are you here?" she wondered.

"I haven't had the chance to call anybody, yet. I wanted to see that you were all right first. I'll call Nino for you and he can contact your parents," he suggested.

"You still haven't answered my question, Fonz," she insisted.

"What?" he evaded.

"Why are *you* here?"

"I was at the park when you collapsed," he admitted.

"Fonz . . ." Laura pressed her head back into her pillow, closing her eyes to try to keep her blood pressure from escalating. "Alfonso, what were you doing at the park? Don't lie to me. Tell me the truth," she demanded.

"So, if I tell you I went there to go sledding you won't believe me?" he tested.

"No. The truth, Fonz."

"Ice skating?"

"Fonz, don't make me raise my voice. If you're going to dodge my question, I'm going to tell you what I think you were doing there," Laura pushed.

"I'd love to hear your theory," he teased.

"Oh!" Laura flustered. "I think you came there on Nonno's orders to keep an eye on Tony."

"Good one, but not quite," he teased.

"This is not a laughing matter, Alfonso. You have to stop meddling in my business!" she insisted.

"If I hadn't been there, both you and the baby would still be in grave danger," he stated calmly.

"I understand that and I am so grateful to you for being there, regardless of your motive. Still, your intention for being there scares me," now Laura confessed.

"Laura, I love you. I'm not going away. Especially, not after the way that . . . that . . ." Alfonso put a finger between his teeth to keep from speaking. He looked away, his other hand still holding hers. "That man you claim to love left you alone, in the dark, knowing full well that you were near hysterics."

Laura's heart raced. He told her he loved her. The situation was more serious than she anticipated. She had to set it straight without stressing herself. "Fonz, you don't love me. You barely know me and you need to remember that I *don't* return your feelings. I care about you and I'll admit that I enjoy your company. But . . ."

"But you love *him*. He's not worthy of you. He's the reason you almost lost your baby, tonight. Oh, and by the way, yes, I do," he claimed.

"Fonz, you better go. I don't know how to make you understand that you can only be my friend. Nothing more; nothing less."

Alfonso appeared hurt. His eyes swelled with unshed tears. "I'm going to just assume that the Demerol is affecting your ability to reason. You know I'd make a far more stable husband for you, than that *pazzo*. When you finally come to your senses, I'll be here. Like I said, I'm not going anywhere." He rose and stalked out of the room.

Laura lifted her hands to her face, careful not to pull on the IV. She took two deep breaths, forcing the tears away. The problem was only escalating. Laura extended her free hand and was able to reach the telephone. Dialing home, she was able to contact John and Marlene, who were at the hospital within 15 minutes.

Marlene dashed into the room, tears already freely falling. "What happened to you?" she cried.

"We're okay—the baby and I. We're okay now," she reassured.

Marlene hugged her and cried, "We should have never let you go alone! I'm so sorry!"

John stood behind her seething. Laura could see that he was angry with himself for permitting her to go. "What did he do to you?" he spit through clenched teeth.

"Dad, I'm sorry to scare you. It was my fault this happened. I wasn't taking . . ."

"Do not blame yourself!" he raged in a mounted voice. "Tell me what exactly happened."

Laura explained what she could recollect of the blurry evening. "He said that the wedding was off. I called him out on Beth. He did not deny it. When I started to emotionally fall apart, he said he could not handle it and he left. I remember looking for my keys. I think I lost them. Suddenly, a pain shot across my back all the way around to my abdomen. I don't remember much after that, only that someone helped me. It turned out . . . it was Alfonso."

"What! That's it. I'm calling Sam. This has got to stop. You're not going to Nino's anymore, while that man's in the picture."

"What was he doing there?" Marlene questioned.

"He's stalking her. He's keeping tabs on her. Laura, I don't want to worry you, but are you aware of the seriousness of this?" John roared.

"Yes, I am, but in the meantime, I'm really grateful that he was there, because he saved our lives. I know you probably think I'm gullible, but I believe that he does not intend to hurt me. If he did, he wouldn't have saved my life and the baby's." Laura touched her round abdomen.

"You couldn't be more wrong," shouted John. "Why, I have a mind to . . ."

Disrupting the conversation, Dr. Packard entered. "I hate to interrupt, but we do have patients sleeping next door. Can we keep it quiet in here?" he chided.

"Forgive me, Doctor, I'm just trying to talk some sense into this thick head," John stormed, pointing at Laura.

"That's quite alright," the doctor chuckled. "I understand your frustration with our little patient. She got herself into quite the pickle," he joshed. "Actually, I'm surprised you didn't end up hospitalized sooner, Laura."

"Why?" she searched.

"I sent out for the test results stat and have them here. There's a combination of reasons you went into labor tonight," he began.

Marlene took a seat near Laura's bed. Her face paled and she looked frightened. John stood behind her with his hands on her shoulders. "What's wrong with my daughter?" she uttered in a small voice.

"Laura was brought in critically dehydrated. This is detrimental to the baby's health. If the child runs low on amniotic fluid, there can be dire consequences for the baby. Abnormalities, deformation—I don't mean to scare you, but you need to understand the importance of eating right and drinking amply. Now the dehydration was not just brought upon by your own doing, gestational diabetes is a contributing factor."

"What?" Laura cried. "Diabetes?"

"Yes, the urinalysis and the blood work have confirmed the diagnosis. The good news is, this is something that can be taken care of with proper diet and exercise. I will not be prescribing any meds for this, yet. I trust you'll take care of yourself, from now on. Plenty of rest, eat right, drink sufficiently, exercise, and Laura—no stress. Are you under strain in your personal life? I understand with Paul's death that it hasn't been easy for you."

"Yes, I really miss him." Laura whispered, tears instantly brewing.

"Well, he would have wanted you to take better care of yourself. He sincerely cared about you and your baby. Enough to sacrifice his life. Don't let his death be a waste."

"I understand," she managed.

"Well, if you want to deliver a healthy baby, absolutely follow my orders." Dr. Packard insisted.

"Oh, don't you worry, Doctor. She'll not be leaving our sight!" John reassured.

The doctor stayed a moment longer, going over some informational pamphlets that described the symptoms and how to care for herself with gestational diabetes. Laura listened carefully, absorbing the information. Dr. Packard exited the room, leaving Laura with John and Marlene.

"This is unreal!" Laura exclaimed. "No wonder I've been so dizzy and feeling parched and shaky all the time. This all makes sense."

A knock at the door startled her. Nino rushed into the door with concern on his face. "Laura, Laura what happened to you?" he cried, embracing her. Laura explained what the doctor had discovered. Nino listened intently, while holding her hand in his. "I passed Alfonso in the waiting room and he told me you almost die! *Amore*, you must take care. I can no lose you, too," he moaned. Taking a handkerchief from his pocket, he wiped his moist eyes.

"I'm okay now, Nonno. I'll take better care of the baby and myself. I promise," she vowed.

"Look Nino, I don't want to ruffle any feathers, but Laura was found by your employee, Alfonso. It wasn't a coincidence. If you are having either her, or Tony, followed by this guy, you need to call him off," John warned.

"*Mama mia*," Nino exclaimed. "John, I understand you concern. I did no tell Alfonso to follow Tony or my granddaughter. If he was pursuing Laura, it is no by my hand. I will talk to him again, and tell him to leave you alone," he promised, directing the last statement to Laura. "In the meantime, it is no Alfonso you need to worry about. Tony Giacalone is responsible for this!"

"He's an ill man and has enough stresses of his own. I don't approve of how he abandoned Laura tonight. But I'm sure if he knew she was ill, he would've never left her," John defended.

"You mean to tell me you defend that guy! If he love Laura, he would never leave her!" Nino expressed.

"I agree, but we don't know what he's going through. It's no excuse, that's for sure. But he's the father of this child and I believe he should know that Laura's in the hospital," John insisted. "Laura, would you agree?"

Laura shrugged unsure. Nino huffed, "When he comes, I no want to see him."

"Well, no one is keeping you here," John spat.

"Dad," Laura pleaded. "Please, don't fight. I want you all here with me. If you think we need to call Tony, well, I guess it's only right. If he comes . . . well, if he comes, I'll be surprised. If not, that's fine, too."

Nino leaned forward and kissed Laura's forehead. "I'll be in the waiting room, if you need me. *Ti amo, amore mio*," he whispered his love. He walked away, shaking his head, and mumbling words in Sicilian that Laura could not comprehend.

John watched with disdain as Nino left. "I'm sorry. I shouldn't have been rude to him. He has no right to judge Tony, though. Like he's so perfect."

"Dad, just get it over with and call Tony."

John did exactly that and called Tony's home. There was no answer and so he tried calling Uncle Frank. He was able to reach Frank, who promised to relay the message to Tony.

Hospital visiting hours were ending and Tony had yet to arrive. John and Marlene kissed Laura goodnight and promised to be there first thing in the morning to take her home. Nino refused to leave the hospital, periodically checking in on Laura from in the waiting room.

Laura finally nodded off to sleep, allowing the Demerol to help her rest.

****

Tony entered the hospital room, after explaining that he was the child's father and that he had just been notified of Laura's condition. They argued with him, stating that the father was already present, resting in the waiting room. After providing proper ID and confirming it with Laura's hospital records, they allowed him to enter her room for a short period. He tiptoed in, hoping not to disrupt her sleep.

Guilt tore through him at the sight of her small pale face. The nurse on staff had already explained her condition to him and he cursed himself for being the source of additional stress. He gazed at her closely. He could recall the first time he laid eyes on her and how he wondered what it would be like to kiss her lips. He missed her kisses. Tony gently leaned forward and pecked her lips. She was still as sweet as honey.

A sudden turmoil erupted inside him. He loved her. There was no denying it. *How could he try to live without her?* He was lying to himself, if he believed he could. Life without Laura would not be life; it would be death. *Did he do the right thing by walking away?* Looking at her and picturing his life empty, his heart shouted a deafening, *'NO'!*

"Oh, Jesus," he whispered. "What did I do? How do I fix this? Help me, Lord," he cried.

He pulled the chair up next to her and sat. Tony put his hands together in prayer.

* * *

Nino entered the room. His blood recoiled upon seeing Tony sitting in the chair next to his granddaughter. He had nerve, Nino would give him that. If it had not been for the situation with Alfonso, Nino would not be thinking of having the conversation he was about to have with Tony. He quietly cleared his throat. Tony's head shot up and their eyes met. Contempt was apparent in Tony's glare. The feeling was mutual. Nino nodded giving him a signal to leave the room. Tony quietly stood and followed Nino into the waiting room.

* * *

Tony stalked passed the old man into the room. Nino hastily closed the door. Thankfully, they were the only people there. That's what Tony thought, until he realized that Alfonso rested, sprawled out on a sofa. He grumbled under his breath at the sight of the man. "What's he doing here?" Tony hissed.

Alfonso's eyes flew open. He immediately jumped to his feet and sprung at Tony, grasping his shirt. "You miserable punk! You left her to die! I should kill you!" Alfonso threatened.

Tony's arms instantly went up grasping Alfonso's shirt as well. "Don't threaten me, you gorilla. You've got guts accusing me and you've got nerve claiming to be the father to my baby!"

"Boys . . . Boys!" Nino cried, prying the men apart. "Laura would no want this! Stop, before they throw us all out."

Alfonso pushed Tony and Tony pushed right back. Tony and Alfonso glared at each other. "What's he doing here?" he asked Nino again.

"I saved her life, no thanks to you!" Alfonso shouted.

"What?" Tony questioned.

"You heard me. I found her on the cold ground, after she collapsed because of you," Alfonso accused.

"What were you doing there? Following me, per your boss's orders?" Tony charged back. His eyes raked Nino's. "Haven't you caused enough pain? You gonna do to me what you did to Paul? You gonna send me 'sleeping with the fishes', because I've failed to make Laura happy?"

Nino put his hands up in peace. He looked to Alfonso and ordered him to retreat and take a seat. Alfonso reluctantly sat down. His infuriated gaze never left Tony's. "Please, Tony, sit down. Let's talk like men, not boys."

Tony refused to sit. Nino sat down, anyway, allowing a loud sigh to escape his lips. He rubbed at his chest. "We are gentlemen, no animals. We all have the one thing in common—*Laura*. If she knows we are fighting, she would be furious with us. Let's talk. Tony, I understand that you call the wedding off, tonight. Why?"

"It's none of your business, old man. What I do, is none of your business!" Tony spouted.

"I ask you one thing . . . do you love her? Do you have the other woman?"

"I don't have to answer you, Nino. I have my reasons for breaking up with her and they're no business of yours. But I think you know that I love her and only her. I couldn't look at another woman. Why would I? Laura's all I'd ever need and more and that's precisely why I let her go. Let's put it this way, I finally agree with what you used to tell her. I don't want to burden her with all my problems. I want her and my baby to have a good life. I don't think I can give her that," Tony admitted.

"I agree, so drop dead and make room for those of us who can!" Alfonso suggested.

"*YOU*? You think you can give her a better life? You think your Mob ties won't eventually bring harm to her or my baby? I'd rather die than see her with you!" Tony avowed.

"We can arrange that!" Alfonso confirmed.

"Gentlemen!" Nino nearly shouted, standing again. "Stop this! No one is going to die. Tony, Laura is in love with *you*. She has waited for *you* for all these years. Why do you want to throw this away? Make it work!"

"I can't, Nino! There's too much pain from my past. Too much hurt that I don't know how to overcome," Tony professed.

"So, you will lose the love of you life? This no make sense! You know you will never bring harm to her or to the baby," Nino insisted.

"My father probably never intended on hurting his kids and he did! He did more than hurt us, he damaged us for good. Had my sisters not died in the fire Galante ignited, they would've grown up totally messed up. I can't take the chance that I might mess up a child. No way!" Tony claimed.

Alfonso laughed aloud. "Well, you know what they say, the apple don't fall too far from the tree!" he exclaimed.

"Shut up, pig!" Tony shouted.

"Shh!" Nino cried, still holding his chest. "Please, I don't want to have to drive home and be away from my *nipote*. Be quiet and let's discuss this rationally!" He turned to Tony again. "Tony, I'm sorry for you that you have so much pain. Only you can control youself. If you say you going to be the good father, you will be the good father *and* the good husband. Do you no have control over youself?"

"Yes, I do now," Tony confessed.

"Then why are you afraid? Why you risk you future? You are to be the head of this little *famiglia*! It is time you took the control," Nino commanded.

"It's so easy to say!" Tony exclaimed.

"It's easy to do! You take the reins into you hands and fight this! Fight for you family!" Nino declared.

"I had every intention of doing that! Don't you think I want to finally stand up and be a man? That animal deserved to suffer the same pain he put me through. I let him get away with hurting my sisters, my brother, my mother. You're right about one thing, it's got to stop! I won't let him have that kind of power anymore. I've got to make this right—for Laura—for myself. I can't allow any more room for pain. Laura nearly died because I failed to care for her. I need to protect her, not allow harm to come to her." Tony swore.

"Then you stick to the original plan. Keep Laura safe. She has had too much pain and it is time to have peace! There is only one way to do this. Do what you got to do, Tony!" Nino encouraged.

* * *

Perfect! Alfonso got just what he needed to set his plan in motion. His rage flared. He hated the men before him and he would do what he must to get rid of them. They are what stood in his way of happiness with Laura—his fortune. They must go. He stormed out of the waiting room, disgusted. Both men stared at him as he left.

Entering the bathroom, he made sure he was alone. He withdrew the small recorder from his pocket. Rewinding it, he played back the last part of the conversation Nino had just had with Tony. He could not have planned a more perfect set-up. Hitting 'play', he listened.

". . . You are to be the head of this little famiglia! It is time you took the control,"

"It's so easy to say!"

"It's easy to do! You take the reins into you hands and fight this! Fight for you family!"

"I had every intention of doing that! Don't you think I want to finally stand up and be a man? That animal deserved to suffer the same pain he put me through. I let him get away with hurting my sisters, my brother, my mother. You're right about one thing, it's got to stop! I won't let him have that kind of power anymore. I've got to make this right—for Laura—for myself. I can't allow any more room for pain. Laura nearly died because I failed to care for her. I need to protect her, not allow harm to come to her."

"Then you stick to the original plan. Keep Laura safe. She has had too much pain and it is time to have peace! There is only one way to do this. Do what you got to do, Tony!"

Alfonso laughed out loud. He would play this recording back for Mario Galante and Mario would assume that Tony was talking about him. Mario would assume that Nino was encouraging Tony to take over the family and protect them. Mario would believe that Nino and Tony were a threat and that they needed to be eliminated. He would give him the help he needed to finish them off and Alfonso would walk away with everything.

Laura would need comfort—a shoulder to cry on and Alfonso would be there. He would pick up the pieces of her shattered life. She would inherit Nino's fortune, and after marrying Alfonso, he would have it all. Love, money, *and* power.

CHAPTER 17

2 Thessalonians 2:12

"All will be condemned who have not believed the truth but have delighted in wickedness."

The next morning, Laura munched on the scrambled eggs that were part of the breakfast delivered to her room. After Dr. Packard's morning visit, she was relieved to find that she and the baby were out of harm's way, and able to go home. Thanking Jesus for the good news, Laura promised to set her priorities straight. The baby came first. Everything else came second, including Tony. She was sorry for the suffering that he had been subjected to, but after the way he had abandoned her, she realized that he was nowhere ready to be a husband and father.

Tears formed in her eyes. She felt so disappointed—so depressed. She had many hopes and many dreams that included Tony. After his miraculous return the day of her falsified wedding to Paul, she was certain they were meant to be. Yet, he had been unfaithful to her. Their love did not mean to him what it meant to her. She was saddened by this reality.

Sniffing her tears away, she concentrated on her breakfast, drinking the non-sweetened juice and plenty of water. The baby moved within her and she touched her belly lovingly. "Do you like your breakfast, little one?" she asked her unborn child.

"If he or she eats anything like you do, you're going to need a second job," Alfonso interrupted with a taunt. "Good morning, how do you feel?" He sauntered into the room with a fresh face, clean clothes, and a smile. His cloak was thrown over his arm and his Italian hat was in hand.

"I can't help it if I love to eat and that I'm not picky. When you grow up eating meager meals, you grow to appreciate real food," Laura expressed with a smile. "Good morning, I feel much better, thank you," she added.

He stood at the end of her bed and extended a hand to touch her blanketed foot. His eyes grew sincere, losing their amusing shimmer. "I'm so glad. You had everyone worried—especially me."

Laura uneasily looked down, avoiding his stare. "I can't thank you enough for saving us. You're a hero. But don't let it go to your head, now. You were still there for your own agenda, so don't think I've forgotten that," Laura warned.

"Hey, I told you," he claimed, still serious, "I have nothing to hide anymore. I want you to be a part of my life. I'll do whatever it takes."

"Fonz," Laura sighed, finally meeting his eyes. "I am so flattered, but it can't happen."

"Why not? Tony's obviously out of the picture," he painfully stated.

Laura flinched.

"I'm sorry, I didn't mean for that to sound so insensitive. I know you're hurting. I can help you forget about him. Please, let me," Alfonso begged.

"You're right. Tony may be out of the picture, but that doesn't mean he's out of my heart. I will not jump into a relationship to try to forget him. *That's* a disaster waiting to happen. It'll be a long time before I can move on—if ever," Laura explained.

"I have all the time in the world," Alfonso declared.

"Boy, are you ever persistent! Nonno is right; you do have a hard head!" Laura laughed, nervously.

"Don't forget it. By the way, I put your keys in the closet with the rest of your things," he clarified. "I better go before someone walks in and sees me here. They're bound to throw the book at me since I'm such a criminal and should stay away from you," he said sarcastically.

"It's for your own good that you stay away, for now, Fonz. I don't want you to get in trouble with the law," Laura advised. "Just a couple questions for you before you go. How did you find my keys and how did you get an ambulance there so quickly?"

"Before that first contraction, when you were crying and searching your purse for your keys, a man called to you. He'd found them in close proximity to where you had walked with Tony. When I came to your help, he ran to a nearby house and called an ambulance," he explained.

"And you just happened to be there?"

"Did I say sledding or ice skating?"

Laura smiled, not really feeling much for joking, anymore. She quizzed seriously, "I know you were keeping an eye on me, but have you also been calling me? Are you my prank caller?"

A look of fear came over his face. "You're being pranked?" he questioned with sincerity.

"Yes, I assumed it was you, Fonz. Are you telling me it's not?"

"Laura, I think I've been pretty up-front about how I feel. Why would I prank you?

"I don't know. To keep tabs on my whereabouts?"

"No, sweetie, I have not been pranking you. You better be careful, there are some sick people out there," he warned. He stood still for a moment. Peeking at the door, he dared to come to her bedside. "Can I kiss you goodbye?" he whispered.

Laura froze. She did not want to lead him on. Yet, he had saved her life and she felt indebted. A simple kiss on the cheek could not hurt. She nodded and he leaned forward. Laura leaned in, as well, and kissed his cheek, as he kissed hers. She leaned back, but Alfonso remained close. His nearness suddenly scared her. His large body was intimidating. He bowed closer, grasping her chin between his fingers.

"Don't," Laura whispered, her heart beating abruptly.

He ignored her and kissed her fully on the lips. Laura pushed him away.

"I said, don't! Don't ever do that again," she warned, growing angry. "You better leave!" Laura commanded. Alfonso straightened his poise. An eerie smile fell over his face, sending shivers down Laura's spine.

"You'll get used to those kisses," he predicted. "See you soon." Alfonso turned and walked out of the room.

Laura shook in her bed. She wanted so badly to believe he was a good guy. Somehow, he still spooked her.

A short period later, Marlene and John came by to bring Laura home. They sat in her room discussing the next few months, waiting on the doctor's okay to discharge her. John and Marlene both agreed that Laura needed to put her health and the health of her unborn child first.

"Are we all agreed?" John stated. "This baby comes first, no unnecessary sugars, plenty of water, healthy foods on a four-hour schedule, checking your blood sugar consistently, and rest. Rest . . . do you get that one?" he teased Laura.

"Yes, SIR!" she saluted with her right hand. "Anything else, SIR?"

"Quit that, you rascal. If you think I'm being strict now, you haven't seen anything yet!" he warned.

"Help me, Mom!" Laura pretended to cry.

"Are you kidding me? I'm going to be worse than him!" Marlene claimed.

"I'm in big trouble!" Laura complained.

"Better believe . . ." John's words halted mid-sentence. His eyes rested upon someone at the door.

Laura turned in time to see Tony enter. He looked disheveled. His hair was tousled, his clothes wrinkled, and his face stubbly with after-five shadow. Nino accompanied him, not looking his clean-cut self, either.

"Just in time," John added sardonically. "We were discussing how Laura's going to see to it that she's absolutely, positively, putting this baby first. Meaning no stress . . . amongst other things. That's your cue . . . to leave," he insisted.

Laura's heart doubled in rhythm. She could not believe her eyes. Tony and Nino came in together. *What was happening?* Tony looked at her. His eyes were remorseful and full of concern.

"Please!" Nino began, "Nobody wants to make Laura stress. But we love her, too, and we want to see that she is okay."

"She's better, as long as you two leave," John insisted.

Laura remained mute. She did not know what to say. Perhaps John was right, Tony needed to leave, but Nino could stay.

"I need to talk to Laura," Tony insisted as well.

John lifted his hand in protest, and then placed a finger on his lips. He seemed to be struggling with keeping his cool. "The last time you insisted on talking to my daughter, you left her outside in the cold and contributed to the start of premature labor. I think you've had your chance. Now—get—out." John whispered through clenched teeth.

"Laura, I'm sorry. Please, give me five minutes to explain," he begged.

"John, Marlene, please," Nino intervened. "We need to give these two time alone."

"Since when do you speak on behalf of Tony, when yesterday you blamed him for Laura's condition?" John quizzed.

"I can say the same to you. You defend him, yesterday. Now you kick him out? I took the time to listen to Tony. You should do the same thing!" Nino persisted.

"Laura, I'm sorry for yesterday. I was wrong. Give me a chance to explain," Tony pleaded, his eyes infiltrating hers.

Laura felt in a tug-of-war. She wanted more than ever to hear him out. At the same time, she could not trust him. He had waffled back and forth too many times. *Could she risk giving him another chance?*

"Laura has been through hell. You made your decision yesterday, when you abandoned your future wife and child. If you'd cared about her, you'd have known that Laura's in real danger. She shouldn't have been left alone. Someone's stalking her and I let her meet you, believing you would keep her safe. But because you've been so distant and because you continue to push her away, you were unaware of that now, weren't you?" John took in a deep breath.

Tony astoundingly looked at Laura, seeming oblivious to the news of her being stalked. He tore his stare away, guiltily.

"You couldn't even care enough to spend the holiday with her," John continued. "Why should she give you another chance? You keep blaming your behavior on your past and what you've discovered. No one is sorrier for what you've suffered than this family. We promised to love and support you through it. Yet, you pushed Laura and the rest of us away."

"Dad, stop," Laura finally interjected. She could see how John's words were afflicting Tony. Despite the mess he had created, she felt sorrow for him. "Please, I can't take this anymore. We've all made mistakes. I hate that everyone is at each other's throats. I just want peace, now. Can we try to get along? I love all of you."

"I'm sorry, Laura *mia*," Nino was the first to confess. He took hold of her hand and kissed it. "*Ti prometto*," he promised, "that I will keep trying to make the peace for you."

John reached forward and caressed her cheek. Marlene had a soft hand on his back, silently encouraging him to do the same. "I'm sorry, love. I don't want you to be hurt anymore. I'll try to be more civil," he pledged. He reached for Marlene's hand. "We'll give you some time to talk with Tony, *if* that's what you want."

Laura felt nervous about being alone with him, but nodded at John's suggestion.

"*Bravo*," Nonno clapped and complimented John with a genuine smile on his face. He kissed Laura's cheek and left. John reluctantly followed Marlene out.

Tony approached her bedside. "Thank you. I don't deserve this."

Laura peeked at his face. His eyes seemed sincere. "Well, I don't know what you can possibly say to excuse your recent behavior. But I've kicked myself in the past for not allowing you to get things off your chest. So, here's your chance," she offered.

"Well, before I begin, please tell me what's going on with you about this stalking thing," Tony requested.

"I don't really know what to tell you," Laura began, "I only know that someone has been pranking me by phone and a few times I felt I was being followed."

"Any idea who?" Tony probed.

"No," Laura fibbed, not wanting to get Alfonso into trouble unnecessarily. Especially, since she had no proof that he *was* her stalker.

Tony blew air forcefully from his lungs. "This is crazy. Just when I thought the danger was over."

"I don't think it's as serious as John and Sam believe it to be. Nevertheless, it does scare me," Laura confessed.

"I'm so sorry. I should've never left you. Do you forgive me? Please, say you do." Tony beseeched.

"I've told you a thousand times that I forgive you. That hasn't changed. But I really would like to understand the reasoning behind *your* actions. I really would love to know why you would betray our love with anyone, *especially Beth*," Laura emphasized.

"Laura," Tony exclaimed. He pulled the chair to her bedside and sat, grasping her hand. "The truth is, I . . . I lied," he confessed.

Laura looked at him questioningly. "About what?"

"About Beth. I was *never* with her. Yes, she somehow found that I was in White Plains and came to my hotel room, but I *never* let her in. Uncle Frank was with me. He's my witness. But yesterday, when we met and you accused me of cheating, I deluded myself into believing that if I allowed you to think that, then maybe it'd be easier for you to move on without me. I was wrong. I hurt you, and I'm so sorry for that," Tony expressed.

"You're sorry right now," Laura doubted. "What happens when you have another change of heart? What happens when you have another flashback or a dream? Are you going to push me away again? I can't live like this. I can't trust you anymore. One minute, we're in love and the next, you are breaking up with me. That kind of stress is putting our baby at risk and I won't chance that. We almost lost our baby, yesterday. I can't take that kind of gamble anymore."

"I don't blame you. I don't expect you to run into my arms after what I've done. As I've said before and I'll say again, I don't deserve you. You *are* too good for me. That's why I was trying to break it off! But, I was wrong! I see that, now. I *do* love you and I *am* the father of this baby. I'm ready to fight for you. I'm ready to put my fears aside and prove to you that I can be a good husband and father. I just ask that you give me the chance to prove myself."

"What about Beth? How do you feel about her and why did she meet you in White Plains?" Laura examined.

"Laura, I swear, you can ask Uncle Frank and he'll tell you the truth. I don't know how she knew I was at that particular hotel. The only thing that Frank and I have presumed is that she listened in when I called for hotel reservations. When she knocked on the door, I told her that she needed to leave and never talk to me again. She's getting more and more persistent and I don't know what I'm going to do. Either way, you have to believe that I love only you.

"Laura, *I can never love another.* I've just been so terrified to admit and accept my past. That's the only reason I've been pushing you away. But no more, I promise. I'm going to see you out of this hospital and I will prove my love for you all over again," he insisted.

"I'd love nothing more than for you to prove yourself to me. But you have a lot of work ahead of you. The past few weeks, even a stranger like Alfonso, has shown more concern over me," Laura accused.

Tony's back stiffened at the mention of Alfonso's name. "I don't like him, Laura. I'm sorry, but if he's showing you interest then that confirms my fears about him. When he brought you in, he claimed to be your husband. They wouldn't let me enter your room, until I verified my identity. Once they confirmed it with your file, they realized that he was falsely claiming to be your spouse. This is not good," Tony warned.

Laura's insides twisted. Her instincts about Alfonso's strange behavior were right on. She needed to stop protecting him and trust the people she loved. "Honestly, I am starting to get concerned as well," Laura confessed.

"Oh, Laura," Tony uttered, "I should've never let you out of my sight. I should've known that Nino's goon had an ulterior motive to his sudden career change from hit-man to chauffer. Something doesn't ring true about him and I'm not going to sit around and wait for something bad to happen." Tony stood and grabbed his jacket from a nearby chair.

"Wait, where are you going? What are you going to do?" Laura raised her voice in fear.

"Don't worry about anything. I'm going to take care of this. You just take care of our baby, okay? I love you, Laura." He kissed her cheek.

"Tony, wait!" she called to him.

"What is it?" he returned to her bedside.

"You should know that John already contacted Chief Sam. His purpose was to have you investigated, assuming you were being unfaithful to me with Beth . . ."

"So, that's how you knew Beth followed me to the hotel?" Tony interrupted.

"Yes. Please understand John's reasoning. He was only looking out for me," she explained.

"I know. John is a good man. He has every reason to be angry with me. I've created a catastrophe of our lives," Tony admitted with remorse. "But that's going to change. I promise you!"

She smiled at his persistence. Despite his haggard presence, his rugged good looks reeled her in. Finally taking a moment to look at him, she realized he was still in the same clothes as the night before.

"You're still in yesterday's clothes," she blurted aloud.

"I came here as soon as Uncle Frank called me, last night. You were sleeping when I got here. I didn't want to wake you, so I sat in the chair all night, praying you both would be okay. God's good to me, even when I'm not worthy of Him," he admitted.

"You were here all night?"

"Yes, I left for a moment to speak with your grandfather. I don't want to jump the gun, but we actually might be seeing eye to eye," Tony affirmed.

"I saw that. I'm impressed."

"Well, it wasn't that clean-cut. Alfonso and I almost came to blows. When I saw him in the waiting room, something inside me exploded. I don't like him and I don't trust him!"

Laura shifted, making herself more comfortable, before dropping the next bomb. "Tony, the reason the private investigator couldn't confirm that Beth entered your hotel room was because of a distraction. Sam confirmed that Alfonso was also present at the hotel. He caused a disturbance that lead the investigator away from the original suspect."

She could see that Tony was becoming more nervous. "Baby, you have got to stay away from this man. Something fishy is going on. Either Nino is using him to cause problems between us or he's doing it of his own free will. Either way, this isn't good. Is there anything else you need to tell me?"

Laura studied Tony's face. He looked thinner. Dark rings circled his eyes. Beneath his unshaved beard, she spotted his sweet dimple. She could easily fall into the temptation to give her heart wholly to him—to tell him everything. She wanted nothing more than to erase the past few weeks and plunge into his arms.

She looked at his heaving chest, still strong and solid underneath his cotton shirt. She could envision him chopping wood in the summer of '76, when they became engaged. His arms would flex with every blow of the axe. The blistering sun would make his skin glisten with perspiration. He would work endless hours for winter firewood.

If she continued with this line of thinking, she was likely to fall right into his arms, and that could not happen. Not yet. She did not know if she could trust him. Not because he would intentionally hurt her, but because his sordid past continued to wreak havoc on them. Until he was certain, she had to keep her heart safe.

"Laura, are you with me?" he asked with concern. "You zoned out for a moment there. Is there something more you want to tell me?"

Laura snapped out of the daze. She decided to trust him on the issues with Alfonso. "Yes, Tony. Alfonso sent me the roses with the strange card." She explained the connection she felt Nino's Christmas gift had to the strange card and how convenient it had been that Alfonso was consistently bumping into her. She admitted that he was openly pursuing her now, including the kiss he forced on her.

"He kissed you? He kissed you!" he repeated again. Tony clenched his hands.

"Tony, please, stay calm. I told him to never do it again!"

"Laura," Tony whispered, trying to remain cool. "This is worse than I thought. I feel like taking you outta here right now. You need to be under police surveillance. Laura, let me take you to our safe house," he begged.

"Tony, our safe house has been compromised. Alfonso can easily find out where I'm at. Remember, my grandfather has complete faith in him," Laura reminded him.

"Then you need to warn him."

"I have. Nonno knows all of this. Except Fonzie's recent attempt at kissing me."

"I'm going to kill him!"

"Tony!"

"I'm sorry. My blood boils at the thought of him touching you. He better not come near you again." Tony warned. "I'm calling John and Marlene in and we're going to figure this out as a family." He stalked toward the door and then suddenly stopped. He turned back around and walked back to the bed, tenderly pulling her into his hold. "I'm so sorry I hurt you. I love you. I'll make it up to you."

Laura stiffened. She could not let it happen. She was so afraid of being hurt. Yet, his arms were warm and his hug welcoming.

With that, he suddenly exited the room.

Laura burst into tears. She was fearful for so many reasons.

* * *

"I can't believe you turned on me, boss," Alfonso complained. "You folded on me like a cheap deck of cards!"

"Alfonso, you have to *capisce*! Tony is the father to that baby. He makes my *nipote* happy. I have no choice but to help this marriage," Nino implored.

"It's NOT a marriage, *yet*. And he doesn't make her happy. He's done nothing but hurt her and he'll hurt her again. You mark my words!" Alfonso exploded.

"I pray that you're wrong, my friend."

"All the praying ain't going to make a spit of difference when your granddaughter ends up hospitalized in worse condition. I'm telling you, he's lying through his teeth about . . . this Beth."

"Alfonso, if you say this, you have to back it up with proof. Prove to me that Tony is with this Beth and I will use all my strength to get rid of Tony," Nino promised.

Alfonso seemed to breathe a bit easier. Perhaps, the situation was not too far gone. Perhaps he could keep Nino on his side for just a while longer. "I'll give you the proof you need. I'll stay out of Laura's hair for now, if that's what you want; but when I find the proof you need, do you give me your blessing to pursue her?"

Nino seemed to squirm in the restaurant chair. Their breakfast had long since grown cold. Alfonso would stop at nothing to see his plan through. It was all coming together perfectly.

"Alfonso, I can no speak for my *nipote*, but if you have the proof . . . if you prove to me and to Laura that Tony is a cheat, then I leave it in God's hand. Okay?" he asked.

"How can she turn down this face, ehh?" Alfonso unexpectedly joked.

* * *

Nino cracked a smile. The situation was becoming more dangerous with every passing hour. He did not want to believe that Alfonso might not be playing with a full deck of cards. He was showing signs of misdirected emotions and Nino was growing concerned. Yet, he could not help but see Alfonso's point. He really could not stand to see Laura marry Tony. He had so many problems, no reliability, no honor, and no integrity. She could do better.

But Alfonso was certainly out of the question. She could never be with him. If he had to, he would reveal why, when and *if* they crossed that bridge.

****

After seeing Laura off to her home and after getting in contact with Sam, the local police decided to keep Laura at the Knight home, under their care and supervision. If the Knights suspected the slightest worry, they were to report to them. The Albany police also promised to keep Sam up to date. The following morning, Tony ran to his daily counseling appointment with Dr. Parnell.

He explained the circumstances involving Laura, including what had occurred at the park and afterward. Doc carefully listened.

"Do you see where you allowed your fears to consume you?" he asked.

"Yeah, Doc, we almost lost our baby because of me," Tony confessed.

"Tony, unless you forgive yourself, unless you come to the understanding that you were only a child when your sisters endured the sexual abuse, you'll continue with this self-destructive behavior. You also cannot blame yourself for Max's actions. If he went to the Galantes, it was to protect you and your sisters. Even Max was deceived into believing that the Galantes would only dispose of your father. He did not think that far ahead.

"If Max wanted, he could've forced you to face the abuse alone. He could've let you deal with it by yourself. Instead, he suffered for you and for your sisters. Max is actually quite noble and selfless."

Tony laughed aloud with sarcasm. "That's pushing it, even for you, Doc."

"Why can't you see Max as your helper?"

"I realize I created him to not have to face what was happening to me, but he's in no way noble or selfless. He was happy to be rid of my family and wanting to be rid of Laura, too," Tony exclaimed.

"Ask yourself, why? Why did he want to dispose of them?" Doc challenged.

"Heck if I know!" Tony shrieked.

"Who did Max want you to take care of?"

"Nobody, but me," Tony shouted.

"That's right. Max wanted you to finally care for yourself. You've always been so busy taking care of your mother, your sisters, your brother, Laura, Uncle Frank. Well, what about Tony? When are you going to start taking care of little Tony, your inner child, the boy within you?" Dr. Parnell disputed.

Tony thought about that for a moment.

"Tell me, Tony. The child within you needs you. Are you going to start caring for him—for yourself—and allow your heart to be happy? Or will you keep putting yourself on the back burner?"

"I don't know how to care for myself, at least not emotionally," he admitted.

"Let's start with what you want out of life. What does that inner child need? What are *your* goals? What do *you* really want?'

"My inner child needs to be loved. *I* want to be happy," he simply stated.

"Tony, you are loved. Laura loves you. Uncle Frank loves you. John and Marlene love you. Most importantly, as you've so openly professed, God loves you. Who's left? It's time *you* loved that inner child. Stop blaming him for everything and just love him."

Tony nodded, realizing for the first time that what he really needed was to just love himself. A tear silently paraded down his cheek. He was speechless. What he had just learned was so profound, so incredible. He held the power to heal his hurting heart right in the palm of his hand. All he had to do was take hold of that inner child . . . and love him—the way he had loved his siblings, the way he would love his own child.

Interrupting his thoughts, Doc pushed further, "Now, I ask you, what makes *you* happy?"

"Laura makes me happy. Loving her makes me happy. Doing good for others makes me happy. Helping people who are hurting, makes me feel like I'm pleasing God."

"Precisely, bud! Take your own advice and do the things that make you happy. Marry Laura, love her. Help out those who've been through the same sufferings as you, the same way you helped your cousins in White Plains. Take the bad that's happened and turn it into good. You can do it. You have to believe in yourself."

Tony left the office with a new perspective. For the first time in a long time, he was sure he had a calling—a purpose. God was calling him to help those who have suffered child abuse. *He felt excited!* He was going to run back to the Knights and tell Laura everything. He suddenly could not wait. With renewed energy, he raced to be by his future bride.

CHAPTER 18

Proverbs 14:22

"Do not those who plot evil go astray?"

Laura rose Friday morning, feeling refreshed and rested after sleeping in her own bed. With the days seeming to blend together, she hadn't noticed the vast physical changes occurring to her body. Not only was her abdomen obviously protruding, Laura could feel her hips expanding. As she dressed that morning, she concluded that maternity pants were an absolute necessity. There was no chance of squeezing into regular jeans anymore. She was also surprised to find that one of the blouses she had recently worn, no longer fit. Laura tossed on a large knit sweater that hugged her rounded belly.

Because she planned not to leave home, she quickly tied her hair into a ponytail. She studied her profile in the mirror. Her face was still small in comparison to everything else. Having her hair pulled back though, she felt her cheeks looked slightly fuller. Her complexion was still pale and she applied a light coat of makeup to her face.

Smelling the aroma of Marlene's cooking, she descended into the kitchen. She had prepared a large breakfast for her, making Laura feel cared for like a child again.

"Mom, stop fussing over me. Don't get me wrong, I'm not complaining. I just don't want you to overdo it."

Marlene wiped her hands on a kitchen towel. "Do you know how I longed to do this? To dote on a child of my own? Let me take care of you. This is what I live for!" she argued. Marlene gracefully walked across the kitchen nook and kissed Laura's head. Laura scooped a forkful of scrambled eggs into her mouth.

Despite the strain of circumstances she was under, her appetite had suddenly grown. She finished Marlene's breakfast in record time.

"Gosh, you were hungry!" Marlene giggled.

Laura smiled. "I guess so!"

"I'm going to have to tell, John. He'll be so pleased to hear you're taking such good care."

"Mom, you crack me up. You act like I just came home from kindergarten with my first drawing!" Laura teased.

"Hey, I can't help but feel excited that you two are both okay. You nearly gave me a heart attack on Wednesday," Marlene cried.

Laura let out a long sigh, suddenly serious. "I thank God that we're okay," she said.

"Me too, darling," Marlene agreed.

The doorbell rang and Marlene scurried to answer it. Laura cleared her dish and placed it in the sink to wash. She lathered dish soap onto the sponge and turned on the warm water. She could hear Marlene open the front door and whispering voices followed. She hurriedly rinsed the dish, glass, and fork, and placed them in the draining tray. Wiping her hands on the dishtowel, she entered the foyer.

Laura found Marlene and Tony in an intense conversation that quickly ended with her entry. Tony's eyes met hers and he smiled. Laura's heart leapt. *When would the time come that her heart would not skip a beat every time he entered the room?*

He sported a black leather jacket, mid-drift, complete with silver zippers and buttons. His jeans were tucked into a pair of black boots. He had slicked his hair back in a modern fashion, similar to those of the characters that played on TV programs. His face was freshly shaven and a wicked smile tinkered on his lips.

"Afternoon, young lady," he called, interrupting her gaze.

"Afternoon? It's still morning, isn't it?" she asked.

Tony pulled back his coat sleeve and glanced at his watch. "Well, I'll be darn, it's still morning. I guess I've had a full day already," he stated with a grin. He ambled past Marlene and planted a kiss on Laura's cheek. "How are you feeling today? You look beautiful."

Laura could not help but blush. He was really trying, but she still did not feel comfortable with the flirting. "I'm fine. What are you two whispering about?" she directly questioned.

"Nothing gets past you, does it?" he continued to razz.

Marlene looked at him with annoyance and tugged at his coat. "I told him not to lay it on too thick and that you needed time," she disclosed, while hanging his jacket in the foyer closet.

"I told her that I wasn't going to just sit back and let some goon snatch you away from me!" Tony revealed, removing his boots and setting them on the foyer carpet.

Laura let out an unexpected giggle. Both Marlene and Tony looked at her. She suddenly laughed harder, placing a look of surprise on their faces. "What? What did I say?" Tony quizzed.

Laura tried to suppress her laughter. Unable to speak between giggles, she pointed to Tony's feet. Everyone glance downward, suddenly catching on. Tony had mistakenly put on two different socks of the same color. One had paisley swirls running through it, the other had checks and stripes. Marlene burst into giggles, while it was Tony's turn to blush.

"It was dark in my room, this morning. I guess I can't even dress myself without you. See how much I need you?" he insisted.

After their fits of laughter ended, they entered the kitchen. "Tony, have you had anything to eat?" Marlene enquired.

"Actually, I'm on my lunch break. I had my therapy appointment this morning. I figured I'd squeeze a visit in with Laura before I head back to that rental dwelling that needed repairs. I can pick something up on my way in," he suggested.

After putting the dishtowel in her hands down, Laura sat down at the nook table and watched the two converse.

Tony immediately found the chair next to hers. A smile continued to play on his lips.

"Well, that's ridiculous. You're already here, let me make you something," Marlene suggested.

"No, don't go through any trouble, please," Tony insisted.

"It's not trouble. How about an egg-salad sandwich?" she offered.

"Your famous recipe?"

"Of course!"

"Awesome!"

Laura could not help but roll her eyes. "Brown-noser," she whispered.

Tony caught her facial expression and laughed. "What?" he probed.

"Forget it," she whispered.

"Why don't you two go sit in the living room. I'll prepare lunch for Tony and bring it out to you when it's ready," she insisted.

Laura half-heartedly followed Tony, who had clutched her hand, as he led the way. He plopped down on the couch, patting the seat next to him. She sat down putting extra space between them. Sitting too closely, she was liable to forget that he had yet to gain her trust.

"I saw Doc, as I mentioned earlier," he confirmed. "I had a great session."

Laura was sincere. "I'm glad. Your spirits appear lighter than I've seen in some time," she agreed.

"He helps me to keep things in perspective. I think I'm ready to finally accept what happened when I was a kid," Tony rendered.

"That's good news, Tony. You've suffered so much. It's time to put the past behind you," she stated.

"I realize now that I was stupid to think that you'd think differently of me, because of what happened. That was just a defense method I was using to support my fear of losing you. I was trying to actually protect my heart. Stupid, isn't it—the way our subconscious works to protect ourselves."

Or our conscious. "No, it's not stupid. I completely understand it," Laura confessed, amazed at how she had adapted his same behavioral patterns.

"Laura, I want you to know what I've learned. I want you to . . ."

The doorbell rang, interrupting Tony. He sighed with frustration.

Laura struggled to rise from the couch. Tony chuckled and gently assisted her by placing a hand on her bottom to help push her up.

"Hey!" Laura yelled, swatting his hand away.

"Just trying to help," he offered with a laugh.

"You try gaining 20 pounds and see if you can get up with ease," she pouted.

Laura could hear Tony's laughter from in the foyer. It sounded like music to her ears. She peeked through the sidelight window and recognized Nino's figure immediately. She opened the door and welcomed him in.

Placing his coat in the closet, Nino followed her into the living room.

"Tony," Nino greeted with a stiff handshake.

"Nino," Tony returned.

"How is my *bella*?" Nino asked turning to Laura, who sat next to Tony.

"I'm feeling much better now, Nonno. I'm happy to be home," she added.

Nino sat down on the sofa chair and reached forward to pat her arm. "I'm so happy. You look beautiful," he complimented.

"See, I told you," Tony tossed in.

"Suck up," she insisted in whispers.

Tony outwardly smiled.

Marlene entered moments later, to bring Tony his lunch. Nino rose and attempted to be courteous to Marlene. He extended his hand. Marlene shook it apprehensively.

"Thank you for allowing me into you home to see my granddaughter," he expressed.

"We'll do anything for Laura," Marlene replied.

"She is blessed to have you," Nino stated.

"Thank you, but it's the other way around. We're blessed to have her."

"We all are," Tony finally added with sincerity. He lifted his plate and followed Marlene into the kitchen to eat at the table.

The doorbell rang again. Laura sighed, forcing her limbs to move. She immediately recognized Alfonso's form in the window.

"Nonno," she called.

Nino moved swiftly. "What, *amore*?" he questioned.

"What's Fonzie doing here?" she asked nervously. "If Tony sees him here, it won't be pretty," she warned. "He'll contact the police, immediately!"

"He drove me here. I told him to come back in half-hour. Don't worry. I'll take care this." Nino opened the front door. "Alfonso, *che cosa*?" he questioned what the matter was.

Alfonso met Laura's gaze. "I need to talk to you immediately, boss," he whispered. His eyes never left hers. "That important information that I told you I would find . . . well, I just got it."

Nino stepped out of the house and closed the door. Laura's curiosity was aroused. *What kind of information was he speaking of?* She quietly opened the door just enough to hear the conversation on the porch.

"*Ma, che dice*, Alfonso? What are you saying?"

"I just got the proof you need. My informant met me, just down the street, after I dropped you off. That punk *is* cheating on her. The evidence is at the rental dwelling he claims to be repairing. I want you to see it," Alfonso revealed.

Laura's heartbeat doubled in rhythm.

"*Madre mia*! I can no believe it. *Sei sicuro*? Are you sure?" Nino nearly cried.

"Boss, would I lie to you? Don't you trust me?"

"*Si*, but he is here. He try to make this work," Nino insisted.

"He's playing her. He doesn't love her. He's messing around with that Beth at the empty apartment on Beamer Drive. My informant followed Beth this morning, and found them there together. He's a liar!" Alfonso accused.

Laura's legs trembled. *Was it true?* She entered the kitchen stunned. Nino reentered the house moments later and suddenly kissed her goodbye, claiming to have an important meeting at a warehouse. He walked himself to the door.

She stared at Tony from the kitchen entryway. He talked to Marlene about something, then bit into the sandwich—eggs sliding down his chin. Her mind played a flashback of the day Paul took her in for her maternity test. She recalled the way she wiped his chin for him, afterward, at lunch, and how he claimed that he needed her to be his wife and that they would be good together. He had already cheated on her with Tammy, and though Tammy had been killed by that time, she felt second best—last resort. She suddenly found herself in the same dilemma. She was being betrayed by someone she loved.

Tony quickly wiped his chin. His eyes unexpectedly met hers. The smile faded from his face.

"Laura?"

He was cheating on her. He was meeting with Beth behind her back, of all places, in John's rental dwelling. He was lying. He did not love her. He did not want to marry her. He probably continued the farce for the baby's sake.

"Laura?"

"Laura?" she heard them question.

The door to the garage opened. Tony promptly stood and went to her. His hand felt her forehead. Suddenly, Laura snapped.

Her fists flew up and struck at his chest. "How could you?" she screamed. "You're a liar and a cheater!" Her little fists flailed. He tried grasping her arms.

"Laura, what are you talking about?" he reasoned.

"Laura," Marlene cried. "Think of the baby. Stop this."

Solid hands reached from behind her to clasp her hands. She felt John pull her into his arms, while she hysterically cried. "What is going on?" he screamed.

"I don't know," Tony explained. "One minute we were fine, the next she's throwing fists at me. Please, Laura, tell me what happened," Tony begged.

"Alfonso was just here. I overheard him talking to Nonno on the porch," she cried. "They followed you this morning! You met up with Beth!"

"What?" John shouted. "That's not true. Beth was at work this morning."

"Laura, you can call Doc; he'll tell you I had an appointment with him this morning. Alfonso is lying!" Tony shouted.

Laura stood shaking her head. The tears coursed down her cheeks uncontrollably. "You lie! He said he has proof. He took Nonno to Dad's rental dwelling on Beamer, where you meet up with her!" she accused through sobs.

"NO! It's a lie!" Tony's eyes crashed with John's. "I swear to you on my own head, I'm telling you the truth!"

"Something isn't adding up here," John admitted.

The telephone rang. Everyone stood still, unsure what would happen next. Marlene answered the telephone. Covering the receiver with her hand, she whispered, "It's Beth."

John released his hold over Laura, making sure she was steady on her feet. Laura stood nearly swooning from the blow of Alfonso's words. Tony's arms were outstretched prepared to take hold of her if need be.

Moments later, John hung up. His face was pale. "We need to call Sam, now!"

"What? What's going on?" Tony insisted.

"I believe you may have just been set up."

John quickly explained how Beth received a call from a prospective renter interested in the vacant apartment on Beamer. She claimed that they were hoping to meet Tony there in a half-hour.

"What a coincidence. Wouldn't you say?" Tony jested with a serious face.

The telephone rang again. This time John answered.

* * *

John quietly listened to Sam go on about something. Tony could not tear his eyes from Laura. She was pale and her body shook uncontrollably. He had never seen her so hurt, so upset. It was killing him to know that she believed that gangster over him. He wanted to take her in his arms and comfort her. He wanted to take away her pain, but she was confused and not sure whom to believe. He would have Nino and Alfonso's heads for the pain they were causing her.

" . . . I don't believe it, Sam," John continued. "Yes, he's here. Please explain to him everything you just told me." John handed the telephone to Tony and then helped Laura to a chair. He took a seat next to her, pulling her into his arms.

"Chief, what's going on?" Tony enquired.

"More than you'll want to hear," Sam stated. "Listen to me carefully. *Do not* go to Beamer Drive. It's a trap. Do you understand?"

"A trap?"

"We've discovered that Alfonso *is* Laura's stalker. We've also found that he has aligned himself with the Galantes." Sam stated.

"Oh, Jesus, not the Galantes," Tony cried.

"He seems to have a vendetta against Nino and you. Apparently, he wanted to be the next 'Don' of the Valente *famiglia* and when Nino turned face, Alfonso felt betrayed. As for you, we're guessing he wants you out of the picture for obvious reasons—Laura," Sam revealed.

"God help us," Tony whispered. "We gotta get Nino out of there."

"Leave that up to us. I'm going to contact the Albany Police Department and give them this information. We're waiting on a warrant and then we'll take Rengali in for questioning. There's more . . ."

* * *

Laura's body trembled. She sipped on the glass of sugar-free apple juice Marlene handed her. Both her parents stood aside her, loving and supporting her. The tears had stopped, allotting room for a grave fear that left her trembling. Something was happening and her grandfather's life was at risk. From what she could comprehend of the conversation Tony was having with Sam, Alfonso *was* a serious threat. Her heart felt as though it was breaking. She could no longer take the lies and the deception. She hated all the secrets and corruption.

Tony hung up the telephone. The earlier humor that outlined his eyes was long gone. "I've got to go," he stated.

"Where? Why?" Laura questioned with a quiver.

"There's trouble and Nino might be in danger," he admitted.

"Leave it to the authorities, Tony. Don't endanger yourself. Sam said to stay put!" John ordered.

"What kind of danger? What's happening?" Laura insisted.

"Alfonso's not the friend to Nino that Nino believes him to be. He's setting Nino up and I just can't stand around and do nothing about it," Tony whispered. He softly pulled her face into his hands. "Don't doubt my love for you. I'll see to it that Nino will be okay. If for no other reason than because *I love you.*"

Tony dashed into the foyer and quickly put on his boots. John chased after him. "Don't do this, Tony. Leave it to the authorities. Alfonso's dangerous. He won't be afraid to kill you! We can't take another death in this household!"

Laura was immediately behind John. "Tony! Don't go! Alfonso hates you. Dad's right, he will kill you! Please, I know you love me. Don't do this just to prove it to me. I won't be able to live with myself if I lose you!" she sobbed, watching John run into the kitchen.

Tony knelt on the foyer carpet, tying his boots. "Nothing bad is going to happen. I'll be okay. Trust me." He stood and gripped his jacket from in the closet.

"Please, don't do this!" she begged.

Laura could hear John asking for Sam, over the phone.

"I promise you, I'll be okay. I know you don't trust me anymore and I don't blame you. But I have to do this and I promise you, Nino and I will be okay." He took two steps backward, placing a hand on the doorknob. His eyes piercing hers, he whispered, "I've always loved you Laura Ann Marcs Knight. Don't you ever forget it!" He slipped out the door, leaving Laura numb.

Marlene's warm arms pulled her in. Laura rested her head on her shoulder. Marlene's face was wet with tears. "He's so stubborn," she whispered. "Yet, I can see why you love him so much. He's as beautiful on the inside as he is on the outside."

Laura stared at the closed door. She could not just sit back and wait to see what would transpire from this. Alfonso could be talked down. She felt a special connection to him. If Tony went there without her, he was as good as dead. If Laura could talk to him—if she could reason with him, this did not have to end with dire consequences.

There was only one problem. She would have to find a way into John's briefcase, locate the Beamer address, and slip out of the house unnoticed. *Could she do it?* Laura guessed that she had no other choice.

****

Tony sped across town as fast as the traffic would allow. His heart raced with a fear and an unknowing that nearly paralyzed him. Yet, something needed to be done. He could not permit anything to happen to Nino, even if he despised the man. He was Laura's grandfather and she loved him, in spite of his flaws. Finally, arriving at the vacant dwelling, everything seemed at peace. Nino's vehicle was parked alongside the street. They were in the apartment.

Tony bowed his head in prayer. "Father, I'm scared. But I know You're with me. Forgive me for failing You in the past. Please, send Your angels to keep Nino and me safe. Keep us from grave physical harm. If there is a way to have us all walk away from this alive, I beg of You, let Your will be done. In Jesus' name. Amen." He quickly crossed himself and exited the car.

Tony ran up the walkway. The brisk wind fanned his face. He shivered, while placing a hand on the doorknob. Turning it, he found it unlocked and entered. The room was dim. Two figures stood between the kitchen and the family room of the small apartment. A light illuminated and Nino and Alfonso stood adjacent to one another.

"I'm happy to see you could make it," Nino announced.

"Does this mean . . . you're not interested in renting?" Tony commented.

Alfonso raised a gun and pointed it at him.

"No one does to my *nipote*, what you have done to her. NO ONE!" Nino shouted with fury.

"Before you accuse me of anything, stop and think this through. Alfonso has an ulterior motive. He wants Laura for himself and is framing me. Nino, don't let him con you into thinking that I'm the enemy. We received a call from the Chief of Police of Cicero. They have proof that Alfonso is Laura's stalker."

"Shut that hole in your face, punk," Alfonso spit.

"I see with my eyes that you have used this apartment as you 'get-away' with that tramp! You are no man with honor! *Disgraziado!*" Nino swore in Italian.

"Where's your proof? What did Alfonso plant in here that's mine?" Tony pressed.

"I didn't have to plant evidence, it was already here. Your ring and Beth's lingerie was all the proof we need to know that you cheated on Laura."

"*My ring?* You son-of-a-gun! You *were* in White Plains. You took my ring and planted it here! Give it to me!" Tony bellowed.

Alfonso dug a hand into his pant pocket and withdrew the ring. "You're not worthy to wear this."

"Nevertheless, Laura gave it to *me*. I said give it to me!"

"Come and get it," Alfonso goaded.

"Stop this! I will no have this! We are here to confront what you have done. No more lies!" Nino insisted.

"Nino, I know you've never liked me, but if it's true that you've given your heart to God, then allow the Holy Spirit to lead you. You're a smart man. Don't let your love for Alfonso blind you. I *know* what he means to you," Tony persuaded.

Nino appeared to take a moment to assimilate Tony's last statement.

"You know nothing!" Alfonso shouted. "You know only how to hurt Laura. But no more. This ends right here!"

Tony laughed maniacally. "You've really fooled yourself into believing that you have a chance with her, haven't you? You think that if you kill me that she's going to jump in your arms. And *y'all* think *I'm* crazy? You couldn't be more wrong. Laura has already seen past you. She wouldn't give you the time of day!"

Alfonso lowered his gun, tucking it into his coat pocket. Removing his coat and placing it on a chair, he gave Tony a devious smile. "I won't need that . . . yet," he explained. "First, I want to take the pleasure of busting your head in with my bare hands."

"Go for it!" Tony encouraged.

"STOP!" Tony heard Nino shout. Alfonso plowed toward him. His large body struck Tony's with full force. It took all of Tony's strength to stand firm. The men wrestled until they ended up on the floor. Their bodies tumbled about the family room. Tony clenched Alfonso's arm and twisted it behind his back. He forced his fingers open and reclaimed his ring. He punched Alfonso's back. Alfonso kicked and squirmed, suddenly grasping hold of Tony and pinning him to the floor.

Nino continued to scream for them to stop. In all the confusion, Tony somehow noticed that Nino was gasping for air and that his hand was clutching his chest. Suddenly, a blow struck his face and he heard a crack. Blood spilled, while Tony struggled with Alfonso. At last, he got to his feet, quickly placing the ring back on his finger.

Putting his hands out, he shouted, "Stop! Wait! Something's wrong with Nino. Nino, what's the matter?"

Alfonso paused a moment directing his gaze at Nino. Nino was gasping for air and held a hand to his chest. Tony ran to where he stood just near the kitchen.

"I'm okay. Just stop this. We're here to talk; no fighting. Please," the older man insisted.

"This is going to be easier than I thought," Alfonso suddenly claimed, after grasping his coat back off the chair he had placed it on. He withdrew his gun again and pointed it at both Tony and Nino. "You might be a little tougher to get rid of," he directed his comment to Tony. "But at least I won't have to fight off this feeble old man while I do it."

Nino looked confused. He sat down on a wooden chair in the kitchen, trying to catch his breath. "Alfonso, *che fai*? What are you doing? What are you saying?"

"What am I doing? I'm going to kill you both," Alfonso ultimately revealed.

"No!" Nino cried. "What do you say? Why you do this?"

"You promised me title of 'Don'. I was entitled to *all* of your fortune, since you had no one else. You promised me!" Alfonso shouted in anger. "Suddenly, your precious granddaughter steps into the picture. It's a good thing for you that I fell in love with her, or I was going to kill her, too, to get what I wanted. Now I see an easier way. I will pin your deaths on none other than the Galante *famiglia*. She's going to believe that I tried to save you both from them, but failed. That's right, don't look so stupid, Nino.

I've been in cahoots with them for months—your enemies. I've given them the proof they needed to think the two of you were planning on retaliating. Mario gave me the order. Now I'm seeing it through."

Alfonso slowly walked backward toward the door, continuing to point his gun at both Tony and Nino. Nino's breathing was heavy, while he continued to rub his chest. Tony actually felt sympathy for Nino. The man was surely having early symptoms of a heart attack, on top of Alfonso's ultimate betrayal. He placed a hand on Nino's shoulder reassuringly.

"I'll get us outta here," Tony whispered, still breathing raggedly, while holding a hand to the cut on his bleeding cheek.

Nino's eyes filled with remorse and tears fell forward.

Alfonso opened the door to the apartment. Shielding his body with the wall, he peeked out. His gun was drawn, ready for fire. He placed his fingers between his teeth and whistled. Waiting a moment, he opened the door wide enough to allow another in.

A man in a full-length wool coat entered. He strutted toward the kitchen where Nino sat and Tony hovered. His gloved hand held a gun. A fedora hat covered his face.

"Gentlemen, let me introduce to you . . . Gino Galante," Alfonso presented.

The mafioso lifted his head and removed his hat with his free hand.

Tony sucked in his breath.

Gino Galante had a large mole under his left eye.

A sinister smile played on his mouth. "It's a pleasure to see you again, Mr. Giacalone."

CHAPTER 19

Proverbs 19:5

"A false witness will not go unpunished and he who pours out lies will not go free."

Laura prayed, while her vehicle took her down the narrower streets that led to Beamer Drive. She managed to slip away unseen, but regretted deceiving her parents. She did not want to upset them, but they would never understand that she was the only one who could resolve the problem. She was the only one who might be able to bring peace to her loved ones.

* * *

Tony charged at Gino. The gunman was not anticipating the force. Catching him off guard, Tony was able to disarm him with a kick of his booted foot. Alfonso lifted his gun, trying to aim at Tony. Nino could not allow him to bring harm to Tony. As much as he loved Alfonso, as much as it hurt that Alfonso had undermined him, Nino knew what he must do. In spite of the dull pain of his chest, he scurried toward Alfonso and put himself in front of the gun.

"Get outta my way, old man, or I'll kill you as sure as you stand there," Alfonso threatened.

"Alfonso, you must stop this! You are still in time, my son. Please, I beg of you. Don't do this! Think of God. Think of Laura. They would want you to do what is right!" Nino begged. He glanced at Tony and Gino as they wrestled from the family room floor into the kitchen. He was worried for Tony, hoping to help him, but his chest burned with fire and he was beginning to feel faint. Sweat poured from his pores.

"MOVE!" Alfonso pushed him away. Nino stumbled aside.

Gunfire suddenly deafened his ears.

"NO!" Nino screamed.

* * *

Tony had managed to disarm Gino and tackle him to the kitchen floor. The gun fell, sliding across the linoleum into the corner. Tony pummeled Gino's face with blow after blow, releasing years of pain and rage toward his family's murderer. Gino's arm still tried stretching back to grasp for the gun.

"Oh, hell no!" Tony shouted, grasping at Gino's extended arm. Unexpectedly, Gino threw a punch to Tony's gut with his free hand. Tony doubled over, giving Gino just enough time to scramble out from under him, crawl to the corner, and grasp the gun. Gino moved quickly to his feet. Tony stood swiftly and lurched at Gino, pressing him against the kitchen wall, while grasping his armed hand and pulling it up, pointing the gun toward the ceiling.

He could hear Nino and Alfonso arguing, but he could not allow his attention to deter. He was struggling to keep Gino from pointing the gun at him. Gino lifted his knee and kicked at Tony's groin. Concentrating on the gun, while ignoring the horribly painful strike, Tony whacked Gino's hand against the wall. Another wallop to his groin and Tony lost his hold over Gino's hand.

Gino pointed the gun at Tony's chest. Tony punched his arm, but it was too late, the gun exploded. A stabbing pain shot up his thigh.

"NO!" Nino cried.

Tony screamed out and fell to the floor, grasping his thigh in pain. Alfonso pushed Nino down next to Tony. Both men raised their guns. Tony and Nino lay sprawled on the kitchen floor.

"Wait! Before you kill us, I think you should know something," Tony tried to stall, placing pressure on his wound with his hand.

"I don't want to hear another word outta you!" Alfonso warned.

"Tell him Nino! Tell him who he really is!" Tony shouted, grasping at straws to keep them alive.

Nino looked at him questioningly.

"Tell him!" Tony roared. "It may be our only chance."

"Nothing you tell me will keep me from killing you," Alfonso reassured.

Tony looked at Nino, pleading with his eyes. Nino still would not divulge.

"NINO! Tell him!"

"Enough," Gino shouted. "Let's take them out. I want Giacalone."

"I'll take Valente." Alfonso and Gino lifted their guns.

"You'd kill your father?" Tony finally spilled.

Alfonso lowered his gun slightly.

Nino lifted his knowing gaze to meet Alfonso's.

"You're a liar!" Alfonso accused.

"No! It's the truth. Sam Desanti, the Cicero Police Chief, confirmed it. Why do you think your mother sent you to Nino? Why do you think Nino was going to make *you* the next 'Don'? He had an affair with her during his marriage to Vita," Tony revealed.

"No!" Alfonso bellowed. "Is that true?" he questioned Nino.

Nino hung his head low. Tears fell down his cheeks and onto his dress suit.

"IS IT TRUE?" Alfonso screamed, making the older man tremble further.

"Yes—yes, it is the truth."

"How? Why would my mother want an old man like you?"

"Twenty-five years ago, I was no old," Nino gasped, as he spoke.

"How did it happen? What would make my mother turn to *you*? TELL ME!" Alfonso shouted.

Nino slowly shook his head. "I cannot breathe good!"

"I don't care! I want to know. Tell me, now!" he commanded.

Nino swallowed, desperate to suck air into his lungs. "When Gabe came to work for me, he had just married Paola." Nino began. He placed a hand on his chest, gently rubbing. He coughed, but then continued. "But after a couple years, they tried to have babies. No babies came. They went to the doctor. The doctor tell you momma that Gabriele was sterile. He could have no babies. They started to fight. Gabe came to me to talk. I told him to adopt a baby. He said he no want the baby without his blood."

Alfonso's stare was agony. His teeth were clenched and both hands held the gun in a white-knuckling clasp. "This is not true," he whispered, still insisting.

"Does it matter? Pop him, Rengali. You have your orders," Gino pushed.

"I have to hear this. I need to know. Trust me, I'd like nothing more than to put a bullet between this pig's eyes!" Alfonso seethed. "Continue," he demanded.

Nino swallowed again, struggling to breathe. "Paola would come to me and Vita, crying every day. She begged us to tell Gabe to adopt a baby for her. She wanted a baby so much. Little by little, she came to me to talk. I feel so sorry for her. The matrimony was going bad. After months of trying to convince Gabe, Paola give up. She come to me *una notte*. That night, she tell me she was going to kill herself. I begged her no. I wanted to go call my Vita to see if Vita could help. But Paola insist she wanted to talk only to me. That night you were conceived."

Nino coughed, grasping his chest—desperate for air.

"Put him outta his misery! That's an order!" Gino commanded.

"Shut up!" Alfonso finally yelled.

"You listen to me," Gino stated in a low-menacing voice. "Remember who I represent. If I see fit, I'll take you down with them and there will be no love lost."

"I'm with you, man. But, I need to hear from his mouth, how I came to be. " Alfonso insisted.

"I'm giving him three minutes and I'm pulling the trigger," Gino pressed.

"No," Nino cried in a weak raspy voice. "You got to hear all the story. It is true. I started to fall for you momma. I felt a connection to her. We start to spend more and more time together. Vita was always so mad to me, because she wanted me to forgive Cara for leaving our *famiglia*. I was too tired to hear this all the time. Paola was the breath of fresh air to me.

"One day, Vita discovered the truth. She threatened to leave me. She was my wife for so many years. I could no let her go. I promised to break up with Paola, but she was insistent that I leave Vita and she leave Gabe. She insisted we stay together. I must confess, I did no want to leave Vita. I realize I make the mistake. But it was too late."

"What? She told you she was pregnant, so you shipped her off to California?" Alfonso assumed.

Nino took in a few ragged breaths, seriously wheezing. "No," he continued. "She told Gabe I took advantage of her. Gabe was furious with me. He wanted to kill me. *Una notte*, he sneaked onto my property. He was planning to eliminate me. My men found him in the garden. He tried to talk his way out, but they killed him, before he could kill me."

"You coward," Alfonso indicted. "You didn't have the courage to have a face-off with him, so you sent your men to do your dirty work!"

"No! I no want to kill Paola's husband. I tell her to go back to him and to leave the state, the country, go anywhere but New York. Gabe was a *testuni*! A hard-headed man! He wanted to see me die for taking his wife. My men did what they were supposed to do. They protected me."

"So, what happened to my mother?" Alfonso pressed, keenly aware of Gino's impatience.

Nino leaned his back against the wall and closed his eyes a moment. His chest rose and fell faintly. His color was pale and Tony wondered if he was going to die.

"Nino, are you okay?" he examined.

Nino nodded. He opened his eyes. Fresh tears spilled forth from them. "I know you will no believe me, but I love you, Alfonso. I missed all the years with you. I'm sorry for this."

Suddenly, Tony felt the need to silently pray. He begged for God's protection. He could not see a way out. Alfonso was clearly struggling with his emotions. The large man fought back tears. Sniffing, he shouted for Nino to tell him what happened to his mother.

"She was mad with me when she found that Gabe was dead. I tell her to go, that our relationship was no meant to be. She was so mad. A week later, I come home and find her in the kitchen with Vita. She told Vita everything—that we killed Gabe and that she have the baby.

"My Vita, she was such a good Catholic. She promised to help Paola. She let Paola move into our *casa* until you were born. Vita took you momma to all the doctor appointments. Vita took care of Paola like a momma take care of her child. When you was born, we give you momma $300,000 to move to California, and make the new life with you. We sent her money for years."

Alfonso scoffed. "We struggled for so many years without money. How can you say you sent money to us?" He interrogated.

"I can show you the proof. My bookkeeper has record of all the checks of $2,000 a month we send to you."

"What did she do with that money then, because we lived in the poorest neighborhood, in the cheapest house? You obviously didn't give her enough!"

"Does it really matter at this point? Your old man drop-kicked ya," Gino painfully stated. "Kill him and get it over with, already."

"You're right, Gino. This man may be my biological father, but he has been nothing but a means to an end for me," Alfonso affirmed. They lifted their guns.

"Lord," Tony prayed in the secret of his heart, "If this is it for me, if my time is now, receive my spirit. Take me to Heaven with You. But if You see that I may still have unfinished work here, if You feel that I can make a difference for You, then spare us. Send an angel—protect us and I'll forgive these men and make peace with all of my enemies and with myself."

The door was suddenly thrust open. Tony opened his eyes to see Laura standing in the doorway. His heart filled with fear. She let out a scream and ran to Tony and Nino, squatting on the kitchen floor, looking over Tony's bloodied leg.

"Laura! Get outta here. Go—this is no place for you!" Tony whispered.

She turned, her glare meeting Alfonso's.

Gino closed and locked the door.

Laura turned her gaze on him. Her mouth fell open. Her face paled. "*You*," she whispered.

"My, how you've grown," Gino sang. "Now that we're all here together, I can finally finish what I came here for."

"You know him?" Alfonso quizzed.

"He killed my family," she continued to whisper, in shock.

"Ding ding ding! Two points for Goldie. You remember me, ehh? I thought I killed you. You play dead very well. I didn't think you'd recognize me, the way I blasted into your so-called house and annihilated that thief you called 'father'," Gino admitted.

"You also killed a beautiful teenager and a little girl," she informed with pain in her voice.

"Which should give you the inclination that I've no qualms about killing a pregnant woman," Gino stated.

"No! The girl lives. We'll take out the others . . . but not her," Alfonso demanded.

"The girl dies! She's an eye witness. We can't leave any loose ends," Gino argued.

"I'll keep her quiet. She won't speak," Alfonso promised.

"Alfonso! Don't do this!" Laura cried. "Walk away from it. Tell this man to go home and we'll pretend this never happened. You can change. I know you have good in you," Laura pleaded.

"We can't pretend this never happened," Gino exasperated. "You're all in too deep! You're going to die! Say your prayers!" Gino cocked the gun and aimed at Nino.

"Wait!" Alfonso cried out. "Don't shoot him, yet. I want him to tell Laura the whole truth. I want her to hear out of his mouth what he did!"

Laura stood. Tony pulled on her arm to try to keep her down, but he was feeling too weak from the blood loss. "Laura, what are you doing? Get down," he whispered.

"Alfonso, I don't know what you're talking about, but whatever it is, it doesn't matter. We can make this right," she begged.

"No, don't you see? We can't be together anymore! I'm your half-uncle!" he shouted.

"What are you talking about?"

"Tell her," Alfonso bellowed. "Tell her how you cheated on your wife with my mother. Tell her how you impregnated her—your enforcer's wife."

Laura turned to Nino, who was squeezing his eyes closed in pain. His chest rose and fell slowly. A hand was clenching his chest.

"Nonno?" Laura kneeled near him and felt his forehead. "He's cold and clammy. He's having a heart attack. We have to help him. He needs a hospital! Alfonso, please! If it's true, what you've told me, then don't let your father die!"

"My father? Where was he when I was growing up? Where was he when we were struggling to make ends meet?" Alfonso yelled.

"ENOUGH!" Gino shouted. "Keep your gun on that one," he commanded, pointing at Laura. "I'll settle this once and for all!" He suddenly left the apartment, slamming the door closed behind him.

Tony immediately unbuckled his belt, removed it, and tightened it above the wound in his leg, making a tourniquet. "Laura, go! Run! Get out of here, now!" he shouted.

She shook her head in no. "Fonzie, this is your chance. God's giving you this chance to make a choice. Don't let us die here! I know you won't do this. I've seen how caring and kind you can be!" Laura coerced.

The gun trembled in Alfonso's hand. He held it up, directing it at Laura. "Only to you! Because I love you! But now, I can't be with you. You're my niece! I might as well let you die here with them, because it'll be easier to see you die, than to know you're alive and that I can't have you!"

"No, Alfonso," Nino begged in a weak voice. "You want to kill me, kill me. Let Laura go. She is innocent! She has suffered enough."

"Alfonso," Tony finally intervened, his head careening from the pain in his leg. "It's me you want. Let her go. Get her outta here, before Galante gets back."

Suddenly, the door collided open. Gino entered with a gasoline can.

"What are you doing?" asked Alfonso, slightly lowering his gun.

"I'm finishing this, right now." Gino began saturating the rooms with gasoline.

"Please," Laura pleaded in a whisper. "Don't do this. If you love me, you won't kill my grandfather or the father of my child."

Anger outlined Alfonso's eyes. His face contorted in a pain-filled snarl. He tore his stare off Laura and turned to face Gino. "I don't want them to be able to get away. Let's tie them up."

"No, Alfonso!" Laura pleaded.

"Shut up! I can't listen to you anymore. It's better this way," he insisted.

"How? Who wins? You're going to be able to live with yourself knowing that you killed your father and your pregnant niece?" she screeched.

"Shut her up, Rengali! Or I'll do it for you," Gino instructed.

"Don't say another word or move from that spot, or Dracula here, will be put out of his misery," Alfonso affirmed, pointing the gun at Tony, now.

Laura slowly rose from the squatted position she had been in and watched in terror.

Alfonso grasped Tony by his jacket collar. Tony tried to fight him, but the bullet wound had drained much of his blood. He dragged his body toward a kitchen chair, leaving a bloody trail. Laura wept, as he tied up Tony's hands and legs. The stench of gasoline began to fill the rooms.

Gino finished dousing the rooms and helped get Nino to his feet, pushing him to walk toward the kitchen table. Placing another chair next to Tony's, he forced Nino down at gunpoint. Nino begged for him to spare Laura.

* * *

Laura could not believe what was happening. She watched in devastation, as a man that she had grown to care about planned to murder her fiancé and her grandfather. *How had it come to this?*

"I thought you were better than this," she could not hold back. "I can't believe how conniving you are!" she accused, slowly moving toward the family room. "I bet it *was* you who tampered with Paul's friend's car. *You* killed Tammy!"

Alfonso looked up at her. He twisted the rope around Tony's ankles. "Actually, you're right. You want a full confession? I'll give you one. Nino gave me the orders to go ahead and give Paul his final warning. That's right, your loving grandpa, here, gave the order to have him killed. I followed through. No, I didn't know that Tammy would get in the car. But it was just as well. She was only one more person who was getting in the way of what I really wanted . . . you!"

"Aww, how touching," Gino ridiculed.

Alfonso tossed him an irritated scowl. He turned his attention to Laura, who looked at him with disgust. "You are sick and twisted," she accused.

"That's right. I would follow you wherever you went. Call you and hang up. I wanted you for myself, so bad, that I even killed. You know that sweet little old lady that used to work for John? She took one too many shots of insulin that morning when she died. How convenient for me that charming Beth was interested in her old crush, Tony Giacalone. How convenient that she had secretarial skills that she could apply toward her new job, where she would have access to Tony daily. How convenient that she was desperate enough for the money I offered her to cause a major distraction."

He finished tying up Tony and slowly began to walk toward her. Laura backed away into the adjacent family room area. "And you fell for it," he continued. "You believed that Tony was interested in her, when he already had you. As much as I hate him, I knew he wasn't stupid enough to fall for Beth after having you. But she made one heck of a diversion, didn't she?"

Laura clutched a pillow off the couch and tossed it at him, as he inched toward her. He swiftly dodged it, laughing aloud. "You're terrible," she cried. "How could you do that to me? You pretended to be my friend, to be a decent man," she sputtered, while coughing from the overpowering odor of gasoline.

He continued to circle the family room furniture in pursuit of her. His laughter was haunting and ominous. Laura quickly glanced at Gino who was nearly finished tying up Nino. She noticed Tony fighting the ropes, his eyes never leaving her, as he struggled to try to help her.

"Me? Decent?" Alfonso interrupted her train of thought. "Look at my father. The apple doesn't fall far from the tree, does it? It was so easy to lure Nino in. Once I got rid of his driver, that opened the door for me to be at his beck-and-call. I had him at my mercy and he told me everything. He told me he was going to have a talk with Tony at the hospital and so I came prepared. I brought my handy-dandy recorder and taped the most perfect conversation to bring to Mario Galante as proof of the Valente and Giacalone union."

Laura stood behind the couch, confused. "My grandfather and Tony are not in union. Until now, they have been at odds," she revealed.

Gino stopped what he was doing. He stood and pulled his gun from his coat liner. He gave Alfonso a deadly glare. He stalked into the family room. "What did she just say?"

Alfonso turned around and entered the kitchen, his gun erect, directed at Gino. Gino pointed his weapon at Alfonso. "You heard her right, Galante. I set you up, too. I couldn't do this alone. But now that you've helped me to neutralize my enemies, I won't be needing you anymore," Alfonso quickly fired, before springing behind the kitchen wall for protection.

Laura screamed and quickly dropped down behind the sofa. Gino leapt behind the same couch untouched. He grabbed her. She could hear Tony and Nino shouting and screaming. Gino put the gun to her head and forced her to stand.

Sirens suddenly bellowed and tires came to a screeching halt outside the door. Orders were being spouted through a megaphone for the armed men to let the hostages go.

Gino cursed and pressed the gun to Laura's temple. She cried out, as did Tony and Nino.

"No!" Alfonso yelled from behind the kitchen wall, where he hid for safety. "Don't hurt her."

"Come out or I'll blow her brains clear across this room," Gino warned.

Laura's heart raced faster than it had ever. She cried out, "Jesus, please help us. Save my baby!"

"Laura," Tony cried, rocking the chair with his might to loosen the ties.

Nino was gasping and coughing. His eyes were filled with tears of pain.

Suddenly, Alfonso stood out in the open. "Let her go," he whispered.

At first, Laura was confused. *Why was he making himself such an open target?* Suddenly, it dawned on her. She understood that the only way for Gino to release her was so he could aim his gun at Alfonso. It was suicide.

In one swift motion, Gino threw her to the floor, aimed his gun, and fired.

"No!" Nino cried. He choked and gasped, unable to fill his lungs with air.

The piercing sound echoed in Laura's head, as it had so long ago, the day the same man fired his gun and killed her family.

Gino stalked toward Alfonso's wounded body and picked up the gun that had fallen from his hand when he fell to the floor. He spit on Alfonso where he lay. "You're a disgrace to the Mafia," he bit. Entering the hallway closet, he used a chair to try to remove the attic entry door as an escape.

Laura whimpered and knelt before Alfonso, who was struck in the chest. Tears blurred her vision. The blood immediately began to pool beneath him.

More commands to surrender were shouted from the law enforcement outside.

Laura did not know what to do to help him. She whispered in his ear. "Now I know where you get your stubbornness from! Why did you do that? You knew he'd kill you!" she cried.

"I don't know," he whispered, trembling.

"Ask Jesus for forgiveness, right now. Ask Him to accept you and He'll save you. You acted like a Christian. You laid down your life for mine. Now become one," Laura begged.

Alfonso struggled to speak. "J-Jesus, I'm so sorry. I'm a horrible man," he gasped, blood spilling forth from his mouth.

Laura tried to wipe her tears, as she watched Alfonso dying before her. "Go on," she encouraged.

Nino was openly weeping. "*Figlio mio*," he whispered.

Tears coursed down Tony's cheeks, witnessing Laura's boldness.

"God," Alfonso coughed, "help Laura." He raised his head to look toward Gino, finding that he was distracted with preparing a get-away. Lifting a trembling hand, he reached into his sport coat pocket. Withdrawing a small handgun, he slowly slid it toward her. Laura instinctively snatched it and hid it between her knees, before Gino could see. "Save yourself." A tear slipped down Alfonso's face. He breathed his last breath.

Laura wailed, "Fonz! Fonz! Don't die!"

Nino let out a pain-filled howl that tore a hole in Laura's heart. "No!"

"How moving," Gino unexpectedly stated, clapping his hands. He stood in the kitchen watching the last scene, unaware that Alfonso had slipped her another gun. He held something in his hands. He played with it, twisting it between his fingers. It was a book of matches.

Laura's chest began to heave. He was going to set the place on fire and she would never be able to get everyone out in time.

"Don't look so panicked," Gino encouraged. "I'm not that cruel. I won't let you burn to death. I'll shoot you first."

"NO!" Tony cried. "Let her go!"

"Oh, shut up! You're going to be the first to go."

From where Laura knelt, she had a straight shot at Gino's body. She could use Alfonso's gun to wound him and then get Tony and Nino to safety. *She had to find the courage or they would all die!*

Gino tore a match from the book and walked into the family room area. Striking it, the match ignited. Slowly, he brought it toward the window curtain.

"Don't do this!" Laura begged. She silently prayed for God to give her the courage to protect her loved ones. *Would Jesus want her to kill this man who had chosen not to follow God? Or was it better that they died, having known and loved Jesus?* She was torn. Jesus wanted not one soul to perish. She could not shoot him.

The flame touched the curtain and instantly burst up the living room wall.

"Oh, God," Laura cried.

"God can't help you, anymore. Say goodbye to your fiancé." He strode toward the kitchen and raised his gun. Gino pointed it at Tony's head. He cocked it back and pulled the trigger. The gun clicked, but did not fire.

Before Laura could think, before she had a chance to consider any other option, she withdrew the gun Alfonso had slipped her. Taking only a split second, she raised the gun and fired. The gun kicked, bouncing Laura backward. Gino's gun exploded this time. Terror gripped her.

She quickly scrambled to her feet. The heat from the fire had already reached her. Gino lay sprawled out on the floor with a hole in his head. Laura immediately hurled. Her insides heaved and spilled forward from the grotesque scene before her. The stench of blood mixed with the smell of smoke, gagged her further. She could hear Tony screaming for her to help them. *He was still alive!*

Blocking the horrible vision from her eyes, she crawled to Tony and Nino. Laura panicked to find that Nino was unconscious. With new energy, she tried to untie the rope around Tony's hands.

The smoke was now thick and she breathed through the collar of her sweater. "Hurry," Tony shouted.

"I can't do it," she gagged. "It's so tight."

"Look through the drawers. Find a knife," he suggested. "Stay low. Use a towel to cover your nose and mouth."

Laura quickly crawled to the cabinets, trying to find the drawer with the silverware. On the counter, she noticed a butcher block. Thanking God, she gripped a large knife and made her way back to Tony.

By this time, the family room was engulfed in flames. The only way out was through the kitchen window. Laura sawed at the ropes with all her strength. Finally loosening them, Tony was able to help her remove the rest.

When his ankles fell free, he rose, shifting his weight to his unharmed leg. He pulled her into his arms and held her. They quickly exchanged a hug.

"It's a miracle!" Laura exclaimed. "The gun didn't go off!"

"God really does love me," Tony proclaimed. "Let's get out of here. Come on!"

"Nonno," Laura cried.

"I'll come back for him. You need to get out of here. The smoke's bad for the baby."

"We can't leave him!"

"We won't! I promise to come back for him. You need to get out!"

"Nonno," Laura cried. "I love you! Hang in there! We'll get you out of here!" she shouted, as Tony assisted her to the window. They were both profusely coughing, for the fire was consuming what little air remained. The window was jammed. She could feel her head getting lighter. The harder Tony tried to work on the window, the more severe her coughing became. She struggled to get air in. Tony backed her away from the window.

* * *

This was all too familiar. He had tried to out run a burning building one too many times. This time the outcome had to be different. He could not let anyone die . . . least of all the love of his life. Tony grabbed a chair and smashed it through the window. Glass splintered everywhere. He tore the tablecloth from the table and threw it over the window ledge. He could see the mess of police vehicles surrounding the building. They had blocked the area and their guns were drawn.

"Laura, come on baby, get outta here! Laura?" He turned to find her collapsed on the floor. "Oh, God!" Tony cried. He limped toward her, called out to her, but she was unconscious now as well. "Oh, Jesus, help me. Help me to help her." He struggled but managed to lift her and carry her to the window. "Help!" he shouted.

"Put your hands up!" they hollered through a megaphone.

"Please, help," Tony cried. He was becoming angry at their stupidity. He sat on the windowsill with Laura in his arms. Swinging his legs over, Tony jumped. A grisly pain ripped through his thigh and he screamed, falling to the ground with Laura still in his arms. He landed on his knees.

He looked up and found that John and Marlene, along with a dozen police officers, were running toward them. EMS rushed to Laura's aid, instantly placing an oxygen mask over her face.

"Where's the fire department?" Tony hollered over the loud sirens and the shouting coming from the law enforcement officers.

"They're pulling in," John yelled. "Are you okay?"

Tony ignored his question and rose to his feet. He hobbled to the window.

"What are you doing?" John demanded. "Don't go back in there!"

"I can't leave Nino to die in there. I have to help him," Tony insisted.

"No, you'll never make it out alive. Don't!" John shouted.

But it was too late. Tony jumped back into the fiery kitchen. Nino was still unconscious, tied to the chair. The fire had not reached him, but the ceiling had begun to give way and fall down around them. Tony moved as quickly as his leg would allow. The pain was so intense he actually felt sick. He ignored it and begged God to give him the strength to get the old man to safety.

Using the same knife, he sawed at the ropes quickly loosening them. Nino fell forward onto the floor. Tony touched his neck, praying for a pulse. It was weak, but he could see Nino's chest faintly rising and falling. Scooping his arms under Nino's, he lifted the man by his shoulders and dragged him to the window, coughing and gasping for air.

Unexpectedly, a flame licking the ceiling above him caught the drapery around the window, sending a blaze of fire forward. Tony felt an intense heat and dropped Nino to keep from becoming consumed. The window was blocked with an inferno of fire and Tony found that there was no way out.

"Run . . . get outta this place," he heard Nino utter.

"I gotta get you out of here!" Tony shouted.

"Save yourself! Leave this ole man to die."

"God didn't spare me from a bullet to the head, just now, to let me die in a fire. Besides, how am I going to live with myself knowing I let my fiancée's favorite *nonno* die?"

"I was wrong about you," Nino confessed.

"Save your breath for later, old man. I need to figure out how to get out of here."

Seeking help in the kitchen area, Tony found a broom. Getting as close to the window as he could, he pried the broom handle under the curtain rod and pushed up on an angle. The rod came loose and the burning curtains crashed to the floor. Tony grasped the tablecloth from the window ledge and tried to snuff out the nearby flames. Placing the smoked tablecloth back on the windowsill, he dragged Nino to the window. Two firefighters appeared at the window and helped Tony to pull Nino out. Tony jumped from the window . . . exhausted.

CHAPTER 20

1 Corinthians 13:6-7

"Love does not delight in evil but rejoices with the truth.
It always protects, always trusts, always hopes, always perseveres."

Laura woke to the sound of John's voice warning Tony not to re-enter the blazing apartment. She shooed the paramedic's hand away and tried to sit up, while they wheeled her toward the ambulance. They held an oxygen mask to her face and Laura struggled to remove it to get a better view.

"Ma'am, you must keep the mask on," the young man insisted.

"Tony!" she shouted through the mask.

"Please, take in deep breaths. Lay back down," he persisted.

"Laura, listen to him!" Marlene shouted. "Think of your baby!"

Laura had not noticed John and Marlene standing on either side of the gurney. They both kept their eyes on the building falling down in flames.

"Mom, Dad! They have to get them out!" she cried.

"The fire department's here. They'll help," John assured.

"The fire has consumed the apartment! Only God can get them out safely!" Laura sobbed.

"Then have faith that He will," Marlene encouraged.

It seemed an eternity before they saw Tony struggling to lift Nino to the window. Two firefighters helped pull him through. Paramedics immediately assisted Nino. Tony jumped from the window and fell to the ground. He let out a loud cry and collapsed.

* * *

The paramedics quickly picked up both men and began to work on them.

"He's having a heart attack," Tony informed those working to resuscitate Nino. His head was fuzzy and he felt he was near unconsciousness.

"How long ago did his symptoms start?" one asked.

Tony coughed, feeling as though he had inhaled sand. "Less than half-hour ago."

The one who had asked the question, quickly ripped Nino's shirt open. He listened to his heartbeat through a stethoscope. He spouted orders to another paramedic to prepare a nitroglycerin tablet and for an EKG. They quickly wheeled Nino into the ambulance and placed the tablet under his tongue.

Tony closed his eyes and thanked God they were alive. The paramedics working on him gave him a shot in his leg and immediately inserted an intravenous needle into his arm. They began wheeling him into the ambulance

"Laura?" he asked. "How's Laura?"

Someone suddenly clasped his hand. He opened his eyes to find John standing over him. "You saved her life. She's going to be okay," he reassured.

"I wanna see her," Tony mumbled, suddenly feeling extremely drowsy.

"They're giving her oxygen, right now, but she's okay. You just rest and let these people help you. We're right here for you. Uncle Frank's on the way to the hospital. He'll meet us there . . ." John's voice started to fade and Tony felt himself fall into unconsciousness.

* * *

"Tony!" Laura called out, but he did not hear her. She painfully watched him pass out. "Is he going to be okay?" she questioned anyone who would answer.

"He's in good hands now. They'll do everything they can for him," Marlene reassured.

"But he lost so much blood!" she cried.

"It's going to be okay."

Laura finally allowed the tears to come. The paramedics moved to lift her into the ambulance. She cried near hysterics at all that had occurred. Alfonso's death, her grandfather's heart attack, and Tony's near death experience, were more than she could already bear. The raw truth of her grandfather's past actions weighed even heavier on her heart. He truly was responsible for Tammy's death. But what shook Laura's self-confidence, what un-nerved her to the very core, were her own actions.

Laura had taken another man's life. She had killed someone's husband, someone's son, someone's father. *How could she live with this on her conscience? Had she made the right choice? Was her obligation to save her loved ones first or had God called her to make a choice between their souls?* If so, Laura felt she failed. In her selfishness, she could not bear to live without Tony and Nino. Therefore, she made the choice to send a soul to Hell, when had she let God's will be done, Gino's soul might have been saved.

This was more than she could handle. When Laura arrived at the hospital, they admitted her and lightly sedated her.

****

Her cries were breaking his heart.

"Should we wake her?" he questioned. "She's so restless."

Marlene sat perched on the edge of her chair, clasping Laura's hand, as she lay tense on the hospital bed. "I don't know," she answered John's question.

John watched on, while Laura's head rolled back and forth in torment. Her body trembled with sobs and she continually cried out.

"I'm calling for a doctor or nurse . . . someone," he insisted.

"I killed him," she cried. "I killed him."

"Oh, God," Marlene whispered. "This is terrible. This is going to haunt her for the rest of her life," she wept.

"How can we help her?" he pressed.

"She'll need to speak to a therapist again," Marlene sighed tearfully.

"I think she needs Father Bill."

****

After all the nightmares that haunted her, Laura was happy to be coming out of her slumber. She could hear murmuring in her hospital room. Forcing an eye open, she tried focusing in on those around her. Marlene and John sat next to her, whispering to someone. Laura slowly sat up and rubbed her swollen eyes. She swallowed and gasped. Her throat was horribly raw.

All heads turned her way and she recognized Father Bill sitting behind John. A lump rose in her throat, making it ache further. Tears swelled in her eyes and her chest began to rise and fall with short breaths.

"Tony? Nonno? Are they okay?"

"Everyone's okay. They're resting here at the hospital," Marlene quickly answered, rushing to her side.

"Oh, thank you, God. Thank you," she cried. She looked at both of her parents and immediately noticed their tired eyes. "I'm so . . . so sorry," she bawled.

John quickly rose to be at her side as well. "What are you sorry for?" John immediately quizzed.

"I disobeyed your orders. I left without telling you. You got more than you bargained for when you adopted me. You could've adopted someone with fewer troubles. Someone who wasn't constantly putting everyone in danger." The tears spilled down Laura's cheeks like an endless waterfall.

"And miss out on all this action? No way!" John teased through tears. His hand was gently rubbing hers. "This is better than the best episode of *Baretta*, any day!"

"Dad."

"Laura," Marlene interrupted with a slight rise in her voice. "That's the furthest thing from the truth! We love you. We adopted wanting to help and make a greater difference in someone's life. I know the Lord brought you to us and I wouldn't change that for anything," Marlene insisted.

"But . . ."

"There's no 'buts'. Yeah, you're grounded for the rest of your life, but at least we'll know exactly where you are at all times," John continued to jest.

Laura cracked a smile, and then suddenly burst into further tears.

"What did I say?" John whispered, raising his shoulders in question. Marlene shushed him.

"You're just so wonderful to me," Laura continued to cry. "I don't deserve either of you. I don't deserve to be your daughter. I've made so many mistakes and have embarrassed you and disgraced our family name."

"Where do you come up with this stuff?" John exclaimed.

"Laura, no. You're the light of our lives. We're so proud to be your parents. You're a great blessing to us," Marlene insisted.

"I'm a sinner! A fornicator! I killed a man! I sent a soul to hell! I'm a horrible person!" she screamed.

John and Marlene looked to Father Bill. He stepped forward and reached out for her hand. Marlene stepped aside and he sat next to her bedside.

"Hi," he smiled.

"Oh, Father Bill, I've failed God," she wept.

"Laura, I have gotten to know you throughout the past year and a half and I pray you feel close enough to me to hear me out," he began.

She nodded, taking a tissue from Marlene who now stood at the other side of her bed, next to John. "But Father Bill, I've sinned."

"We all sin, every day," he added.

"But I got myself pregnant before marriage. I killed someone. I took a life."

"Laura, you've repented already for having been with Tony before marriage. God has already forgiven that sin. Why do you continue to punish yourself? You've kept yourself pure since that time, have you not?"

"Yes, I swear to you," she confessed.

"Then forgive yourself and let it go. As for what happened tonight, do you remember the story of David and Goliath?" Laura nodded again. "When David slew his enemy, he had the blessing of God on him. It wasn't because David had such great aim or vast skill that he killed his enemy with one blow. It was God who guided and helped him. Gino Galante was the enemy. I'm sure that throughout his lifetime, he had plenty of time to repent and didn't. He was going to take your lives and walk away as if he'd killed nothing more than a couple of insects. God knows your heart. I don't imagine you had evil intent. Were you looking to kill him?"

"No! No! I just wanted to wound him so I could get Tony and Nonno out of the fire. I didn't even look at where I was shooting. I just raised the gun . . . almost like a reflex. I didn't want to kill him. But I did! I hit him in the head! I didn't just wound him. I killed him!"

"It was his time, Laura. You were protecting your loved ones. If Gino Galante's soul is in Hell, it's his own doing. God didn't want him to perish that way. But He gives us free will and Gino chose to sin against God. Your heart is pure. You want good for all around you. I heard what you did for Alfonso Rengali. Tony told us how you led him into prayer before he passed. You did well."

Father Bill reached over and pulled Laura into a hug. She silently wept. "Father God, help this child to understand You. Heal her heart of its wounds. Bring her peace and joy, once again. Continue to protect her against every evil and bring her the desires of her heart, in accordance to Your divine will. In Jesus' name, Amen."

Laura felt additional arms around her. John and Marlene embraced her as well. She felt inside that she *really* already had the desires of her heart.

"Laura Ann Knight, you are absolved of all of your sins, intended or not. In the name of the Father, and the Son, and the Holy Spirit, Amen."

Laura crossed herself. "Thank you, Father Bill. Thank you for coming to talk to me."

"Laura, anytime you need a friend, I'm here for you," he claimed. He kissed the top of her head, wished the Knights good night, and exited the room.

"Mom, Dad, tell me the truth. How's Nonno?" she asked.

They exchanged glances and John leaned forward on the bed rail. He pulled a stray strand of her hair back and gave her a brief smile. "He's very weak, babe. They immediately performed open-heart surgery on him, but he has damage to his heart. It'll be some time before he recovers. But the doctors said he could recover, so long as he eats right and exercises. He's in the cardiac unit on the second floor."

Laura's heart ached. Despite everything, she could not lose her grandfather. He had become too important to her. "Will you take me to see him?"

"If the doctor says you're all right, then yes, I'll take you," John agreed.

"There's someone else who's dying to see you," she heard Uncle Frank's voice beckon. He strolled into the room with a bouquet of beautiful flowers in his hand. Laura's heart jumped at the sound of his voice. It had been weeks since she had seen him and she did not realize until that moment how much she missed him.

Tears immediately filled her eyes. "Uncle Frank!" She stretched her arms forward and pulled him into her arms. "I miss you so much!" she cried.

"I've missed you too, love. I'm glad you're doing better. You need to stop fussing about everyone else and take care of yourself. Although I must admit, I'm glad you were there to save my boy's life," he stated.

Laura looked down. "I did no such thing. He saved me. He carried me out of the fire with a gunshot wound to his leg. I know he lost a lot of blood. Please, tell me he's okay."

"He's very weak. They gave him blood, but the doc says he'll be fine. He needs lots of rest and he'll need therapy for quite a while. That bullet shredded his quad pretty bad. They performed surgery to remove the bullet and repair the muscle. He's still in recovery and already asking for you."

Laura absorbed the information Frank had given her. Her heart wanted to get up and run to his bedside. Her head told her that there were still too many issues between them. "I'll give him some time to recoup and then I'll go visit. First, I'd really like to talk to Dr. Packard, make sure the baby's okay, and then, go see my nonno."

****

It was not long before Dr. Packard made his rounds and was in to see Laura again.

"Back again, are we? What did I tell you about staying out of trouble?" he chastised.

"I know, Dr. Packard, but I couldn't leave Tony and my grandfather to die. I had to do something," she insisted.

"Well, thankfully for you, it all turned out well and you and the baby weren't seriously harmed. Aside from the rawness you feel in your throat, the smoke did little damage. You and the baby both are okay. I checked your blood sugar levels and they still need improvement. I don't want to have to put you on meds, but you're leaving me no choice if you can't take care of yourself. When I say no stress, I mean . . . no stress. Eat right and rest or you'll be back in here in premature labor. I can't guarantee to stop it, next time, Laura. Go away for a while. Go somewhere where you can ease your mind and rest your body. Can you do that?"

"Go to Cicero," Uncle Frank, who was still in the room visiting, suggested.

"That sounds wonderful," Marlene added. "Would you like us to take you there, even for a few days? When the doctor says so, of course."

The thought of being in the house where she fell in love with Tony actually did not seem like a good idea. If things had not been going the way they had, she would have jumped at the idea of spending time there. Although, with all the memories that the house held, she did not want to go. She could easily see herself falling deeper into a depression.

Of course, one look at Marlene's face and Laura could see that a visit to the house would do *her* good. She just could not be selfish after what she had put them through. She would grin, bear it, and go with her parents to Cicero. "Sure, Mom, if you both want to get away, and Uncle Frank doesn't mind, we can go there."

"Laura, you know that the house is as much yours as it is Tony's. Go up and get some rest. I'll take care of Tony here," Frank offered.

Since Dr. Packard had given her a somewhat clean bill of health, Laura was discharged that evening. As soon as the arrangements could be made, the family was heading off to Cicero. In the time being, Laura's concern was for her grandfather. She insisted on seeing him before they left for home.

Laura removed the hospital gown, showered, and put on the fresh clothes Marlene brought her for her departure. Once the paperwork was signed, John wheeled her out of her room and into the hospital corridors. It was already late evening by this time and visiting hours were soon to be over.

"Dad, please take me to see Nonno now," Laura whispered.

"Will do, honey," he whispered in return. "Just remember, no stress."

"No stress, I promise."

Finding Nino's room, John pushed the wheelchair to the door. He slipped on the wheel brake and helped Laura out of the chair. She entered the room alone. Laura's heart nearly stopped. Nino lay lifeless on the hospital bed. His face was pallid. His eyes were closed. Laura let out a muffled whimper, covering her mouth with her hand. The room was silent but for the monitor's continual chirping and beeping, indicating Nino's heartbeats and oxygen levels.

She pulled up a chair and sat next to him. Visions of the night Tammy died flashed before her eyes. Sitting at his bedside in that same manner, she wondered if she would have to watch his life slowly slip away. Laura could not bear that kind of pain again. She just could not handle one more death. Tears silently slid down her cheeks. Nino had truly become one of the most important people in her life. She loved him . . . no matter what.

"Nonno," she whispered. "I'm here."

His eyes suddenly fluttered open and he came to focus on her. They immediately filled up and tears spilled down the sides of his face.

"Shh! Don't cry. You're going to be okay," Laura whispered to him.

"*Bella mia*," he managed in a very raspy voice.

"I love you, Nonno. You have to get better fast," she urged.

He knowingly nodded.

"You better promise me. You're my only blood relative. I can't live without you, Nonno." Laura wiped the tears that slid down her cheeks, as well as his.

"Me too," he uttered with a weak smile. His smile faded and he managed to whisper, "I'm so sorry. Fonzie . . . he . . ." Nino could not finish.

"Please, don't cry. Don't get upset. Alfonso's with Jesus. He sacrificed his life for mine. I'll never forget that. He was good way down deep. Just very misguided."

Nino shook his head and tried to contain his emotions. Laura wiped his tears with a tissue, trying not to bump the oxygen tubes near his nose. "I'm a bad man," he wept.

"God has forgiven you for your past sins. Don't think about it anymore. He's still working on you. He's working on all of us, who love Him."

"So sorry," he cried.

"Shh. Rest Nonno. I'll visit you as often as I can. But I must tell you, the doctor's insisting that I take some time off to rest myself. My parents want to take me to the house in Cicero. I don't know when we're leaving, but I'll try to postpone it until I know you're better. Okay?"

"*Amore*, go."

"No, not until I know you and Tony will be okay. I'll come and see you as soon as I can. I love you, Nonno." Laura bent forward and kissed his wrinkled cheek.

Nino extended a trembling arm and clutched her hand. He whispered, "You forgive me?"

"Yes, Nonno, I forgive you. I know you love me and that you're only looking out for me."

"*Bella, grazie.*" Tears poured from his tired eyes. Laura embraced him and kissed him again. "Tony?"

"Tony had surgery on his leg. They removed the bullet. He has a great deal of damage to his muscle, but he'll be okay with therapy," Laura informed. "God spared him from Gino's gun. It's a miracle the gun didn't go off, or he would have been killed."

"Only God," Nino whispered.

"Yes, only God. He must have a reason for keeping him around. I'm more than grateful!" she whispered in return.

"He risked his life for me."

"And for me," Laura added tearfully.

"I was wrong . . . about him. He is a better man . . . than me," he said between wheezes.

"Yes, he's a good man. I'm glad you see that now. Maybe now, you can understand why I love him so much."

Nino nodded and weakly squeezed her hand. "*Amore*, you no need it . . . but you have my blessing . . . to marry him." Nino struggled to finish the last sentence. "He proved to me . . . that he loves you more . . . than his life."

"Shh. Enough Nonno," Laura whispered. "And thanks. I'm glad you approve. But I don't know what's going to happen. I'm leaving it in God's hands," she frowned.

"You do that. God will help."

"Okay, Nonno, you better get some rest. I'll see you soon, okay?"

"*Si, amore. Ti amo,*" Nino whispered, his voice fading.

"*Ti amo*, Nonno," Laura returned his love. She kissed his forehead and walked out of the room.

John and Marlene patiently waited in the corridor. Laura move toward them.

"How is he?" Marlene asked.

Laura sat back down in the wheelchair and John began to push her toward the elevators. "He's very emotional. He cried the whole time, expressing his remorse for what happened. I feel so sorry for him," she answered.

"You're a good Christian, Laura. God has given you a compassionate heart," John complimented.

"Thanks Dad, but I don't always feel that way," she whispered.

Marlene rested a warm hand on her shoulder. "We're only human, sweetie. You mustn't be so hard on yourself."

"I hope I can find the courage to put my fears aside and give my relationship with Tony another try." Laura confessed suddenly. "I'm so scared."

John pushed the wheelchair into the elevator and hit the button for the fifth floor.

"Why are we going back up?" Laura questioned.

"To see Tony, of course," John stated.

"Tonight?"

"Don't you want to go see him? You have to face him sooner or later," Marlene suggested. "He's asking for you, like Frank said."

"Yes . . . well . . . I . . ."

"Spit it out already," John teased. "You're going to leave a wounded man hanging?"

Laura finally laughed. "I guess not. I just don't know what to say to him."

"Don't say anything. Just be with him," Marlene advised.

"Yeah," John jumped in, "No stress, just be good company. I'll only give you 15 minutes, though. You're tired and you need to rest, too."

"Okay, that's fine," Laura agreed.

As they approached Tony's room, butterflies began dancing around in Laura's stomach. She was sure to vomit before she approached the door. Frank paced outside the room. A smile fell upon his face at their arrival. John slapped him a high five. She caught their sly smiles. John pushed her into Tony's room.

She stood and suddenly gasped as her eyes fell on him. John quietly slipped out with the wheelchair.

She walked to Tony's bedside and gazed down at him. *How could it be possible that someone could look so incredibly beautiful with a stitched gash in the cheek and bruised face? Why was it that regardless of time, of distance, of angry words and painful hurts, that she could still love him so fully, so completely?*

A lump rose in her throat, once again. As quietly as possible, she pulled a chair up to his bed. She sat down and set her gaze on him. She decided that she loved to watch him sleep. He looked so peaceful. A slight upward curve to his lips made him look angelic. Suddenly, his eyes flickered open.

He cleared his throat and whispered, "Am I in Heaven?"

"No," Laura whispered.

He cleared his throat again, winced, but continued. "Then why is there an angel before me?"

Laura could not help but blush. He was such a schmoozer—always knowing the right thing to say to break the ice and win her over. "I'm no angel," she finally answered.

Suddenly, his voice became stronger and he clarified. "You don't understand. Just before you arrived, both Alfonso and Gino had their guns on your grandfather and me. We were this close to death," he described, with a tiny space between his thumb and pointer finger. "I prayed to God and asked Him to take me if it was my time. But if I could still be of some use to Him, I prayed that He'd send in an angel. You walked in one second later. You saved our lives, baby."

"Tony. . ." Tears slipped from Laura's eyes upon realizing that she had been an answer to his prayers. God used her to spare their lives. Yet, she still could not let it go that she took Gino's life.

Interrupting her train of thought, Tony continued. "You know," he whispered in a hoarse voice, "We've already confirmed that I've been a big jerk to you. You never deserved what I've dished out and I'm so sorry for hurting you." He coughed and Laura quickly offered him a glass of ice water. He sipped from the cup and continued. "I hope and pray that I've not completely severed all ties to you."

Laura did not know how to respond. Her heart was racing, as well as her mind. When Tony realized that she was not going to comment, he went on. "I've been pretty messed up. You've been my rock. You're always there to save the day. You stormed into that apartment today, on a white horse." He flashed her a dimpled smile.

Laura looked down with a frown. "I almost got us all killed."

"If you hadn't come, Nino and I would be dead. Alfonso would've made sure of that!"

"I'd like to believe that he would've come to his senses the way he did and stopped before it was too late," Laura thought aloud.

"Laura, he planned the whole thing for months. He connived and lied. He was hell-bent on revenge. He joined an alliance with Mario Galante. There was no turning back for him. Gino wouldn't have let him."

"Yet, ultimately, he saved all our lives," Laura defended.

Tony coughed again to clear his throat. "How do you figure?"

Laura offered him more water and answered his question. "He made himself a target so Gino would let me go. He slipped me a gun. The one I pulled out and fired to save your lives."

Tony looked deeply into her eyes. "Do you regret that?"

"Of course not, but if I had to do it again, I would have aimed for a limb, not his head."

"He got what he deserved," Tony mumbled.

"He was still a human. Someone's husband, father, son. I took a life."

"But if you hadn't shot him, we all would've died, Laura."

"I know. Yet, I may have opened up a whole new can of worms now," she insisted.

Tony thought about that for a moment. He nodded his head and whispered, "Mario isn't going to be happy about this. I just hope this vendetta between the Valentes and the Galantes ends here."

"Well, I know it won't be Nonno who retaliates."

"Don't be so sure."

"Tony, I'd like to believe the best of him."

"Me too," Tony stated. "I saw the pain in his eyes when he realized that Alfonso had betrayed him. Yet, he'd been lying to Alfonso for over 24 years. That's a hard pill to swallow."

"You deemed my Nonno's life worthy enough to save. You went back in the burning building to save him," Laura pointed out.

"I know how much you love him," Tony uttered.

"Thank you."

"I'd do it all over again, if I had to, Laura. I love you."

"I love you, too." The words fell out of her mouth like second nature.

Their eyes collided and Tony pulled her hand into his. He slowly leaned forward, minimizing the space between them. Laura panicked. One kiss from him and she was sure to fall, as she fell the first time. A kiss would hurl forth a torment that was sure to leave her in more pain than she cared to feel.

Closer.

She had to think. The temptation was too great. *To kiss or not to kiss?* To kiss would mean that she trusted him and that she would be willing to take that risk of being hurt. To not kiss would torture her further, because her heart longed for nothing more than to be his.

He closed his eyes. One more inch. Laura instinctively lifted her hand and placed two gentle fingers on his parted lips. Tony's eyes opened, catching hers. He looked confused. She shook her head.

"I'm sorry. I better go." She quickly rose and dashed out of the room. John and Marlene seemed startled by her sudden appearance. "Can we go now?" she asked in a little voice.

John and Marlene brought their daughter home.

CHAPTER 21

Proverbs 3:5

"Trust in the LORD with all your heart and lean not on your own understanding."

Saturday, December 30

The next morning, John drove Laura to the hospital. As he parked their vehicle, she walked toward the cardiac unit where he promised to meet her. The hospital corridors bustled with energy. Laura made her way to her grandfather's room. Nurses and doctors scattered about making their morning rounds. Servers, orderlies, and other staff members carried out empty breakfast trays, cleaned vacated rooms, and wheeled patients to their destinations.

Laura's mind was racing, while she casually moved down the hall. She wanted to do what was right. *But what was right?* For now, she would visit with her grandfather and then she would go to the fifth floor and briefly visit Tony. The thought both excited and scared her.

Would he try to kiss her again? And if so, would she let him?

No! Not yet. She would have to make the visit quick and to the point. She would not step near him. She would simply make sure he was well and then leave. Laura was not ready to jump back into a relationship with Tony. He had wounded her too deeply. *How could she be sure he would not hurt her again?*

Temporarily distracting her thoughts, she entered Nino's room to find that he was asleep. She sat with him a while, praying for him, as she waited for John to come. When more time passed, Laura rose and went to the nurse's station. She asked to speak to Nino's doctors. The nurses informed Laura that Nino had a restful night and that he did seem slightly improved. But his doctors would not be available until early afternoon. Laura had some time to kill.

She sat quietly again waiting for John in Nino's room. Her mind began to work overtime. Perhaps John had understood that she was visiting Tony first. She left a note on Nino's nightstand and took the nearest elevator to the fifth floor. As Laura approached Tony's room, she could hear John's voice. He sounded angry.

"You have gall!" he declared. "We let you in, we trusted you, and yet, you had your own agenda!"

Laura quickened her pace, ready to enter the room and stop John from grilling Tony. But as Laura stepped into the room, she quickly realized that it was not Tony he was lashing out at. It was *Beth*.

Tears streamed her face. Her chest, wrapped in a skin-tight seductive blouse, heaved with every gasp. "You don't understand," she tried to explain.

The conversation came to a screaming halt when Laura entered. "You . . ." Laura whispered. "What are you doing here?"

"She was just leaving," Tony interjected.

"Tony, if you'd just let me explain," she pleaded.

"There's nothing you can say that'll justify your actions or your motives. You were willing to put other people's lives on the line to get what you wanted. I swear if I wasn't a Christian man, I would toss you out of here on your butt," John stated.

"I never wanted anyone to get hurt. I didn't know that Alfonso killed the employee I replaced. He met me one night in a bar. He'd already done his homework and found out that I was Tony's old classmate. It wasn't by chance that he found someone who had a crush on Tony Giacalone. Half the girls in our class would've done anything for a date with him. So, when he asked me if I could use some extra cash to try to woo Tony away, I jumped at the chance. I didn't realize that lives could be at stake," she sobbed.

"Maybe not physically, but you were ready to help destroy a relationship between two people. You had no regard for others' feelings. Only your own!" John argued.

"Well, then the only thing that I am guilty of is being selfish. We're all selfish in some way!" she defended.

"Perhaps you're right," John added. "Regardless, I'd like you to pack up your things, first thing Monday morning. My trust in you is broken and I cannot have you working for me and my firm if I cannot trust you."

"This is unfair! I always did my job in a professional manner. Won't you give me a second chance to prove myself?"

"Beth, I'm sorry, but I can't have you working for me after the way you intentionally set out to hurt my daughter. It's time for you to go. I will see you Monday morning, at the office," John confirmed.

Beth threw her purse over her shoulder and stalked toward the door. Before passing Laura, she abruptly stopped and faced her. "Well, skinny, looks like you got your man. Let's see how long you can hang on to him, this time."

"If it's real love, I won't have to hang on. It will surpass all understanding, all knowledge, and *all evil*," Laura emphasized.

"Humph!" Beth spun on her heel and left.

Laura watched her stalk down the hall in her tight mini-skirt and heels. She prayed that that would be the last she saw of Beth. Suddenly, a clapping broke out in the room. Laura blushed.

"Burned her," John praised.

"Thanks, I always hoped I'd have the last word," Laura confessed.

"Well, you spoke the truth," Tony agreed. "Our love *can* and *will* surpass all things."

Laura did not know what to say to that. She was suddenly at a loss for words. Thankfully, John saved her and explained his delay. "I'm sorry it took me so long. As I was making my way for the elevator from the front desk, I spotted her. I followed her up here and caught her trying to explain away her behavior to Tony."

"I wondered what happened to you. I thought maybe you misunderstood me and thought I was coming to see Tony first."

"How is Nino?" Tony questioned.

"Nonno seems to be doing a tad better. He was sleeping when I arrived, so I didn't get a chance to talk to him. The nurse says the doctors will be in early afternoon. I'd like to talk to them and see what's next," Laura explained.

Tony nodded. Laura really looked at him for the first time, that morning. His color looked better and he appeared rested. "How are you?" she asked.

"I feel great on these meds. But the doctor says I won't be able to put any weight on my leg for a week or so. He'll probably send me home in a few more days. I start therapy immediately."

"That's great. Do whatever they tell you. You'll get better quick."

Laura suddenly felt uncomfortable. A silence fell over the room. John shuffled his feet and finally broke the silence. "I'm going to take a step out and give you two some time alone."

"You don't have to leave, Dad." Laura immediately jumped in.

"That's okay. You kids should probably talk. I'll be back soon." Laura watched helplessly, as John left the room.

"Has it come to that?" Tony unexpectedly whispered.

"Come to what?"

"You don't even want to be left alone with me anymore?" he dug.

"No, it's not that I don't want to be left alone with you. It's . . . just . . ." Laura stood there, holding her purse, afraid to step in any further.

"You can come closer, I won't bite," he teased.

Laura blushed. She put her purse down in the chair and walked closer to his bed, folding her hands together.

"Won't you even kiss me hello? Have I hurt you that deeply?"

Laura leaned forward—still unable to answer any of his questions. She briefly kissed his cheek. He suddenly grabbed her arm and held her, just inches from his face. Laura froze, afraid he would plant a kiss on her lips. But he did not; he just held her close.

"Am I lost to you, forever?"

This last question felt as though the breath had been sucked from her lungs. Finally, she found her voice—tiny and shaky. "I don't know."

He released her arm and immediately covered his face with his hands, roughly rubbing his stubbly cheeks. "God, I am so sorry. How can I take it all back? How can I erase what I've done to you? I can see the confusion in your eyes. I just pray that you haven't fallen out of love with me and that you had no feelings for Alfonso."

Laura was shocked at his last statement. "Feelings for Alfonso? Is that what you think? You don't get it, do you? You don't understand, even still?"

Tony looked at her with uncertainty. "I pushed you away. I wouldn't blame you if you did."

"Antonio Giacalone you are so clueless. What I'm feeling has nothing to do with another man. If you believe that then you really *don't* know me. I have so much to take in; so much to digest. The distance you put between us that affected our relationship in a grave way is a big part, but to think that I no longer love you—that's nuts!"

"You've every right to be upset with me. I hurt you. But I know that once you hear what happened, once you know the truth, maybe you can understand?" he begged.

"You're probably right. I *would* understand that you've been through Hell and back. But just as John told Beth, it's the trust issue that's the problem. I can't trust you, Tony."

Tony sat up, wincing. "Listen to me," he pleaded. "I was wrong. I should've never shut you out." His words flew forward, and for the first time, Laura could hear serious desperation in his voice. "I was ashamed to come forth and tell you what happened. But I'm not afraid anymore.

"You need to know that during the first session, we found that my father was sexually abusing my sisters and that I knew about it for two years and did nothing. I felt—a coward! I let it go on, afraid for my own life and because two years went by before I did anything about it, I lost all self-respect. I believed you'd feel the same way about me. That you'd see me as a weakling."

Laura's chest rose and fell with acceleration and her breathing came faster with Tony's explanation. Tony continued, "It wasn't until my father called little Rosie into his room, that I finally snapped. I didn't care what the consequences would be. I just wanted him to stop abusing my sisters. And so, I stepped in."

"Oh, Tony," Laura whimpered.

"First, he beat me, and then . . . he raped me," Tony revealed.

"No, Tony," she cried.

"Over and over and over, it would happen," he revealed. "I created Max to escape the reality I lived in. For a year, he gave me the choice—it was me . . . or my sisters. I wouldn't let him touch my sisters anymore."

Laura had to find a chair and sit. Her breathing was becoming erratic. She had imagined that something horrible had happened to Tony. *But not this. Not something so unthinkable.*

Tony did not seem to notice her breathing. He was in a trance, while he continued to explain why his behavior toward her had been so unpredictable. "And then, while under the influence of the drugs, Max and I began to argue. We finally were able to converse. But I found out two vital pieces of information that shook my world and shattered my self-worth even more. I found that I was responsible for the death of my family. I found that Max was the one who informed the Galantes of the life insurance policy that could pay them off. Max knew that they were going to kill my father. Instead, they killed my entire family. *I* was responsible for their deaths. How could I live with that on my conscience? I was devastated."

Laura's stomach churned and twisted at the thought of the hell he suffered. "I'm so sorry. So sorry," she repeated.

"If that wasn't bad enough, Max finally came forth and blurted your father's reasons for wanting to move you and your sisters to Mexico. I discovered that I'd actually convinced Max to take you girls in, to save you from Matt's evil plan—the plan that he so casually revealed to me while I was in his prison."

Laura suddenly looked at Tony in confusion. "Mexico? What are you talking about?" she inquired.

Tony looked at her, finally centering in on her. "Maybe, I've said too much. I don't want to upset you more."

Laura tried to control her breathing. Her stomach was tied in knots. Her chest ached with anxiety. There were more secrets, more pain to an already clandestine and sordid past. This web of lies and deceit seemed to never end.

"You can't stop now. Tell me! What are you talking about?" she insisted.

"You look pale. We can discuss the rest in therapy," Tony suggested.

"NO!" she suddenly stood and shouted. "Tell me, now!"

Tony shook his head in understanding. "I know how you feel. I wanted to know the whole truth, yet I feared it." He sat up and grabbed her hand. "Laura, brace yourself. The reason Max went to the house the night of the murders . . . was to take you and your sisters and bring you to the 'abandoned' house. He was following my command to bring you to safety."

Laura felt ill. "Why, Tony? What was my father going to do to us?" Her legs threatened to buckle beneath her, trembled with apprehension.

"The truth is . . . your father was planning on selling Patty and Sabrina—Patty as a servant to a rich family for $25,000 and Sabrina to a family unable to have children of their own for $100,000."

Laura pulled her hand from his. Her head spun. "That's sick, crazy . . . sell us? What about me?"

Tony looked down at his empty hand. He blew the air from his lungs forcefully. Looking back up at her, he reached for her again. "Laura, you better sit for this," he recommended.

"Spit it out, Tony!" she demanded, shivering with alarm.

"Prostitution. He was going to keep you and sell you out for prostitution."

Laura took in a breath and immediately fell to her knees, spilling forth the remains of her breakfast. "No!" she gagged.

Tony struggled to get up to help her. He stood on his feet and unexpectedly shouted out in pain. He collapsed to the floor, behind Laura. Still, he reached out a hand to try to comfort her. "Laura?"

At that moment, John entered. Seeing Laura and Tony on the floor, he rushed to their aid. "What happened?" he cried. "I leave you two alone for 15 minutes and I find you both in a heap on the floor! Laura, are you okay?"

"Oh, God," she cried. "Oh, dear God."

"Laura," Tony cried. "I'm sorry. I should've never listened to Doc. He told me you should know the whole truth."

"What are you talking about?" John demanded. He helped Laura to a chair and pressed the button on Tony's bed to get the nurse's attention. He helped Tony back to his feet. Within moments, a nurse entered demanding to know what had happened. They assisted Tony into bed.

"Can you take a quick look at my daughter, please? She's pregnant and looks as though she's about to pass out."

The nurse quickly checked Laura's pulse. "How do you feel?"

"Sick. Sick to my stomach," Laura admitted.

"Sir, I believe you better get this young lady to see her doctor, immediately," she recommended.

"Will do. Come Laura. Are you strong enough to walk?" John asked.

"Laura, I never wanted to hurt you. Please forgive me? Give us another chance. I love you!" Tony cried. John slowly walked her toward the door.

John stopped and turned around a moment. "Get some rest, Tony. You can see her again when you're both better." He turned and continued to guide her.

"Laura?" Tony cried.

She turned and gave him one last glance. His eyes penetrated hers. She felt her soul being torn. Her heart beat wildly in her chest.

"Laura?" he called again.

"Goodbye," she whispered.

****

Laura swore she would never forget the tortured look in Tony's eyes, as she left the hospital room that morning. Those eyes haunted her for the next week, while she stayed home, inactive. Dr. Packard insisted that she get rest, therefore New Year's passed uneventfully and January of '79 rolled in.

He also recommended that she get help to better handle the stress, for her emotions still reeled with all of the truth that Tony set free and with all that had happened. Nightmares continued to haunt her about the murder. Finally, she decided to see Dr. Parnell for help.

Dr. Parnell was an immense support. He was glad to hear that Tony had finally opened up to her, though he wished that Tony had waited to break the heart-wrenching news in therapy. Laura understood his need to get it all off his chest at once and was quick to forgive him. Still, she would need quite a few sessions with the doctor to work through all that had occurred.

After a week, Tony was released into the care of Uncle Frank. Frank, who called Laura every morning, told Laura that Tony was determined to regain the strength back in his leg and vigorously worked out in between physical therapy sessions. He was already walking, but with the assistance of a cane.

Nino was discharged after a week as well, into Josie's care. A nurse made daily visits to his home. Still weak from the surgery, he was in need of continuous assistance. Laura explained to him that she could not visit yet, per doctor's orders. She was not to leave her house, with the exception of doctor visits. Nino understood and wanted her not to worry, but to care for herself. She promised to come see him as soon as the doctor gave her the okay.

One week of perpetual supervision from John and Marlene was giving Laura cabin fever. It was then that they decided to pack up for a weekend and go to Cicero.

****

Sunday, January 6

Laura was right. Staying at the old house in Cicero actually made it harder on her. Around every corner lingered a memory that had something to do with Tony. Though they had long since upgraded the home—fresh paint, new trim, a queen bed in the spare bedroom for guests, such as John and Marlene, a TV in the living room, and a larger table in the dining area—it was still the house that carried so many memories of the most bittersweet days of Laura's life.

She could not get her head out of the past. With a blanket on her shoulders, she entered the kitchen that early morning and stared at the window that she had gazed out of so many times while washing and drying dishes at Tony's side. She could recall other times watching Tony work outside, while she prepared a meal.

One memory in particular came to her at that moment . . .

"Did I tell you who stopped by the store today?" she recalled Uncle Frank asking Tony, one summer day, two months prior to their first kiss. They both worked outside, planting a few shrubs around the side of the house, for landscaping. Laura had entered the kitchen, at that very moment, to prepare lunch for them, when hearing Uncle Frank's question through the open kitchen window.

She watched Tony press his arm against his forehead to wipe away the perspiration that trickled downward. "I don't know. But I'm sure you're about to tell me," he teased.

Uncle Frank pressed his foot down onto the shovel, piercing the ground. "It was your girlfriend, Silvia."

"My girlfriend," Tony sneered.

Laura stepped back away from the sink, afraid to listen any further. It had suddenly dawned on her that Tony could have possibly wanted a life outside of caring for her. *Was she holding him back from pursuing other women and possibly finding a future wife?* Laura felt her breakfast threatening to come up.

"Well," Uncle Frank continued, "She comes in almost three times a week and I don't think it's our produce that she's interested in."

Tony laughed. "Uncle, you have an active imagination. I think you should be paying closer attention to Ms. Torino, who comes in daily. She ain't just coming in for our cold cuts."

Uncle Frank suddenly became serious, vigorously moving the dirt out of the hole. "Tony! Don't even go there. You know that there will never be another for me for as long as I live. Your Aunt Margherita was it. She's gone. End of story."

"Okay, okay," Tony quickly exclaimed. "Don't get so mad. I just thought I'd give you a taste of your own medicine."

Uncle Frank lifted more dirt from the hole that he had already dug. "You're young. You got your future to think about; who you're going to spend it with, what you want to do for a living. It's time to get your head out of the clouds and plan."

Tony lifted the small arborvitae and placed it in the hole. "I like my life just the way it is," he claimed.

Laura recalled going through the rest of her day nearly immobilized. She was happy to hear that he liked his life the way it was. But she knew how selfless he was. She knew his noble qualities. While she was in the picture, Tony would not pursue his future. Perhaps even a future . . . *with Silvia.*

Laura remembered the awful emotions that tormented her that evening. After Uncle Frank departed for the night, Laura sat on their porch bench, lost in thought. Night fell before Tony exited the front screen door to find her sitting in the dark.

"There you are!" he sighed. "All this time, I thought you'd gone up to bed or something. What are you still doing out here?"

Laura looked up at his perfectly chiseled face and tried to smile. "Just enjoying the cool breeze," she covered.

"Can I join you?"

"Of course," she whispered. Laura moved to the side of the bench and made room for Tony. He looked down at her and frowned.

"What's up?" he quizzed.

Laura quickly looked away, hoping he would not sense her sadness.

"Not much," she claimed. He continued to gaze at her. Laura gave him a quick glance. "What?" she probed.

His eyebrows came together. "I don't know. You tell me," he urged.

Laura leaned her head back and looked up into the night sky. Millions of little stars speckled the darkness. She gazed into the Heavens, praying for wisdom.

"Tony?" she finally asked. "Are you happy with your life?"

A look of surprise came over his face. "Happy? Of course I'm happy!" he cried with a laugh.

Laura finally turned to find his eyes. "No, I mean . . . don't you want more for your life?"

Tony's eyes searched hers. "I wouldn't change a thing about my life. Why do you ask? Where is this coming from?"

Laura looked away and out into the night. "One day, some girl is going to come into your life and you're going to want to date her. How are you going to explain me? How are you going to expect any woman to be okay with you fostering me, knowing we live here by ourselves, under the same roof . . . in the same bed?" she whispered.

Tony tried to suppress a laugh. "Laura, did you happen to hear the conversation between Uncle Frank and me today?"

Laura quickly admitted it. "Yes, Tony. I was starting to prepare lunch when Uncle Frank mentioned this . . . *Silvia*," she muttered, trying to hide the disdain in her voice. "Do you know how terrible I feel knowing that I may be stopping you from having a normal dating life?"

"Are you serious, right now?" Tony pressed. He gaped at her in disbelief. Suddenly, a devilish grin fell across his face. "Well, honestly? I figured, when I was ready to start dating someone, I just wouldn't bring them around until I thought it was someone I'd consider spending the rest of my life with. Is that okay with you?"

Laura suddenly became flustered. "What? You'd bring another woman to our house?"

"Does this bother you?" Tony urged.

Laura felt a sinking feeling overcome her. *He did want to date others.* She tried to hide her pain. "Well . . ." She did not know how to answer. "I . . ."

Tony finally burst out laughing.

Laura caught on to his jeering and was instantly angry. *Two could play at this game.* "I guess I'd be okay with it," she suddenly added, "As long as you were okay with me bringing other men here."

The laughter fell from Tony's face. Their eyes locked and Laura suddenly could not contain a giggle. She burst into laughter and Tony understood. They both laughed.

"Laura, you don't understand, do you?" He finally interjected.

She calmed her giggles and sought his face. "What?" she finally probed.

Tony let out a long sigh and stretched his legs out before him. He reached his arm around her and pulled her to him. "Laura. When I say I wouldn't want to be any other place in the world, it's not because of this adorable little house." He looked down at her lovingly. "Nor is it the quiet of the woods. Or this quaint little town."

Laura gazed into his dark rich eyes.

"It's not the store," he continued, "Nor the strangers coming in to see me."

"Then what?" her voice barely audible.

He squeezed her tighter and let out a low rumbling laughter. "Remember a few weeks ago, that night when I tried to sleep in my own bed?" Laura nodded with remembrance. "What did I tell you that night?"

Laura recalled perfectly what he had said. "You said that you had to keep reminding yourself that . . ."

" . . . That I'm fostering you and not pursuing you. Remember?" he cut in.

"Yes," she answered in a small voice.

"Laura, I'm waiting for the right time. You don't have to worry about me wanting to go out and date anyone else or find the person I'm going to spend the rest of my life with. Because I don't have to go very far to find her. She's literally right under my nose."

He pulled her closer and she rested her head on his chest. She could clearly hear the accelerated beating of his heart. She closed her eyes and sighed with contentment.

It was irrefutable. Laura was insanely in love with Tony. The thought of losing him to another woman was proof. What made it even more evident, were the feelings that were awakening every time he held her so close. She recalled the racing of her heart that evening and the excitement she felt at the possibility of spending the rest of her life with him.

Regardless of everything, Laura ultimately could never forget the three precious years that bound them so intensely close together. She could not deny that what had manifested in that same little home, was a union that God had joined and that no one man could put asunder. She loved him . . . with no conditions.

Now, as she moved from the kitchen to the living room couch holding her rounded belly, she yearned for those simpler times. Still, after learning all that Tony revealed at the hospital, her thoughts continued to travel down the path of 'what-if's'.

What would have happened if Matthew had gotten away with stealing the money? What if he really did sell Sabrina to another family? How would Laura have lived wondering whether her baby sister was left in good hands or not? What if Patty had been sold as a servant? Laura could not fathom that kind of pain. The idea that Matthew had planned to sell her out for prostitution sickened her even more, every time she thought of it. *What kind of father would do such unspeakable evil to his children?* And then . . . her thoughts returned to Tony.

Her heart literally ached when she imagined the horror he withstood—the kind of burden he carried. It was no wonder he broke. *How can one man carry such a cross?* Yet, he was doing it. He was seeking help and working on getting better. *What strength! What determination!* She felt proud of him.

The week and a half away from him, with only time to process her thoughts, was really what she needed. Sitting in the house where their love blossomed from a deep friendship to an everlasting love, was confirmation that she did *not* want to be without him.

"Are you just going to sit there and stare into that fire all day long?" John announced, startling her.

"Oh, hey Dad."

"You look comfy under that afghan. Can I join you?"

"Sure, have a seat." Laura made room for him next to her, covering his legs with the knit blanket.

"You know, the doctor did say rest, but you're wasting away. It's a beautiful sunny day. Want to go for a walk outside?"

"Too cold, Dad. I hate the cold," Laura grumbled.

"Come now, it's almost 40 degrees! For January, that's like 80."

There was no way he was going to let her alone. "Okay, fine," she finally agreed.

"Well, don't look so glum. It just may cheer you up," John suggested with a certain twinkle in his eye.

Laura gave him a weak smile and rose from the couch to prepare for the outdoors. They left Marlene alone to read in her room and departed from the house together. Laura decided that John was right, it was a beautiful day. They walked down the old trail, which they now plowed regularly to get to and from the house from Crabtree Lane. The sun shone brightly and the birds sang. Laura actually felt her spirits lifting.

John whistled a sweet tune and held her hand while they strolled down the street. "Hey, let's take the trail to the lake," he suggested.

"Dad, I don't know."

"Come on, I'm curious to see what it looks like in the winter."

"It's frozen water, Dad."

"You're turning into such an old fart. Where's your sense of excitement? Adventure?"

"We're taking a walk, Dad. How adventurous can that get?" Laura questioned with doubt.

"You just never know. Come on." He pulled on her hand and quickened his pace, leading her onto the narrow path of trees that they had long since marked with tags. Passing through the naked brush, they entered the open field that sloped downward toward the lake. Laura gasped. Even in the dead of winter, the scene stole her breath.

"Isn't this where Tony popped the big question?" John asked, knowing perfectly well that it was.

Laura sighed aloud. "It was the most magical day of my life. I wish life was that simple again."

"You've had a rough road these past few years. But God's with you and He's seen you through them."

"Yes, He has. He sent Tony to me just in the nick of time, five years ago."

"It's amazing—God's timing, isn't it?"

"It is."

They slowly descended the slight hill that led toward the water. John brought her to a large boulder and they both sat staring out at the frozen lake. He placed his arm around her to keep her warm. "I love you, Laura. I want to see you happy. What's it going to take?"

Laura let out another long sigh. "Dad, I'm happiest when I'm with Tony."

"Well, you've both been through an incredible ordeal. It's been one thing after the other with you two. Are you going to let Satan get the best of you? Or are you going to fight for your man?"

"Dad, it's not up to me. I never stopped loving Tony."

"Yes, it is. Tony's ready to recommit to this relationship," John insisted.

"How do you know for sure?" she questioned.

"Why don't I let him tell you?" John pointed toward the opening of the path.

Laura squinted against the sun. She raised her hand to shade her eyes. A dark figure stepped out of the path and into the opening. Laura's heart raced. She stood from the boulder and watched him hobble downward toward her. His feet crushed the few inches of snow left on the ground from the previous snowfall.

John kissed her cheek and trekked back up the small incline to greet Tony. They shook hands and hugged. John blew her a kiss and headed toward the path opening to leave. *That little trickster!*

Laura gradually took in Tony's presence. Her heart felt like bursting from her chest at the mere sight of him. Using a cane, he made his way to her. He wore his leather bomber jacket, jeans, and his snow boots. His hair was gelled back, and he sported a week's growth of facial hair, giving him a rugged look. *But it was his eyes that caught her attention!* They sparkled with a renewed hope that Laura had not seen in weeks.

He stopped but a few feet from her. A smile fell across his lips. "Nice day, ehh?" he asked.

"Beautiful," she whispered.

"*You're* beautiful," he returned. She blushed and lowered her gaze. "I couldn't wait, anymore. I had to see you. How are you?" he questioned.

She looked up and their eyes locked. "I'm good," Laura admitted. "How about you? I see you're up and around. Your leg better?"

"Thanks to you, I'm alive and kicking."

"I can say the same."

"God is good, Laura. He works everything out for us in the end, even if we cannot see it right away."

"He *is* good. When I think of how he saved you, all we've learned, and all we've been through—it's crazy that we're still here."

"Again, God's mighty hand," Tony admitted.

"Yes," Laura agreed.

They stood a long moment looking at one another. Laura was not sure what to say next. Looking at him the way that he looked, she wanted nothing more than to wrap her arms around him. Still, she waited.

Tony cleared his throat. He lifted his hand as if to reach out to her, but then withdrew it. He let out a sigh and finally whispered. "Laura, look. I've made a decision and I need you to hear it." His voice suddenly strengthened and he began again, "Coming that close to death and making it out alive, by the grace of God, I've got a new look on life." He paused a moment and collected a shaky breath. "I'm not letting you go without a fight! You're all I've ever wanted and no matter how much I tried to convince myself that I was bad for you, I was wrong. I love you! I may not do it perfectly, but I love you."

Laura unsteadily exhaled, fighting tears.

He continued, "Unless you can convince me that it's truly over and that you no longer love me, I'm not going anywhere! Because if I've learned anything from all of this, it's that I can't live without you." He paused again, lifting his hand to run it through his hair. He threw his hand down in frustration. "Laura, living without you . . . it's not living—it's dying."

Laura immediately choked up. Her eyes filled with unshed tears and she shook her head in agreement. "For me, too," she confessed. She wiped away a tear. A look of confusion crossed her face. "I just have to ask you one thing. How could you ever believe that I could fall out of love with you? Tony, love is not something you fall in and out of. It's a choice. And I chose to love you for the rest of my life, almost two and a half years ago, at this very place. Do you really believe that my love for you is so frivolous?"

He shook his head, loosening a few strands of hair onto his forehead. "No! But I've given you every reason to want to move on. You almost did with Paul, and Alfonso was just waiting in the wings for you to dump me."

"I thought you were dead when Paul came into my life. Even then, I wouldn't let him into my heart. He ended up turning to Tammy. As for Alfonso, he could've waited all he wanted. No one will ever replace you for me. Our three years together here, they were the best days of my life—not for any other reason . . . but you. It was always you!"

Tony finally took a step forward. A smile fell across his lips. He sniffed and blinked a tear away. Stretching out his free hand, he grasped her waist. "Will you just shut up and kiss me, already?"

Laura was suddenly floating. She flung herself into his waiting arms. Tony received her, suddenly losing his balance. Slowly, they both stumbled onto the cold snow laughing. He held her close—her body pressing against his. Their eyes met. Tony's grin slightly faded and a seriousness materialized in his eyes. He focused on her lips. Slowly, his head leaned forward. He closed his eyes.

At last, his lips met hers in a strong fervent kiss. Laura melted against him. *It was so right, so perfect.* When Tony pulled his lips from hers, he whispered with a rugged breath, "Laura?"

"Yes, Tony?" She held his face in her hands.

"Will you marry me on February 24?"

"Only if you promise me that kissing you will always be this incredible," she smiled.

"I don't know about you, but it will be for me." His lips curled up into a grin.

"Yes, I'll marry you," she whispered.

"Yes!" He grabbed her face and kissed her again. "Yes! Yes! Yes!" Laura let out a giggle and they rose to their feet. He brushed the snow off her and kissed her again.

Spontaneously, Tony shouted into the woods, "We're getting married!"

Epilogue

February 24 came quicker than I thought it would. Thankfully, Mom never cancelled any of the wedding plans with the hope that Tony and I would make things work. So, the wedding went off without a hitch. We had a small ceremony performed by Father Bill at our church. The reception was at a nearby banquet hall with only our closest family and friends. Tony looked like a male model in his black and white tuxedo. My dress looked like something out of a fashion magazine. Mom had it specially ordered and tailored to fit around my rounded belly.

Nonno was well enough to make it to the wedding. He came with Josie, whom he was growing very close to. She was doing a wonderful job nursing him back to health, which meant no more heaping bowls of pasta for Nonno.

The night of the wedding, after our last dance together and plenty of goodbye kisses, Tony drove us to the airport hotel in Nonno's borrowed Cadillac. I felt like a princess with my knight in shining armor. He opened the doors for me and when we arrived at our hotel room, he carried me over the threshold. After freshening up in the bathroom, taking down my hair, and slipping into an elegant nightgown, I stepped into the room. Tony sat waiting for me at the edge of the bed. He welcomed me warmly and we made slow love the way it was meant to be as husband and wife. It was perfect in every way.

The eight days in Mexico, for our honeymoon, were incredible. We enjoyed the hot sun at the beach and relaxation at the pools. The resort we stayed at was a dream. Palm trees and beautiful sunsets made for such romantic scenery that neither Tony nor I would soon forget.

Finally, we returned home to our beloved family. Uncle Frank had a 'welcome home' party for us at his house. Before long, we slipped into routine as a married couple living in our new little house. I went back to work for Mr. Stone until April, then took a leave of absence to prepare for the coming of our baby. Tony continued to work for John, meanwhile continuing therapy for both his mental condition and his leg.

On the morning of May 10, I woke with an unexpected cramp. I cried out, startling Tony. From there it was a race against morning traffic to get me to the hospital in time. The family met us there, anxiously awaiting the baby's arrival.

Kara Maria Giacalone was born that day, weighing a bouncing eight pounds and two ounces. God blessed us all with her presence. At last, John and Marlene had an infant to love and help care for. Uncle Frank, our best man and Godfather to the baby, was gaga over her, too. Nonno Nino . . . well, he cried every time he looked at her. His prayer was to stay healthy so he could watch her grow up, as was mine.

Because Nonno previously led a life of crime, he had robbed himself of any real joy. Now that he finally closed the door to corruption and opened his heart to the Lord, I wanted nothing more than to help him make up for lost time. The sadder part of it was that the temptation to fall into old patterns was too easy—especially when his family was being threatened.

After I accidentally killed Gino, Mario Galante wanted answers. He consulted with the Fontana family (normally a neutral family) and tried to convince them to join forces against the Valentes. Thankfully, the Fontanas convinced Mario to end the vendetta, after talking to Nonno, who explained that he was no longer a threat and that his only heir was his harmless granddaughter—me. Don Giacomo Fontana went back to Mario Valente to continue to keep peace, but Galante warned Fontana that it was the harmless granddaughter that killed his nephew, Gino. Fontana, already knowing the truth, explained that Gino's murder was not intentional. Nevertheless, Mario called my grandfather.

"My nephew is dead, thanks to your son and granddaughter," he stated.

"I was not aware that my son had planned revenge against me. But if you wanted to keep the peace, I could say that you had ill intentions too! You went along with Alfonso's plan to take me and Tony down. Why you no come to me to give me warning?" Nonno grilled.

"You're my enemy. Why would I help you?"

"Then I could say the same. You should no have expected *mia nipote* to let your nephew kill her nonno and fiancé! Tony and I no have the intentions to harm Gino. Alfonso did, without my knowledge or consent. *Mi capisce*? Do you understand? I am out. Done."

"Perhaps, you are. But that does not change what has gone down. I will not go against the other family's wishes to keep the peace. But if you or any of your family crosses my path again, you'll be sorry."

"I am already sorry for what has happened in the past between our *famigli*. I hope that God changes you heart, Mario, the way He changed mine." Nonno insisted.

"Take your preaching elsewhere, Valente. I don't buy into it. Just consider yourself warned."

Mario Galante hung up on Nonno, leaving him quite frustrated and very sad. Yet, Nonno reassured me, we would not be crossing paths with the Galante *famiglia* ever again and that was fine with me.

My family is all that I could ever need. Having Tony, baby Kara, my parents, Nonno, and Uncle Frank, in my life, has made up for all the grief and all the pain I've ever had to endure. Now the future looks bright and new. My marriage to Tony is everything God intended it to be. We're crazy about each other. It's like old times at the 'abandoned' house— steady, yet exciting; unwavering, yet spontaneous. I just never know when Tony's going to come home and whisk me up into his embrace to carry us off for a weekend in Cicero or off to our bedroom for some alone time, while the baby sleeps.

So far, it has been a wild ride with Tony Giacalone; a ride that has led me through breathtaking paths, as well as down uncertain darkened alleys. God must have known exactly what I needed as he guided me on that wild ride, for it was worth it. Because that wild ride ultimately brought me on a crash course into Tony's arms.

Of course, God has a plan for everything, doesn't He? In Jeremiah 29:11-13, He tells us, "*For I know the plans I have for you, plans to prosper you and not to harm you, plans to give you hope and a future.*"

Yes, I'm counting on that!

CPSIA information can be obtained
at www.ICGtesting.com
Printed in the USA
FFOW05n1603210916

9 781457 548833